Pawns and Puzzles

DAROS CHRONICLES
VOLUME ONE

Sarah Ettritch

NORN PUBLISHING
TORONTO, CANADA

Contents

Friends Torn Apart

Erryn glanced around the bustling bazaar while Fi examined the pair of earrings that had caught her eye. There were too many people within striking distance of Fi. They should never have ventured outside the castle walls without protection. "We should go back to the castle. We shouldn't be out here, not alone."

"We're not alone." Fi held the earrings up to her ears. "We're with Cedric."

Erryn looked at the elderly guard standing stiffly to Fi's right. He turned to her and quirked a brow. "I know what you're thinking, Erryn. You're thinking I'd be useless in a fight." He patted the hilt of the sword hanging at his left side. "Don't you worry. I know how to use this."

Erryn nodded but continued to scan her surroundings. Fi should know better. Erryn understood how Fi wished she could walk among the common folk without the royal guard surrounding her, how she longed to drink anonymously in a tavern and attend the outdoor theatre unrecognized. But the opulence in which she lived came with a price. Erryn agreed to these dangerous excursions because Fi hadn't chosen her life, and Erryn adored her.

"What do you think?" Fi asked.

Erryn stopped scanning the bazaar long enough to give Fi's prospective purchase an appraising look. "Very nice."

"Very nice." Fi scowled. "That's all?"

"All right, they look beautiful, but do you really need another pair? You already have thousands."

"I don't have thousands." Fi lowered the earrings. "Hundreds, maybe." Her sly look made Erryn smile, but only for a second. "Why don't you look for a pair?" Fi asked.

"No." Unlike most women, Erryn didn't wear earrings often. She also preferred trousers and shirts to dresses. She wore the latter only to banquets and balls, and hated every minute of it. "We really should get back."

Annoyance flashed across Fi's face. "Oh, all right." She handed the earrings she'd chosen to the merchant. "I'll take them. Please wrap them and deliver them to the castle."

The merchant bowed. "Yes, Your Highness."

"Come on, then." Fi looped her arm through Erryn's. "The fastest way back is through the delivery lanes."

"No."

Fi pouted.

"Erryn's right," Cedric said. "Too many shadows. Too many ambush points."

Fi blew out an exasperated sigh. "What is the point of leaving the castle when I'm stuck with two worry warts? Fine. We'll walk the main road. I'd like to see the people, anyway."

Erryn gave her an indulgent look. Fi would like the people to buzz around her, and they'd be happy to oblige.

The walk back to the castle took twice as long, with children rushing up to hand Fi flowers, women curtsying before moving out of her way, and men stopping to doff their caps. When one darted toward her and asked for a kiss, the tip of Cedric's sword changed his mind. "You see?" Fi said with a laugh. "I'm safe here. Nobody is out for my blood."

Perhaps she was right. Erryn saw only interest and respect in the eyes of those craning their necks for a look at the princess, and those following the trio back to the castle were keeping a respectable distance. "Are you eating with your father tonight?" she asked Fi.

"Probably. Why?"

Erryn wanted to talk to her about a subject that had preyed on her mind for several months. She wanted to stop wondering if Fi would laugh and stroll along the road with her when she knew of Erryn's true nature. Would Fi still call her a friend? Was their bond that strong? "I want to talk to you about something."

"Talk to me now," Fi said, her eyes alight with curiosity.

"I can't. It's private."

Fi leaned in to her. "In that case, I must find out what it is today, or I'll never sleep. I'll come to your bedchamber after supper. We'll talk then."

Erryn's heart thumped. "All right," she said, hoping the conversation that evening wouldn't be their last. What would happen if Fi reacted badly? Maybe Erryn shouldn't tell her, but she wasn't used to keeping secrets from Fi. Doing so had cast a shadow over their friendship. It wasn't the secrecy, per se; it was the growing conviction that Fi should know who her closest friend really was. Erryn wanted their friendship to be based on honesty. She hadn't lied to Fi, but not telling her about—

"Death to the Lyos wench!" shouted someone behind them. Erryn whirled. "Death to the royal whore!" A masked man ran at them, a sword in his hand. A boy not more than fourteen darted into his path. With one smooth motion, the man lopped off his head. Screams pierced the air. Cedric drew his sword. Erryn pulled her arm from Fi's and stood in front of her.

Fleeing townsfolk jostled them. Cedric's sword clashed with the attacker's. "Erryn!" Fi cried. "Behind. He's coming from behind."

Confused, Erryn shouted back, "Behind?"

"Help me!"

Erryn looked over her shoulder. Her breath caught in her throat. The man fighting Cedric was only a distraction! A second assassin was running toward Fi, his blade glinting in the sun. No, he wouldn't reach her. Erryn clenched her fists. *Zayvang! Come!*

The air shimmered. A saber-tooth cat leaped into

existence. The assassin's eyes widened. He faltered. Erryn gritted her teeth and held the image of the assassin in her mind. *Kill.*

Zayvang launched into the air and hit the assassin full in the chest. The man slammed onto the ground, his sword skittering across the cobblestones. He screamed and raised his hands to protect himself, but it was too late. Zayvang bit into his neck and tore away his throat, abruptly ending the assassin's cries of terror. Blood sprayed onto the road. The man's arms and legs stilled. It was done.

To me. Zayvang loped to Erryn and sat obediently before her. Blood dripped from the cat's muzzle. *Thank you. Return.* Zayvang shimmered and was gone.

Erryn drew a ragged breath and dropped her eyes to the bloodied assassin. Then the silence rushed at her—everyone was staring at her, including Fi. Erryn winced at the shock on her face.

"Erryn," Fi whispered. "No." She backed away.

Erryn reached for her. "Fi, don't . . . please, don't."

"She's a Beast Master," someone shouted.

"Protect the princess!"

"I was going to tell you," Erryn said, hoping Fi could hear her. Then a push from behind forced her to her knees. Another one left her splayed, facedown. Cobblestones dug into her ribs. She tried to speak, but someone was on her back, pinning her down.

"Don't hurt her!" Fi cried, sounding far away.

Boots thudded on the cobblestones. Erryn was able to lift her head enough to see the trousers and boots of the royal guard. The pressure on her back eased. Hands roughly grasped her arms and hoisted her to her feet. Angry, contemptuous faces swam before her.

"Heathen!"

"Cursed by the Seven."

"Animal!"

Erryn wanted to hang her head, but her desire to find Fi was stronger. When the guards ordered her to walk, she could only shuffle. The voices around her swelled. She could no longer distinguish one shout from another, and she no longer cared. She'd spotted Fi. *"I'm sorry,"* she mouthed.

Fi shrank into Cedric, her eyes filled with fear.

Tears blurred Erryn's vision. She'd no longer have to wonder about how Fi would react. She had her answer. The friendship she'd cherished was over.

King Oswald Beron Lyos the Fourth of Daros took a moment to digest Cedric's account of the assassination attempt on his daughter, and Erryn's part in saving her. He leaned forward and clasped his hands on top of his oak desk. "Are you sure she summoned Zayvang?"

"As sure as I'm standing here in front of you, Majesty. I turned around just in time to see Zayvang sit and look to her for guidance."

When the royal primate stepped forward and drew breath, Oswald motioned for him to remain silent. "I thought you were fighting the other assassin," he said to Cedric.

"That's just it, Majesty. Erryn not only saved the

princess, she gave me the opening I needed. I had my back to her, you see. I didn't see Zayvang ... arrive. But he saw—the one I was fighting. Shocked him for a second, and that was all I needed to run him through. Then I turned around and saw her. Zayvang."

"And you're sure it was Erryn?"

"Yes," Cedric said. "As I said, she went to Erryn after ripping out the throat of the second assassin. If Erryn hadn't been there ..."

Oswald nodded. Erryn, a Beast Master. His jaw tightened.

Primate Enkelo raised a finger. "If I may speak, Your Majesty."

"Please do."

"Erryn saved the princess's life, but Beast Masters cannot act selflessly. She had a reason that had nothing to do with protecting the princess. In daring to summon Zayvang, she has angered Zhikinden. We must demonstrate our disgust with her."

Oswald didn't have to ask him what he had in mind. Why did it have to be Fi's closest friend and a girl he'd promised a dying man he'd look after? He'd never understood why Garon hadn't disposed of the whore he'd gotten pregnant. Oswald had offered to do it for him, but Garon had wanted the child, perhaps because he had no others. The whore had died in childbirth after bearing a daughter, not a son. Garon had hidden his disappointment well and had doted on the babe. Eight months later, he'd died from the wasting disease, but not before Oswald had leaned over him, straining to hear his final words: "Take care of Erryn. Please, Oswald. You owe me that much."

Oswald had agreed, and he'd honoured his promise. Erryn lived in the royal castle, had wanted for nothing, had been educated by the same tutors as his own children. She was only a year older than Fi. They were practically sisters. If not for Fi . . . Oswald heaved a sigh.

"We need Zhikinden's favour, Your Majesty," Enkelo said. "The hunt—"

Oswald's study door slammed open. Fi marched into the room. "She's in the dungeon? She saves my life and you put her in the dungeon?"

"What were you doing outside the castle without the royal guard?" Oswald shot back. "And why did you agree to go with her?" he said to Cedric. "If you'd had the guard with you—"

"It would not have mattered, Your Majesty," Enkelo said. "Erryn would have summoned the Fallen another day."

"If she'd saved me any other way, you'd hold a feast for her, not treat her like a criminal," Fi shouted.

"Fi, she's a Beast Master," Oswald said, hoping his mild tone, though forced, would calm his daughter.

"I know, Father, but the dungeons? You couldn't confine her to her bedchamber?"

"We don't know what her intentions are, Your Highness," Enkelo said. "She summoned Zayvang for reasons known only to her."

Fi's eyes flashed. "She did it to save my life."

"Perhaps to gain your trust. Next time, she could summon Zayvang to kill you."

"She already had my trust," Fi snapped. "And if she wanted to kill me, she's had ample opportunity." She folded her arms and glared at Enkelo.

Oswald could see her conflict through her anger. "Did you know?"

Fi's brow furrowed. "What?"

"Did you know?"

"Of course I didn't know," she shrieked.

"And now that you do?"

Fi dropped her arms to her sides and sank into one of the plush chairs, the only person present who could do so without Oswald's permission. "It's Erryn, Father. I know . . . I know what Beast Masters are, but it's Erryn. Maybe she didn't know until today. Maybe she called on the Seven to save me and Zhikinden sent her Zayvang." She looked sharply to Enkelo. "Is that possible?"

"No," Enkelo said with a regretful shake of his head. "The Holy Texts are clear, Your Highness. She has been cursed since the day she was born. It was only a matter of time before the Fallen used her to enter our world. They won't stop. She won't want them to. Every time she summons one of the Seven's pets, she puts us all in danger of suffering the Seven's wrath." He turned to Oswald. "We must show Zhikinden that we condemn Erryn's action."

"I agree. I'm sending her away."

Fi leaped to her feet. "What? Father, no!"

Enkelo's eyes widened. "Your Majesty—"

Oswald cut him off. "Step outside for a moment, Enkelo. I'd like to speak to my daughter alone. You too, Cedric."

"Yes, Sire." Cedric saluted and strode from the study. Enkelo hesitated, then bowed. "Yes, Your Majesty."

Oswald waited until the door had closed behind him, then motioned for Fi to sit back down. "You know things can't go back to what they were," he said gently. "The primate is right. We can't trust Erryn anymore."

"She saved my life."

"But we don't know why. She isn't like us. Her soul doesn't come from the Seven, but from the Fallen. She has a bestial nature, Fi. She's dangerous."

Fi shook her head. "I don't know. I—I can't see Erryn doing anything to harm me—harm us. But I saw Zayvang. I know what Erryn is. And the primate would chide me, but part of me doesn't care."

"I know how close you are."

Fi's chin trembled. She lowered her head.

"She can't stay. You can't be associated with a Beast Master. You won't rule unless we lose Henrick before he has a babe, and I pray to the Seven that we don't. But you need a good marriage, and no man will tolerate a Beast Master anywhere near his wife."

"I know, Father."

"I was going to make a good marriage for Erryn, as well. But now . . ." Oswald briefly closed his eyes. *I'm sorry, Garon, but you would do the same in my place.* He should have ignored Garon and killed the whore. Instead, his weakness had allowed the wench to bring a cursed child into the world. He wouldn't make the same mistake twice.

Fi lifted her head. "Where will you send her?"

"To Rion Province."

"Rion? Why?"

"They're more tolerant of Beast Masters there," he lied. "There are more wild folk in Rion. They don't always heed the Holy Texts."

Fi's face grew troubled. "Wild folk? Erryn has lived in the city all her life."

"Erryn will learn new ways." Oswald softened his voice. "It's the best I can do. As it is, I'll anger Enkelo. He'll argue that only Erryn's death will appease Zhikinden, and he may be right."

"You wouldn't—"

Oswald raised his hand. "If it was anyone else, I'd order an execution. Instead, I'll have men I trust escort Erryn to the Rion border, where they'll give her a generous amount of coin and a letter of recommendation with the royal seal. From there, she'll have to forge her own way."

"Thank you, Father," Fi mumbled. "Thank you for sparing her. I wish she didn't have to leave, but . . . May I go and see her?"

"No," Oswald said flatly. "Remember her as she was yesterday. Seeing her won't make you feel any better. Let her go, Fi. There's nothing more to be said or done."

Fi nodded miserably. "I'm going to my bedchamber. I'll take supper there tonight."

"I'll let Bydan know. On your way out, tell Enkelo and Cedric to come back in." Cedric. Oswald inwardly sighed.

Fi had the old fool wrapped around her finger. "You did a foolish thing today, going to the bazaar without the guard. I know you're upset about Erryn so I won't punish you or Cedric, but don't do it again."

"I won't, Father." She rose and tried to smile at him, but failed.

Oswald winced at her red eyes. When she returned to her chamber, she'd weep until her throat was hoarse and she had no more tears. The servants would take away her untouched supper. She'd cry herself to sleep. It would be worse if she knew the truth. She must never know the truth.

Erryn sat hunched in the corner of a gloomy cell and replayed the assassination attempt in her mind for the hundredth time. She hugged her legs to her chest and rested her forehead against her knees. She'd had no choice but to summon Zayvang. If she hadn't, Fi would have been lying in a pool of blood, not the assassin. But for Fi to find out that way . . . her shocked face . . . Erryn should have told her earlier. She would have had a chance to explain, to tell Fi that she hadn't sought the Fallen. They'd found her.

Approaching footsteps set her heart racing. She lifted her head, then scrambled to her feet and moved closer to the cell door. Several guards stopped in front of it; one inserted an iron key into the lock. The door creaked open. The guards parted. Erryn dropped to one knee when the king strode into the cell. She inclined her head. "Your Majesty."

Silence. She didn't dare look up. A prisoner's moan reached her ears. Someone coughed. "Look at me," the king finally said, his voice quiet and hard.

Erryn met his cold eyes and withered under his gaze. They'd never been close. When the king wasn't occupied with matters of state, he was grooming Henrick to one day replace him on the throne. He hadn't had much time for his daughter or the orphan he'd promised to raise, but he'd always been kind to Erryn. She'd never sensed hate from him.

"How long have you known?" he asked, his voice trembling with anger.

Erryn swallowed. "A few months."

"A few months."

His backhanded blow took Erryn by surprise. Pain ripped through her right cheek. Her ears rang. She thrust out her left hand to steady herself.

"All that time, you were with my daughter."

"I would never harm Fi," Erin croaked.

His fist smashed into her mouth. The hard metal of his ring tore her lower lip. She hunched on the floor, blood trickling down her chin. "Princess Filmona," the king thundered. "Say it!"

"Princess Filmona," Erryn whispered through the pain.

The king flexed his fingers. "I should kill you. If not for the princess, I would kill you. I can't deny that you saved her life, and she doesn't want you executed. But you can't stay here. I'm sending you to Rion."

"No, please. If I could just explain—"

"Keep your lies to yourself. You're an animal. You're filth.

I took you in, and this is how you repay me. You lie to me, to the princess, to all of us!" The king's jaw set. "I won't allow you to take advantage of anyone else." He looked toward the door and nodded. Two guards marched into the cell and pulled Erryn to her feet.

Was this it, then? She was to be banished immediately? She couldn't leave without seeing Fi. Expecting the king would strike her again, she braced herself. "May I say good-bye to the princess, Your Majesty?"

He stared at her. "Do you think you're to depart now? Oh, no, you'll leave on the morrow, after we've ensured you won't fool anyone else. You will go with these guards. If you dare summon any of the Fallen, they'll put you down like the animal you are."

She wanted to tell him that she respected his authority and wouldn't attack him or his guard, but he wouldn't believe her. When he looked at her, he saw the Fallen.

A third guard joined the others. Erryn looked on in confusion as he clapped her wrists and ankles in irons. Was she to be put on public display and pelted with rotten fruit before they drove her from the Royal Province?

"Walk," one of the guards growled. Panic rooted Erryn to the spot. The guards dragged her to the cell door. "Walk!" the guard repeated.

As they made their way down the dank, narrow passageway, Erryn's chest tightened until she could barely breathe. Her apprehension reached a fever pitch when they escorted her into a sweltering room with a forge, anvil, hammers—no!

The smith turned away from the forge. "Put her on

the worktable.""No. You can't," Erryn cried, her survival instinct forcing her to struggle. "Don't do this to me. I'm not a threat to you."

One of the guards pushed her against the worktable. She fell onto it when another lifted her feet from the floor. She tried to sit up, but they were too strong for her. She lay trembling on the table. Hostile faces peered down at her. She closed her eyes, told herself it would be all right, she'd get through it, but fear tensed every muscle in her body and now her breath came in quick gasps.

"Hold her head still." The smith paused. "Unless you want me to take out her eyes?"

"No." The king's voice. "I want her to see it every time she looks in a mirror."

Rustling. Erryn whimpered. A gloved hand held her throat. She sensed heat near her forehead. She pushed back against the table, but there was no escape. "Please, no," she whispered. The hot metal pressed against her skin. *Searing pain*—her hands balled into fists. The stench of burning flesh assaulted her nostrils. She thrashed about and screamed for mercy.

The pressure against her forehead eased, but the agony remained. The guards hauled her to her feet. Her cheeks felt damp. She gritted her teeth but couldn't stop shaking.

The king cupped her chin and appraised the smith's handiwork. "Good. Now everyone will know."

"A wise action, Your Majesty."

Erryn looked past the king. The royal primate stood in the doorway.

"Do not look at me, Beast Master," the primate spat. "You are heathen."

The king slapped her throbbing head. "Do as he says. Cast your eyes down."

She swayed and lowered her head.

"Take her back to her cell," the king ordered. As she shuffled into the passageway, she heard the king say, "Come to my study in half an hour, Enkelo."

Her head felt as if it were on fire. Squinting heightened the pain. She let the guards lead her to her cell and push her inside. The iron door clanged shut behind her. Still in irons, she sank to the stone floor and quietly wept.

"You want me to look into the assassination attempt?" Cedric said, his eyes wide. "Begging your pardon, Majesty, but I thought I'd lost your favour." His voice dropped. "Justifiably so."

"I'm not pleased that by giving in to the princess's whims, you put her in harm's way." Not pleased? Normally Oswald wouldn't forgive Cedric's lapse in judgement, but he had a daughter to appease. "Now that you'll be occupied investigating the attempt on the princess's life, you'll be too busy to do her bidding. I trust you'll tell her so, if need be."

"Yes, Majesty."

"Use the guard. Depending on what you uncover, we may involve the Ferrets. But not yet. You may go."

Cedric saluted him with a fist over his heart. As soon as he'd left, Oswald waved Enkelo and Reed, a trustworthy guard who'd performed clandestine tasks for him before, into the study. He motioned for them to sit. "I wanted you to be present when I spoke to Reed, Enkelo." He turned to Reed. "You know about the Beast Master."

Reed shifted in his chair. "I've heard you'll give her safe passage into Rion, Sire."

"I'll give her safe passage to the border. You'll take her. Select three men you trust can be discreet. Treat the Beast Master well. Make sure those in towns and villages along the way see her. When you get to the border, kill her."

Enkelo's brows shot up. "You branded her, Your Majesty. I was under the impression you intended to let her live." His mouth pressed into a thin line. "I didn't agree with you, but I always respect your decisions."

"I want Fi to have the same impression you did. She can never know. Do you understand, Reed? The princess can never know. On the morrow, she'll see the Beast Master ride through the castle gates wearing fine clothes. Everyone you encounter will witness the same. If Fi should converse with a travelling merchant, or a visitor to our city who lives along the same roads you'll travel, I want them to tell her they saw the Beast Master and she was well."

"But if the princess encounters anyone from Rion who lives near the border, they won't say the same," Enkelo pointed out.

"I said I'd escort the heathen to the border. After that . . ." Oswald shrugged. "Fi won't hold me responsible for whatever happens to her after that." Not directly. He stared at Reed. "That is why word can never get back to the princess. Tell whoever you choose that if they breathe a word about the Beast Master's death, I will cut off their balls, stick a hot poker in their eyes, slit them open from throat to groin, cook their bowels, and then kill them."

Reed and Enkelo exchanged glances. Reed cleared his throat. "I'll do as you ask, Sire, though I'd feel better if we killed her now. She could strike at us before we reach the border."

Oswald nodded. "I know. Only two of you should sleep at a time."

"If she calls several of the Fallen at once . . ."

"She'll lose control of them," Enkelo said. "If she told the truth about how long she's known about her corruption, she'll not be able to control more than one. That's why we need to cut her down now, before she becomes more skilled."

Oswald steepled his fingers. "Put her in her own tent. Talk to her. Gain her trust. She won't expect you to strike."

"It's unfortunate that the princess doesn't understand how dangerous the Beast Master is," Enkelo said.

"She understands," Oswald snapped. "But she's attached to the woman." He should have separated them long ago, sent Erryn to the country. But he'd been content to let Garon's bastard entertain his daughter while he groomed Henrick. Fi would be angry with him for sending her friend away. But over time, she'd recognize that it had to be done. Oswald was now more convinced that it was time for Fi to marry. Surrounded with suitors, she'd soon forget the friend who'd betrayed them all.

Enkelo scratched his cheek. "The princess has a sharp mind, but little time for the Holy Texts. It would be prudent for her to undergo a period of guided reflection. She spent so much time with the Beast Master."

"Are you implying that my daughter could be cursed?" Oswald thundered. Then he leaned back in his chair and rubbed his forehead. "Don't answer that." He couldn't fault Enkelo. When he'd learned that Erryn was a Beast Master, his thoughts had turned to Fi, as well. She claimed she hadn't known, and Oswald believed her. Perhaps he should order a public execution for Erryn, but even if he did, there would still be whispers about Fi. When they eventually stopped, he wanted the respect and love of his daughter. The only way to remain in Fi's good graces was to secretly kill Erryn and ensure that Fi never found out. His thoughts returned to Enkelo's suggestion. "I want you to spend time with the princess, preferably in public. Let the people see that she honours the Primacy."

"We shall discuss the Seven. I'll avoid passages regarding the Fallen."

"Good. Start today."

"Today?"

"Go for a walk with Fi. Explain to her why we had to brand Erryn. I'd tell her, but she won't listen to me."

"As you wish."

"Remember that Fi has to believe Erryn will live." He waved them away. "Go, go, both of you. You know what you have to do."

Enkelo and Reed rose. Enkelo bowed; Reed saluted. After they'd left, Oswald buried his head in his hands. He'd be happier when the Beast Master was no longer in the city. He'd failed to protect his daughter. Never again. As soon as he'd seen the heathen through the gates, he'd summon nobles with sons who would make suitable husbands for Fi. Erryn would become a distant, unpleasant memory for both of them.

Erryn ran her tongue along her swollen lip, then rolled over on her makeshift bed—a pile of hay a guard had thrown into the corner. The same guard had removed her irons so she'd be more comfortable. If the king had told her the truth, she'd only be imprisoned for one night. Still, she longed to be in her own soft bed, resting her thumping head on a feather pillow.

She cracked open an eye. In the light cast from one of the flickering torches outside her cell, she could see her untouched supper. The runny stew would be a far cry from whatever Fi and her father had eaten. Had they supped together? What had they said about her over the roast and wine? What did Fi think? Her shock and fear kept running through Erryn's mind.

She could sense Zayvang and the others, but she wouldn't call any of them. All they'd do is share a cage. Erryn had no intention of harming anyone or escaping.

"Erryn," a voice hissed.

Despite her agony, Erryn almost chuckled. Now she was imagining Fi's voice.

"Erryn!"

Wait. Erryn peered into the gloom. A shadow crouched outside her cell door. "Fi?" she croaked.

"Yes. It's me."

Fi. Tears prickled at Erryn's eyelashes. She pushed

herself up, crawled on her hands and knees toward the cell door, and sat next to it, with her back pressed against the stone wall. "I didn't think I'd see you again," she whispered. "Are you supposed to be here?"

"No. But don't worry about that. Are you all right?"

Erryn's fingernails dug into her palms. "I'm fine."

"You don't sound fine." Fi paused. "I can't see you. Let me see you."

Erryn swallowed. "No."

"I know what they did to you. Enkelo told me. I know Father ordered it. They're frightened of you."

"Are you?" Erryn asked, despite being afraid of the answer.

"I—no. If I was, I wouldn't be here."

Erryn blinked back more tears. The tremor in Fi's voice betrayed her words.

"Let me see you," Fi said.

"No."

"Erryn, I want to see you. Please."

Erryn closed her eyes. "I don't want you to see me like this."

"Right now, the last memory I have is of you and Zayvang. I need to see you again."

Erryn hesitated, but only for a moment. She wanted to see Fi, too, wanted to see if the fear and shock were still there. She twisted toward the door and knelt in front of its bars.

Fi raised her lantern and gasped. "No. Oh, Erryn." Fi's eyes glistened. "Who did that to you? Which guard was it? Tell me, and I'll make sure he's punished."

"It doesn't matter," Erryn said, after realizing Fi was referring to her swollen lip and cheek.

"Yes, it does," Fi said, her eyes now flashing. She reached through the bars to touch Erryn's face.

Erryn shied away. Fi's touch would hurt in more ways than one. "Nothing good will come of you punishing a guard," she said, hoping Fi would drop it. "What about my forehead? How bad is it?"

Fi grimaced. "It looks like a mess."

This time, Erryn did chuckle, then she winced at the sharp pain that shot through her head.

"Here." Fi dangled a pouch through the bars. "There's some ointment and a piece of willow bark."

A lump rose in Erryn's throat. "Thank you." She set the pouch on the ground. "What's on my forehead?" She'd gingerly traced the raw brand with her fingers but hadn't puzzled out what it depicted.

Fi's gaze sharpened. She frowned. "It's the Beast Master's symbol, Erryn."

Shit. Everyone would recognize the outline of a wolf's head and know what it meant.

"When we were at the bazaar, you said you wanted to tell me something. Were you going to tell me about . . . what you are?" Fi asked.

Erryn nodded. Had it only been this afternoon that Fi had held the earrings to her ears? Tears threatened again. She lowered her head and held onto the cell door's bars for support. "This time last night, we were up on the wall, gazing at the moon. If I'd known what would happen today . . ." She would have told Fi the two secrets that had become a heavier burden each day. One was out, with disastrous consequences. Given what had happened, she dared not breathe the other.

Having mastered herself, she gritted her teeth and lifted her head. "If I'd told you, what would you have done?"

Fi set the lantern on the ground and bit her lip as she pondered the question. "I'm not sure." She jutted her chin toward the cell. "Not this, though. Enkelo and Father, they say you have a bestial soul. I don't believe it. I know it's in the Holy Texts, but I know you. I *know* you." Fi wrapped her fingers over Erryn's, which clutched one of the bars. "I wish we had more time to talk. I know if you explained . . ." She trailed off.

"I didn't choose this," Erryn said quietly. "The Fallen came to me. I didn't have a choice. Nobody would choose this. Nobody would choose something they know makes them an animal, a heathen, in everyone's eyes."

"Father says they won't mind you so much in Rion. With the coin and his letter, you'll—" Fi's voice choked off.

"I'll be okay, Fi," Erryn said, sounding more confident than she felt. "Don't worry about me."

"Father says we wouldn't have seen much of each other, anyway. I'm to be married soon. While you're off on your adventure, I'll choose a husband. You would have married soon, too."

Erryn was almost glad she'd be gone, and she appreciated Fi's optimism, however misplaced and shallow it was. Fi always chattered when she was worried.

"Give it a year or two and then come back, when everyone has calmed down."

"I'm a Beast Master, Fi," Erryn said harshly. "Your father, Henrick, your husband—they'll never allow me near you."

"You saved my life," Fi said. "That's why you summoned Zayvang."

"Yes, and I know it shocked you." Erryn's words tumbled out. "I didn't want to frighten you. The truth is, I didn't think at all. I saw you were in trouble. There was nobody between you and the assassin. I—" She stopped when Fi squeezed her fingers.

"I was surprised. Maybe I felt a little betrayed." Fi raised her other hand. "But I wasn't angry. I knew why you did it. And afterward, when I had time to think . . . I wished you'd told me. I wished you'd trusted me. Perhaps it wouldn't have come to this."

Erryn was convinced it wouldn't have made a difference. Even if Fi had kept her secret, eventually it would have come out. The Holy Texts wouldn't have changed. The royal primate would have called for her execution. The king would have complied. Saving Fi's life had saved her own. But she held her tongue. "Fi, I need you to do something for me."

"What?"

"There's a diary in my bedchamber, behind the bookcase. You have to destroy it. Please don't read it. Toss it into the fire without reading it. Promise me."

Fi's brow furrowed. "What's in it?"

"It's my private diary. Please don't read it, and don't let anyone else get it. Throw it into the fire."

"All right."

"Promise me you won't read it. Promise me."

"I promise." Fi's shoulders heaved. "I'll miss you. I'd tell you to write, but I suspect you'll refuse."

"You're right." Erryn forced herself to meet Fi's eyes and say the heart-wrenching words she'd never, ever thought she'd say to her. "Don't remember me. Forget about me."

Fi shook her head. "I won't. Ever." She gulped. A tear spilled down her cheek. "I have to go. May the Seven guide and protect you, Erryn Fyler." She fled down the passageway, the light from the lantern bobbing until Erryn could see it no more.

Erryn stared at her fingers, still curled around the bar. They felt cold. "And you, Fi," she whispered. She bit back her grief. As much as she wanted to cry and rage and hurl herself against the stone wall, she didn't have the strength.

Instead, she dragged the pouch back to the hay and lay on her side. She pulled out the bark. Chewing on it lessened her pain, but she couldn't sleep. In mere hours, she'd leave the only home she'd ever known and the only people she'd ever loved to travel to a foreign province with coin and a letter. Would they shun her? Beat her? Hang her? Or would they allow her to live among them? But doing what?

She'd been raised to marry a respectable gentleman and run a household. She would have hated it, but she would have known how to do it. What would she do in

Rion? Was the king showing her mercy by sending her away, or was he condemning her to a slow and gruesome death?

Fi strode along the wall to stop beside Father and look down at the courtyard below. Guards and grooms fussed around five horses. There was no sign of Erryn. The promise Fi had made to her friend weighed on her mind. Right after leaving the dungeons, she'd gone to Erryn's bedchamber, only to find the door locked. The servants she'd asked didn't have the key. Fi suspected it was in Father's desk. There was no point asking him for it; he'd refuse to give it to her. She'd have to keep an eye on Erryn's chamber if she was to find the diary before anyone else did.

"You didn't have to come outside," Father said. "You could have watched from inside."

She stared at the door from which Erryn would emerge. When Father put his arm around her, she shook it away.

"So you're going to be like that, then," Father said. "You'll be silent until you need coin for a dress."

"I have my own coin!" Shit, she'd been determined not to speak to him for at least a day. She folded her arms.

The door that led to the dungeons flew open. Two guards entered the courtyard. Fi unconsciously leaned forward, pressing her lips together when Erryn walked out with two guards on her heels.

Father pointed. "You see? She's not in irons. She's not in sack cloth. She'll be on one of our best horses, and one of my best men will escort her. He'll see that no harm comes to her."

"Like no harm came to her in the dungeons?" Fi shot back.

"Primate Enkelo explained why I had to brand her."

She hadn't meant that, and she had to be careful, or she'd get the guards who'd looked the other way last night into trouble.

"I've instructed the guards that they're to punish anyone who throws fruit at her on the way out of the city."

Did he expect her to thank him? He'd be disappointed. She unfolded her arms and leaned through a crenel. The part of her that wanted to shout or wave to Erryn battled the part that said she shouldn't publicly support her. Her association with a Beast Master, as Enkelo had put it, thereby dismissing a friendship she valued beyond all others, could cause some to suspect that she, too, was heathen. She'd have to spend an hour every day with the boring man, listening to him drone on about the Holy Texts. But her penance paled in comparison to Erryn's.

Erryn mounted one of the horses. Fi couldn't see her face from this distance, but the slouch of Erryn's shoulders said she was tired. Had she slept last night? How would she survive in Rion? She'd lived in the castle her entire life. Could she ever come back? Fi couldn't accept that she'd never see her again. Who would she talk to now? Who could she confide in? Erryn was the only one she trusted. Erryn was the only one Fi knew loved her for herself, not for what she could do for her, or so she could say that she was friends with the princess. Erryn never played games. Erryn was always honest with her. Erryn had saved her life. Erryn was a Beast Master. Erryn was banished from the Royal Province. Life had been turned on its ear.

"The banquet next week will take your mind off recent events," Father said. "All the nobles will bring their sons."

Did he honestly think that one banquet and the attention of men who wanted prestige and power would make her forget Erryn?

Hooves clattered on cobblestone. The group of five, two mounted guards in front of Erryn and two behind, walked their horses toward the gatehouse. Fi's throat tightened. Still failing to find the strength and will to call out, she ran along the wall, hoping Erryn would spot her. But Erryn gazed steadfastly forward, and to her credit, held her head high. Fi blinked back tears when the last of the riders entered the gatehouse and disappeared from view.

Father caught up with her. He cleared his throat. "You see, she's gone, safe and sound."

"Her life is ruined, Father," Fi said, grief strangling her voice. "Nobody will want anything to do with her. She won't survive."

"It had to be done. I had to protect you, Henrick, the people. Everyone wanted me to execute her, but I didn't. I was merciful. Don't worry about her. She won't be scrounging for food, I promise you that."

She met his eyes for the first time that morning. "Why should I believe you? You also said those in Rion will be more accepting of her."

"They will be."

"Then why did you brand her?" She strode away, not caring about his answer. Erryn was gone. Fi should have waved or shouted; now Erryn would think she hadn't cared, that she'd still been fast asleep in her luscious bed, her friend already forgotten. Next time Fi looked in the mirror, she'd see the shallow princess she'd vowed not to become, someone more concerned with her reputation than with honesty and honour. She should have cried out! She should have made sure Erryn knew that she cared, that she was here, watching and weeping.

But she was the princess. She couldn't align herself with a Beast Master. What would everyone think? Bah. Usually she thanked the Seven that she'd been born into the Lyos family and lived in luxury, wanting for nothing.

Not today.

Erryn lifted her tent flap and peered at the two guards sitting near the fire. Were they guarding the camp, or protecting the two sleeping guards from her? Probably both. She let the tent flap drop and lay down. Her head ached, as it had all day. The relief the bark had offered had already worn off when she'd awakened, and she hadn't had time to stick it between her teeth again.

Not wanting Fi to get into trouble, Erryn had buried the pouch in the hay when she'd heard the guards coming for her. Hopefully it wouldn't be discovered when the hay was removed. If it was, Fi should have the good sense to hold her tongue, but she'd probably confess to prevent someone else from being falsely accused. Erryn hated that she'd no longer be there to advise Fi and calm her down. Fi could be hot-headed. *Don't do anything silly on my behalf, Fi. No good will come of it. Forget about me.*

Perhaps Fi already had. Erryn hadn't seen her this morning, but she hadn't looked for her, either. She'd wanted to ride through the gate with her chin up, not sniffling like a baby.

Fighting melancholy, she gingerly touched her forehead and traced the brand she could feel, but hadn't seen. She'd applied the ointment sometime during the night but doubted her forehead would heal any faster. Fi had said it looked like a mess. It must be red, and swollen, and ugly. According to the Holy Texts, everything about her was ugly, including her nature. She had a bestial soul. But how she felt inside hadn't changed since she'd first summoned one of the Fallen several months ago, in one of the castle's dusty chambers that nobody visited. As far as she could tell, she experienced the same emotions, desires, and needs as those around her. Did they feel differently inside? Could someone with the soul of a beast laugh, and cry, and love?

She knew those around her couldn't sense the Fallen, as she did. Since she'd given in that first night, they were always there, as if hovering in her peripheral vision. She could forget about them. Yesterday, she'd learned that pain could mask them. But they were always there, always waiting for her to summon them. Why had they chosen her?

She'd sneaked into the primate's study and read some of the passages the Primacy never read during lessons and services. The Fallen hadn't always been the Fallen. At one time, they'd served the Seven and occupied a privileged place in the heavenly hierarchy. But then they'd grown arrogant and offended the gods and goddesses, and so the Seven had transformed them from beloved servants into obedient pets. Now the Fallen used those cursed by the Seven to manifest into reality.

One passage said that each age could birth only a single Beast Master. Another had spoken of Beast Masters gathering together. Which one was right? Was she the only one who walked the land, or were there others? Why was she cursed? What had she done? Was it because of her mother, or because she was a bastard? She'd gone from a bedroom in the royal wing, two doors away from Fi's, to a dungeon, and now to this tent. At least her belly was full. She'd sat around the fire with the others and supped on delicious rabbit stew and a crust of bread.

She hadn't known what to expect from her escort. As she'd lain awake in her cell last night, she'd imagined scorn, beatings, and worse. But Reed, the guard in charge, was treating her well, and the other guards were following his lead. Of course, there was still time. The border was at least a week away. But Erryn wanted to believe they'd deliver her there in one piece and unscathed.

Her escort was her last connection to the only life she knew. She had no idea what she'd do when they sent her on her way. Try to find a village or town? Who would want to offer her board? What would she do when her coin ran out? Would she become one of the wild folk and live in the forests? Who would teach her how to survive?

As the Holy Texts taught, she, a Beast Master, had been abandoned by everyone but them. The Fallen.

The day after Erryn's departure, Fi left the primate's study and breathed a sigh of relief. She'd managed to keep her eyes open, but if Enkelo were to ask her what they'd covered, she'd have no answer for him. What should she do now? Go to the bazaar? That would only remind her of Erryn. Visit the stables? Erryn. Go to the music room? Erryn. She hadn't realized how much they did together, because unlike most others, Erryn had never bored her. Spending time with her hadn't been an endurance test, or an obligation, or an activity that made her want to gouge her eyes out. They'd squabbled, but never seriously. The last time Fi had been angry with her for more than a minute, she'd been four years old, and Erryn five. Never seeing her again . . .

Erryn was on a tour of the countryside. Yes, that was what she was doing. She didn't know when she'd be back. She could ride through the gates at any moment, bound up the grand staircase, burst into Fi's bedchamber, and drag her up to the wall to gaze at the stars—

It wasn't working. Perhaps time would allow Fi to go through her day without everything she saw, touched, or considered bringing her friend's face to mind. Today, she'd retire to her bedchamber, where only a servant, and possibly Father, would disturb her. But first . . .

She hurried to Erryn's bedchamber. Her heart leaped when she saw the open door. Several servants were inside, bustling about. A pile of clothing sat on the rug. A servant left the chamber carrying bedclothes. "What are you doing?" Fi shouted.

The servant jumped. "The king told us to empty the Beast Master's chamber, Princess."

"It's Erryn. Erryn's chamber." Fi brushed past him and stood in the doorway. "Get out, all of you."

Nobody moved.

Fi pointed to her left. "Out! Or I'll make all your lives miserable."

"But the king," one of them whispered, her eyes downcast.

"Come back in an hour. You can finish then."

The servants glanced at each other, then filed from the chamber. Fi grabbed one servant's arm. "Where are you taking her things?"

"We're burning them, Your Highness."

Her jaw clenched. She let go of the servant's arm; it wasn't his fault. So it was to be like this, then—every trace of Erryn eradicated. Father could pretend that Erryn had never existed, but nobody could touch Fi's memories.

She entered Erryn's chamber and pushed the door shut. The walls were bare. Had Father ordered the paintings burned? Was he that determined to destroy everything Erryn had touched? Drawers were pulled open and empty. Erryn's wardrobe was bare. Her shelves: empty. Her chest . . . someone had broken the lock. Fi crouched and lifted the chest's lid. Empty. Not a single scrap of parchment or clothing.

Still crouching, Fi turned toward the bookcase. Good, it was still there. She grasped the protruding book and pulled it from its hiding place. Then she sat on the bed with the book on her lap. She didn't have to blow away dust before she lifted the book's cover.

Erryn had written her name in the top right corner of the first page. The date from several months ago was written in the same place on the next page. Fi read the first paragraph Erryn had written, then closed the book and sprang from the bed. She'd promised Erryn that she'd burn the diary without reading it, but her curiosity was too strong to resist.

She opened the door a crack and peeked into the hall, then swung the door fully open and hurried into her own bedchamber. She'd have to hide the diary and read it in the wee hours of the morning and late at night. Father didn't always knock when he knew she was awake and dressed. She unlocked her chest using the key on the bracelet she wore and slipped the book underneath her own diary. She couldn't wait to read it. She'd nap now, so she could read by the light of a candle after Father and the servants had retired. If Erryn's diary was nothing more than a recounting of her days, Fi would still treasure it. It was all she had left.

Erryn kept her eyes forward as she and her escort cantered along the dirt road that cut through the middle of a village. Nobody shouted. Nobody threw anything. But they were watching—and judging. If she were to look at those who'd stopped to watch the group pass, she'd see the same anger, hate, and revulsion she'd seen when they'd ridden through the first villages they'd reached.

She didn't bother looking anymore. Not everyone scowled at the sight of her. Some appeared curious, even sympathetic. But most would gladly run her through. And that was why she was growing wary of the guards in her escort.

It should have been the other way around. The longer she was with them, the more she should have trusted them. After all, they fed her well, stayed out of her tent, chatted with her along country stretches, and threatened town folk and travellers who dared to shout names at her, or throw stones and fruit. The king would have ordered them to deliver her to the border in one piece, but that was a task they could accomplish without behaving as if they were lifelong friends. Instead of filling her bowl with a smile, they should be struggling to control their dislike.

Some folk lived their lives by the Holy Texts and revered the Primacy, especially in the Royal Province, where the Primacy's High Council resided. Others had no time for ancient texts. Most were somewhere in between, and most would shun her. The writings about Beast Masters were rarely taught, but everyone knew about those cursed with a bestial soul, who invited the Fallen into the world and angered the Seven. They'd all snickered at the obscene drawings and listened to the bards' tall tales. Ugly rumours abounded.

Erryn was of two minds about the exaggerated stories. On the one hand, they painted her a monster. On the other, they could help to keep her alive. Few would dare to challenge her. The guards in her escort likely believed she was cold-blooded and amoral, and would be difficult to kill. Nothing could be further from the truth.

When the Fallen manifested, they weren't invincible. A well-placed sword thrust couldn't kill them, but it would banish them, as would any other attack that would normally prove fatal. Also, Erryn couldn't summon all seven at once—or rather, it would be difficult to command all seven at the same time. Thus far, she'd only ever summoned one. She was afraid to summon two or more at a time. She still half expected them to turn on her.

She was a Beast Master, but she was vulnerable. If the men escorting her were gathering their courage to defy the king and kill the beast, she would face four armed and skilled guards. They could also slay her while she slept. Erryn would have to hope they remained faithful to the king, because they'd reach the border on the morrow.

Fi stifled a yawn as she watched two potential suitors show off their skill at musical fencing. One triple-stepped to the music the quartet in the corner of the banquet room played. With momentum on his side, he delivered a killing blow to his opponent's chest. The other man looked down to where the wooden sword had struck, then nodded and bowed. Fi clapped along with the others and smiled when the two men doffed their caps to her.

If only Erryn were here. Rather than struggling to keep her eyelids from sliding shut, Fi would be exchanging witty observations with her, and they'd bet on who would win each match. Though after reading Erryn's diary, Fi admitted that perhaps it was better that Erryn was gone.

Still, she wished Erryn had ridden through the gates because she'd wanted to leave, and not because Father had banished her.

Fi had thought they'd shared everything with each other. Apparently not. She wasn't sure how she felt about Erryn's second secret. It almost unsettled her more than the knowledge that Erryn was a Beast Master. Disappointingly, Erryn's diary contained no details about when she'd known, or how the Fallen had enticed her. *I need to see you again, friend. There's too much left unsaid between us.* When Fi was married, she expected to tour the provinces, so the people could see her with her new husband. *Please, Erryn, find me.* Could she somehow spread the word that she wished to meet with the Beast Master and offer a reward to anyone who could provide a clue to her whereabouts, or would doing so put Erryn in jeopardy?

Those at her table were clapping again. One of the next two competitors would likely have her hand in marriage. The Duke of Tolin's eldest son was Father's favourite. Tolin belonged to one of Daros's oldest, most respected, and most loyal families. Viren, his eldest son, was a bit older and wider in girth than Fi would have preferred. But he was well educated, wealthy, would give her whatever she wanted, and expect her to run the household. All she had to do in return was provide him with an heir. Marrying for love wasn't for princesses, and she'd observed that love's ardour cooled after a time, sometimes leaving behind bitter, hateful enemies. She and the man she married wouldn't have any illusions.

Someone leaned over her shoulder. "See anyone you fancy?"

Fi didn't turn around. "I have to say Viren, don't I?" she said to Henrick.

Henrick chuckled. "He's a decent man, Fi. Every girl here would accept his proposal."

"Don't worry, I won't be difficult."

"If Erryn were here, she'd try to talk you out of it."

Fi had to restrain herself from twisting in her chair so she could see his face. Had Erryn confided in him? "No doubt," she said levelly. "If you don't mind, I don't want to talk about Erryn."

"Father had to banish her. He had no choice."

"I know, Henrick, and I just said I don't want to talk about her. Where's Surann? Is she with child yet? It's been a year."

Henrick tutted. "There's no need for that."

Fi finally turned around and saw the scowl she'd expected. "Is she?"

Henrick shrugged and walked away. Fi stared after him with hope in her heart. Everyone in the kingdom was waiting for Father's heir to have a son. It was an understandably touchy subject for Henrick, yet he hadn't fought back.

More clapping. Fi turned her attention to the competitors and clapped extra hard when Viren accepted his opponent's congratulations and doffed his cap at her. All right, now that he'd competed, it was time for what she'd planned to do while everyone was occupied. She murmured her pardons to the two ladies seated next to her and glided from the banquet room. Fortunately all the servants were busy seeing to the guests—except one.

"Thank you," she said to the servant who'd kept a roaring fire alive in the bedchamber. "You've done well."

The servant curtsied and scurried away.

Fi pushed her door closed, then went to her chest and slid Erryn's diary from its hiding place. Gathering her resolve, she held it in her hands for a moment, then threw it into the roaring fire. She sat on her bed and watched the diary's pages and its flimsy parchment cover curl in the flames. *What were you thinking, Erryn? You knew not to write anything about being a Beast Master. Why couldn't you have exercised the same caution when it came to your heart?* If Erryn had, Fi wouldn't be watching the fire destroy her only tangible link to her dearest friend. She supposed she could have torn out and kept a page or two, but it was better that no trace of the diary remained.

When the fire had completed its work, she doused it and left her chamber with a heavy heart. She'd intended to return to the banquet, but felt compelled to climb the stairs and go out to walk the wall. She sighed. She couldn't remember ever feeling lonely. When she'd wanted for company, Erryn had always obliged. She was glad she was to marry. Father was right. Getting to know her husband and running a household wouldn't allow her time to miss Erryn. Then there would be children to raise and—

"Good evening to you, Princess."

Fi gasped. Her hand went to her throat.

"I'm sorry. I didn't mean to frighten you."

Following the direction of the voice, she looked up. A

man stood on top of the parapet. "What are you doing up there? Get down!"

He grinned at her and pirouetted.

Fi's heart thumped. "Stop it! You'll fall."

He continued twirling.

Fi could hardly bear to watch. When he teetered for a moment, she sucked in her breath. "I don't care what happens to you, but if you fall into the courtyard, it will shock those below."

He froze and pouted. "You don't care what happens to me? I'm hurt."

"Shouldn't you be inside taking part in the competition?"

The man leaped off the parapet and landed in front of her with a thud. He swayed for a moment, then bowed deeply before her. When he straightened, she could see that he was young, perhaps twenty, the same age as her. "I'm not competing for your hand, Princess. That honour has fallen to my older brother. We'll be related, though. I am Dann, third son of the Duke of Tolin." He lifted her hand to his lips and kissed it. "I am pleased to make your acquaintance, Your Highness."

"And I, yours," Fi said, "though I haven't accepted your brother. He hasn't yet proposed."

"He will." Dann's blue eyes met hers. "I envy him."

"I'd imagine you do. I'll take your words as a compliment, and not as jealousy of your brother." As the eldest son, Viren would marry well, be granted land, and sit on the council. Dann would marry the daughter of a lesser noble and live a quiet life in the country. He wouldn't have a hand in guiding the kingdom. He'd come to the castle perhaps once a year, and Father would ignore him.

"Do you often come up here and gaze at the stars?" Dann asked.

"Yes." Her throat tightened. "Though usually with a friend. I don't think I'll be doing it much anymore."

Dann's brow furrowed. "Your friend . . . the one who was banished?"

She wasn't surprised that he knew of Erryn. News of a Beast Master at the castle, and so close to the princess, would have spread faster than a plague. "Yes. But I don't wish to speak about her with you. What are you doing up here? You don't have to be vying for my hand to take part in the fencing competition."

"I must confess, and I feel comfortable doing so because I know I can't have your hand, I must confess that I enjoy quieter pursuits. I would rather read than wield a sword."

Fi raised her brows. That was a bold confession, indeed, and probably the most honest words a man had spoken to her all evening. "Do you hunt?"

"Of course. But not for sport. I don't consider it a fair competition, especially when hunting with a group."

Fi didn't know what to make of him. "And you enjoy gazing at the stars?"

He nodded. "Though I'll admit, I usually read by the moonlight and a lantern, rather than—"

"There you are, Your Highness," a voice interrupted. Viren stepped from the shadows. "One of the servants told me you might be up here." He frowned at Dann.

"You should return to the banquet hall, brother. You'll be missed."

Dann didn't protest. His eyes lingered on Fi's face, then he bowed and strode away. Viren shook his head. "The boy needs to learn some manners. I apologize on his behalf, Your Highness."

"There's no need. And please, call me Filmona."

Viren smiled. "Filmona." He offered her his arm. "Let me escort you back to the banquet hall."

She rested her hand on his arm. They strolled along the wall. "What were you doing up here, Filmona?"

"I come up here to look at the stars."

"I used to do that as well, when I was a child. Now I have too many duties. You will, too, when you marry and run a household. You'll find there won't be much time for daydreaming."

"I hope to always dream, sir."

Viren grunted. "I came looking for you because I would like to invite you to sup with me at my father's home."

"That would be lovely. I accept." Fi wondered if Dann would be at the table.

Erryn lay on her bedroll and stared toward the tent's flap. All was quiet, but she couldn't shake the sense of foreboding that hung over her. Before she'd retired, the guards had seemed edgy. Reed hadn't given her the coin or letter from the king, but she assumed he'd do that on the morrow, when they reached the Rion border. She was likely seeing shadows where there weren't any, but the

Fallen had also been whispering to her, warning her of danger and pleading with her to summon them.

She didn't quite trust the Fallen yet. The first time she'd summoned Zayvang, she'd held her breath, expecting Zayvang to kill her. But Zayvang hadn't. She'd sat and studied Erryn with unblinking eyes. Then she'd lain at Erryn's feet and hadn't flinched when Erryn had carefully reached out and patted her head. Since that first night, Erryn had called three more of the seven Fallen. She couldn't summon the remaining three within the castle's chamber. The Fallen were larger than other members of their species, or so the Holy Texts said. At one time, Erryn would have accepted what they taught without question, but now she wondered.

As for tonight . . . she gave in. *Zayvang.* The saber-tooth cat leaped into existence, almost landing on Erryn's chest. Uncertain whether Zayvang could see her in the darkness, Erryn put a finger to her lips. *Quiet, Zayvang. Guard me.* Silence, then the large cat lay down next to her. Erryn pressed against her for warmth. Rion was north of the Royal City. The nights had grown cooler. If innkeepers weren't willing to rent her a room, she could spend many cool nights in a tent.

She dozed off.

Snarling. A scream! Erryn's eyes snapped open. She sat up. It was still dark. Something was thrashing. Her stomach roiled. Zayvang was . . . eating. *Stop! Sit!*

Zayvang obeyed. Erryn crawled toward the shadowy shape. Her hands felt wet. She turned them palms-up. She didn't have to see them to know what was on them.

Blood. Zayvang suddenly darted past her and out of the tent. Erryn stumbled to her feet and went after her.

Stop! Don't kill! But she was too late. Zayvang ripped out the throat of the other guard who'd been on watch. *To me!* Zayvang loped over to her.

"On your knees, Beast Master," a voice snapped.

Erryn looked to her left. One of the remaining two guards had come out of the tent he shared with the others. He brandished his sword. "Dismiss your cat."

In her peripheral vision, she saw the other guard circling around the fire to get to Zayvang. Should she surrender? Reed must be the one in her tent, dead. Had he entered it to slay her, or to merely speak to her? She'd told Zayvang to guard her, not to kill. "Reed came into my tent," she said, hoping the nearest guard would offer a hint of what Reed had intended.

"You killed him."

Where was the other guard? *Stay.* "He shouldn't have come into my—"

Movement, behind her. She whirled. As Erryn had commanded, Zayvang stayed. The guard Erryn now faced ran Zayvang through. She disappeared. "Kill the Beast Master," shouted the one Erryn had been talking to.

Two against one. Erryn didn't have time to think. *Cheturrak!*

The force of Cheturrak's arrival drove her to her knees. The mammoth roared and stomped toward the nearest guard. He froze for a moment, then dropped his sword and fled. Erryn looked over her shoulder, expecting the other guard to take advantage of her vulnerable position and take off her head. But he was also on his knees, his mouth hanging open and his eyes wide. "Don't kill me," he pleaded. "Please don't kill me."

Cheturrak had returned to her side and spotted the guard. The mammoth lumbered toward him.

Stay! Erryn barked, her heart pounding and her mouth dry. She half expected Cheturrak to ignore her, but he stopped. She slowly pushed herself to her feet and stood in the shadow of the great beast.

Still on his knees, the guard lay down his sword. "I would have let you go across the border, I swear. But we had our orders."

"From Reed?"

"From the king. Reed was only doing what the king asked of him."

No. "So he came into my tent to kill me while I slept?"

The guard lowered his eyes and nodded.

Then she couldn't blame Zayvang for slaying him. There wouldn't have been time to do much else.

"Please, Beast Master," the guard whimpered. "I was only following orders."

She wasn't a killer, but he wouldn't believe her. "Take a horse and go."

He looked up at her.

"Go!"

He hesitated, then scrambled to his feet and untied one of the horses. Eager to get away, he mounted and kicked it into a gallop. The guard who'd fled on foot could come back and kill her, but he was more than likely halfway to the nearest village.

Erryn braced herself and turned toward Cheturrak. *Thank you. Return.* Cheturrak vanished.

She sat next to the fire and stared into it, listening to it crackle. She felt numb, and afraid. Only when the sun rose did she return to her tent. Reed's lifeless eyes stared up at her. His fingers were clenched around the hilt of his unsheathed sword. Erryn looked at the mess that used to be his throat and stumbled from the tent, retching. She doubled over and heaved, but nothing came out. It wasn't only Reed. It was the other guard with a shredded throat, too.

She had to get away. Forcing herself to go back into her tent, she grimaced and fished through Reed's pockets. A few coins, and nothing else. She went into the guards' tent and searched Reed's bag. No coin. No letter from the king. The plan from the start had been to kill her. Did Fi know?

She drew a ragged breath and left the tent. Her eyes settled on the dead guard again, splayed on his back. From where he was lying, she could tell he'd been heading for her tent. The two guards who'd escaped would denounce the savagery of the Beast Master and her pets, but she'd had no choice. They'd left her and Zayvang no choice. They'd been the aggressors, not her. If she hadn't heeded the Fallens' warnings, hadn't trusted her sense that she was in danger . . . She didn't want to see everyone as a potential threat. She didn't want to live that way. But she was branded.

She lifted one of the swords the fleeing guards had left behind, then dropped it. Never having trained with the weapon, she'd be more likely to hurt herself than anyone else. She went back into the guards' tent. Not surprisingly, her escort's food supply had dwindled. They'd planned to replenish it on their way home, at the last village they'd passed. Erryn added the meagre supplies to the clothing in her bag, then put out the fire and freed the remaining horses. Her blood-spattered tent would remain behind, protecting Reed from the sun.

She mounted her horse and looked in the direction of the Royal City, Fi, and the only life she knew. Then she rode toward the border, with a few coins in her pocket, food that would soon run out, and a brand on her forehead warning everyone that she was bestial and cursed. She was a Beast Master. She was an animal.

On The Run

Hoping he'd misunderstood their report, Oswald stared at the two subdued guards standing in front of his desk. "Reed, dead?"

One of the guards nodded. The guard captain with them cleared his throat. "Jenkins is also dead, Your Majesty."

Oswald was sure Jenkins had been an upstanding and loyal guard, but Jenkins hadn't performed countless messy jobs for his sovereign and kept his mouth shut over the years. Reed had been a rock. Oswald had trusted him with his life. "And the Beast Master escaped?"

The three men nodded.

"What happened?" he croaked.

The two guards glanced at each other. "She summoned Zayvang," one said.

"And Cheturrak," the other said, wide-eyed.

Cheturrak? Oswald swallowed. May the Seven help them all.

"It was the night before we'd have reached the border. After she'd gone into her tent, Reed told us he'd take care of her while she slept. He—"

"It should have been easy," the other guard said. "All he had to do was run her through. She wouldn't have had time—"

"Obviously she did," Oswald snapped. He massaged his forehead. "Go on."

"Zayvang killed Reed in the tent," the first guard continued. "Jenkins was on first watch with Reed. He must have been on his way to help. He didn't make it." The man grimaced. "His screams woke us. We rushed to his aid, but it was too late. The Beast Master came out of her tent. When we told her to surrender, she summoned Cheturrak." He shifted his weight. "I ran. I know that sounds cowardly, but—"

"I'm sure most men would have done the same at the sight of Cheturrak."

"He was as tall as the keep!" the guard said.

Oswald didn't know whether or not to believe him. "What did you do?" he said to the other guard.

The guard hesitated. "I—I ran," he said quietly.

"Neither of you spoke to her."

"Not after I saw Cheturrak," the first guard said.

"And you?" Oswald said to the second guard.

"No . . . I—I didn't speak to her."

"So she killed Reed and Jenkins, and would have done the same to you, if you hadn't fled."

The first guard nodded. After a moment, the second guard did the same, his eyes downcast.

Oswald looked to the captain. "Do we have any idea where she is now?"

"No. We think she took a horse."

Then she could be anywhere, including on her way back here. "Double the guard at the gates. I want four guards with the princess at all times. Capture the Beast Master on sight."

"Yes, Your Majesty."

He wanted to order them to kill her on sight, but he wouldn't have the guards slay her in front of Fi. She'd never speak to him again. "You may go."

The three men saluted and filed from his study. Oswald beckoned to his steward, who'd stood quietly listening. "Tell the princess I want to see her. And summon Arrick." It was time to involve the Ferrets.

Fi marched into Father's study and whirled toward the door. "You can wait outside," she shouted to the guards who'd approached her in the garden and informed her that the king had ordered them to protect her. She slammed the door shut and felt a modicum of satisfaction when Father winced. "I can guess why you asked to see me." Fi pointed at the door. "Will they go to the privy with me, too?"

"Fi—"

"What's happened? Why do I have four guards following me around like lost puppies?"

Father blew out a sigh. "Erryn killed two of her escorts and escaped."

No.

"Reed is one of the dead."

She grabbed the back of the nearest chair to steady herself. When Father quickly rounded his desk and took her elbow, she didn't protest.

"I'm sorry," he said, supporting her as she sank into the chair. "The other two guards barely escaped with their lives." He met her eyes. "She summoned Cheturrak."

"Cheturrak," Fi breathed. "But why? Why would she kill two guards? She must have had a reason."

"She's a beast, Fi. She's a beast commanding beasts. She's amoral and savage. She doesn't care about right and wrong."

"She did a good job of hiding it!" Fi said. "She certainly behaved like a human being to me." Either she was the thickest and most gullible person in the land, or Erryn was a woman like any other. Why would she kill Reed and another guard? Erryn had never been aggressive or confrontational. Whenever Fi had been upset and wanting to throttle someone, Erryn had always been the voice of reason. Father had given her safe passage to the border. Why would she turn around and slay two of his men? There had to be more to the story. "Are you sure the two survivors are telling the truth? Maybe they killed Reed and the other guard."

Father's brows shot up. "Why would they do that?"

"I don't know." She wouldn't say that she'd find that

story easier to believe than the one they'd told. "Erryn saved my life, and suddenly she's an animal."

"It was the way she saved your life, and you know it," Father said, a warning edge in his voice. "She likely did it so that when she revealed her true nature, you'd do exactly what you're doing now. Defending her. Ignoring the Holy Texts' teachings. She didn't do it because she cared about you."

Fi was certain Erryn had done it because she did care and had truly wanted to save her life, but Father's ears were closed as far as Erryn went.

"Under other circumstances, I'd admire your loyalty to her," Father said. "But I can't let you be loyal this time. She could be coming back."

Fi had figured that out the moment Father had told her Erryn had supposedly slain two guards. She hadn't asked him if Erryn was dead because the four guards now following her around provided the answer. She'd liked Reed and was sorry he was gone, but her loyalty remained with Erryn. "What are you going to do about her?"

Father moistened his lips. "The guard and Ferrets are searching for her. She'll be brought back here for a trial."

Fi snorted. "Trial? She'll be convicted and executed."

His face tightened. "She killed two guards. She's not the friend you knew. I know you miss her, but it's time to stop moping about. You'll sup with Viren soon. No man likes a long face."

Well, excuse her for not snapping her fingers and forgetting a life-long friend in an instant! An engagement and marriage would keep her busy, but she'd always wonder about what had happened to Erryn. Not knowing whether her friend was alive or dead would haunt her forever, but it would be more bearable than watching her hang. *Don't come back, Erryn. Run as far as you can, and keep running.*

Erryn plucked her lute's strings and sang as loudly as she could without straining her voice and sounding like a shrew. It was a losing battle. Raucous laughter, shouted conversation, and the occasional whistle drowned her out. She didn't mind much. The tavern's patrons still left her tips at the bar, even though few listened to her. Fortunately she knew the song she was singing inside out, because thoughts of Fi kept intruding. The more Erryn tried not to think about her, the more she saw Fi's face, heard her laugh, ached to see her again.

"You can pack it in now, love," Darla, the landlady, yelled as she passed Erryn carrying a tray loaded with drinks. "Freddy will take care of you. See you on the morrow."

Erryn nodded and finished her song. A few clapped when she bowed; most didn't notice. With a sigh, she threaded her way to the bar. Freddy winked and dropped several coins into her hand. "Good job, Erryn."

"Thanks," she murmured as she handed him her lute to store behind the bar. Her little corner in the cellar had enough room for a bedroll, nothing more.

"Have a drink," Freddy said.

When she shook her head, Freddy did the same. "Even the primates have an ale now and then."

The primates didn't have to worry about summoning

the Fallen and losing control of them because they weren't thinking straight. To think that she used to sneak into the castle's wine cellar with Fi and hope the sommelier wouldn't notice a missing bottle or two . . . Now Erryn wouldn't touch the stuff, or anything that could addle her wits.

"I'm tired," she said to Freddy. "Good night."

"Night," Freddy said absently, his attention already on a thirsty patron.

Erryn went to the cellar entrance and reached for the lantern hanging on a hook beside it, then jerked her hand away when an arm slipped around her waist. One of the regulars pulled her into him and pushed her against the wall. "You don't have to sleep alone, you know," Kell said. His breath stank of ale.

She turned her head away from him, but his calloused hand went to her cheek and forced her face toward his. He grabbed her breast with his other hand. His lips pressed against hers. She mustered her strength and struggled to push him away, but he had her pinned. He pushed his tongue between her lips, trying to force them open. The Fallen called to her. She didn't want to . . . she'd be driven from the town . . . He squeezed her breast hard, bringing tears to her eyes. "Stop!" she wanted to shout, but if she opened her mouth, his tongue would win. The Fallen grew agitated. They called to her. She wanted to resist them, but—

The pressure on her eased abruptly. Freddy jerked Kell away from her and scowled at him.

"What do you think you're doing?" Darla shrieked from

behind Freddy. "We'll have none of that in here. Get him out!"

Kell swung at Freddy, but Freddy easily sidestepped Kell's drunken attempt to slug him. He twisted Kell's arm behind his back and shoved him toward the tavern door.

"Are you all right, love?" Darla said to Erryn.

Trembling, Erryn hugged herself and sucked down air. She desperately wanted to wash, but it would mean going outside and fetching water from the well.

Darla's forehead creased with concern. "Do you want a drink?"

"No. I'm okay." Erryn cursed the tremor in her voice. "I just want to go to bed. Thank Freddy for me."

It took her three tries to light the lantern. Halfway down the cellar steps, she stopped to steady herself and catch her breath. The lantern's light cast a shaky path through the gloom. She carefully descended into the cellar. The leaping shadows, the barrels she could barely see, and the shouts and clatter from upstairs had never frightened her before, but tonight they set her heart racing. She found the corner she called home and sank onto the bedroll. After dousing the light, she hugged her legs to her chest and listened for footsteps.

She could still smell his breath, feel his hand on her throbbing breast, taste his lips. It was her fault. She'd jumped at Darla's offer to stay in the cellar. Every night, she'd come down here and fallen asleep. She hadn't considered, had never thought—nobody would have dared touch her at the castle. One word to Fi would have had the man thrown in the dungeons or banished. Erryn had no protection here—except for the Fallen.

Her bond with them was growing stronger. After leaving behind the two dead guards at the camp, she'd vowed not to call the Fallen again, but she couldn't resist them. Every morning she left the town, found a deserted farmer's field, and summoned them. Not caring whether they turned on her, she'd tried to call two together, then three. She was confident she could call and command four together, perhaps all of them. Of the three she hadn't called all those months ago in the castle's dusty room, only one remained unsummoned. Rachagha would attract attention no matter where Erryn summoned her.

She'd discovered that her bond with Zayvang ran deeper than it did with the other five she'd summoned. When she'd given in and called one of the Fallen into this world for the first time, she'd thought she'd chosen Zayvang, but now she wondered. All six obeyed her, but Zayvang . . . Erryn sensed love from her.

Her sore breast reminded her that she had a problem. She doubted Darla would refuse Kell's coin. Even if she did, Erryn wouldn't sleep a wink in this cellar again, not without a Fallen sleeping at her side. But given what had happened at the camp, she wouldn't risk asking one to guard her. She'd stayed here in Moss too long as it was.

Galloping away from the guards' camp, she'd told herself that she'd have to keep moving to avoid recapture. She'd sold the horse when she'd reached Moss, probably settling for much less than she should have. Every time she haggled with a merchant, she had this sinking feeling they were laughing at her. Her studies at the castle hadn't covered bartering with street merchants over the cost of an apple. But the coin from the horse had kept her belly full. She'd also bought clothing, including a thick wool cloak, and her lute.

She hadn't paid much attention to the street performers when she and Fi had ventured into the city. She'd watched them in this town's square through different eyes. Instead of using her singing and music lessons to entertain visitors at a country estate, she'd sing and play with a cap at her feet. The brand on her forehead wouldn't frighten them away. Outside the first village she'd reached, she'd ripped a strip of cloth from her shirt and tied it around her head. A terrible scar from a burn, she explained to the few who asked. Let everyone think she was vain. The Seven didn't curse those who were vain.

Her performances in the square had usually brought her enough coin to buy herself supper. She'd used some of the remaining coin from selling the horse to rent a safe place to sleep at night. The rest was still in the pouch underneath her shirt. It wasn't much, but she was determined not to spend it unless she had to. There wouldn't be any coin left at all, if Darla hadn't approached her in the square and invited her to play at the tavern. When she'd found out that Erryn didn't have a home, she'd offered the corner in the cellar, "until you're on your feet, love."

Erryn had quickly accepted—and grown too comfortable. It had been easy to spend time with the Fallen in the mornings, play sets in the tavern the rest of the day, and then sleep. Darla and Freddy had been welcome company. But Erryn was a criminal. The king's men would be hunting her. She'd stayed at the tavern for almost three weeks, and it had taken her several days to reach Moss, the closest town to the border. She'd had a head start on the guard, one she shouldn't squander. Messenger birds could travel faster than she could. For all she knew, men were already checking the inns and taverns here. Asking the locals for directions had been foolish. She might as well have left signposts behind for the guard. From now on, she'd let the roads take her wherever they led.

She'd leave on the morrow, when the sun was shining and Kell would be at home, hopefully with an aching head. Until then, she'd sit in the dark and listen, ready to call Zayvang.

Arrick Inel, the Ferret spymaster, clasped his hands atop his desk when the unscheduled visitor his assistant had warned him about stepped into his office. This was turning out to be an interesting day, indeed. First the meeting with the king, and now the royal primate within the spies den itself. Arrick gestured toward a chair. "Sit down, Primate."

Enkelo hesitated, then dropped into the chair. "I'm here on behalf of the High Council."

Arrick waited.

"You heard the king. He wants the Beast Master captured and brought back for trial."

"Yes," Arrick murmured.

"Do you know where she is?"

"I presume you're asking whether we were shadowing her and her escort. The answer is no." There was no harm in being honest with Enkelo on this point. Arrick's agents within the castle had informed him of the king's plan to kill the woman, and the king hadn't requested the Ferrets' aid. The matter had seemed well in hand—four guards against one fledgling Beast Master. The fools had bungled it, something Arrick's agents would never have done.

Unlike his predecessors, this king didn't value the Ferrets. He always called on them last. When Arrick had risen to spymaster, he'd anticipated the king's needs and dispatched agents before receiving a formal request to do so. He still anticipated the king's needs, but he no longer dispatched the agents. The king deserved any consequences that resulted from the Ferrets' inaction.

The Beast Master had escaped, and guards were bumbling around inns and taverns in search of information about the princess's attackers, asking questions too loudly and annoying patrons. When he'd received the king's summons to today's meeting, Arrick had expected the king to finally ask him to look into the assassination attempt. But no, he was more concerned about the Beast Master.

"I don't know where she is, but I'll find out," he said, returning to Enkelo's question. "Wine?"

"Please."

Arrick rose and poured two goblets of vintage red. He handed a goblet to Enkelo. "Why are you here, Primate?"

Enkelo chuckled. "Down to business, as usual." He

sipped his wine and nodded appreciatively. "The king wants the Beast Master brought back for trial. He wants to show the princess that he's being fair."

"You can't blame the man for wanting to remain in his daughter's good graces." Arrick sipped his own wine, and let the liquid linger on his tongue before swallowing.

"The Beast Master's existence is an affront to the Seven and the Primacy. If not for the princess, the king would have ordered her killed, not captured. We've seen what she's capable of doing. It doesn't matter how many men guard her. Anything but killing her is putting the people in danger."

"And offending the Seven," Arrick said.

"Yes. We'd like to help the king, relieve him of his burden. He's asked you to report the Beast Master's location to the guard. We'd like you to kill her."

Well, well, well. "You're suggesting that I go against the king's orders."

"By ordering her captured and brought to trial, the king has effectively ordered her death. The Beast Master will be found guilty. She'll hang. The trial will exist solely to appease the princess. I understand that the king loves his daughter, but a sovereign shouldn't allow emotion to cloud his judgment." Enkelo's voice hardened. "How many lives will be lost so his daughter will continue to smile at him?"

Arrick sipped his wine.

"You can tell the king your agents reported her dead. You don't have to mention that one of them killed her."

"She might very well be dead. She's city born and bred, has been cared for all her life, and she's branded."

"She also has the Fallen at her disposal."

"Which is why an assassination order would require a high price." Arrick raised his brows. "As would defying the king."

Enkelo scowled. "The king—"

"Wants her brought back for trial. But I see your point."

"Thirty thousand in gold."

Arrick snorted. "It was good to see you, Primate. My boy will see you out."

Enkelo's expression didn't change. "In addition, you can choose a bottle of wine from the High Council's collection." He raised his goblet. "This is adequate, but nothing compared to the vintage you'll find in our wine cellar."

Arrick's hands clenched. Adequate? Enkelo was sipping exquisite vintage wine from one of Daros's top vineyards! Imbecile. One who wouldn't get the better of him. Arrick relaxed his fingers and slowed his breathing. "Three bottles."

Enkelo straightened, then his shoulders sagged. "Very well. Bring us her head." He drained his goblet and rose. "I'll see myself out."

Arrick waited until he could no longer hear Enkelo's footsteps, then whistled to the agent who'd listened from the concealed compartment behind a tapestry. Avere emerged from her hiding place and lifted Enkelo's empty goblet. "I'd wondered if you'd poisoned it, until you drank yours."

Arrick gave her an indulgent look. "Killing him would get us nowhere."

"Finding the Beast Master should be a simple matter."

"I've already dispatched the birds." But he was beginning to appreciate that the Beast Master was anything but a simple matter. "I want you on her," he said to not only his best agent, but the only one he fully trusted.

Avere's eyes widened. "Why? I thought you just agreed to kill her."

"And I probably will. But there's more going on here than we know." He didn't believe for a second that Enkelo and the High Council were upset because the Seven were offended. If that were the case, today wouldn't have been the first time he'd had a primate in his office, arranging an assassination.

He pulled a map from the case next to his desk and unrolled it on a table. "Here's where she killed the guards," he said, jabbing his finger on a location near the Rion border. "The king is worried she might be coming back here, but she could be anywhere."

"I'll make inquiries along the way."

"I'll send information as I get it."

Avere nodded. "So I'm not to approach or kill her."

"No. You're to send me her location. Mark it for my eyes only. Then stay on her and wait for instructions."

"I'll ride immediately." Avere strode toward the door.

"Avere."

She whirled.

"The Beast Master has thwarted an assassination attempt and killed two guards. According to the Primacy, her bond with the Fallen will only grow stronger." He poured more wine into his goblet and raised it to her. "Be careful."

"Don't worry, Arrick."

He jumped when the goblet in his hand shattered.

"I don't have to get anywhere near her to kill her." Avere walked past him and pulled her dagger from where it had thudded into the wall. "I hope the wine wasn't *too* expensive."

He watched her slink from the room, then shook his head at the puddle and broken glass on the carpet. That puddle was probably worth more than many folk made in a year, but he was confident Avere would find the Beast Master. If his instincts proved right, he'd be able to afford many more bottles of wine after selling the Beast Master's location—or assassination—to the highest bidder. The High Council's bid would be the first of many. The king would get whatever Arrick decided to tell him.

Fi nodded to the servant and watched him add another piece of cake to her plate. This would be the last one; she didn't want to embarrass herself when the seamstresses measured her for her wedding dress. Not that Viren had proposed, but it wouldn't be long now.

"They should be back soon," Lady Vivien said.

"Any moment, my lady," the servant murmured as he slid cake onto her plate. "They've arrived at the stables and should join you shortly."

"Did I ask you whether they'd returned?" Vivien snapped.

The servant's face flushed. "No, my lady. I apologize."

Vivien picked up her fork and jabbed it into her cake. Fi would have given the servant a sympathetic smile, if she wasn't fretting over Viren's return from that afternoon's hunt. Over several suppers, walks, and outings to cultural events such as the theatre, she'd come to know her future husband better. He treated her kindly, occasionally made her laugh, and they'd discovered a shared interest in the opera. But the passion she'd read about in the books Father would prefer she didn't read wasn't there. No spark. No longing. No counting the hours until she'd see him again. She'd told herself that she was more fortunate than those who were forced to marry cruel men, or men who treated them like possessions. It hadn't helped, because she knew there could be more.

If only she'd returned to the banquet that night. If only she hadn't walked the wall and met the man she couldn't get out of her mind. It was silly. She'd hardly said three words to Dann, and not much more since then. When she was on the Tolin Estate, as she was now, Viren was usually at her side, or both his brothers were away.

She liked Viren. Perhaps she'd eventually love him, as Mother had told her would happen when the time came. "I didn't love your father at first," she'd said, "but it didn't take long for me to fall in love with him." But had there been a Dann for her, a man who set her heart racing whenever she gazed at him?

If Erryn were here, Fi would chew her ear off about Viren and Dann. And if Erryn were here, Fi wouldn't have read her diary and known how much Erryn would have hated hearing about how she wished she could feel for Viren what she felt for Dann. *Where are you? Somewhere far away, I hope.*

She'd managed to persuade her lost puppies that she'd be safe on the Tolin Estate, so it would be all right for them to spend the afternoon at the Tolin guard barracks. Erryn wasn't likely to stride across the lawn with the Fallen at her heels. Fi liked to imagine that Erryn had used the coin and Father's letter of recommendation to buy herself a cottage in a quiet village that tolerated her. She couldn't bear to think of the other possibilities. If the guard captured her and brought her back for trial, Fi wouldn't be among those who watched her hang. She didn't care what Father threatened her with. She would not go.

Vivien squared her shoulders and smoothed her dress. "They're here," she breathed.

Fi glanced over her shoulder. Viren led the hunting group to the ladies taking afternoon tea in the garden. Fi smiled at him when he sat next to her. "Did you do well?" she asked.

"Very well. The steward will be pleased. I believe Lord Eness bagged the most," he said, jutting his chin toward the man who'd pulled out the chair next to Vivien.

"How wonderful!" Vivien squealed. She already loved the man she'd marry.

Fi envied her. Why couldn't she feel for Viren what she felt for Dann? There was nothing wrong with Viren. He'd make a perfectly acceptable husband. She felt comfortable with him. She could be content with him. Comfort. Contentment. Bah.

"Viren was a close second, Your Highness," Eness said.

"I'm impressed," Fi said, meaning it. "You'll have to tell me all about it."

Viren's eyes shone. "I will."

Fi cut away another mouthful of cake. It was obvious that his feelings for her ran deep, which made it all the worse.

Someone nearby guffawed loudly. She lifted her eyes and pressed her lips together. Who was that woman with Dann? She had the face of a hound and needed a more competent seamstress, but she'd made him laugh. Fi's stomach knotted. Dann didn't care about her. He didn't lie awake in bed thinking about her, or remember their brief conversation word for word whenever he looked up at the stars, or wonder if he'd catch a glimpse of her when she came to the estate. He'd marry a woman with a title that didn't count, labour away on a country estate that nobody cared about, and have children who'd carry less weight at court than he did. Oh, how she'd envy that woman!

"Would you like to go for a stroll, Filmona?" Viren leaned toward her and lowered his voice. "You seem to have gone off your cake. Are you bored?"

She frowned at the forkful of cake poised midway between her plate and mouth. "A walk would be lovely," she said, resting the fork on her plate. She didn't want to listen to Dann laugh and watch him flirt with every woman except her. She pushed back her chair and accepted Viren's hand.

"Excuse us," Viren murmured to Vivien and Eness. Fi could feel everyone's eyes on them as they strode across the lawn toward a tree-lined path.

"I hope you don't think me rude, seizing the first opportunity to have you all to myself."

"Not at all. Vivien and I had run out of things to say."

Viren swept out his free arm. "Do you like the estate?"

"It's beautiful," Fi said, finding the question odd.

"Father isn't well. He isn't expected to live out the year."

Fi had heard rumours about the duke's health, but he'd looked all right the last time she'd seen him. Then again, he hadn't participated in today's hunt. Fi had assumed he was otherwise occupied. "I'm sorry."

Viren inclined his head. "The estate will be mine. I'd rather have Father alive and well, of course, but he'll soon be with the Seven." He stopped and turned to Fi. "It's time for me to marry and have an heir."

Viren had finally set her heart racing, but for the wrong reason. She hadn't expected him to propose today.

Viren frowned. At first Fi thought that she'd failed to hide her dismay, but then she heard the footsteps behind her.

"Sir," a man called out. "Sir."

Viren let go of Fi's hand and stepped past her. "What is it?"

The man took a moment to catch his breath. "I'm sorry, sir, but Duke Bale's man is here. He says he has contracts for you to sign, and he's here to negotiate the . . ."

Fi didn't hear the rest of what the man said. Dann was strolling up the path. She forced herself to focus on the conversation at hand.

"Today?" Viren said. "He must have mixed up the date. We were supposed to meet on the morrow."

"When I told him about the hunt, he begged your pardon, sir. Niall suggested that he stay overnight and conduct his business on the morrow, but he said you'd arranged for today, and he has another appointment on the morrow."

Viren groaned. "They're important contracts."

Dann joined them. "Problem, brother? I saw Ross bolt after you as if he had one of the Fallen nipping at his heels."

"It's Bale. His man has arrived early."

"It's all right, Viren," Fi said, silently offering thanks to the Seven. "We can continue our conversation another time." When she'd be more prepared for it.

"If the princess wishes to continue her walk, I don't mind accompanying her," Dann said.

Fi couldn't help but meet his eyes. "I'd—please—if—" What had happened to her tongue?

Dann's mouth twitched. "Is that a yes, or a no?"

"You don't have to," Viren said. "You can return to the tea."

"No, I'd like to become more acquainted with your brothers," Fi said, her mouth finally obeying her mind.

Viren grunted. "I apologize for this interruption. Unfortunately I'll be occupied for several hours. Please don't leave without saying good-bye."

"I wouldn't dream of it. I hope your negotiations go well."

"Thank you." Viren kissed her hand and strode off with his servant. Fi and Dann stared at each other. Dann motioned for Fi to walk. "Shall we?"

They fell into step with each other. The number of times Fi had imagined herself and Dann together, and now she didn't know what to say!

Dann took the lead. "I hope I'm not overstepping, but I heard that the guard is hunting your friend. I know you were close. It must be difficult for you. I've wondered how you feel about it."

Erryn was the last subject she'd expected him to raise. Viren must know about Erryn, but they never talked about her. It was as if she didn't exist. And Dann had wondered about how she felt? Elation that she was in his thoughts almost chased away the sorrow his mention of Erryn had stirred. "It is difficult." She blinked back tears. She'd suffered in silence and held her tongue for too long. "They say she killed two of her escort in cold blood, and so they'll hunt her down and drag her back to the city for a trial that has a predetermined outcome. I can't accept what they say about her. I know she's a Beast Master. I saw her summon Zayvang with my own eyes. But she did it to save my life, and we were close." Speaking of their bond in the past tense made her chin tremble.

She drew a deep breath. "I hope they never capture her."

The moment she said the words, she wanted to take them back. What was she doing, admitting that she disagreed with Father to a man she hardly knew? The Lyoses had to present a united front. She could cry and scream at Father all she wanted, as long as she did it privately.

"What would you do if she came back to the city and found you?"

"I'd talk to her," Fi said softly. "Then I'd tell her to run from the city and keep running. And if you ever tell anyone I said that, I'll deny it."

Dann pressed his hand against his heart. "I won't breathe a word to anyone."

"I know what the Holy Texts say. Perhaps she is cursed. Perhaps if I were to see her again, she wouldn't be as I remember her. Primate Enkelo says now that she's summoned the Fallen, her bestial nature will eclipse any shred of humanity she may have had. But she'll always be Erryn to me. She'll always be my friend. Father would like me to see her for what he believes her to be and forget about her, but I can't. I wish she were here. At the same time, I have to behave as if I don't care."

"Loyalty versus duty. The heart versus the head. " Dann gave her a sidelong glance. "I find myself fighting similar battles lately, so I understand how you feel."

Fi hoped he meant what she thought he meant, despite the warning voice in her head reminding her that her fantasies about Dann would have to remain just that. Anything else would be catastrophic for both of them. She rubbed away a tear that had escaped.

"This walk was a foolish idea," Dann said.

"Why?" Fi said, shooing away the warning voice.

"Because you're upset, and I'd like to comfort you."

She wanted to lean into him and feel his arm around her. Why had she suddenly lost everything she'd taken for granted? Erryn. Her expectation that Father would choose her an acceptable husband and she'd settle effortlessly into married life. Sleeping easy at night. "We hardly know each other," she said, repeating to him the words she'd said to herself hundreds of times.

"Anything we might feel for each other can't be real?"

Fi raised her brows. "That's a bold statement." Duty won out. It couldn't be any other way. "And an impertinent one. You know I'll be betrothed to Viren."

"I don't have much time. I promised myself that when I got you alone, I wouldn't squander the conversation."

"You planned to speak to me?"

"Who do you think arranged for Bale's man to arrive a day early?"

Fi gaped at him. "What? You?" She was both delighted and horrified. "Your brother was about to propose to me when—"

Dann grimaced. "Just in time, then."

"For what?" Fi cried. Despite wishing Dann was a suitable candidate to be her husband, he wasn't. Her feelings for him hadn't addled her so much that she believed they could be together. They couldn't defy Father—the king—and upset Dann's father. "We have to be sensible. I have to marry Viren."

"Ah, so if you weren't the Princess Filmona, you'd consider me?"

"We hardly know each other."

"So what? You expected to marry someone chosen for you, not someone you'd fallen in love with."

"Yes, because I'm the Princess Filmona," Fi shot back. "If I wasn't, I suppose I'd have chosen a husband the way the common folk do." Lucky people. "I'd get to know a man and then decide. But there's no point thinking about that. I'm not common folk. I can't marry according to my heart."

"If you could?"

Fi should demand that they end this conversation right now. But she wanted him to know. Then she'd force sense to prevail. "We only had a brief conversation, but—"

"It's occupied your thoughts since then. I've heard some say that when you meet the person you're meant to be with, you'll know straight away. They're usually telling the happy story of how they met their beloved. I suppose those that didn't get the happy ending don't tell their stories." Dann sighed. "I used to think it fortunate that I was the third son. I wouldn't be saddled with all the responsibility, and I'd have much more say in who I'd marry. I never considered the possibility that the woman I'd want to marry wouldn't have any say in who she married."

A lump rose in Fi's throat. "We can't marry, Dann. I'm glad we've had the opportunity to speak. Perhaps we'll not think of each other so much." Yes, and she'd wake up on the morrow and find out she'd dreamed Erryn being a Beast Master and everything since then. "Now that we've said all that can be said, we must never speak of this again. Let's return to the others." She'd suddenly develop a headache, depart early, and cry herself to sleep.

Dann's Adam's apple bobbed. "You're not betrothed yet. Perhaps we can share a kiss."

She'd like nothing more, but the prospect terrified her. If their lips were to touch . . . Fi would never come to love Viren. His kisses would feel deader than they did now. "We should return before our absence stretches out too long. People will talk." Somehow she found the willpower to turn away from him and walk down the path. When he caught up with her, they walked in silence, Fi acutely aware of him at her side.

"Did you really arrange for Bale's man to arrive early, or were you just saying that?" she finally said, not wanting her rejection of him to be the last words she spoke to him today.

"I arranged it. It was rash, but I had to speak with you." His voice lost its vigour. "But you're right. From now on, I'll be Viren's loyal brother, who you occasionally see at family gatherings. We'll sometimes speak, but never alone."

Fi's throat was too tight to reply. She'd thought she was prepared to marry the man Father chose for her. Her betrothal would be far more difficult than she'd expected.

Avere walked her horse to the campsite where the Beast Master had slain two guards, carefully avoiding the wards and offerings those from nearby villages had left. Chains, muzzles, whips, sticks, the Beast Master symbol scrawled on blood-spotted parchment. Charming. She could judge the cravenness of each villager by where he'd dropped his gift. Not many had reached where she was now. When she dismounted in the camp, she hadn't spotted an offering for several minutes. Everyone had warned her not to come here. One villager had pressed a bear's claw into her hand, "to ward off Cheturrak." As if it would. Zayvang should hunt Cheturrak, but the Fallen weren't really animals. They were heavenly beings who'd offended the Seven.

Fortunately for her, the villagers' silly superstitions had kept them away. The camp was undisturbed. She'd ignore the decomposing body she could see lying outside the tent farthest from her for now. Inside the nearest tent, she found two bedrolls and a bag lying on its side, half its contents spilled on the ground. The Beast Master had searched this tent. Avere left it and looked at the second tent. According to what Arrick had told her after he'd met with the king, the guards had given the Beast Master her own tent. Interesting. She would have expected them to chain her outside like a dog. Perhaps they'd worried that she'd summon the Fallen.

Before leaving the Royal City, Avere had brushed up on Beast Masters. She was sure the primate of the temple near Ferret headquarters wouldn't mind that she'd helped herself to two books from his study while he was elsewhere. The Fallen weren't invincible. One of her daggers could send them back to the heavenly plane. The Beast Master could summon them again, but Avere had more than one dagger, and killing the Beast Master would instantly banish any Fallen she'd called.

A single dagger wasn't likely to kill Cheturrak, but he didn't worry Avere—or rather, the sight of him wouldn't paralyze her with fright. The only Fallen she hoped to never see was Iss. If the Beast Master were to summon Iss . . . Avere shuddered. She'd grit her teeth and hope her aim was true.

She pulled a handkerchief from her pocket and pressed it against her nose and mouth, then stepped into the Beast Master's tent. The Beast Master had left her bedroll, but there was no sign of the bag in which the guards had allowed the heathen to carry clothes and fruit. Swatting away the flies buzzing around the body, now unrecognizable, Avere crouched next to the faceless guard and frowned at the sword clutched in his hand. What had he been doing inside the Beast Master's tent with his sword unsheathed? Had he come inside to force himself on her? To kill her? Had she invited him in and the conversation or sex had turned ugly? According to the surviving guards, Zayvang had killed both men. There was hardly enough room in this tent for two people and an overly large saber-tooth cat. If the guard had wanted to kill her, he'd been close enough to run her through before she could summon Zayvang.

A wave of nausea made her dizzy. Avere stumbled from the tent and sucked down the cleaner air. She went to the other dead guard. The ruckus inside the Beast Master's tent must have had him running to help, but where was his sword? She spotted it where he couldn't possibly have dropped it. The Beast Master must have moved it. She'd left it behind. Curious.

Avere turned away, then froze. She instinctively reached for one of her daggers, then relaxed her fingers. A footprint couldn't hurt her. This one was huge. The creature who'd left it . . . Avere swallowed. Perhaps she could do without seeing Cheturrak. Best to aim for the Beast Master, if it came to that. Avere was certain it would. If Arrick managed to resist the primate's offer, it would only be because a more enticing one had come along.

She returned to her horse and surveyed the camp. Based on what she'd seen, she believed the dead guard inside the Beast Master's tent had entered it to kill her. Zayvang must have been lying in wait, which meant the Beast Master had feared for her life. Avere doubted the Beast Master had invited the guard into her tent. Why would she do such a thing? Perhaps a more sophisticated woman would have overcome her revulsion and tried to trade her body for freedom, but this Beast Master was sheltered and naive—which would make Avere's job much easier.

She crouched to study the tracks the horses had left behind. One had gone in the direction from which she'd come: back to the village. Three had fled into the forest. If Avere had her bearings right, the other had gone north, toward the border. Those at the castle wouldn't have to worry about the Beast Master riding up to the gates. Rather than riding toward familiarity, she'd galloped toward the unknown. A brave girl. Avere would almost regret driving a dagger into her heart.

* * * * *

Oswald scratched his head and frowned at Cedric. "Nothing?"

"Nothing, Majesty. No markings on the bodies. Swords could have been forged by any smith."

"But the assassins didn't reside in the Royal City."

"No. They stayed at an inn in the artisan neighbourhood. The innkeeper said nothing stood out about them. Unfortunately he'd already rented out their room and sold their belongings. Just clothes, according to him. No papers."

"Did they talk to anyone?"

"They arrived the night before they attacked and went straight to bed. Kept to themselves."

"So the trail is cold."

"Yes, Majesty."

Oswald sighed. In the absence of any evidence to the contrary, he'd settle for the least troubling explanation. "Perhaps it was citizens with a grudge, but why attack the princess? Why not me?"

"You're never outside the castle without the guard," Cedric said, looking distinctly uncomfortable—as he should.

"That hasn't stopped someone off their head from taking a run at me."

"Perhaps someone was upset because the princess wasn't to be betrothed to his son."

Oswald shook his head. "I had yet to make a decision. Everyone's sons were still eligible." He lifted his hands in a gesture of surrender. "Two disgruntled citizens decided to express their grievances by killing my daughter. Their failure reminded us that the princess is to be protected at all times."

Cedric grunted. "Do you want me to ask the Ferrets to pursue the matter further?"

He wanted the Ferrets to focus their efforts on finding the Beast Master and thwarting any future assassination attempts. Arrick and his people usually heard the whispers before they led to action, another reason to believe two citizens acting alone had tried to take Fi's life. "Let's consider the matter closed. It's unfortunate that we don't know who they are, and their relatives aren't likely to claim them. But I don't think we're dealing with a conspiracy. Thank you, Cedric. You may go."

Cedric brought his fist to his heart and left the study.

Oswald was glad to put the nasty business behind him. He'd already had words with Viren about Fi's safety. The man would protect her. Now if he'd only propose.

Erryn nodded when a woman dropped a coin into her bowl. She'd have a decent supper tonight, perhaps treat herself to a meal at an inn, rather than buy a meat pie and apple from a street merchant. She was tired of the street, the dust under her fingernails, the smelly clothes she washed in streams, the restless nights sleeping in an alley with one eye open. Since the incident with Kell, she hadn't slept or played in a tavern. She wanted to be outside, where she could summon the Fallen without worrying about a roomful of drunks. Nor did she stay in the same place for longer than a few days. After supper tonight, she'd leave this town.

She finished her song and wiped her brow. The wide-brimmed hat she wore made her sweat, but it also hid her branded forehead. She adjusted the belt she'd bought to hold up her trousers and started another song. A group of boys stopped to listen to her. She didn't mind at first. People drew more people. But two songs later, their loitering was irritating her. They weren't listening; they were whispering and pointing and giggling. Their antics weren't discouraging others from stopping to listen to the bard, but they were distracting.

Halfway through her next song, the boys strolled away, but Erryn's relief was short-lived. A couple of town guards walked through the square, surveying the merchants and street performers competing for the townsfolk's coin. She'd finish her song and slink away. Her bowl already held enough for today.

She was singing the last line of the light ditty when running footsteps made her turn to look. Someone barrelled into her and swiped at her hat. She stumbled. Her hat flew off her head. One of the boys who'd irritated her sprang away and pointed at her. "I did it," he shouted to his friends, now gathering in front of her. "I—" His eyes widened.

"Look at her forehead!" one of other boys shouted.

"It's the wolf," another said. "She's a Beast Master," he yelled.

A female spectator screamed. The two guards wheeled to look, then marched toward her. One of the boys shouted, "The guard is looking for a Beast Master. Get her!"

Erryn fled. Behind her, boots thudded on cobblestone.

She ducked into an alley, ran as fast as she could, but the footsteps and shouts weren't receding. Bursting from the alley, she ran in the direction that should take her to the northern gate. She glanced over her shoulder. They were still on her tail. She darted down another alley, then stumbled when a cat jumped into her path. The knuckles on the hand that still clung to her lute scraped along the stone—and the footsteps were closer. She turned and threw her lute at the guard who was almost close enough to grab her. He stopped to dodge it, but the guard behind him kept running.

She wasn't going to make it to the gate, not without the Fallen's help. *Quon!* she called as she ran from the alley. The stallion leaped into existence. The guard emerged from the alley. His mouth hanging open, he skidded to stop. *Kneel.* Quon obeyed. Erryn swung onto his back. *Go!* She didn't have to kick him into a gallop. He raced down the road. Townsfolk scattered, some diving to the ground or leaping into alleys. Erryn clung to Quon's neck and directed him to the north gate. Nobody tried to stop the Beast Master with the ugly brand on her forehead. Erryn and Quon flew through the gate and thundered away, kicking up dust in their wake.

When she was certain that nobody was pursuing them, Erryn slowed Quon to a walk. The sun shone, the sky was clear, and she was sitting on the horse that served Queyris in the heavens. But the king was searching for her. He wasn't leaving her to whatever fate the Seven had in store for her. He wanted to execute her. Fi would see her hang.

Tears welled in Erryn's eyes. She'd lost her lute. She had two coins to her name. She was right back to where she'd started, but this time she had no horse to sell. Perhaps she shouldn't have run. Perhaps she should have surrendered to the guard and let them do with her as they willed. What sort of life could she possibly have? She had nothing. She had nobody. She'd spend her life scrounging for scraps of food and hiding in the shadows. From Daros's royal family to a beggar. She truly was cursed.

Fi chattered to Viren as they strolled along the same path on which she'd had the scandalous conversation with Dann a week earlier. He wouldn't be here to save her today. Viren must want to propose in the gardens. She had to admit that the lilies floating on the pond, the butterflies flitting from flowers to leaves, and the sunlight dappling the path would make for a romantic proposal—with Dann. How she longed for Viren to sweep her off her feet and addle her mind!

Would it ever happen? When Dann married, jealousy and anger would likely chase away her feelings for him, but that wouldn't help her today, or at the altar, or on her wedding night, or whenever Viren gazed at her with love in his eyes. Why had she strolled the wall that night? If Father hadn't banished Erryn, Fi would never have known what could have been.

Viren stopped next to a shrub heavy with glorious azaleas and took her hand. Fi forced a smile. Viren was a kind and cultured man. He treated her well. He would make an excellent husband. She'd always thought of herself as the most valuable catch in Daros, the woman every man would want, but Viren deserved a woman who loved him. They were both trapped by the circumstances of their births.

The eldest son would receive the princess's hand. The princess would do her duty. She'd always accepted that in exchange for the luxury in which she lived, she'd have little say in who she married, but now the price she'd pay would be high, indeed. But she was a Lyos. She'd do what had to be done and make the best of it.

"This is one of my favourite spots in the garden," Viren said.

"I can see why. It's beautiful. My compliments to the gardener."

"I often roll up my sleeves and help him. I planned this pond and the arrangements around it."

Fi was genuinely surprised and impressed. She could be friends with this man. Perhaps that would be enough. It would have to be. "You're a man of many talents."

"We're clearing an area for another fountain. A fountain that will be dedicated to my wife." Viren dropped to one knee and reached into his pocket. He opened the box in his hand, revealing a ruby ring—her favourite stone. "Princess Filmona, would you do me the honour of becoming my wife?"

Fi hoped Viren would interpret her trembling and dismay as nervousness. Decorum and her dedication to duty took over. "I will," she said, loudly and clearly.

Viren nodded and lifted the ring from its box. Fi couldn't help but think of Dann as she watched Viren slip the ring onto her finger. Here she was standing in a beautiful garden with a decent man, but it felt like a bad dream! If only Erryn were here. Fi would pour out her heart to her, tell her about Dann and her worry that she'd never come to love Viren. Erryn wouldn't have wanted her to marry anyone, but she never would have said that. She would have hugged Fi and told her it would be all right. And Fi suddenly realized that her fretting was selfish and childish. Even in her absence, Erryn was helping her.

How could she be crying inside because the Duke of Tolin's heir was proposing to her, when Erryn was out there with little chance of ever finding a husband? Would any man look past her nature, or the ugly brand on her forehead? Who'd marry a Beast Master? In her diary, Erryn had said she'd hate marrying, that if she couldn't be with the one she loved, she'd rather remain alone. But that would be unnatural for a woman, and when Fi had read those words, she'd imagined herself telling Erryn that her feelings would pass, especially since she couldn't have who she wanted. Now her would-be advice sounded trite. Would it have made it easier for Erryn if she'd known that the object of her desire didn't reciprocate her feelings? Would Fi still long for Dann if he'd rejected her?

Viren rose, dragging Fi back to the present. It would be nice if this moment didn't feel like a state duty, but . . .

Viren's eyes glistened. "My life will be brighter with you in it. I look forward to a long life together, and many children."

"As do I," Fi murmured. The kiss they shared was long but passionless, though she could pretend.

When they parted, Viren's eyes opened and he appeared satisfied. He took Fi's hand and beamed at the engagement ring on her finger. "We must tell Mother and Father the news. They'll want to formally welcome you to our family. Then we'll go directly to the castle and tell the king. We have to set a date. You'll have the most beautiful wedding dress Daros has ever seen."

"I know which designer I'll use," Fi said, determined to throw herself into the arrangements. At the very least, planning a wedding would keep her busy. She'd be too occupied with juggling all the details to think about Dann—except at night, when it was quiet, and she lay awake trying not to dwell on what could have been.

Avere left the home of her Ferret contact in Moss and scrutinized the seal on the message he'd handed her. The pinpoint wax circle appeared intact. If only pigeons could carry longer messages; the seal would be easier to see. She broke it with her thumbnail, unrolled the tiny piece of parchment, and quickly decoded Arrick's words. So, the Beast Master had been spotted in Persh. One word set Avere's heart racing. *Quon.* What had happened to the horse she'd ridden from the camp?

Arrick hadn't provided any other details or word on where the Beast Master was now, but clearly she was moving north. Avere could ride after her now, but the sun had set and her horse needed rest. She'd stay here tonight, tour the taverns and inns for word of her prey. Except for a name and a brief family history, Avere knew little of the woman who could summon the Fallen. If she'd passed through this town and spoken to anyone, Avere wanted to know. Every piece of information would help.

An hour later, she sat at a bar listening to the barkeep tell her about the woman who'd sung at the inn for a couple of weeks, then abruptly left. So, she was using her real name. And the woman who'd grown up in privileged circumstances was now singing for her supper. She'd had the presence of mind to hide her brand, but the girl must be reeling. "Why did she leave?" she asked the barkeep.

He leaned over the bar. "Had a bit of trouble with a fellow in here. Gave her some unwanted attention."

Avere's jaw tightened. She fingered one of her daggers. The Beast Master hadn't summoned the Fallen, or the barkeep would have said. Curious. Avere would have expected a woman with a bestial nature and the Fallen at her fingertips to rip anyone who offended her to shreds.

"When she told us she was leaving, she didn't say anything about Kell. She said she'd only intended to pass through here and it was time to go." He tapped the side of his nose. "But it came on the morn after the trouble, so I think she was afraid to stay."

Avere grunted. "Is Kell here tonight?"

The barkeep nodded.

"Which one is he? I'd like to know who to avoid."

The barkeep lowered his voice. Avere strained to listen. "He's the one watching the men playing cards. I doubt he's following. He's usually blotto by now."

Avere glanced over her shoulder. When she turned back, the barkeep had moved down the bar to serve someone. Good, she was finished with him anyway. She was tempted to sashay over to Kell and teach him a lesson, but it would only draw attention. Then again, she could lie in wait outside and—*focus, Avere.* As much as she'd like to, she couldn't gut every man who couldn't keep his hands to himself. According to the barkeep, the Beast Master was only ten days ahead of her. The heathen shouldn't have stayed in Moss for so long, but she had no street sense or survival skills. Avere swiftly quashed her stirring sympathy. She would probably have to kill the girl.

The next morning, she felt herself feeling sorry for the Beast Master again, much to her chagrin. The barkeep hadn't said anything about a horse, and Arrick's message had mentioned Quon. Fortunately there were only two stables in Moss, and the master of the one she'd just left had delighted in telling her about the magnificent horse he'd purchased for about thirty percent of its value. Avere's fingers had twitched.

As she rode northward, she reminded herself that she had to remain detached. Usually she didn't have a problem viewing her marks as prey, but usually her marks were powerful people who'd offended the wrong person or used their position to take advantage of others. The Beast Master was a woman—a girl—whose circumstances had changed overnight. Avere shouldn't feel sorry for someone the Seven had cursed, but she knew what it was like to suddenly have to scrounge for food and fight for survival, and she hadn't had half of Daros out for her blood.

She wouldn't waste time wondering why the Seven had decided the King of Daros's foster child would become everyone's prey; she'd stopped trying to understand the will of the Seven long ago. Yes, prey. Her prey. She might not attend services and heed the primates as much as she should, but she knew what the Holy Texts taught about Beast Masters. She wasn't hunting a woman; she was hunting an animal. If Arrick gave the word, she'd put down the Beast Master and her pets. This Erryn was just another mark. When one of Avere's daggers pierced her heart, she'd die like everyone died.

Her knees trembling, Erryn shuffled along the mud road toward the cottage she'd spotted. *Please, let there be a vegetable garden, a cow—anything.* She didn't like stealing from farmers' fields and gardens, but with no coin and the mark on her forehead, she'd had little choice. She also had to keep moving. *Why? What's the point?* Was this to be her life until she wasted away from starvation and exhaustion? Why keep struggling to survive? There was no prize to be won.

When she reached the cottage's garden, tears prickled at her eyelashes. Nothing but flowers and bushes. Then she spotted the basket of fruit sitting outside the back door. Her mouth watered.

"It's all right to steal because I'm hungry, Fi. I wouldn't steal if I wasn't so hungry."

Fi glared at her.

"I'm not a thief."

Fi laughed. "Of course you're not, silly. Should we go to the music room?"

"After I've eaten, Fi. After I've eaten."

She crept closer to the cottage, listening for footsteps, a whistle, or a hummed tune. Nothing. She dropped to her hands and knees and skittered to the basket. Unable to wait, she grabbed an apple and bit into it. Glorious! Another bite, then she set it on the ground while she stuffed her pockets. She'd find a spot underneath a tree and—

"What do you think you're doing?"

Her heart leaped into her mouth. She twisted to look, then toppled and fell onto her behind. A man stood with a raised spade, ready to strike. His face was wrinkled and his hair white, but he was no weakling. His shirt didn't hide his bulging biceps. One swing of the spade . . .

He stared down at her. His eyes widened.

Erryn looked away and closed her eyes. "Do it. Hit me. I don't care anymore. Do it. Make it quick. Please."

Silence. She opened her eyes a crack. The man slowly lowered the spade. "All those times I heard the story. I never thought it would happen to me."

Erryn had no idea what he was babbling about, and her sense of self-preservation had kicked in. She pushed herself to her feet—and swayed. The man caught her arm. "You're not well."

"I'm sorry." She turned out her pockets. Apples thudded to the ground. "I'm sorry." She tried to pull away from him, but he wouldn't let go of her.

He dropped the spade. "You must be going to the temple."

"The temple?"

"That's where the other Beast Master was going."

Erryn gaped. "The other Beast Master? There's another Beast Master? Where? Do—do you know . . ." She trailed off when the man shook his head.

"It's a story my grandfather liked to tell, and my father loved to repeat it."

Her disappointment quashed her burst of energy. She slumped against the cottage. "Tell me," she whispered.

The man frowned. "Why don't you come inside? I'll get you something to eat."

Erryn's guard immediately went up. She didn't feel alarm from the Fallen, but this man should be wary of her, not invite her into his home.

"I know what they say about you. But my grandfather told a different story. Come inside. Have something to eat."

She couldn't refuse a meal. "All right."

An hour later, she spooned hearty beef soup into her mouth.

"Slow down, slow down," Rodney, her saviour, said. "You'll make yourself sick."

She didn't care. She wiped away the soup that dribbled down her chin and picked up a thick piece of bread. As soon as they'd stepped inside the cottage, she'd begged Rodney to tell her about the other Beast Master, but he'd insisted that she have a wash and change into an old shirt and pair of trousers. They hung off her, but they were clean. "Tell me the story," she said between mouthfuls.

Rodney sipped the tea he'd brewed and leaned back in his chair. "It was a long time ago, when my father was a boy. My family has always lived in these parts. We have a farm not too far from here. My oldest boy runs it now. The way my grandfather tells it, there was a knock on the door one day. A man stood on the doorstep, wanting to trade. He was in better shape than you are."

"That's easy to believe."

Rodney chuckled. "He wasn't branded, like you are." He paused. "Last time I was in town, I heard rumours about a Beast Master in the Royal Province. Someone close to the king."

"He branded me," she said, wanting to repay Rodney's generosity with honesty. "I saved the—" Her voice choked off. She tried not to think about how unfair it was, but lately she couldn't stave off fits of melancholy.

"So you *did* save the princess. I wondered how tall the tales were. But I'm not surprised. The Beast Master who showed up on my grandfather's doorstep saved his son, my father. Summoned the Fallen to help, not hurt. You did the same."

"This other Beast Master . . ."

"My grandfather never would have known about him, but he stayed for supper, on the same night my father went missing. The Beast Master, I forget his name, told my grandfather he might have a way of finding him quick. Summoned the Fallen. Found him down an old well. Nobody else could hear him crying. Well, after that, my grandfather asked if there was anything he could do for him. He took more food. Said he had a long journey ahead of him. He was going north, to a temple."

Erryn forgot her food for a moment. "What temple? Why? Where is it?"

"I don't know. Details were lost in the retelling, I suppose, and my father's been gone for years. All I know is that he wanted to get to a temple, and it was in the north. He mentioned Loring."

"Loring?"

"It's a city quite a ways from here. Maybe he planned to pass through it on his way, or maybe that's where the temple was—or is."

"I have to go there." After stumbling about for so long, she finally had a sense of purpose, a reason to struggle on.

"It's a long way away."

"I have nothing else to do, nowhere else to go." If only the Beast Master had said why he wanted to travel there.

Rodney's eyes narrowed. "Sometimes when people tell a story, they make events sound grander than they actually were. I can't tell you whether the temple part is true."

"But he did find your father in a well?"

Rodney's eyes twinkled. "You can't embellish when there are witnesses who know the truth. Nobody knew what the Beast Master said to my grandfather in private except my grandfather."

Still, she'd gone from wandering aimlessly to having a destination, a goal to strive for. "How far away is the next town between here and Loring?"

"A few days on foot." Rodney's forehead creased. "You're in no condition to go."

"I—I shouldn't ask, I have no coin, but if—if you could give me some food, I'll pay you back. I'll—"

"You won't make it half an hour up the road. You don't have the strength."

Erryn dropped her spoon into her empty bowl and blew out a long, heartfelt sigh. "I have to try."

Rodney studied her for a moment. "I see it in you. Stay here for a few days. Eat and sleep well. Then I'll send you on your way with a full bag."

She shook her head. "That's kind of you, but they're after me. I can't put you in danger."

"Nobody will look for you here. Now, I can offer you a soft rug in front of the fire. It's not much, but—"

"It'll be more than enough. Thank you." He wasn't a man like Kell.

Rodney's eyes bored into her. "How have you made it this far? Thieving?"

"No, not at first. I had a lute. I sang for my supper. But then the guard chased me, and . . ."

"Even with a full belly, the journey won't be easy. Stay off the main road. It's not unusual for merchants to be robbed. A woman travelling alone . . ." Rodney rubbed the back of his neck. "There might not be a temple, Erryn. You could hide out here for a while. If it wasn't for a Beast Master, I would never have been born, or my children."

"It's a kind offer, but I need to see if this temple exists. My life . . ." She lifted her hands and dropped them to her lap. "I have to understand it."

Rodney nodded. "I suppose I'd feel the same."

A week later, Erryn stood on Rodney's doorstep with stronger legs, a clear head, a bag stuffed with clothes and food on her back, and one of Rodney's hats on her head. He held out a leather purse. "Take this."

"I can't. You've done enough."

Rodney thrust the purse at her. "Take it, Erryn. Buy yourself a lute. You only have enough food for a few days. And tie the hat to your head, if you have to." He hooked his thumbs through his belt. "You'd best be off, then. I reckon I've repaid my debt to Beast Masters, but if you're passing this way again and need my help, you've only to knock on the door."

Tears blurred her vision. She hugged him. After a moment, his shoulders eased and he awkwardly returned her hug. "Thank you, Rodney. You've given me much more than food and clothes. You've given me hope."

He pulled away and pointed north. "Go on, now."

She swallowed the lump in her throat and walked away. She couldn't resist looking over her shoulder and smiled when she saw him still standing on the doorstep. She waved, then resolutely faced forward. *I promise I'll return someday and repay your kindness.* A goal, and a vow. She'd cling to them during the dark moments she'd face. Today, they fueled her determination to find the temple.

Over the past week, they'd discussed why a Beast Master would seek a temple. The Primacy's influence stretched across Daros, and though there was contention around the interpretation of some texts, the broader teachings, including those about Beast Masters, weren't in dispute. Rodney had said there were more wild folk in the north, and while they worshipped the Seven, they used texts written by their own people. But he'd never heard of a text or a fringe group that regarded Beast Masters favourably.

So why a temple? Had the Beast Master asked himself why, as she did? Had he expected to find an answer at the temple? How had he found out about it? Had he been travelling there to speak to someone who was long dead? Did the temple exist?

Erryn had a long and perilous journey ahead of her, but she also had food, coin, determination, and hope. She'd make it to Loring, or die trying. She picked up a branch to use as a walking stick and marched onward.

Blood and Blades

Avere tightened her hold on her horse's reins as she listened to a villager tell her about his encounter with the Beast Master. She glared down at him. "I should report you to the guard for thieving."

The villager's eyes widened. "What?"

"Six for a pie?" she said through clenched teeth.

He shrugged. "She was hungry."

The rein's leather dug into her palms. She should gut him, but she'd have to gut everyone watching, too. Massacring an entire village wasn't her style. "You said she had a cloth tied around her head."

"I think she was soft." He tapped his temple. "Up here."

So he'd taken advantage of her because she was hungry and he'd thought her simple. Avere's fingers twitched. "And this was five days ago?"

"Four."

Good. She was catching up to the heathen. This was the second village the girl had passed through after leaving Persh. Nobody had mentioned Quon, but she must be riding him when she considered it safe to do so.

Avere kicked her horse into a gallop. "Hey!" the villager shouted. Did he expect her to pay him for the information? He was lucky he wasn't trying to plug a hole in his belly.

She rode from the village without a glance over her shoulder, determined to push her horse as far as she could. She was only four days behind her prey!

Two days later, frustration made Avere want to scream. "You're sure?"

The woman behind the fruit stall near the town gate nodded.

Avere sighed. "How much do you want?"

"What do you think I am? If I'd seen her, I'd say," the woman growled. "She's not been through here."

"There's just the one road from the south?"

The woman nodded. "Maybe she passed through when I wasn't here. You could ask the night guard. They come on at eight."

She would, but she suspected the answer would be the same as this woman's and those from the villagers she'd questioned yesterday. After leaving that second village after Persh, the Beast Master had vanished. "Thank you."

The sun was setting. Avere rented a room at the inn next to the stables. After forcing down a meat pie, she went back to the southern gate and asked the guards whether a thin, well-spoken woman, concealing her forehead with a strip of cloth and travelling alone, had entered the town within the past week. Both guards shook their heads.

Avere returned to the inn. As she threaded her way through those drinking and dancing in the common room, a flash of red caught her eye. A woman in a brilliant rose cloak was talking to the barman. She was standing, reinforcing Avere's impression that she wasn't there to drink. She had the air of a religious woman, though Avere didn't recognize the symbol embroidered on the back of her cloak. She stopped to scrutinize it. A lightning bolt striking a book. Curious. The cloak must have cost a fortune. The woman should be careful.

Inside her room, she unrolled her map. She was in Sull, a growing settlement too large to be considered a village but small enough to skirt around. Why would the Beast Master travel through every other town and village but avoid this one? Or was she dead?

Avere hadn't seen any corpses along the road. Perhaps villagers had killed the heathen and lied to cover up the murder. No, killing a Beast Master would be a service to Daros, not a crime, and the villagers she'd questioned had appeared truthful. Bandits? Given the exorbitant amount the Beast Master had paid for a pie, she must be running out of coin. What would bandits have gained from attacking a woman with empty pockets? Had the heathen succumbed to disease or collapsed from hunger?

She could be lying dead or injured, concealed by the trees and thickets next to the road, or she could have deliberately left the road, perhaps seeking food. But why hadn't she returned to the road and continued on to

Sull, where there was coin to be made? Could hunger be addling her mind? Had she ventured far off the road and become lost, or worse? She could be anywhere.

Avere might have arrived here ahead of the girl. If the heathen had left the main road, she could be a day or two behind now. But if she was dead or had decided to bypass the town, waiting here for her would be pointless.

There were no Ferret agents in Sull. Avere studied the map. If she continued north, she'd reach Stronghaven, a bustling city situated at a crossroads, and where a fugitive could blend in unnoticed and sing for coin. If Avere were on the run and heading north, that was where she'd go. Stronghaven also housed a Ferret base where she could refill her purse, send a message to Arrick, and use agents to scour the inns and taverns and watch the southern gates. She'd remain there until she spotted the Beast Master or picked up a rumour as to her whereabouts—or received confirmation of her death. A reply from Arrick could also set Avere on the right path again.

On the morrow she'd ride for Stronghaven and hunt—or wait—for the Beast Master there. If the girl was dead, it would save Avere a lot of trouble. Arrick would be disappointed, though. He'd grumble about not receiving his three bottles of wine.

Erryn squared her shoulders when she spotted what should be the town of Sull in the distance. She'd stayed off the main road, riding Quon when she could, and hadn't run into any trouble. The thought of speaking with people made her stomach churn, but she had no choice.

She'd eaten almost all the food Rodney had given her. The purse he'd handed her was still full, but she'd have to refill her pack here. She should have asked him for pointers about how to barter with the vendors. He might not have been so quick to give her coin if he'd known how inept she was at haggling.

Two guards patrolled the road up ahead. She nodded and kept her head down as she passed them. When shouts didn't pierce the air, her shoulders relaxed. She'd buy food, find somewhere quiet to doze for the night, and continue her journey as soon as the sun rose.

"Oy, you, the one with the hat!" a woman's voice rang out.

Erryn froze. She turned in the direction of the voice and raised her head high enough to see from under the hat's brim.

"Yeah, you," a woman standing behind a fruit stall said. "Come here. I want a word."

Her first instinct was to call back, "What do you want?" but she didn't want to draw attention. Already a couple of townsfolk had slowed to see who was shouting. She sauntered over to the stall. "What do you want?"

"Are you from the Royal Province?"

Erryn blinked at her, then let out a loud sigh, hoping she sounded irritated and bored. "Why?"

"Someone came through town looking for you. Said she was supposed to meet a friend here."

Excitement shot through Erryn. *Fi?* What a foolish thought! Fi wasn't a "someone." If she'd come to Sull, everyone would know. "I'm not meeting anyone here."

The woman's eyes narrowed. "Are you sure? She described you to a T."

"I'm not meeting anyone here," Erryn repeated. "But I'd like to buy some fruit."

Unfortunately her interest in the merchant's produce didn't distract the woman. "She said a well-spoken woman around your height, thin, wearing a strip of cloth or a hat or something else on her head or forehead." The woman peered at her. "Why do you cover your forehead?"

"What was her name?"

"Whose name?"

"The woman looking for me."

The merchant drew back. "Well, I don't know, do I? If she were your friend, you'd know her name."

"She's not. I'm just curious." Erryn picked up an apple and turned it around in her hand. "Do you know where she is now?" she asked casually.

"I don't know. I didn't see her after that. Try an inn. We've only got two. Stables, too. She was on a horse. Are you buying that?"

"Yes, and more." Wanting to leave Sull quickly, Erryn didn't haggle. She gave the merchant the number of coins she wanted for a selection of apples and berries, bought cheese and bread at the other stalls situated in the small market meant for hungry travellers, and left town by walking in the direction from which she'd come. When she was sure the patrolling guards could no longer see her, she left the road and pulled the crude map Rodney had sketched from her pack. Travelling around Sull would add days to her journey, but she didn't want to risk running into the woman who was looking for her.

Who was she? Erryn wished she could have asked the merchant for a description, but she'd been too afraid the woman would summon the guard. Silly, because they'd only been having a conversation, but she didn't want to take any chances and hadn't wanted to appear too interested, in case the mystery woman spoke to the merchant again. Was she still in Sull? If not, in which direction was she travelling?

Determined to reach Loring and the temple, Erryn would continue north, but she'd have to be wary. She'd go around Sull, but she'd have to enter the first village she reached afterward to replenish her pack. She wouldn't sleep there, though. She'd keep moving until she reached Stronghaven, where she hoped to lose herself in the city's large population, buy a lute, and perform to refill her purse and pack.

Fi examined the table settings a servant had arranged on one of the rectangular tables in the grand banquet hall. "That one," she said, pointing to a flowered plate. It burst with colour. Viren would like it.

"Very good, Your Highness," the servant murmured.

Another servant, hovering behind the one overseeing the table arrangement, lifted the sheaf of papers in her hand. "The guest list, Your Highness."

Fi accepted it from her and skimmed the names. She recognized everyone until she reached the third page. Minor nobles she hadn't met, followed by tens of primates from all over the Royal Province, and a few from beyond. The men without titles were probably friends of Father, Henrick, or Viren, or those Father hoped to flatter because he wanted something from them. All these people would drink to her betrothal and wish her a long and happy married life.

Sighing, she returned to the first page and read it again. Her eyes lingered on Dann's name. Would he come alone, or with a woman on his arm? Would she resist looking for him when Father formally announced the betrothal and presented her and Viren to the banquet guests?

"Are you married?" she asked the servant who'd handed her the list.

The servant's head bobbed. "Yes, Your Highness."

"Do you love him?"

The woman's brow furrowed. "Yes." Then her face flushed. "He's not a duke—he won't be a duke, as your betrothed will be, of course."

"What does he do?"

"He's a cobbler, Your Highness."

Her husband may be a cobbler, but the woman was richer than Fi would ever be. That sentiment was unfair to Viren; he was a good man. But one couldn't force love. She wished he was the right man for her. She'd always feel as if she were letting him down. "I'll need time to look this over properly."

"Of course." The servant grimaced. "The king has already—"

"I know. I won't ask that anyone be removed. I'll only make sure there are no oversights."

"Thank you, Your Highness." She curtsied and scurried away.

Another servant quickly took her place. "The head seamstress is ready for you, Your Highness. I've directed her to the blue receiving room."

"Thank you. I'll—"

"I see everything is proceeding smoothly," a voice boomed.

Fi looked past the servant and forced a smile. "Viren. What a lovely surprise!"

He lifted her hand and kissed it. "I heard the last bit about the seamstress. I won't keep you. I'm here to see your father, but I couldn't resist the opportunity to see you."

"I'm flattered, but—"

"Yes, yes, your seamstress is waiting, and I mustn't go with you. I don't want to accidentally overhear anything about your wedding dress. I want to be surprised." He stepped out of her way and swept his arm toward the doorway.

She patted his other arm. "Perhaps we can go for a walk in the garden later," she said, knowing she had to try. "I don't know how long I'll be."

"However long it takes, I'll still be here." He jutted his chin toward the doorway. "You don't want to keep the head seamstress waiting. She'll oversee the creation of the most magnificent wedding dress Daros has ever seen."

Fi broadened her smile, then strode from the banquet hall. The moment she was out of his sight, her smile faded.

* * * * *

Standing next to the fire in his study, Arrick read Avere's latest message. She'd lost the Beast Master—well, she'd never actually found her, but she'd been on her trail. Waiting in Stronghaven was a sound strategy, unless the Beast Master was no longer travelling north. He had agents in the largest cities. If she still lived, one of them would eventually spot her, or hear about her. The heathen would summon one of the Fallen again. It was only a matter of time.

Someone knocked at the door. He tossed the message into the fire. "Come in."

Emen slipped into the study and pushed the door shut. "Sorry to be bothering you, sir, but I thought you might want to hear this."

Arrick motioned for Emen to sit and settled himself into his own chair. "What is it?"

"I know you didn't ask us to sniff around about the assassination attempt on the princess's life, but I happened to overhear something and decided to look into it."

"What did you hear?"

Emen dropped his voice. "Someone mentioned that the Pig and Pie's landlord was throwing coin about. Got the wife an expensive pair of shoes. Commissioned a chair at Arthur and Sons."

The failed assassins had stayed at the Pig and Pie. Arthur and Sons catered to families with bulging purses and bank accounts, not innkeepers.

"I warmed a stool at the bar there," Emen continued. "I was generous with my coin and my compliments. One of the girls told me that on the evening of the assassination attempt, the innkeeper let someone into the assassins' rooms. Of course, she didn't know at the time they were assassins. She only found out later, when the guard came asking questions. She didn't tell them anything because she didn't want to lose her job and figured the assassins were dead anyway. She also recognized the man and that frightened her a bit. But it's pricked at her conscience since then. She wanted to talk."

Arrick leaned forward. "Who was he?"

"A lad named Gerry." Emen met Arrick's eyes. "He was a runner for the High Council."

"Was?"

"He's dead. Fell down a flight of stairs. Accident, apparently."

"Did it happen on the High Council's estate?"

"No. When he was out and about."

So, a runner for Daros's most powerful primates had been sent to clean up after the assassins, and then someone had shut his mouth for him. "When he left the inn that day, was he carrying anything?"

Emen scrunched up his face. "She said he went upstairs with a bag and came down with a bag. She couldn't say whether the bag was more full when he left."

Arrick grunted. "You've done well. Next time you collect your wages, there will be a little extra for you."

"Thank you, sir."

"Leave this with me. If you hear anything else, let me know, but not a word to anyone," Arrick warned.

"Yes, sir." Always a perceptive fellow, Emen knew it was time to go. He nodded to Arrick and left the study.

Arrick closed his eyes and steepled his fingers. Emen's information didn't mean the Primacy was responsible for the attempt on the princess's life. It constantly hosted nobles, powerful merchants, and visiting dignitaries on its large estate. Anyone could have made a naïve or ambitious runner an offer he couldn't refuse. But Arrick's gut told him the Primacy was involved. Enkelo? He was the closest primate to the Lyoses. But why would he want any of them dead, and why target the princess? Unless . . .

Arrick's eyes snapped open and he bolted upright. Everyone had assumed the assassins had wanted to take the princess's life. What if the Beast Master had been the target? As the king's foster child, she was—had been—a member of the royal family. The words the assassins had shouted had suggested they'd wanted the princess's blood, but they could have meant the heathen's.

There was only one flaw in his hypothesis: nobody had known Erryn Fyler was a Beast Master until that day, or so they all believed. She'd told the king she'd known about her corruption for several months. Had someone discovered her secret, unbeknownst to her? Or was Arrick making a connection that didn't exist because the royal primate had sat in the same chair Emen had just vacated and asked the Ferrets to kill the Beast Master?

If only he'd known about the runner when Enkelo had come to him. But the king hadn't wanted the Ferrets to look into the assassination attempt. Instead, he'd used the guard. The fools had believed that anyone with information would share it because it was their duty and they loved the land and the Lyoses. Emen had known better and been liberal with his coin.

Arrick had a problem. He'd never been able to penetrate the High Council. Twelve primates sat on it—thirteen if one counted the grand primate, who appointed the others. When he died, the twelve selected the new grand primate from among themselves. Every primate on the High Council had a university degree and had served for years as a temple primate. None would risk the prestige and power High Council members enjoyed to become the Ferrets' eyes and ears. Their servants were compensated well, and so were temple primates. Arrick had people among the estate workers, but nobody close to those in power.

He didn't believe the High Council would order the assassination of the princess, but the Beast Master would have been a different story—if the High Council had known about her. As the royal primate, Enkelo spent most of his time at the castle. Had he seen something that had alerted him to the girl's true nature? If so, why not have her killed quietly? Why not go to the king, who would have dealt with the information in a way that protected his daughter and preserved his relationship with her?

It was more likely that the assassins had wanted to slay the princess, but Arrick would keep an open mind regarding both the assassination target and who'd been behind it. At the moment, all he had was the connection to the High Council.

He already had a list of those who called the High

Council's estate home. One of his people recorded every visitor and dropped off the list once a week. Another Ferret would have checked every name on those lists, but now Arrick had something to look for. He'd comb through the lists himself. Accusing anyone associated with the High Council of stealing so much as a single coin would require absolute proof. Arrick couldn't trust anyone with his suspicions—not yet. Whoever had ordered the assassination of the princess or the king's foster daughter wouldn't think twice about snuffing out a Ferret's life.

Avere dropped a coin into the barkeep's hand and sipped the ale she didn't want. She'd sit and observe the common room for a few minutes, then leave her drink at the bar, knowing another patron would quickly claim it.

So, the Beast Master hadn't come to Stronghaven—yet. The guards at the southern gates hadn't seen her. The barkeep she'd just chatted with was the sixth one she'd gently questioned since she'd arrived in the city. Tales of the Beast Master who'd saved the princess had reached this far north, and they'd all grown taller with each telling, of course. But nobody had spotted her. No messages had arrived from Arrick, either, which meant that none of her fellow Ferrets had a lead on where the heathen had gone after Persh. Was she dead, or on her way to Stronghaven, or had she changed direction? If the latter, Avere would have to wait for a bird to arrive. A Ferret would hear news of her eventually.

A woman stumbled past her, ale slopping over the sides of the mug she held. Avere frowned at the sword hanging at the drunk's side. She could understand using a sword when nothing else was at hand, which was why she'd been surprised that the Beast Master had left behind the sword at the camp, even though she'd picked it up. But women should stick to daggers. They were easily concealed. A woman could get close to a man and stick a blade in his belly without him ever seeing a weapon. Why announce one's intentions and skill with a long blade?

But this bumbling woman was one of the wild folk. Subtlety wasn't one of their strong points. Avere watched the woman drop into a chair and swig her ale. Half of it ended up on her leather tunic, but the two men she was with didn't care. One was asleep with his mouth hanging open and the other had a whore on his lap. Avere wrinkled her nose in disgust. Would the Beast Master please hurry up and pass through Stronghaven? She'd like to deal with her while civilized folk still outnumbered the barbarians.

It was time to move on to the next tavern. Avere slid off her stool and started threading her way toward the door, then suddenly stopped. The woman moving purposefully toward the bar . . . she wore the same type of cloak that had caught Avere's eye in Sull. She hadn't made a point to see the woman's face at the time because there had been no reason to take a special interest in her. But the cloak was definitely the same. It was a brilliant rose red, and a lightning bolt striking a book was embroidered on its back.

Was this the same woman she'd seen in Sull? If so, seeing her again could be a coincidence. Sull and Stronghaven were on the same trade route. That cloak, though . . . Avere had never seen one like it. She retraced her steps and watched the woman speak to the barkeep without buying an ale or pushing the cloak's hood off her head. A minute later, the woman walked straight past her without giving her a second glance, but Avere glimpsed her face. She was older, intelligent, determined—and hadn't come into the tavern to drink. Avere followed her out of the tavern and shadowed her to the next one.

An hour and a couple of taverns later, the woman climbed the stairs to one of the inns that catered to the wealthy. Avere returned to her more modest room in the Ferret base and quickly sketched the symbol on the woman's cloak. She'd try to find out more about it on the morrow, and then she'd return to the woman's inn and have a quiet word with her. She wasn't worried the woman would leave Stronghaven in the meantime. At the final tavern the mysterious woman had visited before returning to her inn, Avere had beaten her to the bar and strained to listen to her conversation with the barkeep. The woman had provided him with an accurate description of Erryn Fyler.

At least Avere had something to do while she waited for the Beast Master to show up. If the red-cloaked woman intended to harm the heathen, Avere would slit her throat. Nobody would deprive Avere of her prey. Nobody.

Erryn told Quon to slow to a trot when she spotted something farther up the dusty trail she'd followed since she'd cut around Sull. Hardly anyone travelled this route.

She'd only had to dismiss Quon twice since leaving Sull behind.

She squinted. She could see a wagon, but—movement caught her eye. A man was crouched inside the wagon, sorting through its load. Fortunately his back was to her. She dismounted, dismissed Quon, and darted off the trail into the woods. She'd skirt around—

"No!"

The shout set Erryn's heart racing. She whirled in the direction of the voice. Someone was whimpering. Sobbing. Her first thought was to move deeper into the woods, away from the sound, but what if the stranger needed help? Was she that selfish, that she'd pass someone by in favour of saving her own skin?

"We want the woman," another voice growled.

Erryn crouched and crept toward the voices.

An anguished scream stopped her in her tracks. She caught her breath and carefully took a step, then another, then—she could see a man through the trees, kneeling on a narrow dirt path. Blood ran down his cheek and neck. Another man was crouched at his side, holding a bloodied sword. One of the bleeding man's ears was— Erryn's stomach lurched.

"Give us the woman, or we'll start cutting off fingers," the man with the sword said.

Erryn craned her neck. Now she could see the three other men standing behind the man they held prisoner. She presumed the man with the sword was their leader.

The captive shook his head. "Don't give in," he croaked.

Trying to see who he was talking to, Erryn carefully

shifted her position. One snapped twig would give her away. A man and woman stood about ten paces away from the bleeding man, facing the leader and his three companions. Both their swords were drawn, but they were outnumbered. A woman with a sword, the leather tunics, the pale skin . . . they must be wild folk. "If ye want me, ye'll have to kill me," the wild woman spat.

"Very well." The leader straightened and lifted one of the man's hands. "Take the forefinger," he said to one of his companions.

"No. Please," the captive whimpered.

Why was he torturing the poor man? If the thugs fought the wild folk, it would be four against two. If he wanted the woman, he could just take her.

One of the other men pulled a dagger from his belt and grasped the captive's finger. Erryn turned away. Her teeth clenched when the captive screamed.

"I want the woman," the leader said. "Now."

Erryn looked back. The captive man was hunched over, clutching his bleeding hand and sobbing.

"Ye'll never have me," the wild woman spat. "I'd rather go to the Seven than be taken by a pig."

"Now, now, don't ye be insulting pigs," the man at her side said.

The leader's face darkened. "In that case." He drew back his sword and ran it through the captive's back. The sword's tip emerged from the man's chest. Blood bubbled from the wound. Erryn's mouth dropped open.

The leader pulled his sword from the captive's back,

kicked the dying man forward, and turned to his men. "Kill him. Take her."

The four thugs charged the two wild folk. Swords clashed. While one man kept the wild woman busy, the other three focused on her companion. The wild man was clearly skilled with a sword, but so were the thugs. Three against one, and once the wild man was slain, the woman would be at the mercy of the leader. Erryn couldn't bear to think about what he'd do to her. The Fallen were agitating. She didn't need much encouragement.

Zayvang. The saber-tooth cat leaped into existence. *Lerxis.* The dire wolf heeded her call. Erryn pictured the wild folk in her mind. The details were sketchy, but they were the only two wearing leather tunics, so hopefully . . . *Protect.* The two Fallen raced into the fray. Both took down a thug so quickly that Erryn didn't think their prey had glimpsed them. Now the wild man had only one opponent to worry about, but everyone still standing stopped fighting, confused by the sudden appearance of the wild animals.

"It looks like one of the Fallen!" the thug leader shouted.

All stood rooted to the spot, a fatal mistake for the thug leader. Perhaps he raised his weapon before Zayvang took him down; Erryn couldn't see from her vantage point. Lerxis didn't have to deal with the remaining thug. The wild woman took advantage of his shock and distraction and ended his life with her sword.

Now the wild folk were slowly stepping away from the carnage. Assuming defensive stances, they warily eyed the Fallen. Zayvang paced around the four dead thugs.

Lerxis stood as still as a statue and stared back at the wild folk. Without thinking, Erryn burst from her hiding place and stood several paces away from the man and woman. Hoping to calm them, she raised both hands in a gesture of surrender. "It's okay. They won't hurt you. I called them to help you. It wasn't a fair fight."

They didn't move. Their eyes remained on Zayvang and Lerxis.

Sit.

Both Fallen obeyed her.

"I told them to protect—"

The woman suddenly leaped to Lerxis and drove her sword into the dire wolf's eye. Lerxis vanished. "Ha!" she shouted, and shot the man a triumphant look.

Erryn had assumed the wild folk would appreciate her help. In the second it took for her to realize they might be as ruthless as the thugs, the woman was bearing down on her.

Stop her! But it was too late. The wild man's sword banished Zayvang to the heavenly plane. Erryn backed away—then stumbled and fell onto her back, squashing her bag. The woman loomed over her, the tip of her sword at Erryn's throat.

The man peered over the woman's shoulder. "Now, now, let's not be hasty."

"She's a Fallener," the woman growled.

"A Fallener who saved our lives." He stepped to the woman's side and sheathed his sword. "Are ye going to murder her in cold blood?"

The woman stared down at Erryn, her mouth set.

"Ye aren't like that. I know what they say about ye, but ye aren't. So sheathe yer sword. We have to help Jon."

"He's dead," the woman murmured.

Erryn swallowed. The sword tip grazed her throat.

The woman lifted her sword, using the tip to slowly raise Erryn's hat enough to reveal her forehead. "A warning. One we should heed."

The man bent over to look at the brand. "With Jon gone, it's just the two of us. Maybe she can help us."

"We don't need any help," the woman snapped. She pointed her sword at Erryn's throat again.

The man straightened. "Where are ye going, stranger?"

"Stronghaven," Erryn whispered, being careful to remain still. One twitch and the woman wouldn't hesitate.

"Stronghaven." He turned to the woman. "Don't ye think it would be better if we travelled together? Ye know that, if not for her, I'd be dead, and ye . . . What if we run into trouble again?"

"We can handle ourselves."

"Even the strongest warrior can be defeated by numbers. Don't be stubborn. We're only about a week from Stronghaven. Let's travel together and get there alive." He nudged Erryn with his foot. "If that's all right with ye, stranger."

"Yes, let's travel together," Erryn said, despite feeling ambivalent about it. On the one hand, he was right. If there were more thugs roaming the trails, they *would* be safer travelling together. On the other hand, she could see the bloodlust in the woman's eyes. The direst threat to Erryn's life between here and Stronghaven could be standing right in front of her.

He tapped the woman's arm. "It makes sense. Put yer sword away."

The sword tip pressed harder against Erryn's throat. The woman's eyes narrowed. Erryn desperately wanted to turn her face away, but she kept her eyes locked on the woman.

"If ye summon the Fallen, I'll gut ye," the woman spat.

"Unless we're in trouble, of course," the man said lightly.

Erryn moistened her lips. "I just want to get to Stronghaven."

The woman grunted and lifted her sword. Erryn let out her pent breath. Under the woman's gaze, she slowly rose to her feet and brushed herself off.

"I'm Toetril, but everyone calls me Toe," the man said.

"Erryn."

Toe turned to the woman. When she remained silent, he said, "This is Renn. Now, if ye don't mind, Erryn, I need to see for myself that Jon's dead." He shot Renn a warning look and wandered over to the man lying motionless on his side. The thug's sword had run right through him. If he wasn't already with the Seven, he soon would be.

"I'm sorry about your friend," Erryn said to Renn.

Renn stared at Erryn, her face expressionless. Erryn cleared her throat. She took a tentative step. When Renn didn't whip out her sword, Erryn walked past her to where the thugs had fallen and surveyed the carnage. Zayvang had torn out the throats of two and Renn's sword had finished one. Lerxis had crushed the fourth thug's skull.

Erryn had done this. She'd called the Fallen to protect two people who were already being attacked, and therefore threatened. There had been only one possible outcome: the dead sprawled in front of her. It had been them or the wild folk, and possibly Erryn, if they'd spotted her. They would have shown no mercy. They'd tortured Jon and then run him through. Still, the senseless loss of life saddened Erryn. Would someone with a bestial soul feel sad?

She wrinkled her nose. Something acrid Toe yelped and raced up the path. Renn hesitated a second, then ran after him. Erryn pondered what to do. She could dart into the woods and continue on to Stronghaven alone. Renn certainly wouldn't miss her. Travelling with the wild folk would increase her chances of survival, but that wasn't why she trotted up the path after Toe and Renn. They knew what she was, and yet they were willing to travel with her, albeit grudgingly in Renn's case.

When Erryn emerged from the path onto the trail, she could see the smoke the trees had hidden. Her throat felt scratchy. She covered her mouth and nose with her hand and ran toward the burning wagon—the same wagon she'd seen before leaving the trail. Toe had torn off his cloak and was using it to beat back the flames. Renn leaped into the front of the wagon and stood perilously close to the fire. She tossed a couple of bags onto the trail, then carefully edged closer to the flames. A bundle landed next to the bags.

"Get out," Toe shouted. "It's no good."

He abandoned his effort to put out the fire and picked

up one of the bags Renn had saved. Erryn grabbed the other one. Renn leaped from the wagon and landed on her feet with a thud. Coughing, she dragged the bundle toward the trees, then bent over to catch her breath. Toe went to her and patted her back. Erryn joined them and stood so that Toe was between her and Renn.

Renn lifted her hand. "I'm all right."

Toe straightened. He watched the wagon burn and shook his head. "I wondered what had happened to the other one," he muttered.

"The other one?" Erryn said.

"Five came out of the trees. Four are dead. The other one must have set fire to the wagon and taken the horse. Bastards."

Erryn was still confused. "They ambushed you here, on the trail?"

Toe nodded.

"How did you end up on the path?"

"They grabbed Jon, told us they'd kill him if we didn't go with them. They wanted us off the trail. They didn't want to be interrupted."

"We should have gutted them right then and there," Renn said.

"They would have run Jon through, and then it would have been five against two." Toe blew out a sigh. "We thought staying off the main road would be safer."

Renn grunted.

"We should have hired more men in Sull. Or maybe we shouldn't have agreed to the job. There's a reason not many will run contracts north of Sull. Not without a bloody army with them."

"Contracts?" Erryn said. "They didn't want what was in the wagon?"

Toe's forehead creased. "They weren't thieves. They were slavers. They wanted Renn. She would have brought them a pretty price. Step right up, gents, and ride the wild woman."

"So if they'd captured me . . ." She felt sick.

Renn glowered at Erryn. "I wanted to cut them. I wanted to make them all bleed."

"They outnumbered us and they were as skilled as we are," Toe murmured. "I, for one, am grateful that Erryn helped. I wasn't ready to meet the Seven today, and I don't think ye wanted to be in chains."

Renn's face tightened.

"We lost our horse and our wagon, and poor Jon lost his life. But we're alive." Toe heaved another sigh. "Let's take care of Jon. Then we'll make our way through the forest."

They trudged back to five men who would never laugh, cry, or love again, not in this world. Erryn thought they'd bury Jon, but Toe and Renn, after telling her to leave it to them, lay Jon under a tree. They undressed the dead man until he was in his smallclothes, then covered him with leaves and branches. Erryn watched silently as they knelt next to the mound and bowed their heads.

"Let's go." Toe hoisted the bundle onto his shoulders. Renn picked up the two bags.

"I can carry one of them," Erryn said.

Renn ignored her. She turned to Toe. "Let's follow the river." Toe nodded.

Obviously not wanting to walk with Erryn, Renn took the lead and marched farther into the woods. Toe fell into step with Erryn. "She'll warm up to ye, eventually."

"I don't know. You said we're only a week away from Stronghaven," Erryn said.

Toe's eyes brightened, but only for a second.

"I'm sorry about Jon."

"We didn't know him well. We only met him last week, in Sull. He was so grateful when we hired him to go with us to Stronghaven." His voice dropped. "Poor lad."

"You didn't bury him."

"When one of us falls in the wilderness, we leave him as he came, and as food for the animals."

"What happens when one of you falls at home?"

"If the ground isn't frozen, we bury them. Otherwise we burn them."

"Oh." Erryn supposed that made sense. "You said you're running contracts?"

"Aye. Merchants and others who can afford it pay us well to run contracts between towns. Some roads are safe. Others . . . I should have asked for more for this job." He shifted the bundle on his shoulders. "Why are ye going to Stronghaven?"

"I'm not. I mean, I am, but just to resupply. I'm going to Loring."

"Loring?" The pitch of Toe's voice conveyed his surprise. "That's a long ways away. Why would ye want to go there?"

Erryn wanted to be honest with him. He was treating

her as if she was a decent person. "I heard about a temple. Another person like me was going there, years ago. I want to know why. I have nowhere else to go, so . . ."

Toe opened his mouth to say something, then clamped it shut.

"Have you been to Loring?" Erryn asked him.

Toe shook his head. "But it's one of our settlements. I doubt ye'll find one of yer temples there, but maybe ye're looking for a different kind of temple."

Erryn hoped so. It would be a real letdown if the temple was gone or Rodney's grandfather had made up the story.

"Ye're not what I expected a Fallener to be."

Erryn looked at him. "What did you expect?"

Toe grimaced. "I would have expected ye to kill us all and take everything. But I can tell ye're a good sort. I'll believe what I see over what I'm told any day. Ye saved our lives."

"Thank you for letting me travel with you."

"It makes sense," Toe said.

Perhaps for him. Renn was at least twenty paces ahead of them. Erryn would have to watch her every word, and she wouldn't summon the Fallen unless they were threatened by thugs. It wouldn't take much for Renn to turn on her. She was only one irritant away from cutting Erryn down.

Fi waited for the server to refill her goblet with wine. As soon as he moved to Viren's side, she took a sip, but only the one. She'd already drank a glass. She'd have to pace herself with this one, or she'd wobble when Father presented his daughter and her future husband to those gathered in the banquet hall. When had she begun to fret about being the centre of attention? Oh, about the time she'd become betrothed to one man while in love with another.

When everyone was leaning back in their chairs after devouring a sumptuous seven-course meal, she and Viren would join Father in a toast and lovingly gaze at each other as he showered his future son-in-law with compliments. Fi would struggle to keep her eyes on Viren while her heart urged her to search for Dann. She'd spoken to him once this evening. It would have been rude for him to snub his brother and future sister-in-law at their betrothal banquet, but he hadn't said a word to either of them since then. Thank the Seven he wasn't seated at the royal table.

Her wine beckoned. Not yet. She glanced at Viren, who was sitting between her and Father. Grateful that Father was engaging him in conversation, Fi surveyed those present. When their eyes met, a guest occasionally raised his or her glass to her. She smiled and responded in kind, but didn't drink. Nobody would take it as a slight. If she sipped her wine every time someone acknowledged her, she'd be on the floor in no time.

Most of those here were nobles, primates, or Father's friends. Fi had invited a few ladies, but . . . she'd tried not to think about it, but it was impossible! *Where are you, Erryn? I never imagined you wouldn't be with me at my betrothal banquet.* Father was wrong. Fi would never stop missing her and needed her now more than ever. She'd told Erryn everything. Erryn was the only person Fi had always been honest with. Being able to let it all out without fear of judgement had kept her spirit light. Now she had to bottle it all up. Her genuine smiles were fewer, her heart heavier. When she spotted Cedric standing guard and he nodded to her, her eyes moistened. He was another who'd always cared about her, rather than what she could offer him.

Half the tables in the hall were filled with primates, those who claimed to serve the Seven but vied for the king's favour along with the nobles. Enkelo, in his element tonight because of his place at court, served the High Council's interests, not Father's. Father knew it. They used each other.

A number of the primates wore mitres that were not the blue colour worn by Enkelo and the other primates Fi knew. "Visiting primates from Westerfox Province, Your Highness," Enkelo had said when she'd asked him. "They've come a long way to meet your future husband. You should be honoured."

"I am," she'd murmured, even though she didn't give a toss about primates she didn't know and would never see again.

She focused on those at the royal table. Henrick and Surann seemed tense, which wasn't surprising. Fi's suspicion that Surann was with child had proven false. People were whispering that Surann was barren. If she didn't get pregnant soon, Henrick would take a mistress, if he hadn't already, and because he had no brothers, the Royal Council would legitimize any bastard sons.

The Duke of Tolin and his wife were notably absent. Viren's father had taken to his bed a few days ago and wasn't expected to live out the week. By the time her wedding day arrived, Fi would marry the duke, not the duke's son, and she should stop feeling sorry for herself. She wasn't the only one at the table feeling as if she had the weight of Daros on her shoulders. Viren would have to beam at her and kiss her hand while his father lay dying. He hadn't divulged how he felt about his father's imminent death. Most of her conversations with her betrothed were light and polite. She hoped that once they were married, they'd come to trust and confide in each other.

Light and polite. Light and polite. She wanted to weep.

Combing through the list of visitors to the High Council's estate, Arrick flipped to the next page, then leaned back and rubbed his eyes. So far, nothing had jumped out at him. It would be easier if the man who recorded visitors didn't write in such a small script. Arrick thumbed through the remaining pages. Only four to go until he reached the date of the princess's attempted assassination.

If the assassins had succeeded, the Lyoses, nobles, and primates who resided in or near the Royal Province wouldn't be packed in the banquet hall to celebrate the princess's betrothal while he sat here, hoping to figure out who had tried to kill her. Not that he felt snubbed because his name wasn't on the banquet's guest list. His presence would only have put a damper on things. Conversations would have been shallower. Everyone would have wondered which of their secrets he knew. No matter. He didn't expect invitations to social events. He always had eyes and ears at those that counted, and tonight's banquet was no exception.

With a sigh, he read the list of visitors on the next page, then flipped it to the finished pile and started on the next one. He reached for his wine, then jerked back his hand and jabbed his finger onto the page. Two primates from Westerfox had visited the High Council around the time of the assassination attempt. That in itself wasn't alarming, but—

"Jack!"

His boy stepped into the study. "Yes, sir."

"Fetch me the guest list for the princess's betrothal banquet."

A minute later, Arrick took the list from Jack and skimmed it. There. Five primates from Westerfox. Five? All the way from Westerfox? There was no reason to curry favour with the princess by travelling hundreds of miles to attend her betrothal banquet. A handful of primates had come from Rion and the other bordering provinces, but none from the outer ones—except Westerfox. Was it coincidence that primates from Westerfox had also been in the city when assassins had threatened the princess's life? The instinct Arrick had learned not to ignore shouted no.

He pushed back his chair. "Ready my horse. I want to ride to the castle immediately." Jack scurried from the study.

His heart pounding, Arrick grabbed his cloak and

hurried after him. What move did the Westerfox primates plan to make upon the princess's death? He'd puzzle out the answer later, because if his suspicion about the primates was correct, the princess's life was in danger again. He had to warn the guard. They'd be on duty at the banquet, but none would stop a primate from approaching the princess—and sticking a dagger into her gut.

Erryn swallowed the last bit of the stew Toe had cooked and licked her fingers. She'd shared some of her bread with Toe, but had definitely come out ahead in the exchange of food. Renn had refused the bread with a shake of her head. She was sitting on the other side of the fire with her back partially to Erryn and hadn't said a word to her since they'd left Jon's body, not even a grunt.

"Thank you for the stew," she said to Toe.

The bags Renn had grabbed contained food and utensils. The bundle had turned out to be a tent, which Renn had pitched while Toe cooked. Erryn had offered to help him, but he'd waved her away.

"There's no need to thank me. We're travelling together. And ye need more meat on yer bones." He gazed thoughtfully at her. The glow from the fire illuminated his face and made his eyes dance. "How long have ye been wandering? Where do ye come from? I can tell ye've not been living wild long."

She glanced at Renn, wondering how honest she should be. "I'm from Darroth."

Toe's brows shot up. "The Royal Province?"

Erryn nodded.

He set his bowl on the ground and leaped to his feet. "Charmed to meet ye, lady." He bowed to her.

Renn snorted. Ah, despite appearing uninterested in the conversation, she *was* paying attention. Erryn rewarded Toe with a smile, even though he was mocking her. She wouldn't tell him she'd grown up in the royal castle.

Toe sat back down. "Ye said ye're going to Loring. Did ye come all this way alone? Why isn't anyone with ye?"

Renn snorted again. Toe shot her an indulgent glance. Then his brow furrowed. "When we were in Sull, we heard a story about a Fallener and the princess. Was it ye? It must have been ye. The only time I ever heard word of a Fallener was in the Mothers' stories. I doubt there would be two of ye in the Royal City at the same time."

How much had the story in Sull told them? Would they be more or less wary of her if they knew she was—had been—the king's foster daughter? "I was passing by when the assassins attacked. I had to do something." Erryn swallowed. "When they saw what I am . . ."

"They marked ye and ran ye out." Toe looked over at Renn, then back at Erryn. "If it wasn't for ye, Sull's crier would be shouting about the princess's death. But she's alive, and betrothed. She—"

Erryn could hardly breathe. "Betrothed?" she whispered.

Toe nodded. "To some duke. Did ye not hear?"

"For the past while, I've avoided towns and cities," Erryn said, her throat still tight. Fi, betrothed? She'd known it would happen, but . . . She wanted to crawl away and curl into a ball, punch something, run through the woods and let the branches bloody her face, go back to Sull and summon the Fallen and let the guard end her misery. Her hands clenched. Who was it? Which duke? Tolin? Eldos? Did Fi love him? Tears welled in her eyes.

"Ye're upset," Toe said, his confusion written across his face.

Erryn bit back her grief. "Hearing the news . . . it reminds me of how much I miss home." She drew a shaky breath. "Tell me where you're from."

"From way up north, somewhere ye probably haven't heard of." Toe's voice softened and he gazed wistfully past Erryn. "We haven't been home for a long time. We run contracts, and sometimes goods, in northern Rion and Moore. Roads are dangerous these days. It's not only the thugs like the ones we ran into, but the desperate people coming down from the north."

"Why are so many people coming south?"

Toe's brows drew together. "Have ye not heard in the Royal Province, or do ye not care? Ye should. It's only a matter of time."

Erryn didn't recall hearing anything ominous about the north, but the criers in the Royal City usually announced tidings of the king and Primacy. They spent little time on the goings on in the other provinces. "What's only a matter of time?"

"The land is sick, Erryn. Living in the north has always been harsh, but not like it is today. Our crops die. Our prey is thin, in number and girth. The Mothers—our priestesses—believe the Seven are angry, but they don't know why." Toe's mouth pressed into a thin line. "The sickness is spreading. Eventually those in the Royal Province will be scrounging for food, if any remain alive. If we don't have the Seven's favour, we're doomed."

"Is it because of me?" Erryn blurted. "Am I making them angry?"

"How many years do ye have, Erryn? Nineteen? Twenty? Our troubles started before ye were born."

"But there was another Beast Master before me."

"Beast Master?"

"Fallener. The one who was going to the temple."

Toe shook his head. "There have always been Falleners."

He was right, but Erryn knew she was a blight in the Seven's eyes. Why? Why did they allow Beast Masters to be born? Was it a game to them? Did they enjoy watching each Beast Master hunted, and caught, and killed? Even though she was sitting in the glow of a roaring fire, she shivered. "I haven't heard anything about the situation in the north."

Toe shrugged. "Yer people don't care because it's only the—what do ye call us?" His mouth twisted. "It's only the wild folk who are suffering."

It was more that those in the Royal Province didn't care about those outside it, wild folk or no, but Erryn kept her thoughts to herself. She glanced at Renn's stiff shoulders and back. She must be listening. What was the relationship between her and Toe? They seemed to know each other well, but they didn't strike Erryn as husband and wife. Brother and sister, perhaps? Renn looked to be in her late twenties; Toe was older, in his mid-thirties. If she felt brave, she'd ask Toe about Renn out of Renn's earshot. Did all wild women take up arms? Were they all intimidating and brusque?

She wouldn't try to speak to Renn. She wanted to make it to Loring alive, and now that Toe had stopped talking and was staring broodingly into the fire, the thoughts Erryn had tried to suppress intruded on her again. Fi. Her betrothal. The reality that the life Erryn had known, her place in Fi's life, was gone. Oh, she'd known it from the moment she'd summoned Zayvang to save Fi's life, but the stubborn fantasy that she'd somehow return as if nothing had happened was now dead. Gone. Fi would marry. There was no longer a place for her in Fi's life. Fi was a Lyos, Erryn a cursed woman.

She'd continue to Loring and find the temple, but not for herself. If not for Rodney's kindness and her desire to repay him someday, she wouldn't care whether she lived or died.

Toe lowered himself to sit next to Renn and gazed in the direction she was looking. Erryn lay on a blanket next to the fire, fast asleep. When she'd said she was tired, she'd pulled an old shirt from her bag and rolled it up to use as a pillow. Toe would have liked to offer her a place in the tent, which was large enough for all three of them. Instead, he'd given her a blanket, despite Renn's glare. "We'll be walking all day tomorrow. Ye need sleep," he said to her.

Her eyes remained on Erryn. "I'm on watch."

"Watch? If we all sleep in the tent, we can put out the fire. Everyone sleeps. It's dangerous in the forest at night. The thugs don't—"

"I'm watching her. I'll wake ye a few hours before sunrise."

Toe braced himself. "No."

Her jaw tightened. "She's a Fallener."

"A Fallener who saved our lives. If not for her, I'd be dead, and ye . . ." He didn't want to think about it. "Open yer eyes. If she didn't have the Fallen to call on, the girl would already be dead. I don't know how she's made it this far. Now she's in over her head. If we travel together, we all have a better chance of reaching Stronghaven."

Renn continued to watch Erryn.

"She was sent away, just like ye."

"I'm not a Fallener." Renn jutted her chin toward Erryn. "Maybe she's the reason for the trouble."

"She thought the same, but there have always been Falleners."

"Like the one who was looking for the temple." Renn snorted. "Ye didn't tell her he never made it there."

Toe lowered his voice. "I didn't want to dampen the girl's spirits. She's confused, Renn. If ye listened to her, looked at her, ye'd see."

"Don't make a fool of yerself. She's too young and soft for ye."

Toe drew back. "Ye think that's why—" He shook his head. He wouldn't let her goad him into an argument.

"We should kill her and be done with it." Renn spat on the ground. "What are we doing, helping a Fallener?"

"She saved our lives. I won't repay her by taking hers. We're better than that." When Renn didn't respond, he tapped her arm, then shook it until she turned to him. "I know they were wrong about ye. I don't know what happened, but I know they were wrong."

"Ye don't know anything." She jerked her arm away. "But if not for ye, I'd still be on my own. Ye want to travel with the Fallener, so we'll travel with the Fallener. But any lives she takes will be on yer head."

"She's not a beast."

Renn's eyes narrowed. "Not yet."

"So ye can get some rest."

"No."

Toe sighed. "Fine. But ye better keep up."

He pushed himself to his feet and went into the tent without looking back. Let Renn deprive herself of sleep. They all needed to be on their toes in case they ran into more trouble, but he'd tried. The stubborn woman would have her way tonight.

Given what the Mothers taught, he understood Renn's wariness toward Erryn. But Toe believed more in what he saw with his own eyes than what he was told. Erryn seemed a decent sort. If the Mothers were right and her soul was black and bestial, why had she helped them? Why hadn't the Fallen she'd summoned ripped them all apart? She knew good from bad, right from wrong. Still, Toe hoped the debt they owed her wouldn't grow before they reached Stronghaven.

Fi finally finished her second goblet of wine and nodded

when a servant offered her more. She wasn't drunk, but she was terribly bored. Against her better judgement, she downed half her wine before the servant had finished serving Viren, who stood next to her. This would have to be her last glass, or she'd make a fool of herself. Already, she felt lighter in spirit than she should, because every glimpse of Dann made her want to weep. Why? Why had she walked the wall that night? And why did she keep looking for Erryn? She wasn't here. She'd never be here again. Maybe Fi *would* have a fourth glass of wine. Fortunately Father had already presented the happily betrothed couple to the guests. Fi had managed to keep her eyes on Viren, so she deserved as much wine as she wanted.

The tables had been cleared and the musicians were playing. Those who weren't dancing were drinking and mingling. In an hour, she'd suggest to Viren that they slip away. Everybody would be too drunk to notice by then.

She jumped when someone grasped her elbow. "Come, both of you," Father said. "A group of primates from Westerfox want to meet you."

Fi had conversed with enough boring primates this evening to last her a lifetime. She giggled. "Do we have to?"

Father scowled. "How much wine have you had?"

Not enough. "I'm sober, Father." More or less. Sighing, she took a couple of sips of her wine, then set the almost empty goblet on a nearby table. "I won't embarrass either of us. Should we go and meet these delightful men, Viren?"

"I suppose we should," he said, displaying as much

enthusiasm as she felt. "They didn't come all this way for the banquet, did they?" Viren asked Father as they walked to the primates. Revellers formed a path for them, bowing and curtsying as they moved out of the royal group's way.

"They're here to study in the great library. Interesting gentlemen. Henrick and I were talking with them when they asked to meet you." He gave Fi a pointed look. "Do try to sound coherent. Grand Primate Otane is with them, as well."

Oh, goody.

By the time they reached the group clustered around Henrick and Surann, Fi had managed to appear as if she cared about the Westerfox primates. "Such a pleasure to meet you," she said, when they all inclined their heads to her and Viren. Their mitres weren't as elaborate as those worn by the primates in the Royal Province, but then, Darroth was the jewel of Daros. Everyone who was anyone lived here, and that included primates.

"Congratulations on your betrothal," the one Father had introduced as Primate Ydare said, his voice carrying a slight accent. "A strong royal family is a sign of the Seven's approval."

Father grunted. "The Lyoses humbly serve the Seven, Your Grace."

Grand Primate Otane cleared his throat. "Our brethren from Westerfox would like to see Calen's Text. I thought we could all visit the royal library together." His face tightened. "I've explained to them why the Holy Text is here, rather than in our great library."

"Don't you think the Holy Text belongs where it was

written and discovered?" Henrick asked, a mischievous glint in his eye. He had as much time for primates as Fi did. "The royal castle was built on this very spot because the Seven blessed it. The Text says that Zhikinden herself sat with Calen under the trees and told him of the heavenly plane, a story that's corroborated by Sulor's Text."

Otane's face flushed. "I am aware of the passages in both texts," he said, his voice strangled.

Fi bit back a smile. Primates were so easy to rile.

"The grand primate should be lecturing you, not the other way around," Father snapped at Henrick. "Come, let's go to the library."

Fi wanted to groan. Now she'd not only have to pretend she cared about the primates, but also about some musty, smelly parchment only those versed in the ancient language could read.

Nobody spoke as the group made its way to the hallway that led to the grand staircase. Enkelo spotted them. He broke off his conversation with a noble and moved to join them, but Otane lifted his hand and shook his head. Enkelo stopped short and frowned.

Otane turned to Father. "We should toast Calen and pray to the Seven before we enter the sacred room."

Father beckoned to a servant. "Bring enough wine and goblets for all of us to the library." The servant scurried away.

At least Fi would have another glass of wine before she had to stand before the display case and murmur the appropriate words of awe over an ancient parchment.

"No," Father said, when a guard fell into step behind

them as they moved into the carpeted corridor. "We're going to the library."

The guard nodded and resumed his position next to the doorway. There would be guards inside the library, and there was no need for him to shadow them there.

Irritated with the guards who'd delayed him at the gates and on his way to the banquet hall, Arrick scanned the revellers for the princess, the king, the prince, anyone who belonged to the royal family. His apprehension reached a fever pitch when he couldn't spot anybody. He shoved his way through the crowd, ignoring glares and muttered curses.

Enkelo! Arrick strode over to him. "Where's the princess?"

Enkelo's nostrils flared. "Well, good evening to you—"

"Forget the pleasantries. Where's the princess, the king, anyone?"

"They left with the grand primate."

"Only the grand primate?"

"And our Westerfox guests."

Shit! "Where did they go?"

"I don't know." Enkelo pointed to a servant. "The king spoke to him on—"

Arrick wheeled and darted over to the servant. "Where's the king and his family?"

The servant drew back. "In the library, sir."

Arrick pointed at the guard who stood nearby. "You— gather five or six men and get to the library." The guard frowned at him. "Now! The king is in danger."

That lit a fire under the man. He shouted for two nearby guards to join him and signalled to several others. The commotion drew attention. Alarmed cries and whispers raced through the crowd. As Arrick hurried down the hallway to the grand staircase, the music behind him died. Enkelo managed to catch up with him. "What's happening?" he gasped.

"How long ago did they go to the library?"

"About fifteen minutes ago."

Fifteen minutes. Arrick hoped they weren't too late.

The Lyoses and primates stood around the grand oak table in the main study room. The guards overseeing the library's top floor had raised their brows when the king, prince, two princesses, a duke's son, the grand primate, and the Westerfox primates with their distinctive mitres had strolled past them. When one had moved to trail the group, Father had waved him away.

After three nervous servants had brought in two carafes of wine and enough goblets for everyone, Otane closed the door. "Let us give thanks for this wine," he said.

Still standing, everyone bowed their heads.

"We thank Roosad for the grapes, Queyris for those who laboured, and Samshy for the pleasure of partaking of this wine."

"We thank the Seven," everyone murmured.

"Please continue to meditate upon the Seven while I pour the wine," Otane said.

Fi suppressed another groan. She wasn't in the mood for an impromptu worship service, but Otane seemed determined to stand on ceremony, probably to show off to the visiting primates. When he finally gave permission for them to raise their heads, Fi rolled her eyes at Surann. She could tell that Surann would rather be back in the banquet hall. Everyone else always had fun while they were stuck performing some dreary duty.

Otane murmured more words of blessing as he handed each person a goblet, starting with Father. While Fi waited for her turn, she surveyed those around the table. The grand primate and Westerfox primates stood intermingled with Lyoses and those related to them, or soon to be related to them by marriage.

The grand primate finally returned to his place and lifted his goblet. "To Calen, who recorded Zhikinden's words and now serves her in the heavens."

"To Calen," everyone echoed. Fi wanted to gulp down her wine, but that wouldn't be ladylike, especially in this company. She was one of the last to set her goblet on the table, though.

Primate Ydare, the same Westerfox primate who'd spoken in the banquet hall, swept his arm toward the door. "It's a humbling experience to be here, in this room, with Calen's Text so close by, and in the midst of the royal family." He turned to Father, who stood next to him. "You said that the Lyoses serve the Seven."

Father nodded. "It's by their grace that we rule."

"Yet you allowed a Beast Master to leave your castle and your city alive."

All of the Westerfox primates looked at Father. Henrick glanced at the grand primate. Viren's jaw was set. The tension in the room had definitely risen, but it was more than that. Fi wished she hadn't drunk so much wine. Her head felt fuzzy.

Father squared his shoulders. "The Beast Master in question was close to my daughter. Under other circumstances, I—" His face reddened. "I—" He grabbed his chest and stumbled into the table.

"Father!" Fi shouted. "Father, what's—" Her breath caught in her throat. Henrick had fallen to his knees. Surann clutched at her throat. Primate Ydare pulled a dagger from under his robe and pulled back Father's head. Before Fi could scream, he slit Father's throat. Blood sprayed across the table.

Another primate plunged a dagger into Henrick's chest. Fi backed away. No, this couldn't be happening. A scream—it sounded like Surann. Another shriek—then silence. Fi stood paralyzed.

Someone shoved her toward the door. "Run!" Viren roared.

Confused, she whirled to him. He was all right! He was alive! "Run!" he shouted again. Then he lunged at the nearest primate. "Run, Filmona!"

Fi's legs felt like lead. Blood pounded in her ears. She stumbled toward the door, her arms outstretched. She grasped the handle, then winced when someone grabbed her hair and pulled her away. "No, no, no." *Where are the guards?*

She fell onto her behind. No, she wasn't giving up. With all her strength, she tried to pull away, loose her hair from her attacker's hands. She made it onto her hands and knees. Her knuckles scraped along the hard floor as she scrabbled toward the door.

Her attacker yanked her backward. She screamed again. Another of the Westerfox primates swam into view. She looked up at him and raised her hands. "Please, no," she croaked. "Please."

He smiled and drew back his arm.

Pain.

Darkness.

Place Your Bets

€rryn trudged along a dirt path behind Toe and Renn, straining to hear their conversation over the roar from the river. For once she was grateful for the hat she wore. The trees lining the path provided poor shelter from the heavy rain. The wild folks' hair was plastered to their heads and water dripped from their cloaks. When the skies had opened, Erryn had expected them to seek a dry haven, but neither of the wild folk had suggested doing so.

Toe looked over his shoulder and pointed to his right. "We're moving to higher ground. The rain is swelling the river, and we're getting nearer to the waterfall. This path will take us too close to the water."

It was slippery, too. If she fell into the river and the current swept her away, nobody would mourn for her. Nobody who cared would know. Would she travel to the heavenly plane and meet the Seven? Where did Beast Masters go? None of the many services she'd sat through in the castle's worship room had touched on the fate of those who could summon the Fallen.

As she turned onto the path that would take them away from the river, Erryn realized she was lost. When Rodney had sketched his crude map, they hadn't expected her to travel through the forest. Renn had suggested they follow the river. Erryn assumed it would lead them to Stronghaven, but she didn't *know*. She needed to be more careful and not blindly trust anyone who didn't kill her the moment they saw the brand on her forehead.

This path was steeper than the last. Erryn's legs ached. When Toe stopped and pulled a berry from a bush, Erryn considered finding a walking stick, but her belly was grumbling. She plucked a berry from another bush and—

A slap sent the berry from Erryn's hand. Erryn whirled, but it wasn't Toe next to her, it was Renn.

"Were ye going to let her eat it?" Renn said to Toe, who looked as bewildered as Erryn felt. Renn must have pushed him aside. The wild woman scowled and snapped a branch off the bush from which Toe had picked a berry. "Look closely."

Erryn leaned in.

"Ye see how there are three leaves and then a berry?" Renn handed the branch to Toe and tugged one from the bush near Erryn. "What do ye see on this one?"

Erryn peered at it. "A large leaf and a berry."

"This is a gony bush. Do ye know why they call it that?"

"No."

"Because long ago, it was called an agony bush, and those are agony berries," Toe said. "They're gony berries now, and ye don't want to eat them."

Erryn wanted to inch away from the green berries. "They're poisonous?"

"They won't kill ye, not unless ye eat a bunch. But they'll make ye sick. Ye'd moan and groan for a day."

"Do ye not know anything?" Renn said. "Any three-year-old child knows not to eat gony berries."

Erryn swallowed. "I grew up in the city."

"Did ye not eat berries?"

Toe guffawed.

"We don't have gony berries in Darroth, or at least I've never eaten any."

Renn gave her a withering look. "Ye'd know if ye'd eaten gony berries." Her mouth twisted. "Ye don't belong out here. Ye should be inside, sitting on yer soft bottom while someone else picks yer berries for ye. Ye've only survived out here because of yer pets."

Erryn's cheeks burned. "If I didn't have my pets, I wouldn't be out here."

Renn raised an appraising brow. "When they ran ye out, they expected ye to die."

"They probably did," Erryn said, defiantly raising her chin, despite knowing that without Rodney's help, she'd be dead. Renn was right. She didn't have the knowledge to survive out here. She had to risk entering towns and villages to buy food, but couldn't remain in one place for longer than a few days. Unless she learned how to live in the wild, she'd be running for the rest of her life. "Now I know what gony berry bushes look like and not to pluck berries from them. Thank you for teaching me that."

"We're not yer teachers," Renn said incredulously. "Ye think ye'll learn how to live off the land in a few days? Ye should forget about going to Loring. Ye won't make it. Ye and yer soft bottom should stay in Stronghaven."

Erryn wished she could remain in the city. She wished she could earn enough coin to rent a tiny room in a hovel and maybe make a friend or two, but . . . Her voice quavered. "I can't stay in Stronghaven. I have to go where the other Beast M—Fallener went. I have to find out why he went there."

Renn looked at Toe. His eyes held hers for a moment, then he turned away from her. "Pull out one of the empty food bags," he said. "Let's fill it with berries and be on our way. I'm tired of standing in the rain."

"Let us pick the berries," Renn said.

Frustration clenched Erryn's hands. "I want to help. You've shown me which ones to pick. I won't pick any gony berries. And thanks to you, I won't get sick," she added, wanting to be conciliatory.

Renn snorted. "I only did it so I wouldn't have to listen to yer whining. Here." She gestured toward a bush. "Pick berries from this bush."

Erryn felt like finding another bush, but doing so would be childish, and picking a fight with Renn would be stupid. She went to the bush Renn had chosen for her.

It didn't take long for the three of them to fill the bag. When they set off again, Renn took the lead and Toe fell into step with Erryn. When Renn had put some distance between them, he said, "Don't mind what she says. Mind what she does. She could have let ye eat the gony berry, but she didn't."Erryn wanted to roll her eyes. "Because she didn't want to listen to my whining."

Toe chuckled. "She's not a bad sort, but she doesn't trust easily."

Erryn didn't expect Renn's trust. Renn treated her the way she expected most to treat her, once they knew what she was. Toe was the exception. "Maybe you shouldn't trust me."

"I don't. I trust my instincts."

Renn was probably doing the same—trusting Toe's instincts. "It sounds like you and Renn have travelled together for a while. Are you married?" Erryn asked, even though she didn't believe they were. She hoped Toe's answer would tell her what she wanted to know.

He laughed, making Renn turn around. She glowered and continued on. "No, we're not married." His voice dropped. "I'm fond of Renn, but when I pledge to a woman, I'd like someone a bit less . . . prickly."

Erryn smiled. "You're not brother and sister, are you? You don't look alike."

"No, but we're from the same clan. Renn—" He heaved a sigh.

Erryn waited, then said, "You left together to find work in the south?"

"No." Toe scratched his nose. "Renn's story isn't mine to tell. All I can say is that she was run out of our clan, like ye were run out of yer city."

"Why?" Erryn asked. "Can you tell me that?"

Toe's lips pressed into a thin line.

"Did she do something wrong? Violate a sacred rule? Did she offend someone powerful?"

Toe blew out another sigh. "Ye don't need to know. We'll part ways at Stronghaven."

"I know, but . . ." She took a moment to ponder why she wanted—needed—to know. "I was run out, like you said. I know how it feels. I don't know anyone else . . ."

"Ye feel a kinship with her now."

She wouldn't put it like that, but she understood what he meant. "Yes."

"I wouldn't be telling her that," Toe said, his eyes bright.

"I won't, but I can't help but wonder why. Like you said, we'll part ways. I won't tell her you told me. No matter what the reason was, I'm worse. Everyone hates me, including the Seven."

"Did ye choose to be a Fallener?"

"No."

"Then maybe ye're not worse."

"What did she do? I swear, I won't tell anyone. I won't talk to her about it."

"Ye better not." Toe looked up the path. "She killed another clan member."

"Why?"

"She wouldn't say."

"She must have had a reason. Was she defending herself?"

Toe shook his head. "The Mothers wouldn't have judged her so harshly."

"Who did she kill?"

Toe's eyes went to Renn again. "One of her closest friends," he said quietly.

Erryn shivered, and not from the cold. "Why?" she breathed.

"She wouldn't say. She was only seventeen at the time. So was Ian. Renn never denied that she'd killed him. She admitted it."

"Don't you worry that she'll, uh . . ."

"Run her sword through me while I sleep?" Toe's smile didn't reach his eyes. "I said Renn's story isn't my story to tell. I can't tell it, because I don't know the story. She didn't tell the clan the story. She admitted to the murder and said little else. My kin were close to her kin. I knew her well back then. I believe that if she'd told us why, the Mothers would have understood."

He fell silent for a moment, then tore his gaze away from Renn's back. "Ye're right. She must have had a reason. Renn's a good sort. She has a temper and doesn't make a lot of friends, but she's a good sort. I trust my instincts."

Erryn hoped his instincts were true. Her life depended on it.

Avere squared her shoulders and entered the temple closest to Stronghaven's Ferret base. She hated temples and primates and anything to do with religion. She respected the Seven, but she didn't believe the primates were any closer to the Seven than she was. She'd learned all her important lessons from life, not from listening to a sheltered man in a mitre droning on about how she should live. She only entered a temple when she wanted something, and today was no exception. But today she wouldn't slink inside and pretend to meditate until it was safe to slip into the primate's study. Today she'd have to speak to the dreary man.

A quick scan of the main worship room told her the primate wasn't there. To avoid disturbing those communing with the Seven, or doing what she'd be doing—thinking about something else—she tiptoed around the periphery of the room until she reached a hallway. She found the study two doors down. Usually she'd groan at the sight of the primate behind his desk. While she was in his study, she'd surreptitiously look around, see if there was anything worth—*focus, Avere.* Except for the few times she'd lifted a book that would help her achieve whatever Arrick had tasked her with, she hadn't stolen from a temple in years. She was here to find out why the woman in the rose cloak was seeking the Beast Master, not to make coin.

The primate's head was bare. Most only wore their mitres in worship rooms and when they were out in public. Avere remembered being slapped when she'd asked whether they wore their mitres to bed. She couldn't recall who'd left the red mark on her cheek. She'd been about eleven and on her own. Adults had moved in and out of her life, some who were kind, and some who still made her skin crawl when memories of them intruded. She didn't thank the Seven for much, but she did thank them for Arrick.

She tapped on the study's open door. The primate

looked up from his writing and beckoned her inside. Avere approached his desk. "I'm sorry to bother you, Primate, but I was wondering if you could help me with something."

"What do you want?" he asked, but not churlishly. His eyes shone with curiosity.

Avere pulled her sketch of the symbol on the woman's cloak from her pocket and held it so the primate could see it. "I was in an inn yesterday and I saw this symbol on a cloak. I've never seen it before."

The primate drew back and scowled. "Put that away."

"You know it, then," Avere said, folding the paper and slipping it back into her pocket.

"I wish I didn't. You're not the first to ask me about it." His voice hardened. "Bloody heathen, flaunting her blasphemy. I wish the guard could do something about her, but it's not a crime to offend the Seven, not unless it also violates the law."

"What do you mean? What blasphemy?"

The primate shook his head. "Forget you saw it. If you happen upon her again, spit on her." He lifted his quill and lowered his head.

Bother. "I heard the woman asking about the Beast Master. The one banished from the Royal Province."

The primate's head jerked up. "Does she think the Beast Master is here? In Stronghaven?"

"I don't know. All I know is that she's looking for her."

"If she finds her, her foolishness will be the end of both of them."

"You think she'll kill the Beast Master?"

"Kill her?" The primate barked a laugh. "No."

"What, then?"

"This heathen belongs to a cult that offends the Seven."

According to primates, just about everything offended the Seven. "Why haven't I heard of them before? Why have I never seen the symbol?"

"Because the few misguided souls who belong to the cult call Westerfox their home. I only know about them because we spend five minutes on them during our studies. Of course, there usually isn't a Beast Master walking Daros. I suppose the news of one has them searching for her."

"But why? What do they believe?"

"It's not what they believe. Well, I suppose it is, since that leads to what they do."

Avere resisted the urge to throttle the man. "You said the woman won't kill the Beast Master. Do they worship Beast Masters? Is that what they do?"

"Why do you want to know?" The Primate leaned back in his chair. "You're not enamored of the Beast Master, are you?"

"Certainly not!" She wished she could tell the man she'd likely kill the heathen. Perhaps then he'd tell her what she wanted to know before the sun set. "I'm just curious. I'd never seen the symbol before. I'm surprised you haven't told your flock about the woman. If you all did so, word would spread and she'd be run out of the city."

"We prefer not to offend the Seven by mentioning Beast Masters." He waved a dismissive hand. "The woman's a blasphemer and offensive to all who love the Seven, but she's harmless. Once she's satisfied the Beast Master isn't here, she'll leave."

"In the meantime, she'll flaunt her blasphemy on her cloak."

The primate shrugged. "Few know what the symbol on her cloak represents. Isn't that why you're here?"

Time for a new tactic. Avere leaned over his desk and lowered her voice. "I couldn't help but notice the worn carpet in the worship room. I was thinking that perhaps I might make a donation, but I don't know. I'm feeling frustrated at the moment. I don't feel generous when I'm frustrated. If only I knew what this cult believes. I'll be ever so grateful to whoever enlightens me. I'll certainly want to compensate them in some way."

The primate blinked at her, then rubbed the back of his neck. "The temple would be grateful for whatever donation you can make. And I'm always happy to enlighten those who support it, of course."

Of course. Avere flipped open her purse and dropped several coins into the man's hand. When he shook his head, she added several more. He pocketed some of the coin and added the rest to the donation box on his desk. An honest primate, then. Nobody would expect him to put it all toward a new carpet. "Does this cult worship Beast Masters?"

"No." The primate met her eyes. "They worship the Fallen. This woman sees the Beast Master as a means to an end. She's looking for her because she'll want her to summon the Fallen. Well, I hope the heathen does what the woman wants, right here in the city. The guards will cut them both down."

Avere straightened. So, the woman wouldn't steal her prey and was highly motivated to find the heathen.

The primate rubbed his forehead. "I apologize. Though the Seven would welcome the deaths of the Beast Master and the blasphemer, my enthusiasm for such an outcome is unseemly."

His words reminded Avere of why she usually entered temples to steal. If Beast Masters offended the Seven, why did they allow them to exist? Why allow the Fallen to enter the physical plane? Was it a game? An inside joke? An afternoon's amusement?

The Holy Texts sometimes contradicted each other. But according to tradition, they'd been written by men who'd spoken with the Seven here, in Daros. Why did the Seven no longer walk the land? Had they ever?

Avere would leave such lofty questions to others. She was merely a woman. She couldn't hope to understand the motives of gods. She didn't believe that any primate did, either—not that she'd ever say that out loud. Nobody would point at *her* and call her a blasphemer. At the same time, she wouldn't waste her time listening to men who only understood as much about the Seven as she did.

"Thank you," she said to the primate.

His shoulders hunched. "Please don't bring any harm to this misguided woman. Her presence here is irritating, nothing more. If she happens to find the Beast Master, they won't do anything foolish here. I expect they'll travel to Westerfox."

Not if Avere could help it.

Fi opened her eyes and blinked into the light streaming in through her bedchamber's window. Her head throbbed. She pushed herself into a sitting position and— *Father!* She leaped to her feet. Pain lanced through her forehead. She gingerly touched it, then gasped when she turned to the mirror hanging on the wall. Her right cheek was a red, ugly, swollen bruise. Dried blood marred her forehead. Then she hadn't dreamed it . . . *Father. Henrick. Surann. No! It must have been a dream. It must have!*

Ignoring her pain, she went to the closed bedchamber door. It wouldn't open. Someone had locked her inside her bedchamber. Anxiety snaked through her. No, it hadn't happened. She'd drunk too much wine, fallen, and hurt herself. The blood . . . the screaming . . . she'd dreamed it all. Whoever had helped her to her bedchamber had accidentally locked the door, though they'd need the key.

She lifted her arm. The key was gone! Someone had removed it from her bracelet. Panic coursed through her, and she pounded on the door with both hands. "Let me out! Let me out!" she shouted. Her head ached. She wanted to sink to the floor and weep.

Footsteps, outside. Someone slipped a key into the lock. Fi moved away from the door. Whoever had locked her inside would regret it.

The door swung open. Fi frowned when Duke Eldos stepped into the bedchamber, followed by Lord Eness and several other men who sat on the Royal Council. They studied her, their faces grim.

She swallowed. Her body trembled. *No.* It hadn't happened. "Where is the king?" she whispered.

Eldos raised his hand and stepped forward, but Eness grabbed Eldos's arm. "No. We must do this right."

Had he been about to hit her? Why? Because she hadn't saved Father? *The Westerfox primate . . . blood spraying . . . a dagger protruding from*—Fi couldn't pretend it hadn't happened any longer. Father was dead. They all were. "It happened so quickly. I—" *The Westerfox primate drawing back his arm.* "Why am I alive?" she breathed, more to herself than to anyone else.

Eldos's eyes widened. "I can't believe the depth of your treachery. Even now, you lie. You will pay for what you've done."

Her grief and pounding head must be addling her mind. Eldos wasn't making sense. "I don't understand."

Several of the men exchanged glances. Eness shook his head. "Out of respect for your father, we didn't throw you into the dungeon. I see now that we were mistaken."

"The dungeon?" Indignation momentarily quashed Fi's confusion and sorrow. "Answer me this. Are Father—are the king and the prince dead?"

"Don't play innocent with us. You know they're dead."

"Then I rule Daros."

She drew back when Eldos took another step toward her. "And that's what you wanted, isn't it, Filmona?" he spat. "The throne. You and your betrothed weren't satisfied with a dukedom. Oh, no. You wanted what you couldn't have, not without committing cold-blooded murder."

Fi grabbed her head. "What are you saying? I don't understand."

"Stop pretending! It's over. Your co-conspirator has told us everything."

"What co-conspirator?"

"Again, you play the innocent. Your betrothed."

"Viren?" Overcome with grief for her family, she hadn't wondered what had happened to him. *"Run, Filmona!"* Guilt deepened the grief she already couldn't bear. He'd tried to save her.

"He was quite cooperative, once we had him on the rack."

Her stomach lurched. She backed farther away from Eldos. "What have you done to him?" she breathed. "Viren is a good man."

Eldos sneered. "He *was* a good man. When we had what we wanted, we were merciful."

"You killed him." *No!* "You killed him." Everything and everyone had gone mad.

"He confessed everything. He claimed he'd planned it all, that you knew nothing."

Viren had protected her right to the end. She hadn't deserved him.

Her head and heart ached. She couldn't breathe. She wanted to lie down, sleep, hope to never wake up. But she was a Lyos. She would not let whoever had done this get away with it.

Eldos stroked his beard. "We know he was lying. There were too many witnesses. We can only thank the Seven the guard arrived before you killed them."

Witnesses? The visiting primates were the guilty ones! "The Westerfox primates assassinated the king, the prince . . . " Her voice cracked. "And the princess. They did this." She pointed to her cheek. "Do you honestly believe Viren and I could have overpowered my father, my brother, and six primates?"

Eldos turned to Eness and tutted. "Still she spews her venom." He looked at Fi. "When the guard entered the study room, the grand primate and three of the Westerfox primates were subduing you and Viren. The other two Westerfox primates were dead."

What?

"According to the primates who survived, you, Viren, and one of the two dead brethren assassinated the royal family while the grand primate was blessing the wine. Then the three of you turned on everyone else. They were taken by surprise. You managed to kill one of the Westerfox primates before they could subdue you."

"The grand primate and his brethren killed the treacherous primate," Eness said. "I can't say I blame them. You're alive because they aren't cold-blooded murderers."

Fi couldn't believe her ears. "That's not how it happened."

"You dare to contradict the grand primate?"

"That's not how it happened. Someone drugged the wine. They . . . " But she hadn't clutched at her throat. Neither had Viren.

Eness frowned. "Look at her. Even she doesn't believe her lies."

"The Westerfox primates were the assassins. They—"

"One of the primates was an assassin," Eldos snapped. "His room at the High Council's estate was searched. We found the letters. Stop lying to us. Show some respect for your dead father."

Eness shook his head. "She should be in the dungeon."

"I didn't kill my family!" Fi shrieked. Then she winced and lowered her voice. "Why would I kill them? I . . . I loved them. I don't care about the throne. I never have."

Eldos's eyes bored into her. "Yet you were quick to declare yourself Daros's ruler."

"I . . . " There was no point. They were convinced of her guilt. She'd be put to death, and history would remember her as a cold-blooded assassin and a traitor. Who had framed her? Why? "Who will rule Daros now? One of you?"

Eldos snorted. "You think everyone is as depraved as you are. Not everyone is disloyal, and we do not answer to you. The only question you need concern yourself with is whether you'll make things easy or difficult for yourself."

"No matter what happens, you'll be paraded before the people," Eness said. "They deserve to see the treacherous princess. But how you die is up to you. Spare Daros a disturbing trial. Confess your guilt, and we'll execute you privately and mercifully."

"But if you force a trial, hoping to rally the people to you and sully the reputations of your betters, we'll spare you no mercy," Eldos said, his voice ice cold. "You'll be taken to the city's merchant courtyard, stripped, drawn, hung, and quartered. If there is a shred of your father in you, do the honourable thing. Confess."

Fi swallowed. With Father and Henrick gone, the men standing before her and those who sat on the Primacy's High Council were the most powerful men in Daros. She couldn't fight them, not alone, but that didn't mean they'd beaten her. They would spit on her. They would humiliate her. They would execute her. But they would not force her into confessing to treason. Viren had died protecting her, but more than that, she was a Lyos! She was the daughter of Oswald Beron Lyos and Felicity Regina Lyos. More than a shred of her parents was in her. "You will pay the consequences for executing the rightful ruler of Daros," she said, with all the dignity she could muster. "You will answer to the Seven."

"Does that mean you won't admit to killing your family?" Eldos looked down his nose at her. "I can't say I'm surprised, considering the depths to which you've sunk. You will—"

He looked over his shoulder when several of the men behind him jostled and shifted positions to make room for someone else to enter the room. Fi spotted his mitre before she could see him. Enkelo pushed to the front and stared at her. Despite her certainty that she had the Seven's support, Fi wilted under his gaze. He believed her a traitor. Only the Seven knew what had really happened in the study room. No, that wasn't true! Others had survived. What about the grand primate? Had he also been drugged, and so hadn't witnessed the attacks? No, how could that be? He was the one who'd blessed the wine. Eness had said the grand primate had helped to subdue her and Viren.

"You killed your father, your brother, and your sister-in-law," Enkelo said gravely. "Most would refer to them as the king, the prince, and the princess, but they were more than that to me. I married your mother and father. I held Henrick in my arms when he was only a few hours old. I held you. I watched you grow up. I still can't believe what—" His chin trembled. He cleared his throat. "When did you turn away from the Seven? Was it the Beast Master? Did she corrupt you?"

Erryn? Dear Erryn. If she were here, she would have believed Fi's account of events and stood by her. Tears stung Fi's eyes. "Nobody corrupted me. I didn't kill my family."

"She won't confess," Eldos growled. "It's time to throw her into the dungeon and let the guard worry about her until the trial."

Enkelo turned to him. "Before we lock her up, let me take her to the worship room. Perhaps contemplating the Seven for a time will change her mind."

Eldos grimaced. "She doesn't care about the Seven."

"I know this girl," Enkelo said, making Fi bristle. "She's shallow and impressionable. I don't excuse her actions, but I believe that contemplating the Seven may sway her to avoid the trial none of us want." He jutted his chin toward the doorway. "I have a guard with me, and she'll be in chains, of course."

Fi wanted to smack him. The pompous, arrogant twit. Impressionable, was she? Who believed the grand primate's version of events without question?

The men murmured amongst themselves. "Out of

respect for her father, I would like to give the Seven one last chance to guide her before her path is set," Enkelo said.

Eldos nodded. "Very well. Let it not be said that we didn't do everything we could to help her."

Help her? Please.

"If some of you could step into the corridor to make room for the guard," Enkelo suggested.

Eldos motioned for everyone behind him to leave. Only he and Eness remained inside the bedchamber. Fi sucked down air. She hadn't noticed how stuffy the room had become, and she'd forgotten about her throbbing head. She winced when a stab of pain reminded her of it. She wouldn't beg for some willow bark. She'd grit her teeth rather than give them the opportunity to lord their power over her.

Enkelo raised his voice. "Bring in the chains."

Fi gasped when Cedric walked in. "Cedric!" She grabbed his tunic's sleeve. "You must know I didn't do it. I loved them. You know I've never cared about the throne."

Cedric avoided her eyes. "Hold out your hands," he said gruffly.

She'd thought she couldn't feel any more despair and grief, but she was wrong. Everyone had deserted her. She stood alone. Utterly alone.

Cedric clamped her in irons. Tears rolled down her cheeks. Now she truly understood how Erryn must have felt when everyone had turned their backs on her. Had Fi stood by her? Had she done everything she could to help her? She didn't like the answer. She'd mourned the loss of their friendship, felt sorry for herself, and done little.

"Come." Enkelo strode from the bedchamber. Fi trailed after him, holding her head high, despite how much it hurt. Cedric and the others fell in behind her. The irons dug into Fi's wrists, but she didn't care. Walking down the hallway felt like a dream.

She jumped when a loud wail reached her ears. A moment later the group passed a servant slumped against the wall, a handkerchief pressed to her mouth. Moans, sobs, and cries of, "The Seven have welcomed them with open arms," tore at Fi's heart as she shuffled to the worship room on the castle's ground floor.

After seeing the first servant, Fi didn't look at the mourners she could hear. Their grief made it difficult for her to suppress her own, and she was afraid of what she'd see in their eyes. Revulsion? Disbelief? Sympathy? Were they shocked to see their princess in chains? None had called out words of support. Nobody had spat at her or called her a name, but Fi suspected that would come later, when the initial shock had worn off and her supposed motives had grown more twisted with every whisper. *You'll be paraded before the people.* She shuddered. Only the guard would prevent them from ripping her apart before the executioner cut her open and removed her entrails.

Enkelo wheeled when they reached the worship room. He looked past her. "You will all remain out here. Despite her guilt, we can't violate the Primacy's customs. Anything she says to me or the Seven during her contemplation must remain private."

"If she confesses . . ." Eness began.

"Then the Seven will have reached her. She'll emerge humbled and ready to confess to you."

Eldos frowned. "She killed her family. Do you really want to be in a room alone with her?"

Enkelo's brows shot up. "She's in chains, and we know she's unarmed. But if the girl agrees to it, I'll allow Cedric inside, as long as he remains silent. He'll vouch for any confession." He looked at Fi. "Will that be all right with you?"

"It's fine," Fi mumbled. Cedric wouldn't see or hear anything interesting. There would be no confession.

"Take this man, as well," Eldos said, nodding to the guard closest to him. "This girl isn't an innocent. She's a ruthless killer who ordered and carried out the assassination of her family. She's in chains, but she's resourceful."

"Very well." Enkelo gazed at the men. "Return in an hour. If she's still hardened to the Seven's will, there won't be anything we can do."

"I'll tell the guards to choose a cell for her," Eldos said. The ensuing laughter made Fi ball her hands into fists. To think she'd respected and trusted these men. They'd decided her guilt before they'd spoken to her. With Viren's forced confession, and the word of the grand primate and the Westerfox snakes, she'd been tried, judged, and sentenced without being allowed to utter a word in her defence—not that it would have mattered. Whoever had orchestrated the assassinations and her supposed role in them had done their job well.

Father . . . what would she do without—no, she couldn't wallow in it, not now. She had to keep her wits about her until she was alone again. Enkelo hoped guilt and shame would elicit the words everyone wanted to hear. If the blood that ran through her veins was so cold that she'd conspired to kill her father and brother and watched them die, did they really think that time in the worship room would make any difference? Eldos and the rest of them were agreeing to this because they wanted to tell the people they'd given the treacherous princess every opportunity to confess, but that she'd forsaken the Seven, as well. An assassin *and* a heathen. The day she hung from the rope, gutted and bleeding, they'd dance in the streets.

"It is time for you to face the Seven," Enkelo said.

Without any hesitation, Fi followed him into the worship room.

She wanted to lash out at him when he pressed on her shoulder until she knelt on one of the cushions. He wouldn't have dared to manhandle her like that yesterday! The number of times she'd seen him with Father, scraping and snivelling and babbling, "Oh, yes, Your Grace, I'll do so immediately." He'd bowed to her, moved aside so she could pass, seized every opportunity to stroll with her where others could point and say, "There's the royal primate with the princess." Yet he'd instantly accepted the story his brethren had spun. He believed her capable of murdering her own family.

She glanced over her shoulder. Cedric stood against the wall near the open double doors. The second guard stood watch on the other side. Enkelo nodded to those outside and swung the doors shut. He strode to the front of the room. "Use this time to think about what you've done," he snapped. "Reflect upon the Seven. Let them guide you."

His words provoked a memory of the grand primate directing them to meditate on the Seven just last night, before . . . before . . . She lowered her head. The irons chafed against her wrists, a constant reminder of the nightmare that would never end. Why? Why, why, why? *Why did you let this happen?* That was all she had to say to the Seven.

She lifted her eyes to the mural on the wall in front of her that had been painted hundreds of years ago and touched up many times since then. It depicted Zhikinden, Roosad, Queyris, Samshy, Cesernys, Irnys, and Lleor, as described in the Holy Texts. The writings disagreed on the minor details, but agreed on the important ones: gender, hair colour, physique, height. Fi had always felt drawn to Zhikinden, said to be the oldest of the Holy Siblings, and the one whose wisdom settled any disagreements between them. In the mural, she was drawing back a golden spear, her long black hair, which contrasted with her pale skin, almost reaching her waist. The fur draped over her shoulders didn't hide her bulging biceps. She was the tallest of the siblings, and the central figure in the montage.

Fi had giggled along with Erryn when Enkelo had rebuked Lady Agnes, one of the children in the elite study group that had met twice a week in the castle, for saying that Zhikinden looked like a wild woman. Later, they couldn't decide whose face had been the reddest: Agnes's, or Enkelo's. Zayvang served Zhikinden. Zayvang had saved Fi's life, had appeared right before her eyes, here, in the physical world, and obeyed Erryn's command.

Fi bowed her head. She had nothing to hide or be ashamed about regarding the assassinations, but she felt terrible about Erryn. *I should have done more to help you.* She understood now, understood what it was like for people she loved and trusted to abandon her during her worst hour. She understood how it felt to have those she loved ripped away from her, to have her life change in an instant. Father and the same powerful men who'd turned against Fi had banished Erryn from the only home she knew. Had Fi done little because she'd heeded Father's advice and done her duty, or because she was a coward? Viren had deserved a better woman than her, especially since she'd tried not to think about his brother, but couldn't stop herself from wondering.

What had happened to Dann? If Viren had been declared a traitor, the Tolins would all be under suspicion. Had they arrested Dann? Was he on the rack? She couldn't bear to think about it. Perhaps everyone was right about her and she was a horrible person, because she shouldn't be worrying about Dann, not when her betrothed had died protecting her, and Father was dead . . . Henrick . . . and poor Surann. Maybe she should welcome death. She had nobody. Nothing.

She kept her head down when Enkelo walked past her, his robes rustling. Was he leaving? Had he given up on her already, grasped that she wasn't going to confess—

not because she had a heart of stone, but because she was innocent! She hadn't done—

A sudden noise made her jerk her head up. It sounded like someone— She twisted around to look. Her jaw dropped. The guard Eldos had insisted come with them was stumbling backward. Cedric swung at him again and connected with the man's left cheek. The guard's eyes fluttered closed. Enkelo caught him as he fell backward and lowered him to the floor.

He noticed Fi staring and put a finger to his lips, then came over to her and crouched. "Please don't make a sound, Your Highness—or I should say, Your Grace. Just listen to me for a minute. We're going to take you to safety, if that's what you wish us to do. Understand that if we're caught, we'll be killed. There will be no trial. If you prefer to remain here, we'll defer to your wishes, though I'd advise you to run from the battle today. You must know there's no chance you'll be found innocent. Will you come with us? Will you run today, only because you must?"

She searched his face. Was this a trick? If she said, "Yes, let's escape," would Eldos, Eness, and the others burst into the worship room and proclaim that they now had proof of her treachery? Enkelo had always struck her as a man who aspired to be grand primate. Why would he jeopardize his position—his life—to help her?

Cedric stepped to Enkelo's side. "We'll want to be away as quickly as possible, Majesty. You have to decide now. Every minute counts."

Fi didn't trust Enkelo, but she trusted Cedric, and she couldn't be in any more trouble than she was already in. They were the ones who'd be laying their lives on the line. Hers was already forfeit. If there was the slimmest chance . . . She nodded to them. "Let's be away. But how?" They wouldn't make it to the courtyard, let alone through the castle's main gate and into the city.

Enkelo stood and strode to the mural. He bowed his head. Watching him, Fi jumped when Cedric gently grasped her elbow. "I'm sorry, Majesty. I'll help you to your feet. Try not to let the chains clink too much. I'll remove them as soon as we're somewhere safer."

Her eyes still on Enkelo, Fi rose. Enkelo raised his head and stepped to the left end of the mural. He touched Samshy's head, then Roosad's, then Cesernys's, and stepped past Zhikinden. Then he touched Queyris's head, Irnys's, Lleor's, and moved back to Zhikinden. Fi didn't catch the words he murmured as he touched her head.

A click, then a scraping sound. This time Fi heard Enkelo's words: "We thank you." He went to one of the brilliant tapestries adorning the south wall and pulled it aside. Fi's breath caught in her throat. A passageway.

Enkelo beckoned to them. "I'll be right behind you, Majesty," Cedric said.

Fi's throat tightened. She wasn't alone. There was hope yet. She stepped into the musty passage and stared into the gloom. Enkelo lit a lantern he'd lifted from a hook, then motioned for them to pass him. The tapestry had already dropped back into place behind them. Enkelo pulled a lever. The door swung shut with a thud. His shoulders relaxed. "Now we can speak."

Cedric pulled a key from his pocket. "Let me relieve you of those irons, Majesty."

Fi winced when he pushed the key into the lock and the iron on her right wrist dug further into her skin. He pulled the shackles off. "Thank you, Cedric," she murmured, rubbing her wrists.

"Leave them here," Enkelo said. "If they find the passageway, it won't matter if they also find those. Now, come on. They could return earlier than we hope."

Cedric lifted his elbow. "Hang on to me, Majesty. There won't be much light."

Fi could see that. In the lantern's glow, she'd already spotted what looked like men, or beasts, or monsters that lurked inside dank corridors. She grabbed Cedric's arm and clung to it.

"How did you know about this passageway?" she asked Enkelo as they trailed after him, the lantern in his hand a beacon of hope.

"Royal primates know. It's useful during uprisings, when the castle is stormed. The primate can escape, and sometimes the monarch with him, depending on the circumstances. When they come for us and discover an empty room, I doubt they'll find our escape route. They won't know how we got away, just that we did. I expect the guards will be interrogated. They'll assume some helped us."

"Surely someone else must know about the passage. Otherwise the knowledge would die with you."

"The monarch and spymaster also know. We're rarely in the same room together." Enkelo paused. "When you're on the throne, I'll show you how to open the door to the passage, Your Grace."

Fi wished she shared his optimism.

"They'll close off the city. We'll need to be away before then," Cedric said.

"Will this take us out of the city?" Fi asked, thinking that if it did, the tunnel must stretch a long way.

Enkelo shook his head, his mitre appearing larger than usual in the soft light. "No. It leads to a temple not far from the castle."

Fi had more questions that demanded answers, but she'd save them for later, when they could breathe again.

They moved through the passageway, their footsteps echoing off the walls Fi couldn't see. She shrank against Cedric when what looked like a rat darted across their path. She wanted to close her eyes and let Cedric guide her, but doing so wouldn't protect her from the horrors of her own mind: blood spraying from Father's throat, Henrick falling, Surann's screams, Viren on the rack. Her imagination would taunt her. She couldn't bear—*Focus on getting to the temple.* And then, hopefully, to freedom.

Avere slipped inside the inn where the cultist was staying and searched the common room. A drunk who looked like he was a permanent fixture at the bar no matter the time of day, a couple of travellers, and the woman Avere sought were the only ones there. Even if the common room had been packed, she would have spotted the brilliant rose cloak right away. Its hood was down. The woman's hair was pure white.

She approached the cultist's table. "Do you mind if I join you."

The woman looked up from her soup. Icy blue eyes appraised Avere. "I suggest you sit at one of the many empty tables."

"I would, except I'd like to speak with you. We have a common interest."

"And what would that be?"

"The Beast Master."

The woman rested her spoon inside her soup bowl and cocked her head. "Go on."

Avere pulled out the chair across from her and sat. "We're both looking for her. Perhaps we can help each other."

"I do not need your help."

"Yes, you do, if you hope to see her alive. You may not want to kill her, but plenty do."

"She does not deserve to die. She does not offend the Seven."

Avere wanted to snort. "Only you and those in your cult believe that. Nobody else does."

"My cult." The woman clasped her hands on her lap. "What do you know of my cult?"

On her way to the inn, Avere had decided to be honest about everything except her true intentions regarding the heathen. She wanted to gain this woman's trust. The cultist could have valuable information about the Beast Master and how to subdue the Fallen, and if this cult found the heathen before Avere did, she wanted to know about it before they fled to Westerfox. "Only what a primate told me. You're a blasphemer from Westerfox. You worship the Fallen. You're looking for the Beast Master because she can summon them."

To her surprise, the woman laughed. Her amusement brightened her eyes and smoothed her wrinkles.

"I take it he's wrong?" Avere said.

The woman grew serious. "The Primacy mocks everyone who disagrees with it. It does not listen, does not try to understand."

"What do you believe, then?"

"Who are you? What is your interest in who you would call the Beast Master?"

"My name is Avere. I'm not interested in the Beast Master, per se. I'm interested in coin."

The woman's eyes flashed. "And you dare to say you can help me and accuse me of blasphemy? You are the blasphemer."

"There are many who want to slay her and collect the reward the guard is offering. You must know the king wants her returned for a trial that will certainly lead to her execution. Proof of her death will do just as well."

The woman tutted. "Misguided, all of you."

"How are we misguided? What do you believe?"

"You must take me for a fool. You will not collect the reward through me." The woman lifted her spoon. "Go away, Avere. Leave me to my soup."

Avere narrowed her eyes. "You can't get rid of me. I'll dog your every step. In the meanwhile, my many friends will track the Beast Master and find her, and I'll make sure you never set eyes on her." When the woman's brow furrowed, Avere pressed on. "I don't intend to kill her." Not until Arrick gave the word. "I'll sell her to the highest bidder. I'm offering you the opportunity to be that bidder. Pay me the coin and I'll see that you both make it to Westerfox alive."

"Coin." The woman tossed the spoon down and jabbed her right forefinger at Avere. "How dare you put a price on a woman blessed by the Seven! You disgust me, you people who do not think for yourselves. You let the primates dictate your beliefs and actions."

"Nobody dictates my beliefs!" Avere spat. *Calm yourself.* This woman would not best her. "You have so little faith in your beliefs that you won't state them."

"I do not wish to be mocked. You do not care about what I believe. To you, I am a means to an end."

"You don't wish to sway me to your thinking?"

The woman stared at her. Good. Avere had suspected the religious zealot wouldn't resist an opportunity to spew her nonsense. She looked at her nails, then glanced around the common room.

"Have you ever thought about what the Beast Master truly is?" the woman asked.

Avere shook her head.

"Think about what Beast Masters do."

"They summon and control the Fallen."

The woman pushed her soup aside and leaned forward. "Do you truly understand what that means? The Beast Master, as you call her, can bring the Fallen into the physical plane. The Fallen. The Seven's loyal companions."

"The Fallen. Those who defied the Seven."

"Heavenly beings who sit at the feet of the Seven, and the Beast Master brings them here. Do you think she could do that without the Seven's blessing?"

Avere suspected that Beast Masters were part of a game the Seven played to amuse themselves. *Aren't we all?* Except the Beast Master must be the brunt of a particularly cruel divine joke. The woman across the table wouldn't be interested in such thoughts. "I don't know."

"You have never thought about it. You simply accept what the Primacy feeds you."

Avere's fingers dug into her legs, but she kept her mouth shut.

"We do not worship the Fallen, we worship the Seven," the cultist said.

"But you hold Beast Masters in high regard. If you don't worship the Fallen, why do you seek her? Do you worship Beast Masters? You obviously believe they're blessed by the Seven."

"We seek her because we must escort her to where she needs to go."

This conversation was stretching Avere's patience. If not for worrying that the woman's cult could get to the heathen before she did, she would already have told the old bat that she was crazy. "What do you mean?"

"All you need to know is that no Beast Master has ever made it there. Forces work against them."

"Forces the Seven can't overcome, assuming they want the Beast Master to reach wherever it is she's supposed to go?"

"When I speak of forces, I speak of Death and its disciples."

"But every living thing dies," Avere pointed out, not having the foggiest notion what the woman meant by disciples, and not caring to know.

"And when we do, we go to the Seven, because they prevent Death from snatching us away for all eternity. Imagine if Death won. Imagine that if instead of the Seven welcoming you when you breathed your last, you were snuffed out." The woman snapped her fingers. "Just like that. It is Death that prevents Beast Masters from reaching their goal, and when a Beast Master walks Daros, Death's fury causes events that change the course of history."

Despite her skepticism, a shiver ran up Avere's spine. "Nothing extraordinary has happened."

"Not yet. But it will."

"Why don't the Seven overcome it—Death?"

"Because the Seven and Death are equally matched, Avere. They are both eternal, and whatever the Seven can do, Death can do. There must always be balance. The Elder Gods gave Daros to the Seven, but also gave them Death, so they would not become complacent and spoiled."

The woman was talking nonsense! No wonder the Primacy and the Holy Texts made no mention of this Death or any Elder Gods. The Seven were all-powerful and invincible. They had created Daros and everything within it. But Avere would play along with a straight face. "You still haven't explained why you think Beast Masters are blessed. All right, they can summon beings from the heavenly plane into the physical one. And yes, I suppose the Seven must permit them to do so. But that doesn't mean they're blessed. Perhaps the Seven have a purpose for Beast Masters that we don't understand." She almost snorted again. Of course they didn't understand it. Nobody could deny that Beast Masters existed, but everyone was mute on why they existed. If only she could speak her mind! It was a game. A silly game. Perhaps the Seven placed bets on how long each Beast Master would survive and how they'd meet their demise. Was one of the Seven betting on her daggers? She hoped so.

"All we know is that the Beast Master must reach her destination, that the journey will be fraught with danger, and that Death has so far proven victorious. That is why it is essential that we find her. But there are so few of us now."

"You believe that Beast Masters play a role in keeping Death at bay," Avere stated, having a flash of insight.

"We believe they are supposed to. Unfortunately, none have succeeded in reaching their destination thus far. Death has always found them before we do." The woman frowned. "I fear that this time will be no exception."

"Do you think you can protect her? Forget this Death. There are plenty of regular old people who won't hesitate to kill her or turn her over to the guard."

"The odds are against us, but we must try. We do not know what will happen when she reaches where she will be compelled to go, but we do know that what she finds there will affect all of Daros, and that if a Beast Master doesn't reach there soon, Death will claim this world."

Excitement surged through Avere. She would relish the challenge of getting the Beast Master to the secret destination unscathed. Rather than being one of the hunters, she'd be the protector who outwitted those who hoped to slay the heathen. Too bad it was all nonsense, but now she knew the woman wouldn't steal her prey. She might, however, hear of the Beast Master's location before Avere did. She might also help Avere lure the heathen into a trap. "You must have people searching Daros for her."

"That is none of your concern."

"I can protect her."

"You must think me addled. You will take my coin and then sell her to the first one who offers you more." The woman fell silent, her eyes on Avere's face. She sighed. "I can tell you are persistent. We both want to find the . . . Beast Master. Let us work together and, should we succeed, approach her together."

"Why would you want to work with me? You don't trust me."

"My reasons are my own."

"There's nothing to stop either of us from keeping information to ourselves."

"You are correct, there is not," the woman said mildly.

"There's nothing to stop us from acting on any information alone, either."

"No matter your decision, you will hunt her."

True, and Avere was beginning to understand why the zealot had made her offer. "Fine, let's work together. But I don't want to be tethered to you. I'll meet you back here at, say, six o'clock? We can sup together and share anything we've learned."

The woman nodded. "Now let me get back to my soup. It is growing cold."

Avere pushed back her chair. "Are you going to tell me your name?"

"I am Malina."

"Pleased to meet you, Malina. I'll see you at six." She turned to go.

"Avere."

Avere looked down at Malina.

"You say the Primacy does not dictate your beliefs, but you were instantly skeptical about everything I told you about the woman you call the Beast Master. Ask yourself, where does your skepticism originate? What does the Primacy base its beliefs upon? Where is its evidence? The Holy Texts? We have our own. Why are their texts more credible than ours? If you are as bright as I think you are, you will realize that you have accepted what they have told you without questioning it, that they have no more evidence to offer you than I, and you have no more reason to accept their beliefs than you do to accept mine. If you do not reach that conclusion, then you follow blindly, as the rest do, and regurgitate what you are told."

Avere wanted to tell the old bat to keep her ramblings to herself, but rather than feeling as if she'd come away from the conversation with the upper hand, she felt unsettled. She *had* been quick to dismiss the woman's beliefs. She'd believed that Malina was a zealot and blasphemer before the woman had opened her mouth. She hadn't questioned what the primate had told her. What if Malina was right? What if Beast Masters had the Seven's blessing? What if they did play a role in keeping this Death from overtaking Daros and claiming every living thing within it?

Don't think about it, Avere. Confusing her was exactly what Malina wanted to do. Avere would have to guard against the zealot's attempts to manipulate her. She hadn't considered Malina a threat. Perhaps she'd misjudged. She forced a smile. "Let me give you some advice."

Malina's face tightened. "I will not refrain from speaking about my beliefs. I cannot."

"I was going to say that perhaps you should leave your cloak in your room, but somehow I doubt you'd listen to me, so watch yourself. That cloak would fill someone's purse with gold."

She whirled and strode away, not wanting to hear another word from Malina. The conversation had elicited more than she'd hoped for, but the satisfaction she'd expected to feel eluded her. In its place sat doubt. She hated doubt. It could make her hesitate, not throw the dagger, miss a critical opportunity. But it would not stop her from following Arrick's orders. Avere had never doubted him. When he gave the word, the Beast Master would die by her hand.

Fi coughed into her hand, then jumped when Cedric did the same. Hopefully they'd soon reach the end of the musty tunnel. She could tell she was walking on an incline—a good sign.

Enkelo led them around a corner to a dead end, or so it appeared in the lantern's dull light. He pulled a lever on the left wall. A door scraped open. Light flooded the tunnel. Fi's eyes instinctively closed.

"Hurry," Enkelo said.

Squinting, Fi clung to Cedric's arm. They followed Enkelo through the doorway. A man stood waiting for them in the temple cellar. "I was starting to worry," he said. "No alarm has been raised. How long do we have?"

"If they do as I asked, about forty minutes." Enkelo turned off the lantern that was no longer needed and hung it on a hook inside the secret escape route. Fi shifted her attention to the man who'd lit all the torches in the cellar. She'd occasionally seen him in the castle and remembered Father's grimace when she'd asked him who it was. "Arrick Inel," Father had said. "The Ferret Spymaster. I don't enjoy rubbing elbows with thieves and cutthroats, but they have their uses."

"There's a change of clothes for everyone." Inel pointed toward a doorway that led to another part of the cellar. "Your clothing is in there, Your Majesty. Please leave the clothing you're wearing behind. I'll take care of it after you've gone."

"Where are we going?" Fi asked. Behind her, the door to the tunnel scraped closed.

"To a sympathizer's estate, where you'll be safe until we determine our next step. I'll put out rumours that will mislead the guard about your whereabouts."

Enkelo strode to Inel's side and gazed at Fi. "Putting you on your rightful place on the throne will take time,

Your Grace. We have to gather allies, see who is vying for the throne, possibly raise an army."

Father's face flashed through Fi's mind. She couldn't think about him, about any of them, until she was out of immediate danger. Father hadn't groomed her for the throne, but she'd always believed she possessed the Lyos strength. She must draw on it now. She was the queen! She couldn't show weakness. "Who is leading Daros now?"

"The Primacy has stepped in, Your Grace."

The Primacy! "What about the Royal Council?"

"Begging your pardon, but we don't have time to discuss this now," Inel said. "Suffice it to say that members of the Royal Council and many of Daros's nobles are all candidates to take up the mantle. Grand Primate Otane pointed out that none of them should act as regent. The throne must remain empty until a new king is chosen."

So the Primacy had volunteered to rule Daros until that time. Every powerful noble with a chance would be vying for the throne. It could be months, years, before the matter was settled, and in the meantime skirmishes, perhaps civil war, would tear Daros apart. While chaos reigned, the Primacy would become more entrenched in power. Was that why it had assassinated Father and Henrick? To grasp power? But why? It was already a powerful organization that had the monarch's ear and considerable political clout.

"We intend to put you on the throne, where you belong," Inel said. "Our first step is to get you to safety. I don't mean to be impertinent, but we've spoken enough. All of you must change and be on your way."

On her way, fleeing from her beloved people and city like a dog with its tail between its legs. Father and Henrick dead, the Lyos name sullied, Viren torn apart on the rack, the Tolins ruined . . . Her vision blurred. Her thoughts about the Lyos strength mocked her. She would do what these men asked, even though she sensed she was merely their pawn. If they managed to put her on the throne, she'd be in their debt. What would they ask from her? What would they demand? Cedric was the only one here out of loyalty alone. Everyone else who truly cared about her was dead.

No. Not everyone.

She squared her shoulders and took a deep breath. "I don't want to go to an estate. I want to find the only family I have left."

Enkelo frowned. "Why? Apart from the odd state occasion, you rarely see anyone in your extended family."

"Some may put in a claim for the throne," Inel added. "Those who don't will be wooed by those who do. Nobody will support you, Your Grace. You're a fugitive accused of murdering the king and prince. The evidence against you is strong."

Fi braced herself. "I'm speaking of Erryn Fyler. As far as I know, she's still alive. I want to find her."

Enkelo and Inel exchanged glances.

Fi swallowed. "Unless there's something you haven't told me," she whispered, her throat tight with fear. She looked at Enkelo. "Did my father order you to keep news about her from me?"

"No, Your Grace," Enkelo said.

"Then I want to find her. I know what you think of her, but she's my sister, and a Lyos, in all but blood."

Enkelo shook his head. "Your Grace, finding her wouldn't be—"

Fi cut him off with a wave of her hand. "Do you honestly believe me to be your queen, or is your only concern what I'll do for you if we succeed in putting me on the throne? And what about you?" Her eyes met Inel's.

Cedric placed his fist against his chest and bowed. "You are the rightful Queen of Daros, Majesty. I am in your service."

"Thank you, Cedric." Fi gazed at Enkelo and raised her brows.

He hesitated a beat, then bowed. "I serve you, Your Grace."

Inel quickly did the same. When he straightened, he said, "Your father didn't like the Ferrets. He undervalued and underestimated us. Please don't make the same mistake, Your Majesty. We exist to serve and protect you."

"I admire your candor," Fi said. "I thank all of you for swearing your service to me. I wasn't expecting to sit on the throne. Father tried to interest me in politics and court matters, but frankly, I wasn't motivated to learn." Though she wasn't completely dim-witted when it came to the machinations of court and the Primacy's political meddling. "I'll need the aid of good men like you. You have a plan. You've spoken of raising an army. I'm not a military commander, but I know my role. If you want me to rally troops . . ." Her voice faltered. Her composure was held together with a thread, and a fraying one, at that.

She clenched her hands and steadied herself. "If you want me to rally troops, I need a bit of hope, some good news. Otherwise, I'm afraid my heart won't be in it."

She needed the one person she knew with absolute certainty would support her with no expectation of anything in return. She wanted the dear friend she'd always leaned on, trusted, and loved. It wouldn't matter how many men and women rallied around her. Without Erryn, someone who truly understood her and cared about her, she would feel alone. "We have to find Erryn."

Enkelo scowled. "The heathen may not be alive, and if she is, she won't be the girl you knew. Her bond with the Fallen will have grown. Her corruption—"

Fi jutted her chin toward Inel. "Do you know where she is? Do you know if she's alive?"

Inel moistened his lips. "We believe she's in northern Rion, heading to Stronghaven, but I can't say for certain whether she's alive. The heathen was—"

"Her name is Erryn," Fi snapped. "I don't want to hear her called Beast Master, heathen, blasphemer, or whatever other names you have for her. Is that understood?"

"Yes, Your Majesty," Inel murmured.

"I will consider her to be alive, then. It's settled. If you want me at my best, we have to find her."

Cedric cleared his throat. "Staying on the move might be better than hunkering down at an estate, anyway. But it will be hard, Majesty. We'll have to sleep rough, stay off the roads . . ."

She didn't care. After the horror of last night that would colour her life forever, everything would be hard.

She should have died. If they wanted to frame someone, why not Henrick or Surann? Why her? Because they saw her as the most vulnerable? The weakest? Perhaps they were right. She didn't know how she'd continue through the pain, so what would sleeping on a hard forest floor matter? Or eating stale bread and wearing smelly clothes? She'd look like the beggar she now was, depending on others for sustenance and their silence. She couldn't stomach the thought of sitting in some fat noble's dining room, drinking wine and stuffing herself with meats and cakes. She wanted—needed—a different life, one that wouldn't constantly taunt her with memories of those she'd never see again. She needed to be somebody else.

"Are you sure this is what you want to do?" Cedric asked, his face filled with concern.

Dear, kind, loyal Cedric, the only light in her darkness. "I've just lost three people I loved dearly, Cedric. I have to find her."

"I would advise against it, Your Grace," Enkelo said. "But I will, of course, do as you wish."

Of course he would advise against it. He believed Erryn to be an affront to the Seven. Fi couldn't fault him for that. Perhaps if she'd studied the teachings with a sincere heart, rather than treating her time with Enkelo as a wretched obligation, the Seven wouldn't have allowed her family to be slaughtered. Why did they no longer show themselves? Perhaps Enkelo could explain that to her. But she wouldn't push him, or dismiss his concern regarding Erryn. He'd risked everything to save her. His fate was now tied to hers. The man may irritate her, but she needed him.

"I understand, Primate. I'll trust that, should we find her, you'll ensure she doesn't corrupt me."

"She won't be the woman you knew. Her nature will have grown more bestial."

"If you're right, then at least I'll know. She won't travel with us, and I won't have to wonder." But Fi hoped Erryn was herself. When they found her, because they must find her, perhaps the cold, hard ball sitting inside Fi's chest would thaw. "I'll go change. We must be away."

She went through the doorway Inel had indicated and sagged against the wall. She wanted to slide down it to sit on the floor and cry, but there wasn't time. A bundle of clothes lay on the stone floor, next to a pair of boots. She crouched and lifted a plain brown shirt from the bundle. Underneath it lay a pair of trousers. Travelling through the forest in a dress would hardly be practical, and she was eager to dispose of the bloodstained garment she wore. Any other time, she would have smiled at the thought of how Erryn would react at the sight of her friend in a shirt, trousers, and boots. But smiling wouldn't be fair to Father, Henrick, and Surann. Smiling would mean that life could be joyful without them. Smiling was no longer for her.

Arrick turned to Enkelo the moment the princess—the queen—had disappeared into the other part of the cellar. He dropped his voice. "Leave the Beast Master to my people."

"Why, because if I slip a dagger into her gut, you won't get your wine?" Enkelo glanced over his shoulder. Cedric was off in a corner, changing out of his uniform. "I'd prefer that the girl stay away from the heathen. She can't afford to associate with a Beast Master, not if we're to gather the support we'll need to place her on the throne. But we'll see how long her determination to find the heathen lasts when there aren't any servants to pour her wine and draw her bath."

"And if she's stronger and more determined than you believe her to be?"

"Then we'll find the Beast Master and I'll finish it."

"You'd lose the queen's favour," Arrick said.

"I'll make sure she doesn't know it was me."

"That could prove difficult. If you find the heathen, let me know and I'll have my people take care of it."

"Does it matter who does it?" Enkelo said. "You can still tell the High Council it was you and claim your wine. I won't be here to contradict you, and until the queen is on the throne, my word means nothing."

"Erryn Fyler is dangerous, Enkelo. She has the Fallen at her disposal."

"She has to sleep."

The guard who'd escorted her to the Rion border had thought the same, but Arrick didn't speak his thought. He'd been honest about the Beast Master's last known location only because he'd already reported it to Enkelo. From this point forward, he had no intention of keeping the primate abreast of where the heathen had last been spotted. The guards hunting for the queen and her rescuers wouldn't be the only ones Arrick would misdirect. "If the Beast Master hears news of the assassination and the queen's escape, she might come looking for you. She could find you."

Enkelo smirked. "That would be fortuitous, wouldn't it?"

Not if it endangered the woman changing in the next chamber, but there was no time to argue the point now. "You should change."

"I should." Enkelo looked down at himself. "I don't know if I'll ever wear this robe and mitre again," he said quietly.

A flash of sympathy surprised Arrick. His feelings were raw today. He hadn't liked the king, but he was loyal to the Lyoses, as all spymasters were. He would get to the bottom of this, and *he* would take care of the Beast Master, not Enkelo. He mentally planned the orders he'd give to his people the moment the trio of fugitives were on their way.

"Do I look all right?" a tremulous voice said.

Arrick turned. The queen stood in the doorway. Again, a wave of emotion—sorrow and grief—washed over him. Anyone else would see one of the many common folk who'd gathered at the castle gates upon hearing the unbelievable news of the assassinations and the princess's treachery. Arrick saw his queen.

The woman asking for his approval was not common. She should be in the finest dress, with her hair up, and priceless pieces from the royal collection around her neck, on her fingers, and dangling from her ears. Instead, she looked so sad, and vulnerable, and lost. Someone had used her as a pawn in a deadly game. Arrick would find out who.

He forced a smile. "You look fine, Your Grace. Just fine."

Fi nodded at Inel and cast her eyes downward. She'd glimpsed Enkelo putting on a shirt. Cedric approached her. "Once we're out of the city, we'll stop and have a bit to eat, Majesty."

She wasn't hungry. Eating would be a necessity, not a pleasure, but she lifted her eyes and nodded.

Enkelo came over to them. Fi hardly recognized him in a shirt, jacket, trousers, workman's boots, and the cap he'd plonked onto his head. The reality, the loss, punched through her defences. Her knees sagged. She felt a steadying hand on her elbow.

"We are with you, Majesty."

She mustered her strength. "Thank you, Cedric."

"We must go," Enkelo said.

Inel motioned for them to follow him.

"What about my clothes?" Fi asked, focusing on minutiae to keep her mind off everything else.

"Don't worry about that. I'll take care of everything," Inel said.

Yes, she remembered now.

They climbed the wooden steps to the temple's ground floor and hurried along a hallway. The worship room was empty, save for a man standing near the front entrance. He looked to Inel and shook his head. "Nothing. No alarm."

Outside, a boy waited with three horses laden with stuffed saddlebags. "Anything, Jack?" Inel asked.

"No, sir. Streets are quiet. Everyone's at the castle." He glanced at Fi and gulped. "You should have a clear run to the northwest road."

"Thank you," Fi said.

He bowed. "I'm in your ser-service, Your Grace."

Fi's throat tightened. He shouldn't be. He'd get himself killed. So would Cedric, Enkelo, and Inel. She should stop this madness now, tell them their plan was doomed to failure. Raise an army? Force the Primacy to relinquish power? It was the stuff of dreams.

"I'll help you up, Majesty," Cedric said.

Fi shook herself. She was a Lyos. She was the true Queen of Daros. The men risking their lives for her were her loyal subjects. Today everything seemed impossible, but somehow she'd take the throne, or die trying.

Cedric boosted her onto one of the horses and mounted his own.

"I'll send word ahead of you," Inel said to Enkelo. "Go to the Whistling Pig tavern in Moss and ask for Mick Dunley. Use the names we discussed. He'll tell you where you can find us in other towns and cities, and give you any news I have about the Be—Erryn. May the Seven guide and protect you."

"And you," Enkelo said. He swung onto his horse. "Let's go."

The short ride to the northwest road that would take them away from Darroth was surreal. Everything looked the same, yet everything had changed. Stalls were closed, shops were shuttered, the few people who walked the streets bore the same shocked eyes and expressions. The guards on the city's border didn't give them a second glance. The three horses and their riders thundered past them, leaving Darroth behind.

Fi focused on Enkelo's back. Darroth, her beloved Darroth. Father. Henrick. Surann. She wouldn't be at their wakes, wouldn't file past them as they lay in state, wouldn't be in the temple to say good-bye. Darroth, her beloved Darroth, had claimed all of them. But not Erryn. Erryn was alive. Fi would find her. And cling to her. And weep.

Avere looked at Malina and shook her head. "I haven't heard anything." She breathed in the aroma of the stew in front of her, then picked up her spoon.

"Nor I." Malina buttered a piece of bread. "You thought she would be coming this way. So did I. But she must be heading somewhere else."

"Why did you think she'd be coming this way? Why won't you tell me where she's going?"

"Because I do not trust you, Avere," Malina said, without a hint of malice or mirth.

Avere chuckled. Too bad they were on opposite sides when it came to the Beast Master. She'd supped every day with Malina since their first meeting, and had grown to like her. Malina was still trying to sway Avere to her view of the heathen, but her beliefs were too strange for Avere to accept. Elder Gods? Death a force that worked against the Seven, rather than a natural part of nature's cycle? Malina should have been a bard. Though Avere had to admit that listening to Malina had deepened her appreciation for the Beast Master's ability to summon heavenly beings, albeit fallen ones enslaved by the Seven. Perhaps the Fallen suffered while they were in the physical plane. Perhaps that was why the Seven allowed Beast Masters to walk Daros. It punished the Fallen, and Beast Masters didn't survive for long once their true nature had revealed itself. Their deaths were never natural. Erryn Fyler would be no exception.

"Where did your holy texts come from?" Avere asked.

Malina swallowed a bit of stew. "Have you been to Westerfox?"

"No."

"It is a blessed place. Our texts are older than yours. The Seven visited Westerfox first, after the Elder Gods granted Daros to them."

Avere nodded and spooned stew into her mouth.

"Where do you come from, Avere? Where were you born?"

Her shoulders stiffened. She'd decided she wouldn't use one of her daggers to end Malina's life and wanted to keep it that way. "I know your texts speak of these Elder Gods and Death, but what about the Beast Master? Did the Seven tell your people about the Beast Master?"

Malina's eyes narrowed, but she didn't repeat her questions. "No, they did not."

Triumph surged through Avere. "Then why do you believe the Beast Master has something to do with conquering this Death?"

"Not conquering, Avere. Maintaining balance."

"According to whom?"

"Texts that have belonged to our people for generations."

"But not dictated by the Seven." Victory lightened Avere's mood. Men who'd sat at the Seven's feet and learned from them had written the Holy Texts. Malina's cult's beliefs had resulted from the rantings of madmen.

Malina sipped her wine. "I have studied your Holy Texts. According to them, when the Seven announced they would return to the heavenly plane for a time, they said Beast Masters would walk Daros in their absence."

"And they have." The old woman was arguing Avere's case for her.

"But that is all the Seven said about Beast Masters. Everything else about Beast Masters in your Holy Texts was written after the time of the Seven's departure from this plane."

"By those enlightened by the Seven," Avere said, managing to keep her frustration from her voice. "And by those who observed the first Beast Masters, those who recorded their transformation from human to beast and wrote about their depraved acts. You believe Beast Masters somehow prevent Death from taking over Daros, but no Beast Master survives for long. Yet Daros survives as it always has."

Malina's mouth pinched. "There is trouble in the north. The land is suffering, and so is every living creature that depends on it for sustenance."

Avere waved away Malina's point. "Famines, droughts— we've experienced it all before. It's a cycle. And we're a cycle." She swung her fingers between them. "We two. We're going around in circles. Perhaps we should stick to playing cards and leave the proselytizing to the primates. We aren't going to change each other's mind."

"In that you speak the truth, though I wish you would listen. I suspect the Beast Master would do well to have you at her side."

Avere almost choked on her stew. Time to change the subject. She reached for her wine and gulped some down. "I see that you continue to ignore my advice. I don't suppose I can convince you to leave your cloak in your room."

"This cloak marks me as a disciple of the Seven."

"It also appears to be very expensive. I'm surprised nobody has tried to help themselves to it."

"I am under the protection of the Seven."

Avere wanted to shake Malina. She believed in the Seven, but trusted in her daggers. "Cards, then?"

Malina shrugged. "Why not?"

In a sombre mood, Erryn gazed in the direction of the river, even though she couldn't see it. The glow of the fire was behind her, the river's roar before her. The rain had finally stopped a couple of hours ago, but the river had swelled. Worried that it might overflow its banks, Toe and Renn had chosen to set up camp at the top of a slope dotted with bushes.

As usual, Renn had refused Erryn's offer to help put up the tent, and within ten minutes of stopping, Toe had ducked into the trees and returned with their supper.

Renn had deftly skinned and cooked the rabbit. For the first time, she'd handed Erryn her food, rather than giving it to Toe or leaving it on the ground for Erryn to pick up. She must have been distracted. Renn hadn't spoken to her, though. She was a woman of action, not words.

Watching the two wild folk live, seeing how easy it was for them to survive in the forest, Erryn felt useless. Expecting to live on a country estate where a husband and servants would see to her every need, she hadn't learned the skills required to live off the land. When she and Fi had ridden through the forest outside the Royal City, they'd done it for fun, and with a dozen guards behind them. While nobles had hunted, they'd drank tea and stuffed themselves with sweets.

If she were like Toe and Renn, she wouldn't have to buy clothing. She wouldn't worry about running out of food between towns. If she were like them, if she wasn't a soft bottom, she could avoid towns altogether until Loring. But she was useless out here. They must look at her and shake their heads at the soft bottom who was as helpless as a baby. She deserved Renn's scorn.

That wasn't the only reason she felt down. She hated to admit it, but she missed Zayvang and longed to see her, to pet her head and ruffle her fur. While travelling alone, she'd summoned Zayvang every day, and the cat had sat watch while she'd slept. She missed the others too, except Rachagha, whom she'd never summoned. But she'd forged a kinship with Zayvang, a bond that ran almost as deep as the one she'd shared with Fi.

Someone was approaching. She wasn't surprised

when Toe looked down at her. "Do ye mind if I sit with ye for a bit?"

"No, of course not."

He lowered himself down next to her. They sat for a while, the only sound the river's waters racing toward the waterfall to the south. "Are ye all right? Ye're quiet."

"I know we're only a couple of days from Stronghaven now, but will you teach me the basics of how to survive in the forest? This is where I'll be living for the rest of my life." Erryn swept her arm toward the forest's edge. "Here. Outside. I don't know how to survive out here. I'm lost."

Toe's silence spoke volumes. Even he couldn't come up with a few words of comfort, or deny the reality of Erryn's existence. She heaved a sigh. "I'll always be on the run. This is it for me."

There was no point in having dreams about her future. No point to aspiring to build a life for herself. She would never have a normal life, not with the brand on her forehead and the Fallen scratching inside her mind. While Fi carried on with her life, Erryn would be lucky to live another year. Who was she fooling? "Let's face it, I won't make it to Loring, or the temple." *I'm sorry, Rodney.* She was trying to remain optimistic, but the lies she had to tell herself were too great.

Toe stared at his feet. "What do ye hope to find at this temple?"

"I don't know. I don't even know if it exists. Even if it does, it might not hold any answers for me. I have to believe it will, because it's all I have. But then I think, if someone there can tell me why I'm a Beast Master,

Fallener, why the Seven cursed me, what will knowing do for me? It won't give me back my life." She swallowed. "This is my life now. Running, hiding, nobody to care for, nobody who cares about me. I don't believe I have a bestial soul. I feel the same way now as I always have. But they're not wrong when they say I'm cursed. I am. But this is the curse."

Erryn pressed her hands against her chest. "This existence. This loneliness. Being torn away from those I love. Being judged by those who don't know me. I just wish I knew why. Why me? Why did the Seven do this to me?"

She drew a shaky breath. "I'm sorry. This isn't your burden to bear."

Toe roughly patted her arm. "I wish I had answers for ye. I wish I could help ye."

"You've done more than most would. Talking to me and letting me travel with you for a bit . . . I appreciate it more than you can know."

Toe's forehead creased with sympathy. "I wish I could teach ye about the land, but we have to deliver the contracts we're carrying to those waiting for them. The sooner they receive them, the heavier our coin purses will be. And surviving out here, it's not something ye learn in a few hours."

He was right. She was being selfish. They were travelling together because there was safety in numbers, not because they were friends. Her desperation had compelled her to ask him for something that wasn't his responsibility. She was alone in this, and always would be. "I shouldn't have asked. I know we have to keep moving."

Toe's brow furrowed. "As we're walking, we can talk about the land, but doing is better than listening."

"Toe."

Erryn looked over her shoulder. Renn was standing behind them. "I need yer help with something."

Toe pushed himself up. "What do ye need?" He trailed after Renn.

Erryn watched them walk away. How long had Renn stood there? She might have heard every desperate word.

Erryn smelled her shirt sleeve and wrinkled her nose. When they camped tonight, she'd go down to the river and wash herself, this shirt, and whatever she wouldn't wear on the morrow. Toe was at the river now, fishing. She would have liked to have gone with him, but he'd said that he liked to fish alone and had suggested she help Renn pack up camp.

The wild woman was pulling down the tent. She'd shaken her head when Erryn had crouched to pull up one of the wooden stakes. So much for warming up to her by the time they reached Stronghaven, which they'd do late on the morrow, according to Toe. A week ago, Erryn would have welcomed the sight of the city's walls, but on the morrow she'd part ways with Toe. And Renn. The gruff woman barely tolerated her, but she was a presence. Soon Erryn would be alone again, her hat pulled down and her eyes on her feet, afraid to speak to anyone and seeing the guard around every corner.

But Stronghaven would be a paradise compared to what was to come. To reach Loring, she'd have to travel through territory occupied primarily by wild folk clans. What if they were all like Renn? What would happen if one glimpsed her branded forehead? She couldn't avoid them all the way to Loring. She'd need to trade.

When she'd left Rodney's, she'd vowed that nothing would stop her from reaching her destination, but now that she was so far from home, she—

A shout pierced the air. Erryn's heart raced. Renn jerked her head up. Their eyes met. "It could be Toe," Erryn said.

Renn dropped the corner of the tent she held and buckled on her sword. "Stay here."

"No, I'm going with you. What if it's slavers, or bandits?"

"Ye need to watch the camp."

Erryn rushed to the edge of the slope and looked toward the river. "I don't see him."

Another shout.

"It's coming from the south." Renn moistened her lips. "We don't have time to argue this." She grabbed Toe's purse and hooked it onto her belt. "The contracts are in here," she said tersely. "Nothing else matters. Come on." She ran toward the river. Erryn took off after her.

They reached the riverbank in less than a minute and looked to the south, but nobody was there. Renn's brow furrowed, then she headed south. Erryn trailed after her and scoured the area for Toe, but she didn't see him. "He couldn't have gone far."

Another cry, almost lost in the roar of the river, reached Erryn's ears. Renn pointed. "There."

Erryn looked in that direction. Her heart leaped into her mouth. Toe was in the river, clinging to the edge of a slick rock jutting from the choppy waters. If he were to let go, the river would sweep him toward the waterfall. He wouldn't survive.

Renn ran down the bank until she was even with Toe and stepped closer to the water.

"No," Erryn shouted, resisting the urge to grab Renn's belt. "The current is moving too quickly. You'll end up in trouble, too."

"We have to help him!" Renn shouted back. "Maybe we can find a branch and hold it out to him. Hang on, Toe. Hang on!" Her eyes searched to her left, then to her right. "There may be something near the camp."

"There won't be. He's too far out. We'd need the trunk of a tall tree to reach him."

"We have to do something!" Renn snarled.

Erryn shrank back, but she wasn't afraid. Fear burned in Renn's eyes, not anger.

"If one of us goes into the water, the other one could . . ." Renn trailed off.

"Push a branch out for the other one to haul in, and then out, to Toe? The branch would be too large, and we can't go into the water. If only—"

A yelp drew Erryn's attention back to the river. *Shit.* Toe's head was underwater.

"Toe!" Renn cried.

His head bobbed above the water again. Renn wheeled to Erryn. "If only what?"

"If only we could get to him without getting into the water," Erryn said lamely. "But obviously—" A shriek tore through her mind, then another one, and another. Erryn grabbed her head and doubled over.

"What's wrong? What's happening to ye?" Renn said, sounding far away.

The shrieking stopped. Understanding, Erryn lifted her head and slowly straightened. "Rachagha," she whispered.

Renn's brows drew together. "What?"

"Rachagha could reach him."

Renn shook her head. "No, we'll find another way."

"What other way? There is no other way."

"No!"

"Do you want Toe to die? Because that's what's going to happen. He'll eventually let go of the rock and be swept over the waterfall. He'll drown, Renn. Or I can summon Rachagha and give him a chance."

Renn stared at Erryn, her conflict plain on her face.

"Will you stand here and watch Toe die because you refuse to accept my help?"

"Not yer help, the Fallen's help." Renn gulped down air. "Do it. But if the Fallen come anywhere near me, I'll gut ye."

"She won't," Erryn said, more confidently than she felt. She'd never summoned Rachagha. Doing so could draw attention, but she couldn't stand by and let Toe die.

Rachagha! Come!

The sky seemed to rip apart, and from within the tear emerged a gigantic eagle. Rachagha let out an ear-piercing cry. Erryn clapped her hands over her ears. Renn drew her sword and assumed a defensive stance. Rachagha circled high above the river and swooped toward Erryn and Renn.

No!

The eagle pulled out of its dive and flew past them. *Stubborn bird.* Erryn pictured Toe in her mind. *Bring him to me.*

Rachagha returned but didn't head for Toe. She crossed the river and circled back, then dove toward them again. Renn gripped her broadsword with both hands and lifted it.

No!

Rachagha flew by them. Erryn sensed her alarm and concern, and suddenly understood. "Sheathe your sword."

"She'll kill us," Renn shouted.

"Sheathe your sword! She thinks you're going to hurt me."

Renn hesitated.

"Do it! Toe could lose his grip at any moment."

Renn's lips pressed into a thin line. She slammed her sword into its sheath. Her wide eyes followed Rachagha as the bird circled high above them.

Erryn looked at Toe, willing him to hang on for a bit longer. She closed her eyes, pictured him clinging to the rock. *Bring him to me, Rachagha.*

Rachagha circled the river, then dove toward Toe.

Renn gasped when the great bird flapped its wings and rose into the air again, with Toe grasped in its talons.

Good. Bring him to me and put him down gently. Erryn could hardly breathe as Rachagha flew over the camp and looped back toward the river. If she dropped him . . .

Though she was certain the bird wouldn't harm her, she couldn't help but tense when Rachagha flew at her. The great bird released Toe when he was a few feet above the ground. He crumpled into a heap.

"Toe!" Renn ran to him.

Rachagha's huge wings lifted her into the air again. Erryn could sense her pleasure, her delight at flying free. She wanted to let her travel through the sky for a while longer. Regretfully, she said, *Thank you. Return.*

The mighty bird shimmered, and was gone.

Tears filled Erryn's eyes. She stared into the sky for a moment, then turned to Toe and Renn. Toe was sitting up and rubbing his head, with Renn hovering over him. His hair was plastered to his head and his clothes were sodden. Water dripped down his face.

"How are you?" Erryn asked.

Shivers racked his body. "C-c-cold." Blood trickled from a wound on his arm.

"Can ye walk? Renn asked.

When he started to push himself up, Renn grabbed his arm to steady him. Toe winced. "I think—my ankle—" He looked at Renn, then at Erryn. "W-w-what happened? I— how did I get here. I was in the water . . ."

"Put yer arm around me. Erryn, go back to camp. We need a fire. Go!"

Erryn whirled and ran, ready to summon Zayvang, Lerxis, and perhaps Sath, but when she stumbled into the camp, her lungs bursting, nobody was sifting through their belongings. Rachagha would probably have frightened anyone nearby away, but if they'd recognized the great bird . . . She couldn't think about that now.

Renn must have already packed the flint and tinder. Erryn rummaged through one of the bags Renn usually carried. By the time Toe hobbled into camp, leaning heavily on Renn, the fire was burning. At least Erryn hadn't failed at that.

Toe groaned as Renn helped him sit down. "Ye need to get out of those clothes," she said. "Erryn, bring us a blanket."

Erryn dug through another bag. She didn't mind that Renn was ordering her around. The woman was using her name and had said more to her this morning than she had since they'd first met. Erryn pulled out a blanket. She turned to—she quickly averted her eyes. She'd thought Renn planned to hold up the blanket while Toe undressed. Apparently not. Her head turned away, she held out the blanket to Renn and felt it leave her hand.

"We should stay here for today," Renn said.

"No, give me an hour or two next to the fire and I'll be fine," Toe said.

"Are ye sure?"

"Yes." Rustling, then, "Ye can look now, Erryn."

She lifted her eyes. Toe had wrapped the blanket around himself. Renn gazed at her, her eyes bright, but she remained silent.

"Renn told me what happened," Toe said." I don't remember. I was freezing, and in and out. All I kept telling myself was not to let go of the rock, hold onto the rock."

"What happened? How did you end up in the river?" Erryn asked.

"I was foolish. I wasn't having much luck from the bank, so I hopped on a rock, then saw another one close by. I stepped onto it and slipped."

Renn tutted and shook her head.

"I might have hurt my ankle when I slipped, or when…" He cleared his throat. "When I landed. Rachagha, she . . ." Toe glanced at his bleeding arm. "I don't know if she did this, or something else did. It doesn't matter." Toe fell silent for a moment, then met Erryn's eyes. "Ye saved me. Ye saved my life—again. I'm grateful to ye."

Renn pressed her hands against Toe's wound. "Thank ye," she said, so softly that Erryn almost didn't catch it.

For a moment, she wasn't stumbling around alone in the dark, looking forward to nothing but desperation and despair. But the Seven had cursed her. She couldn't change what she was. "Don't thank me. Summoning Rachagha might have drawn attention. We're a day away from Stronghaven, but still. If anyone happened to be travelling nearby, we could have the guard on top of us, and perhaps bounty hunters."

With a lump in her throat, she lifted her bag and slung it over her shoulder, then popped her hat onto her head and pulled down its brim. "Toe should rest here today. I'll go. They want me, not you. If anyone comes, you saw Rachagha but it was nothing to do with you. Thank you.

Thank you for letting me travel with you for a time. You don't know how much . . ." Her voice cracked. She took a moment to breathe. "Good-bye." Then she said the words she wanted to say, even though doing so might upset them. "May the Seven protect you."

"No," Renn barked.

Erryn willed herself to walk. She'd said what was in her heart. She didn't want to argue with Renn.

"Don't go."

Erryn stopped short and stared at her.

"Toe says he can leave in a few hours. If anyone comes before then, we'll face them together. Ye saved Toe. Ye saved him," Renn said fiercely. "We said we'd travel with ye to Stronghaven, and we will. Put yer bag down and take that stupid hat off yer head. Then make yerself useful. There's some willow bark in my bag. Bring it here."

A mixture of gratitude, amazement, and relief flooded through Erryn. She pulled off her hat and dropped it to the ground, along with her bag. As she dug through Renn's bag for the bark, she reminded herself that they'd still part ways when they reached Stronghaven. Maybe she should have left them anyway, despite Renn's surprising outburst. Erryn didn't have a bestial soul, but her regret when she'd dismissed Rachagha, her affection and longing for Zayvang, and her admiration of the others . . . she was growing too close to the Fallen. She loved them.

Avere drank the last of the ale she'd nursed for the past hour and slipped off the barstool. She was tired of spending her afternoons and evenings visiting common room after common room, listening for news of the Beast Master. Where was the girl? Nobody had heard word of her. Nobody had seen her. Avere was starting to believe the heathen was dead. How long would Arrick expect her to stay in Stronghaven, twiddling her thumbs? Maybe she should visit one or two houses tonight, for old time's sake.

One of her fellow Ferrets had told her of a fence who was always interested in acquiring art pieces and jewelry. To keep herself sharp, she'd scouted Stronghaven's affluent quarter and had sussed out several residences she could easily dip in and out of unnoticed.

But that fun would come later. First she'd sup with Malina, as usual. She looked forward to her meals with the old woman more than she cared to admit. The zealot's beliefs were ludicrous, but she played a mean game of cards and always told an interesting story or two. Avere had developed a soft spot for her, but her affection for the old bat wouldn't stop her from planting a dagger in the Beast Master's chest, if the heathen wasn't rotting away somewhere already.

She was almost at the tavern's door when it smashed open. Three hunters tumbled into the common room. "Get Olly an ale," one shouted. "He's seeing things. Seeing things!"

One of the other men roared with laughter. The third man, who must be Olly, scowled at them. "I saw it, I'm telling you. It was as big as this bloody tavern."

"He saw a flying tavern." The first man laughed at his own words.

Avere sighed. This city was filled with drunks, and these men weren't wild folk. They were also blocking her path to the door. She started to skirt around them.

"It looked like an eagle, but a huge bloody eagle," the first man said.

Avere stopped. "An eagle, you say. Where did you see it?"

The one needling Olly focused on her. "Look, Olly, this lady's interested in your story."

The second man whistled. "Oy, darlin', I saw a flying bear. Do you want to hear about it?"

"I'm telling you, I saw it," Olly shouted. "It scared my horse."

"Oh, well then, let's ask his horse what it saw," the first man said, evoking laughter from those who'd gathered around the trio.

"And didn't you say it disappeared, Olly?" the second man said. "You said it was flying around, and then it just disappeared."

The first man nudged the second in the ribs. "And he hadn't been tippling. Right, Olly?" They both clutched their shaking bellies.

"You don't believe me, but I know what I saw." Olly pointed. "It was to the south, toward the river."

"We'd go look, but you said it disappeared!"

Avere had heard enough. Excited, she hurried past them and had to force herself to walk, not run, to the inn where Malina was staying, so she wouldn't attract the guards' attention. A giant eagle that had suddenly disappeared? Rachagha. It had to be. The heathen was alive, and nearby! Avere could keep the information to herself, but she wanted to share it with Malina, see her eyes light up and listen to her babble excitedly. She wanted Malina to experience the thrill and excitement of being so close to meeting her idol, and let her revel in her religious fervour—before she betrayed her. Tonight would be their last meal together. Avere would miss her.

At Malina's inn, Avere lifted her hand to wave, then frowned. Their usual table was empty. She glanced around the common room, searching for Malina's rose cloak.

"You just missed her."

Avere turned to her left. "What?"

"Your friend." The landlord lifted two plates from the table he was clearing. "She left with two men."

"Two men?"

The landlord nodded. "I heard them talking—not that I eavesdrop on what patrons are saying, mind. I just happened to be cleaning nearby."

"And?" Avere said, her rising anxiety tightening her jaw.

"I know she's some type of religious nut looking for the Beast Master, but she seems harmless enough to me." His voice dropped. "She wants to meet her. Odd, if you ask me, but her coin is good."

"What did they say?" Avere said through clenched teeth.

"Oh, right. They told her they could show her where the Beast Master is."

Shit. "Do you know where they were going?"

"No, but you just missed them, as I said. They only left five minutes ago."

Avere wheeled.

"I've seen them before. They—"

She didn't hear whatever else he had to say. Her heart pounding, she left the inn and ran south, not caring about the guards. She wanted the guards. Now. "Have you seen an old woman in a bright rose cloak?" she called out to a woman sweeping a shop step.

The woman shook her head. When three other people to the south also hadn't seen Malina, Avere doubled back and headed north. "Have you seen an old woman in a rose cloak?" she asked a man and woman loitering outside another shop.

The man nodded and pointed to an alleyway. "She went down there with some men."

Avere raced into the alleyway. Two men were crouched over a— "Hey!"

They looked up and ran away from her, but not before Avere caught a flash of red in one's arms. She reached for one of her throwing daggers, but her attention was drawn to the heap they'd left behind . . . *No. No, no, no!* Avere skidded to a stop and fell to her knees. Malina looked up at her, her skin already gray and her lips blue. Her cloak was gone.

"You stupid, stupid, woman! I told you—I told you to keep your cloak—" Avere forced herself to look at the blood gurgling from Malina's slashed belly. Her entrails . . . Avere pulled off her cloak and covered the wounds. "I'll get help. I'll—" Her voice choked off.

"Look at me," Malina rasped. "Look at me, Avere."

Avere did as Malina asked. To her amazement, Malina didn't look frightened. She looked resigned, and at peace.

"I . . . go to the . . . Seven. It is up to you now. You must . . . you must help her. Take the book. Take the . . ." The light faded from Malina's eyes. Her head lolled to one side.

Avere fought tears and stared at Malina, then shook herself. The woman had been a silly, misguided fool. She'd been someone Avere had befriended because she needed information. She'd been nothing to Avere. *Nothing. Nobody.*

Avere gulped down air and lifted her cloak. She'd interrupted the thieves. Perhaps they'd left valuables behind. Grimacing, she slid her hand along Malina's belt, then slipped it underneath her body. Ah, she'd fallen on her purse. The thieves must have just finished pulling off her cloak when Avere had ruined their little party. She unhooked the purse and pulled it from beneath Malina's body. "You won't be needing this anymore," she murmured, hooking it to her own belt. Anything else? Avere felt again. Something else hung from Malina's belt . . . Avere pulled it out and studied the leather-bound book. *"Take the book."*

She didn't have time to open it now. She added it to her belt, quickly finished her search of Malina's body, and rose to leave, wanting to get away before anyone else chose to walk this alleyway. But she couldn't move, not until she had one last look. She crouched again. Malina's lifeless eyes gazed at her. Avere closed them. She touched the old woman's hand, then ran in the same direction in which the thieves had fled.

At least five people could describe her to the guard and tell them she'd asked after a woman in a rose cloak, but that didn't worry Avere. They'd have to find her first, and she knew how things worked. The local primates couldn't get the guard to run Malina out of the city, but they could persuade them to look the other way now that she'd met her death. The guard would oblige.

There would be no justice for Malina, even though the inn's landlord could give them a description of the men and might even know their names. But it meant that no guards would be searching for the woman who'd regularly supped with the cultist and had ducked into the alleyway where she'd met her violent end. The Beast Master had finally surfaced. Avere couldn't have risked lying low. She had to find the heathen before anyone else did.

The moment she stepped inside the Ferret base, the man who oversaw the birds came over to her, his face flushed. "Message for you," he said, handing it to her. "I'd read it now, if I were you. If it's anything like the one I got, you're about to have the shock of your life."

She'd had enough shock for today. Malina's purse weighed heavily on her belt, and her conscience. Why hadn't the woman listened to her? Under the protection of the Seven? Fat lot of good that had done. If only Avere had arrived at the inn a few minutes earlier. If only she'd gone north first, instead of south. She'd wanted to tell Malina about the Beast Master, see her face . . .

The Ferret still stood in front of her. "Thank you,"

Avere murmured, and went up to her room. It took her a minute to decode Arrick's message, but only seconds to read it. Were her eyes deceiving her? Malina's death had shocked her, but this . . . She sank onto her bed. Wanting to be sure, she decoded and read Arrick's message again. *King and prince assassinated. Princess on the run. Kill the Beast Master.*

Friend or Foe

Arrick looked up from the message in his hand when Evan, a captain in the royal guard, strode into his study. He quickly pocketed the slip of paper. "I've been expecting you." He didn't offer the man a chair. Evan always shook his head and stood ramrod straight.

"Have you any news?" Evan asked.

"There are rumours everywhere." Arrick had instigated many of them. "It's difficult to sift through the noise, but based on a couple of reliable sources, I believe the fugitives are heading west."

"West? Do you know where they're going?"

Arrick grimaced. "You didn't hear this from me, but I've heard rumblings that Lord Manchester will call for a fuller investigation into the assassination. He has a summer home out that way. He hasn't outright declared his support for the former princess, but . . ."

Evan's brows shot up. "I didn't know he was so loyal to the Lyoses."

Manchester wasn't, but the more everyone suspected each other and squabbled, the less chance someone would end up on the throne. Placing the princess on the coveted seat would be more difficult if someone already occupied it. Best to keep everyone pointing fingers at each other and let the Primacy rule for now. It hadn't made any declarations yet, except to offer a handsome reward to anyone who captured the princess and her two companions. Curiously, the reward would only be paid if the princess was delivered alive. Why would the Primacy not want to kill the only woman who'd be a danger to the throne while she drew breath? Did she have information they wanted? Did they want to make an example of her?

Arrick forced his mind back to the conversation at hand. "Some don't accept that the former princess murdered her father, brother, and sister-in-law. She never showed any ambition, and she claimed to be innocent."

Evan's eyes widened. "They believe her story over the grand primate's? He was in the room. He witnessed it, along with the other primates who weren't involved in the assassination plot."

The man was naive. Only the downtrodden and poor listened to the primates and viewed them as closer to the Seven than everyone else. To the rich, the Primacy was a political machine like any other. The Royal Council believed the word of five primates over the princess, but part of its willingness to accept the Primacy's version of events had to do with throwing in with the stronger party. The Primacy, or a young princess who hadn't expected to rule? They would rue their choice. "Regardless, some don't believe the former princess is a murderer. They'll help her and her companions."

Evan's face crumpled. "Like the royal primate? I feel bad for him. Don't agree with what he did, but he saw the girl grow up. Same goes for Cedric. They'll pay with their lives now. They'll pay with their lives." He shook his head.

"Have you found out how they escaped?" Arrick asked casually.

"We're still questioning the men who were at the castle, especially those at the gates. They claim innocence and don't recall seeing anyone suspicious entering or leaving the castle. The gates were shut because of the crowds. Only tradesmen were being let through, and few of them were working that day." Evan rubbed the back of his neck. "I don't know, someone had to help them. Someone's lying, and I have to find out who. The grand primate's lackey is breathing down my neck."

Arrick clucked his tongue sympathetically. "The grand primate won't stop until he finds them."

"I know." Evan squared his shoulders. "I'll send men to speak to Manchester. If you hear anything more . . ."

"I'll send someone over to you immediately."

"Thank you." Evan nodded curtly and left Arrick's office.

Arrick hoped the grand primate felt as frustrated as he did. He'd heard what Viren had said on the rack—before the pain was too great and Viren had realized no words would save him or his betrothed, though he'd valiantly tried to shelter the princess. He'd insisted that someone had drugged the wine, that the Westerfox primates had pounced on the royal family as they'd clutched at their chests and throats. The interrogator had rightly pointed out that Viren and the princess weren't drugged.

The Primacy had framed the princess, and the grand primate had told the Royal Council he doubted the princess would confess. Not a stretch for someone who knew she was innocent. He'd wanted a trial that could last weeks, perhaps months. What had he planned for her during that time? Would the guard have discovered her cell empty one day? Would she have received visits from the grand primate or someone representing him—under the guise of attempting to bring her back to the Seven, of course? What was the Primacy's interest in keeping the princess alive? The answer was in front of Arrick, but every time he grasped at it, it slipped away, like a word on the tip of one's tongue.

He had people shadowing the "innocent" Westerfox primates, a boring assignment so far. They hadn't left the High Council's estate since the assassination. What were they plotting? Was the Primacy the driving force behind the assassination, or had someone else ordered it? The latter possibility frightened Arrick. If it was true, it would have to be someone powerful enough to control the Primacy and order the assassination of a king.

Avere flipped open her purse, fished out several coins, and plunked them onto the table. The dour man on the other side of it lifted his quill. His bushy eyebrows drew together. "Are you sure? From what I hear, the woman was a heathen and got what was coming to her."

Her jaw clenched. "I'm sure. To pass the time, I occasionally played cards with her. She wasn't a bad sort, simply misguided."

"If you say so." He counted the coins with his eyes, then wrote a note in his ledger, his quill scratching along the paper. "She won't be put into a common grave, then. It'll still be a pauper's burial, but her name and burial spot will be recorded in the cemetery book." He lifted his head. "You can visit her, if you like."

"No, I won't be doing that." Using Malina's own coin to ensure she received a proper burial was sentimental enough. The old bat had gotten under Avere's skin. She'd hardly slept a wink last night, and it wasn't the news of the king's assassination that had kept her awake. "I just don't want to see her thrown into a hole with rabble."

The man nodded, then his eyes narrowed. "The guard who dropped her off said she'd been covered with a cloak. You wouldn't know anything about that, would you?"

If Avere hadn't learned to mask her feelings, her face would have flushed. "No, I wouldn't."

He grunted and gathered up the coins Avere had placed on the table. "Do you want to leave your name, in case family comes looking for her?"

"No. And I don't expect anyone will come."

"You're probably right."

"Is that it, then?" She'd never paid for a burial before. Most of the people she worked with disappeared, or died in dark alleyways or at a guard's hand. Arrick took care of the few who died naturally.

"Unless you have other business."

"No. Thank you, then."

She left the mortuary with a sigh of relief. Now to face the other task she'd avoided. Malina's book. She'd stared at it. She'd lifted the cover once, only to let it fall. What was she afraid of? Malina had talked nonsense.

Back at the Ferret base, she went to the common room and looked for Billy, the Ferret who'd organized several scout patrols for her. "Any word?" she asked him.

"I've had a couple of birds back. One reported a group of hunters. Another glimpsed three wild folk camped in the forest. Nobody has seen a woman travelling alone."

"She has to be somewhere nearby."

"Who is she?" Billy asked. "Is it the Beast Master? You said she'd be wearing a hat or covering her forehead. I heard the king branded her there, may the Seven bless him."

"Never you mind who she is. I'm going up to my room. The moment you hear anything, knock on my door. Understand?"

"Yes, mistress."

Avere strode away. If Arrick were here, he'd chide her for being short with Billy. Frustration was making her surly. She wished she could be out in the forest tracking Fyler herself, but she wanted to be here when the heathen entered Stronghaven. The girl *was* coming here. Not only did Avere feel it in her bones, but where else would the girl go? She wouldn't come this close to the city if she didn't intend to enter it.

Ferrets were on every gate. After she looked at Malina's precious book, she'd stake out one of the southern gates herself. If she were the heathen, she'd enter the city during the day, when the roads were busy and she could attach herself to an unwary group of travellers and slip inside. Avere's breath quickened. She could lay eyes on the Beast Master before sunset and plant a dagger in her before dawn! Then she'd gather her things, mount her horse, and ride back to Darroth and into chaos.

Arrick didn't have to tell her that affairs in the Royal City would be in turmoil, and not only because of the assassination. *Princess on the run.* Why? With her father and brother dead, the princess was the rightful ruler. Avere could remain in Stronghaven and wait for a courier to arrive with a letter from Arrick that explained why the princess had fled the city, but if things went her way, he wouldn't have time to write one before he received a message from her that read: *Beast Master dead. Coming home.* Anticipation lifted her mood.

In her room, she unhooked Malina's book from her belt and held it in her lap. It was probably filled with dull passages about the Elder Gods, or maybe giants and horned pigs. She opened the book. An empty page greeted her. She flipped to the next one and peered at a sketch of a rectangle, with an arrow pointing down at it. In the upper right corner, a spear piercing the sun—the symbol for Zhikinden. Directly underneath it, a saber-tooth cat. Zayvang. In the lower right corner, a skull. Death?

Avere turned to the next page. Another rectangle with an arrow pointing to it, but this time the upper right corner contained a hoe. Queyris. And underneath, a horse. Quon. In the lower right corner, another skull. The next five pages contained the symbols for the five remaining gods and their pets. After that, a drawing that could represent a temple. On the next page, an abstract depiction of a person holding a whip. The Beast Master?

She flipped through the rest of the book. Not a single word. Only pictures. What did it mean? Was it a copy of an ancient text, or a child's art project?

The final sketch in the book unnerved her. If she was interpreting it correctly, it showed Zhikinden blessing the Beast Master. What if Malina had been right and Beast Masters served the Seven, or these Elder Gods of hers? If she killed Fyler . . . Avere strode to the window and gazed out at the city. Malina had said that when a Beast Master walked Daros, Death's fury could change the course of history. The king and prince were dead. The princess had not taken the throne, or perhaps she had and was running because the assassins were after her?

Think, Avere. Malina had been a religious zealot. The fact that she'd parroted the contents of one of the cult's holy books didn't make any of it true. The assassination of the king and prince could be coincidental. She should forget Malina's babble and stick to basics; obey Arrick— he'd never failed her. Then again, he'd hadn't met Malina, seen the certainty in her eyes and heard the passion in her voice. As Malina had pointed out, Avere should give as much credence to her cult's beliefs as she did to the Primacy's teachings. Where did that leave her?

If she killed the Beast Master, she could be offending the Seven and endangering the balance Malina had spoken about. If she didn't, she'd be disobeying the one person she trusted. Arrick was real, but Malina had been real, too—and what about the book? Was it the reproduction of a mad artist's scrawling, or a sacred text?

The Beast Master was within Avere's grasp. She had little time to decide.

Toe stared into the darkness and listened for the sound of Renn's rhythmic breathing. Instead, he heard her roll over and mutter something under her breath. She wasn't sleeping, either. "Renn?"

Silence, then, "What?"

"The ground must be damp. Did ye tell her ye didn't mind if she slept in here?"

Renn grunted. "She didn't want to. She said she likes to sleep outside."

Was it because Erryn was a Fallener? Could she no longer sleep with a roof—or tent—over her head? No, why would that be? Despite the stories and teachings, Erryn was like any other woman. If he had the opportunity, he'd ask her why she wouldn't sleep in the tent, but only because he was curious.

Wondering whether Erryn was comfortable wasn't the reason sleep eluded him. Due to his embarrassing topple into the river, they'd rested here all day. He'd soon part ways with the Fallener who'd saved his life twice. "We'll reach Stronghaven tomorrow. We should give Erryn Jon's share of our payment, but why do that when it will only end up in someone else's pockets?"

Renn didn't answer.

"I don't mean in the pockets of merchants or innkeepers. I mean—"

"I know what ye mean."

Toe swallowed. "She won't survive long. She might make it a day or two from Stronghaven, but then she'll enter clan territory and ye know what they—what we did to the last Fallener."

Stories took on lives of their own, but he didn't have any trouble imagining clan hunters slaying the last Fallener, cutting him up, and feeding him to their dogs. Whether he'd suffered through the torture and indignities the storytellers recited until one of the hunters had killed him with a merciful thrust of his sword . . . Toe used to raise his ale mug and tip the storyteller. He wouldn't do that anymore. "She saved my life, and yers."

"There's nothing we can do for her."

"I doubt the other Fallener approached the clans and spoke with the Mothers. If we were with her—"

Renn snorted. "Ye think they'll let her pass because we're with her? They might listen to ye. They won't listen to me. My name is not to be spoken, Toe. I haven't been more than a day north of Stronghaven since I walked through the city gates when I was seventeen."

She spoke the truth. Banished from her clan, Renn could harm with her presence, rather than help. She could no longer introduce herself as Renn from the Snowlake clan. She was clanless, and therefore had no voice as far as every clan was concerned.

He and Renn were business partners. They always did right by each other. Many of the contracts they had were with wild folk turned city merchants or businessmen who respected wild folk ways, either genuinely or because it was good for trade in these northern parts. They wouldn't deal with a clanless woman. If he left Renn to travel with Erryn to the temple, what would she do? She'd have to work with someone else, but who would give her a chance? Most wild folk would have nothing to do with her, and city folk would treat her like a mindless lackey. He couldn't leave her in the lurch because he wanted to escort a woman they hardly knew to a temple that might not exist. He wouldn't do that to her, but wishing Erryn well tomorrow would be dishonest. She wouldn't be well. If only Renn hadn't killed Ian. "Why did ye do it?" he said softly.

"Do what?"

He wished he could see her face. "Ye know what."

"Last time ye asked me, I told ye I didn't want to talk about it," Renn hissed. "Nothing has changed."

"Ye must have had a reason."

An exasperated sigh conveyed Renn's frustration. "I'm grateful to ye for not turning me away when I asked ye for help. Because of ye, I'm not hungry and scrounging for food . . . or doing something worse to survive. But ye have to leave this be."

Had it been a lover's quarrel? Or maybe Ian had forced himself on her? Why would she kill her friend? It had cost her everything—her clan, her family, her reputation. Almost ten years had passed since she'd approached him in the tavern, dirty and hungry, and begged him to hire her for a contract run. Another man might have offered her work as his personal whore instead, but Toe had known her since she was a girl, and he wasn't that type of man. Even if he'd been tempted, Renn would have refused, or gutted him while he was still unlacing his trousers.

He'd given her a chance to prove herself and still remembered the tears of relief that had brimmed in her eyes, the tears she'd quickly rubbed away. They'd worked together ever since. She was a business partner now. She was his trusted friend. She was also a proud woman. There was nothing wrong with pride, except when it got in the way of common sense and was paired with stubbornness, as it was with Renn. If only she'd told her side of the story. If only she'd tell him. If she confided in him, he'd go to the Mothers, which was why she'd never tell him.

"Okay, I'll leave it be." But he couldn't drop the other subject. "We could run a couple of contracts to Loring. Few will do it. It would mean a lot of coin. I'd deal with the clans. Ye and Erryn could stay out of sight."

"Ye think we can avoid our folk all the way up to Loring? The hunters don't keep to the strongholds and settlements. And some of our folk travel to trade with the city folk, especially now."

Renn was right. He should roll over, try to sleep, and forget about helping Erryn, but he couldn't. "If Erryn kept her hat on and ye use a different name . . ."

"If we run into any of our folk and they ask about my

clan, I can't lie, Toe. Ye can't ask me to lie. I won't do that. I am Renn, shamed by the Snowlake clan. To say otherwise would be to deny myself and disrespect our ways."

"I know." He couldn't ask Renn to lie about her banishment or to risk her life for Erryn, but he couldn't leave her behind, either. He owed Erryn his life twice over, but Renn was his kin. She depended on him for work. She was shamed, but he'd chosen to overlook that so she wouldn't have to beg for food and be mocked and spat upon. He couldn't turn his back on her for a woman he hardly knew, and a Fallener and city woman, at that.

"As we got closer to Loring, there would be more of a chance of seeing someone who knows me," Renn said. "Even if I was willing to lie, it would do me no good. If ye want to help Erryn, don't help her get to Loring."

"It would be a fool's errand, anyway," Toe said, as much to himself as to Renn. "She doesn't know if there's a temple. Even if there is, it won't change her. She'll still be a Fallener."

"A fool's errand is right. If her hat blew off while we're talking to hunters, how long do ye think she'd survive?"

As long as it took one to draw his or her sword and run it through Erryn's belly. Toe rolled over and pulled the blanket over him. He stared into the darkness.

Fi stirred the stew Cedric had cooked and willed herself to spoon a bit into her mouth. It wasn't that Cedric was an awful cook. The first time he'd handed her a bowl, she'd told herself that even if it tasted awful, she must thank him and eat every drop. She needn't have worried. Cedric was a capable cook, but she'd still forced down the soup, as she would the stew. Her stomach no longer grumbled, and her tongue no longer tasted. She lived in a bland world, where nothing mattered. If not for the men who travelled with her, she'd lie down and let the Seven do what they would with her. She understood why animals hid when they were dying. Why fight it?

Cedric poured stew into his own bowl and covered the pot hanging over the fire. Spry for his age, he lowered himself next to her. "Is it all right, Majesty?"

"It's wonderful, Cedric." As she chewed on a piece of meat, she glanced over to where Enkelo sat quietly, his eyes closed. After he'd finished his meditation, he'd fill the empty bowl sitting at his feet. Fi had learned that Enkelo's devotion to the Seven was genuine—not that she'd believed his faith was a sham; she had, however, presumed that his public displays of devotion were an exaggeration of whatever he did in private. He wasn't alone here; perhaps his thrice daily meditations were for her benefit, but she doubted it. She was sitting on a rock in peasant clothes, her hair straggly and dirt underneath her fingernails. The chance that she'd ever sit on Daros's throne was about the same as Father suddenly bursting into their camp and declaring that the assassination had all been a terrible dream. How she wished that were true! How she longed to see Father, and Henrick and Surann.

For three days she and her rescuers had ridden on dusty trails, ignoring everyone they passed and setting up camp in the forest every evening. For the first couple of days, she'd depended on her horse to follow Enkelo while she'd sat numbly in the saddle, staring at nothing. This morning questions had begun to intrude, questions she'd asked herself before the shock had set in.

She wiped her mouth with a leaf and turned to Cedric. "Do you know what happened to the Tolins? Viren's father was ill. I hope they didn't mistreat him. And what about his brothers? Were they all racked?" Her throat tightened. She shouldn't have asked, because she couldn't bear to hear the answer. If Dann was dead . . .

"I don't know, Majesty. After they found you . . . when they said you'd . . ."

She could see his discomfort. "It's all right, Cedric. Speak plainly."

He sighed. "When they went into the main study room and found the king, prince, and princess dead, and you unconscious, and the primates saying that you and Viren and one of the primates were behind it, word spread quickly. Fortunately the royal primate knew I'd always been loyal to your father and believed I would continue to be loyal to you." The smile that played on his lips didn't chase away the circles under his eyes and the gloom that hung over them. "He found me in the banquet hall. We were too busy planning your escape to know what the guard was doing. I don't know who else they arrested."

"Didn't your superior wonder where you were?"

"I always reported to the king. My captain knew that. Most men my age have given up the uniform, but I never married."

Fi looked at him with new eyes. Kind, gentle Cedric had been a constant presence in her life. She couldn't remember a time when she hadn't passed him in the castle, seen him going into Father's study, or barely registered him hovering nearby while she'd played, and later, shopped. He'd been with her the day Erryn had shocked them all. Why hadn't she wondered who Cedric was, where he slept at night, whether he had a wife and children? He shouldn't have risked his life for her.

"I told the captain I needed to be alone. He understood. I don't think he thought I'd be of much help. He probably sees me as a doddering old man. You get that when you're older," he said, looking down at Fi. "They think you can't do anything, but I can still swing my sword. You saw that."

"I did," she said, wanting to ask him how old he was. Well, why shouldn't she? "How old are you?"

His brows shot up. "Seventy-one."

"I didn't think you were a day over sixty," she said, meaning it. She almost smiled when his face flushed. "You should be at home in a nice, warm bed, not here with me, trying to do the impossible." She regretted her words the moment they left her mouth. Cedric and Enkelo had risked everything to help her escape. They deserved her confidence and support. "I'm sorry. I'm not at my best."

His forehead creased with sympathy. "How could you be? You're doing well, Majesty."

"Thank you," she murmured. "Thank you for standing with me."

"I would have served your father until I died. I won't rest until you're on the throne, and then I'll serve you."

She gazed at him. "Did you ever doubt me? Did you believe for a second that I might have killed them?"

He shook his head. "No, Majesty. Not for a second."

She wanted to touch his hand. "You have to stop calling me Majesty. I'm to be Calindra, remember, and you're my grandfather."

Cedric huffed. "That'll take some getting used to."

"We'll get used to it together."

He looked down at her bowl. "You must eat, Maj—Calindra."

She spooned more stew into her mouth and watched Enkelo stretch and carry his bowl to the pot. Fortunately he was to be her uncle, not her father. She couldn't have called him Father. Her father was dead. *Dead.*

Erryn grew silent as she and the wild folk drew closer to the road that would take them to Stronghaven's main southern gate. Within the hour, she'd bid good-bye to her two companions and be back to dodging the guard, haggling poorly with vendors, and dozing in alleys until she had enough coin for two bags of food, a bedroll, and a blanket. First she'd have to buy a lute and try not to waste Rodney's coin by agreeing to an unreasonable price. She wouldn't snatch up the first one she found. She'd request the asking price from several merchants and try to overhear how others bargained with them. Maybe Toe and Renn—no, they wouldn't know anything about lutes, and they wouldn't be with her. They'd be visiting businessmen who regularly hired them and looking for an extra sword or two to travel with them back to Sull. They'd have forgotten about her by this time next week.

Determined not to let them see her dismay, she turned to Toe and pointed at a bird. "Do you know what type of—"

Renn dropped the bags she was carrying. She drew her sword. Toe's sword was in his hand a second later, the bundle on his back now on the ground. Erryn looked at them in confusion, then tensed when two men emerged from the trees. The taller one swaggered toward them. His eyes raked Erryn from head to foot, then flitted to Toe and Renn. "Lower your swords. There's no need for hostility."

The second man rested his hand on his sword's hilt. "We're here for the heathen."

"Whatever she's paying you to protect her, we'll triple." The taller man pulled a bulging coin purse from his belt and waved it at Toe. "Push her over here and I'll toss you the purse, and we'll all continue on our way, our business concluded."

"How do we know ye'll throw the purse?" Toe asked. With his free hand, he motioned for Erryn to get behind him. She did so, preparing to call Zayvang and Lerxis.

"Come now, don't be like that. We all want the same thing. Coin and prestige. You'll get this coin. We'll get coin and prestige." The tall man shrugged apologetically. "The nobles won't honour you at their banquets, so take what you can. Coin is coin, and a heathen is a heathen."

"Go back to Stronghaven," Toe growled. "Ye'll have to find another way to prove ye're men."

The man's face tightened. "Be reasonable. Let's not shed blood over a Beast Master." He whistled. A third man emerged from his hiding place, his sword already drawn.

The second man's hand tightened around his sword hilt. The one doing most of the talking swept his arm toward the newcomer. "Now it's three against two. Do you really want to throw your lives away for a heathen the Seven would spit upon?"

Erryn shouldn't be cowering behind Toe. They wanted her. She wouldn't allow Toe and Renn to risk injury, or worse. She didn't want to fight, but they'd left her no choice.

Zayvang, Lerxis, come. The air next to her crackled. Zayvang and Lerxis leaped into the physical plane. *Protect me.* With the two Fallen at her side, Erryn moved to the fore. "It's not three against two. It's five against three, and I have five other Fallen ready to heed my call and send you to the Seven."

The men glanced at each other. The one who'd shown himself last gulped as he looked at Lerxis, then Zayvang. He gave a curt shake of his head and sheathed his sword. The second man stepped back and lifted both his hands in a gesture of surrender. The tall one's eyes flashed, but he hooked the coin purse back onto his belt. "So, that's how it's to be. You've chosen the heathen over the Seven. They'll show you no mercy, and neither will we. You haven't seen the last of us." He motioned to his men to follow him back into the forest.

"No, walk along the path, where we can see ye," Toe shouted.

The leader turned and made a rude gesture, but he and his men strode down the path. Erryn and the wild folk watched them go.

"When we can't see them anymore, we'll go through the forest," Toe murmured. "There might be more along the path, waiting to ambush us."

Renn grunted her agreement. While Toe and Renn's attention was on the retreating trio, Erryn seized the chance to ruffle Zayvang's fur and stroke Lerxis's muzzle. She dismissed them with a heavy heart.

The men rounded a curve in the path and disappeared from sight. "I wanted to tell him to come closer and show me the purse wasn't filled with dirt, so I could run him through," Renn said. "But if they were nobles, killing one would have brought us too much trouble."

"They weren't nobles," Erryn said. "They were bounty hunters. Every noble has his favourites, and when one brings in a catch, they shower them with coin, gifts, and women."

Toe sheathed his sword. "Ye could tell that just by looking at them?"

"Uh, yeah. In the Royal City, the town crier would always announce when a noble's bounty hunter had captured a criminal. It elevated the noble in the eyes of the king. Sometimes he'd even invite the noble and his man for supper . . . or so I heard. How did you know they were there?" she asked, wanting to change the subject.

Toe's brows drew together. "Ye didn't hear them?"

"No."

"They were crashing through the bush. They would have disturbed the dead."

Renn nodded. "They probably didn't think they were loud, but they were."

Erryn felt stupid. "I only heard birds and insects. I didn't hear them."

Toe and Renn exchanged glances. "Ye'll have to be more careful when ye're going north—listen, look, be more aware," Toe said. "Our folk are much quieter than those flatfoots were, and there are animals that'll want ye for dinner."

"Ye won't make it on yer own," Renn stated. "Ye'll be dead in days."

"Renn!" Toe barked.

"What? She needs someone to tell her the truth. She should give up on Loring and this make-believe temple."

Toe shook his head. "It might not be make-believe."

"Even if it isn't, she won't see it. She won't make it there."

"She might," Toe snapped. "Why do ye—"

"The last Fallener, the one also going to this temple. He didn't make it," Renn said.

Shock stabbed through Erryn. "What do you mean?"

Renn's lip curled. "We killed him. The same thing will happen to ye."

"Why, Renn?" Toe roared.

"She needs to know the truth!"

"I already know the truth," Erryn shouted. "Do you think I don't know that I'll die up there? That the first time I run into one of you will be the last day of my life? I have to try to get to Loring. What else can I do? I have nothing else. I have nobody. At least I'll die trying to do something, rather than hanging in the middle of a town square with people throwing rotten fruit at me. I have nothing to lose. I have nothing." Her chest felt tight. She walked away from them and heaved a sigh.

"Toe and me were talking," Renn said.

Erryn turned back to them.

"We were going to give ye a share of the coin we'll get when we deliver the contracts, but we'd be throwing it away."

Toe's eyes flashed. "Why are ye doing this? She saved my life, and yers. Why are ye being so unkind to her?"

"I'm a Fallener," Erryn said, her disappointment and weariness robbing her voice of any vigour. She'd thought Renn had come around a bit, that her hate had turned to dislike.

Renn's fists clenched. "Ye two need to talk less and listen more. Toe and me, we need coin. Living off the land is difficult now." She cocked her head toward Toe. "We need coin. If we don't run contracts, we don't get coin. There's other work, but running contracts lets us be alone and out of the city most of the time."

Erryn nodded, wondering why Renn was telling her all this.

"We can run contracts to Loring, but there aren't many who want contracts running up to Loring, and not many who'll do it."

"Why?" Erryn asked, a seed of hope sprouting in her heart.

"Loring isn't a city like others ye've been to," Toe said. "Most of the people there are from the clans. They don't trade as much with Stronghaven and the other towns filled with yer kind. They hardly traded at all until the land sickened. Now some do, but not all agree with it. Some of our hunters stalk human prey."

Erryn's hope died. "Not many contracts, and a dangerous route to run."

"Those hunters are a disgrace," Renn spat. "They should be banished."

"But they're not," Toe said mildly. "Every hunter is needed now, and the clans need coin. Most hunters are honourable. It's only a few."

"That's the same as my people," Erryn said. "Most of us don't trouble the guard."

"Yer problem is that every hunter will be a danger to ye, honourable or not." Renn's eyes flicked to Toe, then she looked at Erryn. "Are ye sure ye have to go to Loring?"

"Yes. I need to find this temple, if it exists."

"If it exists," Renn repeated. She muttered something under her breath. "All right. I have a proposal for ye." When Toe drew breath, she lifted her hand. "We'll go with ye to Loring in exchange for the coin we would have given ye."

Erryn's jaw dropped. Toe's wide eyes matched her own. "You—you will? Why? Why would you do this for me, a heathen?"

Renn swallowed. When she spoke, it was to Toe. "She saved yer life. Ye want to help her, and ye saved mine. I owe it to ye. But if we do this, my debt to ye is paid."

Toe's eyes met Renn's. "Ye don't owe me anything, but I understand."

"Are ye sure ye want to do this?" she said to him.

"I can't turn my back."

"Ye didn't turn it on me." Renn's voice softened. "I can't expect ye to turn it on another."

Toe nodded and patted her arm.

"Do ye accept our proposal, Erryn?" Renn asked.

She shouldn't. She should let them carry on with their lives, not draw them into the madness hers had become. But she wouldn't make it to the temple on her own, and she liked them. "I accept."

Toe's eyes lit up. "I'm curious to see what this temple is all about."

"If it exists." Renn picked up the two bags she usually carried. "Now all we have to do is survive until we make it to Loring."

Toe hoisted the bundled tent onto his shoulders. "We'll need a few days in Stronghaven to find a contract or two and gather what we'll need for the trip."

Erryn slipped her bag off her back and fished through it for her coin pouch. She offered it to Toe. "I was going to buy a lute, but use it for supplies, instead."

Toe's eye caught Renn's. "Ye've hired us for this job. It's up to us to get what we'll need. Buy yer lute. Some music will be welcome."

The two wild folk turned and headed into the forest. Erryn swung her bag onto her back and hurried after them with a spring in her step.

Leaning against the guard tower that stood near Stronghaven's busiest southern gate, Avere bit into one of the two apples a scout had brought her and tossed the other to a hungry child. The boy scurried away without a word or gesture of thanks. Avere had always done the same. Whenever someone had been kind, she'd wondered what they wanted. Some hadn't asked; they'd taken. She'd learned to run away. "Anything?" she said to the Ferret at her side.

"Nothing, from anyone."

Avere nodded and looked up. From the position of the sun, she estimated that she'd watched those entering the city for about five hours. She'd need to eat a hearty meal soon, or her attention would wander. "I'll have to be relieved in an hour, and so will everyone else."

"I'll see to it."

She didn't see him leave. Her eyes remained on the travellers coming through the gate. Not all of them were merchants, or folk arriving for a visit or hoping to find work. Over the past couple of hours, more guardsmen had entered the gates, usually in pairs. A bird carrying news of the assassinations had reached the estate of the highest-ranking local noble. Within the next day or two, he'd ride through the gates and announce the grim news personally.

In addition to the bird that had landed at the Ferret base, birds must have reached Stronghaven, but the officials who'd read the messages had known not to breathe a word without the noble's permission. When the noble announced the news, would he also declare himself king? The guards entering the city didn't have the royal crest on their armour. How many would-be kings would Daros have until one defeated the others? How much blood would run in the streets? And what of the princess? That part of Arrick's message hadn't made sense.

With the king and prince dead, Princess Filmona should be sitting on the throne. Why was she on the run? Were the assassins after her? Had the guard escorted her from the castle to a safer place? No, Arrick's wording suggested that she'd fled, and the bolstering of the local noble's presence in Stronghaven indicated the throne was in play. Avere wished she was in the Royal City, rather than watching people straggle through the gates of a city she hoped never to visit again.

A merchant and his young son walked through the gate, with a boisterous dog on their heels. A couple in a wagon trundled along after them and stopped to ask the guard for directions to the nearest inn with a stable. Three wild folk, likely the ones the scout had glimpsed, strode into the city. Just what Stronghaven needed—more wild folk. Avere's eyes followed them as they passed her position. She stiffened. The one in the hat . . . she wasn't wearing a leather tunic. Hat. No leather tunic. About the right height. Thinner, but that would be expected. *Fyler!*

Her heart pounding, Avere pushed away from the guard tower and followed the trio. When they stopped a minute later, she stepped to the nearest stall that waited to greet hungry travellers and positioned herself so she could watch her prey. The woman with the bag on her back was wearing a filthy cloak, trousers, and muddy boots—and a wide-brimmed hat that hid her forehead. Only two wild folk had camped in the forest, not three.

Ah, one of the wild folk had pulled a coin purse from

his belt. Fyler must be about to pay them for escorting her to Stronghaven. The agreed-upon amount must be substantial—or perhaps not. The wild folk apparently believed in the Seven, but how much did they understand? They were a people of limited intelligence; all brawn, with little brains. Maybe they didn't know what the brand on the heathen's forehead meant, or appreciate its significance.

The wild man dropped several coins into the wild woman's hand and wandered away, leaving the two women behind. Curious. Fyler and the woman walked down the road that led to the travellers' quarter, so named because there was an inn on every corner. Had Fyler hired the wild woman to guard her?

Avere left the stall and melted into the crowd streaming toward the travellers' quarter, her eyes on her prey.

Fi glanced around the crowded common room at the Whistling Pig tavern and hunched over the ale Cedric had set in front of her. According to him, the folk dancing, talking, laughing, and drinking were more subdued than usual, but she didn't believe him. News of the assassinations had perhaps shocked them for a second and made them think about their own mortality, then they'd carried on with their lives. Those here sounded as boisterous as she'd expected—not that she had a lot of experience with taverns and their patrons.

She'd only been in a tavern once before, when she and Erryn had persuaded Henrick to play commoner for an evening and go with them to the mysterious place Father had forbidden them from visiting. The moment they'd stepped inside, Erryn had wanted to leave because the tavern was too noisy for her. But Fi had been fascinated and would have stayed all night, if two guards hadn't approached their table ten minutes after they'd sat down. They'd whispered something in Henrick's ear, and he'd motioned for Fi and Erryn to abandon their ales and go outside. The guards had escorted them back to the castle, but had kept their word not to mention the incident to Father. Fi would have risked it again, but Erryn hadn't wanted to. It wouldn't have been any fun for Fi on her own. Plus, Erryn's presence and support had always bolstered Fi's courage ten-fold. *That's why I have to find you. They want to put me on the throne. We'll have to fight for it.*

Would the bard warbling away in the corner eventually sing of her victory, or her defeat and disgrace? He wasn't singing of the assassinations, but that would come after a respectable mourning period, along with tales of the treacherous princess.

She jumped when Enkelo sat on the bench next to her. Cedric leaned across the table. "I have directions to a safe place to spend the night," Enkelo said.

"Any word from the spymaster?" Cedric asked.

"He's given us a contact in Persh."

"Did he tell you where Erryn is?" Fi whispered. She repeated herself when Enkelo pointed at his ear and shook his head.

"No word about her, so we'll keep moving north."

"Did he say anything about what's happened to the Tolins? I feel responsible for them," she said, feeling she had to explain her interest in the family's fate. "Viren gave his life for me."

"He didn't say."

Fi frowned at her ale. Where was Dann? Was he alive? *Please let him be alive.*

Enkelo caught her eye and smiled. "You'll sleep in a proper bed tonight, uh, Calindra."

She managed to smile back at him, but it made no difference to her whether she slept on a soft bed or the forest floor. A roof over her head and a feather pillow wouldn't take away the endless ache deep inside her.

"We'll continue north on the morrow," Enkelo continued.

"He'll know more by the time we reach Persh, I'm sure of it," Cedric said.

But it would take forever to get there. They couldn't ride on the main roads because they had to avoid patrols, and Fi suspected she was slowing them down. Cedric had insisted she wasn't, but he was being kind. She'd have to try harder, push herself, stop dragging her feet when they walked their mounts through densely-treed areas. She wouldn't find Erryn by letting her grief overcome her. Father would expect her to keep her chin up and behave like a queen, even though she was in a dirty shirt and trousers, and her hair probably had birds nesting in it.

"We should go." Cedric downed his ale and plunked the empty mug on the table.

Fi stood without touching hers and didn't protest when Enkelo lifted her mug and swigged from it. He wiped his mouth and picked up his bag.

They'd left the horses at a stable near the gate, so they followed the directions the contact at the tavern had given them on foot. "Almost there," Enkelo said. "It should be right around—"

"Pardon me," a voice called out behind them. "I wish to speak to you."

Fi whirled. Her breath caught in her throat. Several armoured men strode toward them, swords hanging at their sides. Cedric grasped her arm and pulled her away from them. She turned—and froze. More men, behind them. They were surrounded.

"Stay next to me," Cedric murmured, but he didn't draw his sword.

"What do you want?" Enkelo said. "You're frightening my father and niece."

Two men stepped away from the others and studied them. "What do you think?" one said to the other.

His companion nodded. "It's them. It's the princess."

"The princess?" Enkelo rolled his eyes. "What are you talking about?"

"You are the royal primate, are you not?" the first soldier said. "Don't deny it. I've seen you speak several times in the Royal City."

Fi reached for Cedric's hand, not caring that doing so was improper. He couldn't fight so many men, and she didn't want him to. She needed him, and Enkelo. She hoped they'd hang her first, so there would be two men alive who'd mourn her death, if only for a minute. Either way, she would not die a coward. She squared her shoulders and lifted her chin. "Yes, it's true. I am Princess Filmona." *No.* "I am your queen."

Erryn followed Renn from the tavern where they'd eaten a quick supper. Their next stop would be the rooming house Renn called home when in Stronghaven. Erryn kept her head down as she strode with Renn through one of the city's less affluent quarters. Back in the Royal City, she and Fi had never ventured into areas with filthy children begging on corners, men and women slumped in doorways, their eyes glassy from too much drink, and merchants in alleys enticing folk to buy their dubious wares. A few months ago the poverty, misery, and depravity would have shocked her, but now this quarter was where she belonged. She was one of them. Dirty. Every coin she owned in a small pouch. Alive only because Rodney hadn't bashed her head in for pinching his apples. She wouldn't risk sleeping in an alley here, though. Could a rooming house in this part of the city be safe?

The sun was setting. "How much farther is it?" she asked Renn.

"We're close."

"And you're sure we'll be safe there?"

"I stay there every time we're in Stronghaven. I know the landlady. The doors have locks."

That was hardly comforting.

"Through here." They turned in to a narrow laneway that ran between two shops. A minute later, Renn turned another corner. Another laneway, then another corner, and another laneway. More corners. More laneways. It was a maze.

Anxiety snaked through Erryn. "Don't lose me." She might never find her way back to a road. Even if she decided to risk asking for directions, there would be nobody to help her. She hadn't spotted anybody lurking in the shadows since two, maybe three laneways ago. The absence of chatter, shouts, and clattering wheels was disconcerting. Their footsteps sounded unnaturally loud.

"Not long now," Renn said.

Erryn turned to her. "You said the same thing ten minutes—"

"Someone is behind us," Renn hissed. "Listen."

Erryn tensed. She strained to hear sounds beyond their footsteps, her quickened breath making it more difficult. Then she heard them. Another set of footsteps. No, several more.

"Don't run," Renn murmured. "They're probably taking a shortcut, like we are. I'm just telling ye, so ye know."

"I wouldn't know where to go." Now that Renn had alerted her, Erryn could hear nothing but the footsteps of those behind them. They were growing closer. She reached out to the Fallen. *I may need you.* They were ready.

The laneway was too narrow to call on Cheturrak. Rachagha wouldn't make sense and would draw every guard in the city. She wouldn't ask Quon to fight unless she had to. Iss was better suited to killing by stealth, should the need ever arise. That left Zayvang, Lerxis, and Sath, who wouldn't have much room to maneuver, but might dissuade some men from attacking them.

". . . my lead."

"What?"

"They're drawing closer. Follow my lead."

Before Erryn could respond, Renn dropped her bags and whirled. Erryn slowly turned around. A group of men marched toward them. She recognized the one who led the pack.

"Keep yer bag on," Renn said. "It'll protect yer back. Get ready to call yer pets."

Erryn swallowed. If she didn't already know they were in trouble, Renn wanting her to call the Fallen would have removed all doubt.

The leader of the bounty hunters who'd accosted them earlier that day stopped a safe distance away from them and smirked at Erryn. "How many of the Fallen can help you here? Three or four? It will be ten against five or six." He shifted his gaze to Renn. "Or ten against four or five. My offer still stands, wild woman. I don't know why you're helping this Beast Master. Do your people not know what she is, or are you simply too stupid to understand? Either way, I'm willing to bet you understand a jangling purse." He patted the purse hanging on his belt. "Pick up your bags and go, and this is yours. I promise you that none of my men will touch you. Simply go."

Renn drew her sword.

The leader shook his head. "Why are women always so hard-headed? Stupid, too. She can have a purse filled with coin and live, or she can die, and what does she choose?"

The men behind him snickered.

"Well, Daros won't miss an idiot. Kill the wild woman.

Try to take the Beast Master alive, but if you must, strike her down. Her head will do just as well." His sword was suddenly in his hand. He raised it high above his head. "To victory!"

Zayvang, Lerxis, Sath, come!

The air shimmered. The saber-tooth cat, dire wolf, and humongous bear entered the physical plane. *Sath, show them who you are.* The bear reared and roared. Two in the bounty hunter's group fled, tripping over their own feet to get away. Good. Five against eight.

Three assailants rushed Renn. *Lerxis, help Renn!*

The dire wolf streaked past Erryn. The remaining men, including the leader, charged her. Erryn backed away. She braced herself. Zayvang snarled and leaped in front of her. Two attackers lunged at Sath and jabbed at her with their swords. The bear's powerful jaw clamped down on one man's arm. He screamed.

A clatter drew Erryn's attention. Zayvang lifted her bloody muzzle from the neck of one assailant. Five against six and one cripple. The leader plunged his sword into Zayvang's side. She disappeared. He advanced on Erryn with another bounty hunter. She backpedalled and called Zayvang back. The saber-tooth cat returned and leaped on the hunter, but the leader edged closer to Erryn.

She couldn't see Renn and Lerxis. Sweat trickled down her temple. Her left arm stung, making her spin to her left—toward a hunter, raising his sword. Then Sath was there, bowling him over, ripping into his neck. The hunter managed to plunge his sword into Sath's side, and the bear disappeared. *Sath—*

A cry. *Renn!* Erryn strained to see through the melee. Lerxis was gone. Two men lay on the ground. Renn was on one knee, her upheld sword blocking blows from her only remaining attacker. There was blood on her tunic.

Lerxis, come, help Renn!

A flash of black was all Erryn saw. She stepped back—and hit a wall. She glanced over her shoulder. She'd backed against a stone building jutting into the laneway. *Shit.*

The leader thrust his sword into Zayvang with a triumphant shout, then rushed at Erryn, growling, "You don't deserve to live, filth. For my men!"

She shrank against the building, cringing as he drew back his sword. *May the Seven welcome me, despite what I am.*

The leader's eyes widened. His sword clattered to the ground and he sank to his knees. She sidestepped him as he flopped forward, then stared in confusion at the dagger buried in the back of his neck.

She looked up. Renn was staggering toward her, pain etched across her face. But Erryn sucked in her breath for another reason. *Zayvang, come.*

The saber-tooth cat was immediately at her side.

Protect me. Protect Renn. She went to Renn and winced at the blood seeping from a wound in Renn's left arm. Then she turned her attention to the woman strolling toward them with a dagger in her hand.

The woman stopped about ten paces away. "Hello, Erryn." She looked at Zayvang. "There's no need for this. I just saved your life. One flick of my wrist and Zayvang will be gone, so you might as well send her away now."

Renn gamely raised her sword.

The woman chuckled. "You're in no condition to challenge me. Your arm is injured, and you'd never get near me anyway. I have more than one dagger, but I don't want to throw it at you, or Erryn, or Zayvang. Why would I save her life just to kill you?"

"Ye say ye saved her life, but perhaps the dagger in him was meant for her," Renn said, her voice as thin as a thread. "Ye may have missed."

The woman tutted. "I never miss. Now, we can stand around and wait for the guard to arrive, or we can chat somewhere more private. I suggest you tell Zayvang we're all friends and send her back to her real mistress."

Erryn hesitated, then dismissed Zayvang.

The woman inclined her head. "Thank you. Now take the mercenary's sword from her. I don't want her waving it at me. It's unpleasant."

Mercenary? What mercenary? Oh. Erryn bit back a retort. Right now, she was more concerned about Renn than correcting the stranger who'd come to their aid. "Give me your sword," she murmured. When Renn slowly shook her head, Erryn cursed her stubbornness. "She's not going to kill us." Not yet, anyway.

"Ye're hurt," Renn whispered.

Erryn glanced at her arm. "It's just a scratch. You're the one who's hurt. Give me your sword, so we can go to your rooming house and clean your wound." And Renn could sit down. Her face had lost all its colour. "Let me take your sword. Please."

Renn held it out, blade down. Erryn slipped it from

Renn's grasp. The weapon was lighter than she'd expected it to be.

The woman smiled. "Good. I'll just retrieve one of my favourite daggers and we'll be on our way." She planted one foot on the dead leader's back and grasped the protruding dagger's hilt with both hands. "Where were you going?"

"Who are you?" Erryn said. "What do you want with me?"

The woman grunted as she tugged on the dagger, and staggered back a step when it came free. "My name is Avere. As for what I want with you, we'll discuss that when we're out of this laneway." She wiped the dagger's blade using the man's sleeve and slid it back into the leather sheath underneath her cloak. Then she unhooked the purse from his belt. She whistled. "This is a nice fat purse. He was either a very successful bounty hunter, or his master paid him some coin in advance for your life. A bad investment, as it turned out." She straightened. "Now, where were you going?"

Renn hunched over and clutched her injured arm. Erryn's concern for her grew. "To a rooming house. Can we go now? We need to tend to her wound."

"We'll drop her off there and pay her. Then I'll take you somewhere safe and we'll chat."

Erryn's jaw clenched. This woman would cast Renn aside like a piece of garbage. "Renn doesn't work for me. She's helping me. She stays with me, or we don't chat."

The woman's eyes narrowed. "Renn, is it? You keep strange company. Both of you." She focused on Erryn.

"Very well. Sheathe her sword before you hurt yourself with it, and we'll be off."

It took Erryn two tries to slip Renn's sword into its scabbard. She went to where Renn had dropped their bags. One was splattered with blood. Erryn picked it up. She lifted the second one, but could only shuffle back to Renn and Avere. Three bags were too much for her.

Avere held out her hand. "I'll take one. We'll go back the way we came."

"No," Renn said. "We go to the rooming house. We don't know who ye have waiting for us, where ye want to take us."

Avere rolled her eyes. "I knew you'd be the distrustful type. We don't have time to argue, so we'll go to this rooming house of yours." She took a bag from Erryn. "Lead the way."

Erryn went to Renn's right side and touched her shoulder. "Lean on me, if you need to," she murmured. Renn nodded, but walked using her own strength, as Erryn had expected the headstrong woman would do.

They had to pick their way around two bodies before they were free of the carnage. Some poor townsfolk would stumble across the battlefield and be sickened by the dead men, some with their necks torn open and others missing chunks of flesh. Erryn was getting used to it.

Erryn crouched next to the chair in which Renn was slumped and winced at the ugly gash in the woman's arm. She dipped a cloth into the basin of warm water the rooming house's landlady had brought. She could sense

Avere staring at her. The woman was leaning against the wall with her arms folded. She'd already sighed twice while waiting for the water to arrive. The moment they'd stepped into the small but tidy bedchamber, she'd wanted to talk, but Erryn had insisted that Renn's wound be cleaned first. It would also have to be stitched.

The landlady had sent her son to fetch the local doctor. When Erryn had removed her hat, the woman hadn't commented on the strip of cloth tied around Erryn's forehead. It wouldn't have mattered if she'd heard the rumour that the Beast Master's forehead was branded. Folk expected the heathen to be frothing at the mouth, or summoning the Fallen to tear their children apart. Erryn didn't grunt her words.

"This might hurt," she murmured to Renn. Renn sucked in her breath when the cloth made contact with her torn skin. "Sorry."

"Can we talk while you're doing that?" Avere asked.

Erryn twisted to look at her. "If you like."

"I do like. Where are you going, because you are going somewhere, aren't you?"

Erryn plunged the cloth into the water. Blood gave the water a reddish tinge. She wrung the cloth out and continued to cleanse the wound. "What do you mean?"

"It's a straightforward question. Where are you heading? I doubt you're planning to take up residence in Stronghaven."

She caught Renn's eye. "Why do you want to know?"

"Why are you being difficult?"

"I don't know who you are, why you saved my life, or

what you want from me. You said you'd tell me when we were safe. So tell me."

Avere didn't respond. Erryn focused on Renn's wound. "You're lucky it wasn't one of those spurting injuries," she said to her. "You could have bled to death. It's still deep, though."

Renn barked a laugh. "It's just a nick. I'll be fine."

"But sore for a few days," Avere said. "If you run into more men who want to kill or capture Erryn, will you be able to protect her?"

"What do ye want with her?" Renn snapped. "All ye do is ask questions."

"Oh, thank you for saving our lives, Avere." Avere bowed. "No need to thank me. It was my pleasure."

Renn gripped the arms of the chair. Erryn caught her wrist. "I'm not finished." She raised her voice. "Are you suggesting that you'll protect me, Avere? When we were in the laneway, you turned your back on me when you were pulling your dagger out of the bounty hunter's neck. I could have used Renn's sword."

Avere guffawed. "You don't know how to use a sword, Erryn. It took you two tries to sheathe it."

"I sheathed it after you got your dagger."

"Yes, but you left a sword behind at the camp, the one where you killed the guards escorting you to Rion. You picked it up, but left it, because you knew you'd be useless with it."

Erryn dropped the cloth into the water and stood. She turned to face Avere.

"I've followed you all the way from the Royal City. Well,

I lost you at one point, but I deduced you'd eventually come here."

"Why?"

"I'm a Ferret."

A Ferret? How could Avere be on her side? "You work for the king."

"I did work for the king, indirectly. I don't know who'll be pulling the strings next."

"What do you mean? Are you no longer a Ferret?"

Avere blinked at her. "I'm sorry. I should have realized you don't know. The news hasn't reached the common folk here, and you've been on the road."

"Know what?" Erryn asked quietly.

"I'm sorry I have to tell you this. The king is dead."

Erryn blinked at her. "What? How?"

"He was assassinated, along with Henrick and—"

Erryn's heart pounded. The room spun. She sank onto the end of the bed. "What about Fi? The princess. Princess Filmona."

"I don't know how she is. I—"

"What do you mean, you don't know?" Erryn shrieked. "You know about the king. You know about Henrick. How can you not know about Fi?"

"The message I received was short. It said the princess is on the run."

"Why? Is someone after her? If the king and Henrick—" Her voice choked off. It was monstrous. The king had treated her kindly, almost as his own, until . . . And Henrick. They hadn't been close, but he'd always treated her respectfully. "The princess is the heir. She should be on the throne. What did the message say, exactly?"

Avere dug into her purse and pulled out a sliver of paper. She gave it to Erryn. "Read it for yourself."

Erryn went to Renn and held the paper so they could both read it. It consisted of two lines: one was gibberish, but above it someone else had written *King and prince assassinated. Princess on the run. Kill the Beast Master.* Kill the Beast Master? Erryn expected Renn to shoot up from the chair, despite her arm. Renn's face was scarlet, but she didn't move. She also wasn't looking at the paper. She was—Erryn suddenly understood. "King and prince assassinated. Princess on the run. Kill the Beast Master," she read aloud, for Renn's benefit.

Renn started to rise. "Get behind me," she growled.

Avere rolled her eyes. "Sit back down. You're in no condition to face me, and there's no need to. If I was here to kill her, do you think I would have shown you the message? I've had ample opportunity to plant a dagger in Erryn. I haven't." Her voice softened. "And I'll have you know that this is the first time I'm disobeying the man who gave the order."

Erryn wanted to ask why, but she had a more pressing concern. "The message could be referring to Princess Surann." In which case, Fi was on the throne. Should Erryn return to the Royal City and throw herself at Fi's mercy?

"If the message was referring to Princess Surann, it would have said princess by marriage. That's how we refer to them. Princess for Princess Filmona, and princess by marriage for Princess Surann."

Then what had happened to Surann? Was she also dead? Erryn handed the message to Avere and paced. "We need to find the princess."

Avere's eyes flashed. "No. We have no idea what the situation is, and you're on your way to somewhere, aren't you? I've asked you several times where you're going. Wherever it is, it's important that you get there."

"I can go there after we've found the princess."

"For some reason, the princess has fled the Royal City. There are signs that Daros is on the verge of a civil war. Nobles will fight for the throne. Of course, that raises the question of why the princess has been usurped. I'm sure a courier is carrying a letter to me that will answer all our questions, and rumours will soon reach Stronghaven, but I won't be here to listen to them. Wherever you're going, I'm going with you."

Again, Erryn had a more pressing concern than to ask why. "The princess would only flee if she's in danger. If she's not on the throne, then something is terribly wrong. She needs our help."

Renn snorted. "Why would we help the princess? It doesn't matter which soft bottom is on the throne. It won't change anything for us."

Avere's eyes widened. "You don't know. She hasn't told you."

Renn frowned at Erryn. "Told me what?"

Erryn swallowed. She should have been honest with Renn and Toe. They'd helped her when few would, had fed her, travelled with her, and would now risk their lives for her. She'd only recently earned Renn's trust, and that meant something to her. "I didn't think it was important," she began.

Renn's eyes were as hard as flint. "Didn't think what was important?"

Erryn's stomach knotted. Why hadn't she told the truth from the beginning?

Avere let out an exasperated sigh. "You're travelling with the king's foster daughter, Renn. Erryn's name may be Fyler, but she's a Lyos. She cares about the princess because they're sisters. Foster sisters, yes, but as close as blood sisters, from what I understand."

Renn's expression didn't change. Erryn wished it would, so she'd know what Renn was thinking. "I'm sorry. I honestly didn't think it was important. I should have told you."

Renn looked away.

"It doesn't make sense to waste time scouring Daros for the princess," Avere said. "You have to forge on to wherever you're going, and you don't owe the Lyoses any loyalty. You were never truly one of them. They accepted you while you behaved, but the moment you disgraced them, they branded you and threw you away. Do you think the king would have done the same if it had been Henrick, or Filmona? No, he would have found a way to protect them. He certainly wouldn't have made a mess of their forehead, that's for sure."

Fi wouldn't have cast her out. Fi had visited her in the cells, had risked the king's wrath to bring her willow bark.

"I'm going to ask you again, where are you going?"

"To Loring," Erryn said, the handful of words on a slip of paper having drained her of any desire to keep information from Avere. The king, Henrick, and probably Surann were dead. Fi was alive, but . . . "If I wasn't a Beast Master, I would have been with Fi."

"And perhaps dead." Avere moistened her lips. "Why are you going to Loring?"

Erryn shrugged. "I'm looking for a temple."

"A temple? Why?"

"I don't know."

Avere was silent for a moment, then she unhooked a book hanging on her belt. "I have something to show you." She opened the book and thumbed through its pages, then held it out so Erryn could see inside it. "This looks like a temple."

Erryn peered at the drawing. It could be a temple, but she failed to see the significance. "What is this book?"

"I'm not sure. It belonged to a member of a cult that believes Beast Masters are blessed by the Seven."

Erryn gaped. "Really? How do they define 'blessed'?"

Avere chuckled. "How do you know about this temple?"

"Someone told me another Beast Master was trying to reach it. I don't even know if it exists."

Avere's brow furrowed. "Another Beast Master. There's more than one of you?"

"No. This was in the past."

"You don't know why this other Beast Master was going there?"

"No."

Avere turned back several pages. "Look at this one."

Erryn looked at the drawing of . . . Zayvang. What did that arrow mean? And was that a brick, or a slab?

"Do you know what it means?" Avere asked.

"I can see it's Zayvang. Otherwise, no."

Avere moved her thumb across the page. "There's the symbol for Zhikinden."

"Well, she is Zayvang's mistress." Something Erryn tried not to think about. "There's a skull, too."

"Yes. The cult member mentioned something, or someone, called Death."

"Do ye belong to this cult?" Renn said.

Avere looked past Erryn. "Of course not. What would make you think that?"

"Ye seem to know a lot about it. Maybe ye're the cult member."

"No."

"Yet ye're offering to help a Fallener. Why would ye do that?"

"A Fallener . . ." Avere brightened. "Oh, you mean a Beast Master. Why are you helping her?"

Renn shook her head. "I asked ye first."

"Oh, we're playing games." Avere snapped the book shut. "Let's just say I'm keeping an open mind about Erryn. Perhaps we shouldn't accept what the Primacy says about her. Perhaps things aren't what they seem to be." She raised her brows. "Your turn."

Renn didn't hesitate. "She saved Toe's life—twice. And mine."

"Toe?" Avere's face scrunched up. "Who, or what, is Toe?"

"He's her business partner," Erryn said.

Avere snorted. "You mean there's an adult male in Stronghaven who voluntarily answers to the name of Toe? Let me guess. Her other business partners are named Fingernail and Elbow." She didn't wait for anyone to reply. "This cult member thought it was of vital importance that you reach your destination. She knew you would feel compelled to go somewhere. She wouldn't tell me where, though."

Probably because she'd trusted Avere as much as Erryn did. "Ask her what the drawings in the book mean."

"I can't. She's dead." Avere hooked the book to her belt. "I don't know what to make of what she said, so I'm keeping an open mind. I do know that you'll never make it to Loring without help."

"Yer help," Renn stated.

"You've seen what I can do."

"Toe and me are going with her."

"Where is this Toe?"

"He's taking care of some business and, uh . . ."

"Visiting the local brothel. I see. What is your plan?" Avere asked.

"Toe's looking for contracts we can run to Loring. Me and Erryn will get what supplies we need for our travels. We'll leave when we're ready."

"I'm going with you."

Erryn looked at Renn.

"You need as many as you can get to protect you," Avere

said to Erryn. "You were almost killed today. I know you were outnumbered, and I'll admit you fought well," she said, jutting her chin toward Renn. "But Renn won't be in top form for a couple of days, and you can't hang around in Stronghaven. Given what just happened, the guard knows you're here. You must leave as soon as Renn's able. You'll be travelling through what I assume will be hostile territory, unless your people also worship Beast Masters." Avere looked past Erryn again.

"No," Renn said.

"Well, then. You need me."

Avere was right, but what did keeping an open mind mean? Erryn suspected that if they reached Loring and found nothing, or the temple turned out to be insignificant, Avere would kill her on the spot. Of course, that would be moot if they didn't make it to Loring.

"I'll follow you regardless of what you say, so you might as well agree that I'm coming along."

Someone tapped at the door. Erryn spun away from it and tightened the cloth that hid her brand. The door opened. "Sorry it took me so long," a man said mildly. Erryn forced herself to turn around. "There's been some trouble not too far from here," the doctor continued. "Terrible business. They say the Fallen ripped apart—" His eyes narrowed. Erryn's heart pounded. "How were you injured?" he asked Renn.

"We saw it," Avere said. "She—the Beast Master—was coming after us. We barely got away. The woman's an animal."

Erryn's nails dug into her palms. What did Avere think she was doing? She'd give them away.

"Then it's true. She's here, in Stronghaven."

"Oh, yes. She's here."

"The guard will be searching for her."

Renn groaned. "Can ye take care of my arm?"

The doctor set his bag on the floor and studied Renn's wound. "Good, you cleaned it. I'll do it again and sew you up. Your arm will be right as rain." He reached into his bag.

Avere moved away from him and beckoned to Erryn. "I'll return in the morning," she murmured. "Stay inside. I'll have eyes on this place." Louder, she said, "I must go. Thank you for coming, doctor."

"Mmm," he said absently, his attention on Renn's wound.

Avere slipped out, closing the door quietly behind her. Erryn sat on the bed. Fortunately the doctor hardly seemed aware of her presence. She looked down at her bloody shirt and realized why Avere had told the doctor they'd run into the terrible Beast Master. He wouldn't suspect that the animal was sitting in the same room with him. The woman who'd called the Fallen to rip apart those men was insane. Deluded. Cursed. Hunted.

Fi shuffled down the road with Cedric and Enkelo, surrounded by the clink of armour and boots ringing on stone. She wanted to bow her head, but she wouldn't let her captors see her cowed. How much pain would lance through her when the executioner slit open her belly?

Would she be numb with agony by the time they put the rope around her neck and strung her up in front of a crowd out for an afternoon's entertainment? Would the rope scratch? Would she die immediately after the lever was pulled, or would her feet thrash about and her eyes bulge?

She couldn't bear to look at the two men who'd thrown away their lives for her. What would she see in their eyes? Regret? Fear? These armoured men had thwarted their grandiose plan. Fi should never have gone along with it. She should have known they'd never find Erryn, that they'd be lucky to remain on the run for more than a week.

Stop it. She would not be cowed. Cedric and Enkelo had given her a chance to fight. She hadn't cowered in a prison cell and meekly gone to her death. She'd tried. She'd pushed away her grief and tried. They couldn't capture her spirit. The bloodthirsty crowd would see defiance and pride in her eyes, and so would these men.

She studied the man closest to her. No crest adorned his breastplate. A mercenary company, perhaps. That would mean they were escorting their captives to the nearest guard post. The company's leader would leave his name, and within the next few days these men would be spreading coin about in taverns and brothels, and telling everyone about how they'd captured their supposed queen in filthy rags, her hair straggly and dirty. Let them! The Seven would know these misguided and gullible men had interfered with the succession of Daros's rightful monarch.

They rounded a corner. Fi's breath caught in her throat.

Two guardsmen on patrol strode up to them. "Stay silent," one of her captors murmured. What did he expect her to do? Push her way to the guardsmen and turn herself in? She glanced around. Perhaps while everyone was distracted, she could get away. No, the men stood too tightly together. But when they walked again, she'd make a run for it. Losing her life at the tip of a sword would be easier to bear than the indignities to come.

"What is your business?" one of the guardsmen asked.

Fi stood straight and readied herself.

"We were hired by Lord Kenwood to capture three servants who stole from him," the same mercenary who'd called out to Fi and the others said to the guard. "He would like to handle this matter himself."

Fi gave Cedric a sidelong glance.

"This is a matter for the guard," one of the guardsmen replied.

The mercenary flipped open his purse and fished out several coins. "Lord Kenwood would be most appreciative if you would allow him to mete out punishment. He has plans for the woman."

The two guards gave each other a knowing look. One held out his palm. "Very well. But return to the lord as soon as you can. It's not a good time for a group of armed men to be marching about."

"We'll leave Moss on the morrow." The mercenary dropped the coins into the guardsman's palm. "Thank you, sir."

The two guardsmen moved aside. Fi didn't look their way as the group walked past them. She'd met Lord

Kenwood on several occasions. His estate was in Rion, but close enough to the Royal City that he often attended banquets at the castle. Father should have left him off the invitation lists! Kenwood must want to deliver the treacherous princess and her saviours to the Royal City himself. He'd bask in the glory and ingratiate himself with the primates. Maybe he wanted the throne!

Now that they were moving again, she took a deep breath and prepared to dart away the moment she spotted a break in the mercenaries' formation, but they remained close together. They were certainly a well-trained and disciplined company. The way they held themselves reminded her of those who belonged to the royal guard or a noble's personal retinue. Maybe these men were former guardsmen.

They turned another corner. "Halt," the mercenary who always spoke for the group said. They stopped in front of a plain stone residence. "You three, come with me."

The men in front of Fi parted. With as much dignity as she could muster, she went to the mercenary, wondering who was inside. There must be more men, otherwise it would be three against one. She hadn't looked at Enkelo, but she could sense his tension. If they ended up alone with the mercenary, Enkelo would be on him, along with Cedric.

The mercenary opened the door and motioned for them to go inside. Fi stepped over the threshold and blinked into the dim light. A man stood gazing into the fireplace, the flickering flames illuminating his profile.

"We found them," the mercenary said.

The man turned to face them. Fi's eyes were already filled with tears. Her heart had raced the moment she'd seen him. *Dann.*

Erryn's stomach lurched as she watched the doctor gather up the bloody rags he'd thrown to the floor. She normally wasn't squeamish, but seeing him thread the needle through Renn's skin . . . and that was after he'd poured something into Renn's wound that had made her blanch, and her jaw close so tightly that the veins in her neck had stood out. Renn hadn't made a sound while the doctor had stitched her wound. Erryn wasn't sure if Renn had been brave, or the pain had rendered her speechless.

The doctor rose from his kneeling position. He lifted a bottle of liquid from his bag and handed it to Erryn. "Keep her arm clean. If anything oozes from the wound, clean it with this. If it doesn't help, have Ivy fetch me again." He peered at Erryn's tunic, then his eyes went to her forehead. His brows drew together. "Are you all right? Do you need my help?"

"No, I'm fine," Erryn said, moving away from him so she could set the bottle on a small table next to the bed and hopefully make him lose interest in her. "Did, uh, Ivy give you the coin?"

He nodded.

"Thank you for coming so quickly."

"You get some rest," he said to Renn with a shake of his finger. Then he was gone.

Erryn locked the door. "How do you feel?"

Renn shrugged, then winced.

"You should get into bed."

Renn gave her a weary nod. She slowly rose to her feet. "I'm not bowing to ye," she said.

Erryn tutted. "I didn't tell you because I didn't think it was important."

"It wasn't important that ye're royal?"

"I'm not royal. Not really. You should lie down." She stepped forward to grasp Renn's elbow, then thought better of it.

Renn shuffled to the bed and sat on it, then flopped back. "How did ye end up with the king?"

"My mother died in childbirth, and my father died when I was a baby. Oh, and my mother was a whore, if that makes you feel any better." The king and queen hadn't told Erryn about her mother. She'd overheard several conversations between nobles that were usually accompanied by furtive glances in her direction. They must have wondered the same thing she always had: why had the Lyoses taken her in and treated her as if she were their own daughter? Her father and the king had been friends, but Duke Fyler wasn't the only noble who'd left young children behind after his death. Legitimate children, not bastards. Erryn had never had the courage to ask her foster parents. She hadn't wanted to remind them that she wasn't theirs, but a favour, or an obligation.

"Ye haven't answered my question," Renn said.

"No, I suppose I haven't. My father and the king were close friends. That's all I know. Look, I'm sorry I didn't tell you. I didn't think it was important, and I didn't know how you'd react if you knew. I thought maybe you'd not want to travel with me anymore."

Renn was silent for a moment. "I don't know. At first, it didn't matter who ye were. I didn't want to travel with ye."

Erryn tensed. "And now?"

"Now I know ye better. It doesn't make much difference whether ye're a soft bottom or a royal soft bottom."

Her shoulders sagged with relief.

"I don't trust her," Renn said.

"Avere? Neither do I, but she's right. We're going into hostile territory. The odds are against us." And Erryn was being selfish. "If she's willing to go with me, you and Toe don't have to do it. You don't owe me anything. You must know that—" Her voice faltered. Nobody should risk their lives for her. Some cult thought she was blessed? What other nonsense did it believe? "Our chances of making it to Loring are slim. This isn't your journey."

"Ye'll have less chance with her." Renn closed her eyes. Erryn thought she was going to doze off, but then Renn's eyes opened. "Toe wants to see this through. He needs to. Ye saved him. I want to see it through, too." She pointed at Erryn's forehead. "Was she telling the truth? The king did that to ye?"

Erryn nodded. Avere was right. He hadn't tried to protect her. He hadn't let her live under guard to see if her soul truly was bestial. He'd come into her cell and disowned her. She'd thought—well, she'd known he hadn't loved her, but she'd never considered herself a burden to him. Maybe he'd always wanted her gone. If only the queen had still lived. She might have stayed his hand for a time, stopped him from branding her so quickly.

Renn motioned for Erryn to move closer to the bed. She reached out with her good arm and lifted the cloth hiding Erryn's brand. Erryn closed her eyes as Renn traced the brand with her fingers. Renn's touch was gentle.

"Does it hurt?" she asked.

"No," Erryn said, her throat tight. If Renn didn't stop, Erryn would weep, but she didn't want to pull away. When Renn lifted her hand, relief mingled with disappointment. "You should rest," she murmured.

"When ye get to yer room, lock yer door."

"No. I'm sleeping in here."

Renn frowned. "There's no room."

"I'll sleep on the floor. I can sleep on stone. I can sleep on a wooden floor."

"There's no need."

"The guard might search the rooming house, and every bounty hunter in Stronghaven will know I'm here now. Your arm will hinder you for a few days, and you need rest." Erryn pulled a blanket from one of the bags.

"Toe and me were thinking ye can't sleep inside. Ye never slept in the tent."

"I don't like to feel confined," Erryn said, glad her back was to Renn. "Given the choice, I'd rather sleep where I can easily get away."

"Ye're more exposed outside."

But she always slept where there was room to call several of the Fallen without attracting too much attention. Ever since she'd sat in the dark through that final night at the tavern in Moss—she didn't want to think about it, nor did she want to explain why she wouldn't sleep in this rooming house if Renn wasn't here and hadn't vouched for the landlady. She didn't want to tell Renn why sleeping outside wasn't as safe, but felt safer.

"I have to avoid talking to folk as much as possible," she said, hoping Renn would leave it at that. She turned around when Renn didn't reply, and smiled to herself. Renn's eyes were closed again. This time, they wouldn't open so quickly.

Erryn spread the blanket on the floor at the foot of the bed, but sat in the chair. She was too keyed up to sleep, so she'd watch the door for a while. If anyone bashed it open and threatened Renn, she wouldn't hesitate to command Zayvang to rip his throat out.

Avere stood in Renn's room with her arms folded, waiting for Erryn and the two wild folk to pick up their bags and hoist bundles onto their shoulders. Every guard and bounty hunter was searching for two women, one of them wild. Three women and a man should have an easier time of reaching the northern gate, and the Ferrets had lined the pockets of the two guards watching it for the next few hours. A runner had already informed them that a woman matching Avere's description would be passing through with three associates and wasn't to be stopped. The guard would assume they were moving stolen goods or illegal substances. They'd never suspect that the Ferrets were protecting the Beast Master—or rather, one Ferret was. Hopefully Arrick wouldn't be too upset when he received her message. She could have lied to him, and if it had been anybody else, she wouldn't have hesitated to do so. But not Arrick.

The strange trio she'd travel with had stayed in Stronghaven longer than she would have liked. She'd tried to persuade them to leave sooner, especially when Toe had arrived and announced he'd secured a lucrative contract for them to run, but they'd insisted on remaining in the city until Renn's arm was well on its way to mending itself, in case she needed the doctor again. At least Avere had managed to convince them that Erryn and Renn must stay out of sight in the rooming house. She and Toe had gathered the supplies they'd need. She didn't trust him, but she didn't mind him, either. He was an easygoing sort who was good at haggling and patient with surly merchants.

Part of her—the adventurous part that relished a challenge—believed they'd make it to Loring. The other part, the practical part with its feet firmly planted on the ground, would always have an escape plan in mind, including how to get away if she decided to thrust a dagger into Erryn's gut. She wasn't disobeying Arrick. She was merely delaying carrying out his order until she had more information. For now, she was entertaining the possibility that Malina had been right. On the morrow, she might conclude that Malina had been a ranting madwoman and rid Daros of the Beast Master who walked it.

Her travelling companions stood ready to depart. "Ye don't have to come with us," Renn said.

Avere could hear the hope in Renn's voice. "You're right, I don't. But I am. So let's go, shall we? We want to reach the gate while my friends are still on duty."

She pulled open the door and motioned for everyone to leave ahead of her. When Erryn walked through the doorway, Avere's fingers twitched. *Not yet.* She was in control of when the Beast Master would breathe her last. The moment Avere no longer entertained Malina's beliefs or it became clear that Erryn was becoming a beast, she'd end the Beast Master's life. If she had to kill the two wild folk as well, so be it.

Loyalty and Lies

Avere almost drew a dagger when a bird burst from its hiding place within the leaves of a tree. She glanced at Erryn and Renn as it flew away. Their eyes were on the bird soaring through the sky. How much longer would they have to sit around the firepit in a hunters' camp, waiting for Toe? He was on foot. They'd decided horses would make it more difficult to avoid wild folk, so Avere's horse was in its stable in Stronghaven. The Ferret who'd promised to care for the filly had better be exercising her daily.

She peered into the surrounding trees and listened for signs that they weren't alone. Uneasiness snaked through her, even though she didn't see or hear anything. She wasn't afraid of Erryn. The heathen wasn't a coward, but she wasn't aggressive. Avere had watched the brawl in the laneway, had observed that the girl wasn't a natural fighter. She'd only fought to defend herself—or rather, her pets had. Why had the Seven cursed—or blessed—Erryn with the ability to call and command the Fallen? Avere would have expected them to choose someone more suited to the role. They'd done her a favour. She didn't have to worry that her neck would be torn to shreds as she slept, or worse, that Iss would pay her a nocturnal visit.

Now Renn, she was a different matter. She was the one keeping Avere's fingers close to a dagger. The woman was unpredictable. Avere hated unpredictable. Renn often deferred to Toe, but he wasn't here. Had she remained behind to protect Erryn from the newcomer they didn't trust? Avere hadn't thought about it at the time, but now she realized they hadn't discussed who would venture into the nearby settlement to try to find out the general location of any nearby hunting parties. Toe had announced he'd go alone, and nobody had protested.

"Why didn't you go with Toe?" she asked Renn, who was sitting across the firepit, next to Erryn. "When we have to split up, it would be better if we travelled in pairs."

Renn's face tightened, but she remained silent.

Avere stifled a sigh. Talking to the woman was a chore. "I understand why Erryn couldn't go, and I wouldn't have been the best choice. People prefer to deal with their own kind. You should have gone with him."

Erryn turned to Renn. "Maybe you should tell her." "Tell me what?" Avere asked in a level voice.

Renn stared at the cold firepit. "My people won't deal with me."

"Why not?"

"Because they cast me out. I'm clanless." Her voice dropped. "I'm shamed by the Snowlake clan."

Avere blinked at her. "Why? What did you do?"

Renn lifted her head. Her eyes were as hard as flint. "I killed someone. A friend."

A shiver ran down Avere's spine. Curse Malina! If it wasn't for her, the heathen would be dead and Avere would be on her way back to the Royal City, not sitting here with a Beast Master and a wild woman who wouldn't hesitate to run her through for no good reason. "Why did you kill your friend?" she asked as casually as she could.

"That's not yer concern. I killed him. That's all ye need to know."

Avere looked to Erryn, but she shook her head. "Oh, so I'm to be left in the dark?"

"I don't know, either," Erryn murmured. "Neither does Toe. Just leave it be."

The reason didn't matter, anyway. Renn had probably slain her friend while in a drunken stupor, over something stupid. "Why didn't you tell me about this before we left Stronghaven? I thought I'd be travelling with two wild folk who could talk their way past their kinsmen. Instead, I'm with one woman the wild folk will want to kill on sight, and another one they'll want to spit on."

"Ye didn't have to come," Renn said.

Yes, Renn would love to see Avere abandon their misguided and likely doomed journey to Loring and the temple that might not exist. *What am I doing here?* She should have finished Erryn back in Stronghaven without speaking to her. Avere had befriended targets before. Killing those whose trust she'd gained was extra satisfying. Witnessing their sense of betrayal as the light left their eyes was delicious. But the heathen wasn't what she'd expected. Erryn only harmed those who threatened her. Despite her ability to call the Fallen, she was powerless. Avere usually killed the rich, the powerful, the depraved.

Most would argue that Erryn was depraved, but only because the Primacy and its Holy Texts told them so. Malina had opened Avere's eyes to another possibility, but the zealot could have been wrong. If Erryn revealed another side of herself on their journey, or the temple didn't exist, Avere would end her life. For now, she'd continue to keep an open mind and couldn't deny her curiosity about what they'd find when they reached Loring.

"Did your clan mark you, like the king did to her?" she said, jutting her chin toward Erryn. "I don't see anything, but perhaps they marked your palm, or . . ."

Renn shook her head.

"Then you could have gone with him," Avere said, brightening.

"When we meet for the first time, we always greet each other with our names. I am Renn, shamed by the Snowlake clan."

"Yes, but you wouldn't introduce yourself that way."

Renn's brow furrowed.

"For the love of the Seven, don't tell me you would!"

"I would dishonour myself if I didn't."

Avere moved her fingers closer to a hilt. "I'm not

going to be killed because you won't lie about who you are. You've been cast out by your own people because you don't have any honour, so what's one little lie?"

Renn's eyes flashed. "I still have my honour."

"And I'd like to keep my life. Do you want to get Erryn to Loring, or not? What's the point of escorting her there if you'll deliberately antagonize the first wild folk who spot you? We all need to do whatever we can to keep her safe. If we run into any wild folk, you will lie. Anything else would be stupid."

Renn leaped to her feet. "We didn't ask ye to—"

A whistle cut through the heavy air. When Avere drew a dagger, Renn motioned for her to sheathe it.

Toe emerged from the bush, casting a cursory glance at those waiting before saying, "We should head northeast. A group is tracking a bear to the north, and there are hills to the northwest." His brows drew together. "Did ye run into trouble?"

Avere smiled. "No, no trouble. We were just discussing what we'll do if we encounter any hunters. We all know what we'll need to do to survive." She gazed at Renn. "Don't we?"

The wild woman slung her bags over her shoulder and tromped away.

Arrick frowned at the message he'd decoded, then read it a third time. *With Fyler. She may not be what she seems. Letter on the way. Will be out of touch for a bit.* Did Avere mean the Fyler girl wasn't a Beast Master? How could that be? She'd summoned Zayvang on a crowded road, used the Fallen to kill three guardsmen, and fled Persh on Quon's back.

He pushed back his chair and paced his study. Avere had never disobeyed him, never questioned him, never given him a reason to doubt her loyalty. She must have a good reason for staying her hand, but Arrick couldn't come up with a single explanation that made sense, despite turning the problem over and over in his mind. Was she in the Beast Master's company, or shadowing her? Were they in Stronghaven? How was he supposed to misdirect Enkelo's group and navigate the choppy waters the assassinations had created if he didn't know where they were?

Avere should know better. She must have received his message about the assassinations and understood how volatile the situation was in the Royal City. Just this morning he'd received an invitation to meet with the grand primate. A spymaster would pass through the gates to the Primacy's estate and walk the hallowed ground, something that would have been unimaginable before the assassinations. Otane wouldn't dare leave the safety of the estate and come here. Emotions were running high. The guardsmen spent much of their time breaking up fist fights between those who believed the princess was innocent and those who wanted her to hang. Some were uneasy with the Primacy's regency. Those who spoke out against it were quickly silenced. Darroth's people were angry, afraid, and confused. All it would take was one spark.

Regardless of where Avere was, she would have sent

her message before she'd received his letter explaining why the princess wasn't on the throne. She wouldn't know he was flirting with the hangman's noose and one slip could be fatal. He couldn't afford to be distracted, so he'd have to do what he'd always done: trust her. She'd never failed him. This time had better not be an exception.

He snatched the message from his desk and flung it into the fire, then whirled toward the door when someone knocked on it. "Yes?"

The door opened. Evan, one of the royal guard captains, stepped into the study. "Thought you'd want to know that Lord Gentry's wife and children just arrived at the castle, requesting refuge. Lord Gentry was killed last night, and it wasn't an accident."

Arrick's jaw clenched. It was starting.

Fi listened to the discussion taking place between Enkelo, Cedric, Dann, and Terry, the mercenary leader who'd turned out to be a captain in the Tolins' personal guard. Everyone had assembled for this meeting, but the four men sitting around the square table were the only ones who spoke.

". . . need to move," Terry was saying. "We can't stay holed up here forever. I've no doubt they'll eventually conduct a house-to-house search."

"We were heading north," Enkelo said. "We should continue that way."

Terry shook his head. "No. There's nothing up there but wild folk. We need allies. We're not the only ones who want a Lyos on the throne."

"We need an army, yes, but we have another matter to attend to first."

"What other matter?"

"Obeying our queen," Cedric said. Everyone in the cramped room turned to him. "Our queen has lost her family. She wishes to find her closest surviving relative."

"Who will likely be after the throne," Terry said, his voice climbing.

"Not this one. She wants to find Erryn Fyler."

"The Beast Master?"

A cacophony of voices assaulted Fi's ears.

"What purpose will that serve?"

"That's the worst thing we could do. We'll need the Seven on our side if we're to put her on the throne."

"She'll be an animal by now!"

"I thought the heathen was dead."

Fi's shoulders hunched. She should speak up, silence them, announce in a commanding tone that she was the queen and they must obey her without question. But it was difficult to feel regal and behave like royalty in rags, when hunted, and when asking men to risk their lives for something that only made sense to her.

Dann slammed his fist on the table, then did it again when the protests continued. "Silence!"

The men settled down, but Fi could feel the tension in the air. Dann gazed at her. "Is that what you want, my queen?" he asked softly. "Do you want to find Erryn Fyler?"

Fi forced herself to look at him. They'd hardly said two words to each other since she'd stepped inside this house. Men were sleeping wherever they could find a spot on the floor; they were tripping over each other. She'd been offered her own bedchamber, but she'd insisted that Cedric and Enkelo share it, partly because she couldn't in good conscience have an entire room to herself, and partly because she was afraid to sleep alone.

Even if she could manage a private moment with Dann, what would they say? The grief in his eyes mirrored her own. She'd asked after Dann's family, but all he knew was that his parents had been alive when he'd rushed to the Tolin estate after the assassinations. He'd then fled at his father's urging. The whereabouts of his other brother were unknown. Viren had been torn apart on the rack. Father, Henrick, and Surann were dead. Surann's screams frequently intruded into Fi's thoughts and dreams. Even if it wouldn't be completely inappropriate for her to want to close her eyes and lean into Dann for comfort, it would be impossible. Right now, the stone in her chest was incapable of feeling anything but sorrow.

"My queen?" Dann said.

She straightened and held his gaze. If she wasn't to falter, she would speak only to him and not think about the men who didn't know her. "You lost a king, prince and heir, and a beloved princess. I lost my father, my brother, and my sister-in-law. I never expected to be on the throne. I expected to marry, and to support my husband, my father, and Henrick, and for my children . . ." Her voice choked off. She took a moment to compose herself. "For my children to be loved and spoiled by their grandfather and aunt and uncle. They're all gone."

She swallowed. "I have a foster sister who is a true sister to me in all but blood. I need to know if she's alive."

"Why?" Dann asked. "Perhaps that would be a silly question if she weren't a Beast Master. But she is."

"Because she's the only close family I have left. You're all willing to risk your lives to put me on the throne, so you deserve the truth. I witnessed the brutal murders of three people I loved dearly. I should be angry. I should thirst for vengeance. I should want to seize the throne and use every resource to find those who killed them. But I feel nothing. My spirit has been crushed. Opening my eyes in the morning can feel like a chore. How can I rally troops when I can't rally myself?" Fi blinked back tears and kept her eyes on Dann. "Not knowing how Erryn is faring, whether she's alive or dead, weighs heavily on me. I need that weight lifted if my spirit is to have any hope of recovering."

The silence in the room was deafening. Dann rubbed one of his eyes. He looked older than his twenty years. Fi wasn't the only one wondering about loved ones. Maybe her request was selfish, but if she were to give rousing speeches and implore men to sacrifice their lives so she could claim the throne, she needed to know what had happened to Erryn.

"What if we find out she's dead?" Dann asked.

Then all hope would die. Would she be capable of encouraging men to fight for her? She didn't know, and she didn't want to ponder a possibility she couldn't handle. She had enough trouble dealing with the present. What she could say with certainty was that she couldn't carry the day while her heart and mind longed to know whether Erryn was alive. "Then I'll know, and the weight will be lifted," she said to Dann.

"She could be alive but not herself."

"I know."

"May I speak plainly, Your Grace?" Terry said.

Fi nodded. "Of course."

"We have a difficult road ahead of us. We need every advantage we can muster. We need the Seven's blessing. Finding the Beast Master could bring down their wrath."

They didn't understand, and maybe they were right, but Fi had to find Erryn. There was no hope for Father, Henrick, and Surann, but there was still hope for the woman she'd grown up with and considered a sister. Fi could still save her. She held her head up and swept the room with her gaze. "Do any of you not believe me when I say I didn't kill the king, the prince, and the princess? Do any of you not believe me? Speak up now."

She met the eyes of Dann's men one by one, and was pleased to see that none were staring at their feet or avoiding her gaze. "You won't suffer any consequences if you believe me to be an assassin."

"We wouldn't be here if we believed you were responsible, Your Grace." Terry raised his fist into the air. "For the queen!"

"For the queen!" came the thundering response.

Fi's voice grew stronger. "Then listen to me. The only other people in the study room with us when . . . when they were struck down, were primates, and who was quick to seize power? The primates are also the ones who tell us that Beast Masters are cursed by the Seven. I'm not suggesting the Holy Texts are wrong or that we shouldn't listen to the Primacy. Many within it are good men." She looked at Enkelo, who nodded to acknowledge her words. "But last time I spoke to my foster sister, she was herself, fully herself, despite admitting that she had been summoning the Fallen for months. She may still be herself. I respect the Primacy and have never had reason to doubt the Holy Texts. But when it comes to Erryn, I have the opportunity to see with my own eyes whether what they teach about Beast Masters is true. I will not assume."

"May I ask for the primate's opinion on the matter, Your Grace?" Terry said.

"Of course." She turned to Enkelo. He'd grudgingly supported her when she'd first stated that she wanted to find Erryn. Showing him up in front of these men would be an act he wouldn't forgive or forget.

Enkelo cleared his throat. "I believe we need our queen at her best and must support her in every way we can. If finding Erryn will bolster our queen's spirits, then we must find her."

A diplomatic and acceptable answer. "Thank you, Primate." Fi already felt brighter than she had when she'd awakened. "I am a Lyos. I have the Seven's blessing, and I want to find my sister. Not the Beast Master. My sister."

"And if she isn't herself?" Dann asked gently.

Fi understood; he was preparing her for the worst. The men would agree to her wish, but they needed a concession in return, and a difficult but necessary one. "You have my word that if we find her and she's not herself, we will do what has to be done." Her chest tightened. She'd just given them permission to kill Erryn if her soul truly was bestial. Putting her out of her misery would be the right thing to do, but it would sear Fi's soul, all the same. *Please, Erryn, be alive, and you.* She couldn't bear to lose her.

"We need the people to rally behind you, Majesty," Cedric said. "If we find Erryn and you wish her to travel with us, she'll have to stay out of sight. You cannot openly associate with her."

"I understand, Cedric. I don't know what will happen if—when we find her alive and well. We may decide it would be best for her to remain on her own path. But I would know she's alive and herself, and that will help me greatly."

"Then I say we find Erryn," Dann said. "We have to keep moving, anyway."

Cedric scratched his beard. "We should split up. We don't want to attract attention. One group can go with the queen while the other approaches potential allies."

Terry shook his head. "We should all remain with the queen. Protecting her life is paramount."

"We can best do that by keeping her in the shadows. She doesn't dare reveal her whereabouts when we have so few men."

"Cedric is right," Dann said. "Let a small group go with the queen. The rest will go to those we have reason to believe will join us." He met Fi's eyes. "I will go with her."

A lump rose in Fi's throat.

"If we're to sway men to our side, we'll need someone

associated with the queen." Terry twisted to Enkelo. "Perhaps the royal primate?"

Enkelo stiffened. "My place is with the queen, especially since we'll be seeking the—Erryn. And if you'll forgive me, Your Grace, your emotional attachment to your foster sister, while understandable, could cloud your judgement. I understand that you'd like to see with your own eyes how she fares rather than accepting the Holy Text's teachings, but you may need my guidance when deciding her fate."

Fi bit back a retort. She couldn't afford to irritate anyone in the room. Enkelo had agreed to find Erryn, a major concession for him. She must compromise as well. She drew breath to say she agreed, but Cedric spoke first.

"I'll go with the other group. I've met many nobles at the castle. They know me."

"No, Cedric," Fi cried. "I need you with me."

"You'll have good men with you, Majesty. I can serve you better by persuading others to join our cause. Do you trust me to speak for you?"

"Of course I do," she said quietly.

"Then it's settled."

Dann nodded. "Terry, you'll go with him. The queen, royal primate, and I will take two men. We'll leave on the morrow."

The discussion turned to gathering supplies and which noble to approach first. Fi only half listened. She was losing Cedric, a tangible link to Father and a trusted advisor. But she'd have Dann. She'd fled the Royal City with two men who'd die for her. Now there were three.

Erryn sat on the trunk of a tree felled by age and watched Avere drink from a stream. The cool breeze nipped at her skin, making her shiver. She pulled the fur Toe had bought for her in Stronghaven around her shoulders. Last night, she'd slept in the tent. She trusted Renn and Toe, and she doubted Avere would try to kill her before they reached Loring. If she was wrong, sleeping outside the tent wouldn't save her. One throwing dagger would send Zayvang back to Zhikinden. A second dagger would cut Erryn's throat.

Her jaw clenched. By the time Avere came for her, Toe and Renn would be dead. Erryn couldn't allow that to happen. If they reached Loring and nothing was there, she'd have to strike first. The thought made her stomach roil, but she would not allow Avere to take Toe and Renn's lives.

She jumped when Renn sat next to her, her mouth pressed into a thin line. "Ye need to listen and be ready. Hunters could be nearby."

"Sorry. I was thinking." And she'd be useless at it, anyway. Renn, Toe, and Avere would hear or see hunters long before she did. The one who was supposed to be a beast would be the last to sense the predators.

Renn frowned. "What's the matter with ye? Ye've been quieter since we left Stronghaven."

"I'm worried about Fi. The princess."

Renn's gaze went to where Avere was standing. "She was right. Ye can't help the princess. She could be anywhere."

"That doesn't stop me from worrying about her."

They lapsed into silence.

"What's a Ferret?" Renn blurted. "I know what a ferret is, but what did *she* mean by it?"

"You didn't know and it's taken you this long to ask me?" Erryn turned to Renn and wished she could take back her words. Renn's face was red. "The Ferrets are the king's—or the queen's—spy network. Avere's a spy." While they'd waited in Stronghaven for Renn's arm to heal, Erryn had told her about saving Fi from the assassins, being thrown into the dungeon, and being escorted to Rion, supposedly to be exiled from the Royal Province. "She must have been sent after me when I killed the guards. If not for that religious zealot and her book, I'd be dead. She would have killed me in the laneway."

"She may still kill ye."

"I know. I was just thinking that when we get to Loring . . ." Erryn couldn't say it.

"I'll do it for ye."

"No. I can't ask you to kill for me."

"I would be doing it for me and Toe, too."

She should have known Renn would reach the same conclusion about Avere. "Let's not be hasty, though. It will all depend on what we find and how she reacts."

Renn grunted.

Erryn knew that if it were up to Renn, Avere would already be lying dead in an alley back in Stronghaven. Erryn wouldn't make her swear to stay her hand until they agreed it had to be done. Renn was her own woman. She couldn't trust Avere, Erryn couldn't trust Avere, Avere didn't trust them . . . Erryn longed for the days when her only worries were about what to wear, whether to sneak out of the castle with Fi, and who the king would choose to be her husband. The latter matter had been of great concern, but not a life-threatening one.

Toe, who'd gone off to answer a call of nature, sauntered over to the bags. Renn started to rise.

"I've been worried—thinking—about something else, too," Erryn quickly said. She hadn't meant to tell Renn, but suddenly wanted to.

Renn sat back down. "What?"

"Back in the laneway when I summoned the Fallen . . . I usually command them by picturing in my mind who I want them to protect or attack. But everything happened so fast, I just said your name. They knew. They knew who you are."

"They're not animals. I'm not surprised they understand ye when ye speak to them."

"Me, either. I've always spoken to them, but I've never told them your name."

"Ye used them to save me and Toe. I was the only one there they'd seen before."

"That could be it," Erryn said, not convinced. The Fallen hadn't hesitated, hadn't stopped to survey the battlefield and pick Renn out. They were intelligent, but—

Renn leaped to her feet. Avere had a dagger in her hand. Erryn cut through her thoughts and reached for the Fallen.

"We see ye, and we have arrows pointed at ye," someone shouted. Several wild men emerged from the bush, their bows drawn. Erryn thanked the Seven that her hat was firmly on her head.

"We're hunting here," a man with an ugly scar running down his left cheek growled. "Ye need to find somewhere else."

Toe lifted his hands in a gesture of surrender. "We're not hunting, we're passing through."

The scarred man sneered. "Ye have to eat."

"We left a village not too long ago. What's yer name? I am Toe, of the Snowlake clan."

"My name isn't yer concern. Ye stink of the city, and ye have two city folk with ye. Game is scarce enough without ye poaching. Go back to where ye came from. Next time, a stray arrow might find ye."

"Poaching?" Toe snorted. "Ye sound like a city lord."

"Ye've been in the city too long. We've claimed this area. Go back to yer soft bed, and take yer wench and the two soft bottoms with ye."

Erryn glanced at Renn. Her face was taut, but she didn't reach for her sword. Avere stood as still as a statue, her eyes darting from one wild man to another. Her dagger was still in her hand, but she'd lowered it.

"This will be yer only warning. Others will let their arrows speak for them." The scarred man jerked his head in the direction of the bush. The wild men backed away, their bows still drawn.

When Erryn could no longer see the men, she waited for someone else to speak. Avere broke the silence. "Apparently that's the friendliest welcome we'll receive. I'm not liking our odds of getting to Loring in one piece."

Everyone huddled around Erryn and lowered their voices. "It's worse than I thought," Toe said. "I'd heard the stories, but . . ." He shook his head.

Erryn wanted to crawl into a hole. They were out here because of her.

"We still have a ways to go." Toe looked at Renn. "We need the support of the clans, or we'll never make it."

"They won't help us," Renn snapped. "A Fallener? And me?" She cocked her head toward Avere. "And her? Ye're the only one they won't spit on."

"We need the Mothers to mark us." Toe's mouth twisted and he looked to where the hunters had melted back into the bush. "Even hunters like them wouldn't dare harm those who are marked."

Renn shook her head. "They won't help a Fallener."

"They might hear us out. We can explain where we're going, show them the book." Toe jutted his chin toward the book hanging from Avere's belt. "Tell them the Fallener might be able to help heal the sickness that's afflicting the land."

Renn's eyes widened. "It's not true! Why would we—"

"It could be true," Avere said. "My cultist friend mentioned the problems you're having. She believed the trouble will travel south, and east and west, until it reaches every corner of Daros. She believed Death is responsible, and that the Fallener plays a role in keeping Death in its place."

"You mentioned this Death before. What do you mean?" Erryn asked.

Avere shrugged. "Someone or something that opposes the Seven, I think. I'm not sure, to be honest."

"Why are the Seven allowing the land to sicken?" Renn said. "Why aren't they stopping it? Why would they need Erryn?"

"I'm not a primate, Renn. If I was, I certainly wouldn't place my hope in Erryn. But what if she's a Fallener because the Seven wish to use her in some way?"

"That's not what the Mothers—our priestesses—teach." Toe gave Erryn an apologetic look. "I don't mean to offend ye. I'm just telling ye what the Mothers believe."

"I know." Erryn surveyed her companions and drew a deep breath. "I wish I could make it to Loring on my own, so I wouldn't have to drag you into danger with me."

"But you can't," Avere said, "and we're not the only ones risking our lives. You are, too, and I think you'll have to take the biggest risk of all, for us to make it to Loring alive."

"What do you mean?"

"I agree with Toe. We need the support of someone out here, and your clan is our best bet," she said to him. "But we need to hedge those bets. I propose that we approach your clan and tell them we're escorting the Fallener to Loring on the chance that she can reverse the withering of the land and its creatures. If it turns out she can't, they can kill her."

Renn sucked in her breath. Erryn's heart raced, but she instantly knew she'd agree. If the temple didn't exist, or it didn't reveal that she wasn't the cursed being most believed her to be, then why go on living, running, sleeping rough and looking over her shoulder? Let them end her life. There would be nothing for her to look forward to.

Toe's mouth dropped open. "We can't make that promise. If ye heard the stories about the last Fallener, ye wouldn't. Ye couldn't . . ."

Avere gazed at Erryn. "I promise you that if it comes to that, I'll give you a swift death. You have my word." She looked at the two wild folk. "You two must promise the same, in case I can't do it for some reason. We agree that we won't give her to them. One of us will do it."

"No," Renn said fiercely. "We help her get away."

"If we make the deal and then cross the clan, we'll never make it back to Stronghaven." Avere grimaced. "I don't care what you'll want to do when it's time to part ways, but I'll want to get back to civilization."

"Then we don't make the deal."

"No, Avere's right." Erryn stood, feeling lighter than she had for some time. Avere's proposal could work. More importantly, it would increase Renn and Toe's chances of survival. She wanted them to live, to return to Sull and run contracts. "Offering me to them might be enough to persuade them to help us."

"Or they could kill ye the moment they know what ye are," Renn said.

"We'll have to take that chance." Having her companions ally themselves with the clans and against her, albeit for show, felt right. If the journey to the temple proved futile, only she deserved to die. She would accept her fate. It would mean never seeing Fi again, but she'd known in her heart that Fi was lost to her the morning she'd ridden through the castle's gates with the guards escorting her to the Rion border. Seeing herself with the princess again, browsing in the bazaar, whispering at a banquet, or up on the castle wall gazing at the stars, were fantasies. She would never be anything but a liability to Fi. It was time for her to grow up, to face reality and stop being selfish.

"Are ye sure?" Renn asked.

"Yes. It makes sense, Renn." Erryn swallowed. "I'll understand," she said, hoping to calm the apprehension in Renn's eyes.

Avere nodded. "Then it's decided."

"What about me, Toe?" Renn said. "The clan . . ."

Toe blew out a sigh. "I don't know. I'm hoping they'll care more about the Fallener and not give ye trouble. But they could refuse to deal with ye, or travel with ye." His voice dropped. "It could be dangerous for ye. They won't kill ye, but if ye end up on yer own . . ."

Renn barked a laugh. "I'd meet ye in Loring. I'd be waiting for ye."

Toe's eyes brightened. "We have to get to the clan first. That won't be easy."

"Then we'd better be on our way," Erryn said, with renewed determination. The prospect of being thrown to a wild folk clan shouldn't have bolstered her confidence, but it had. It was a plan, and one that would get her what she wanted, no matter what happened.

Erryn's stomach churned as she crept through the trees behind her companions. They were nearing the Snowlake clan stronghold. This could be her final hour on Daros. She should be afraid, especially since she didn't know if she'd go to the Seven. What would happen to her soul? Would she be snuffed out? If that was to be her fate, she wouldn't know. Nor would she suffer a painful and prolonged death. She was suspicious of Avere's motives for travelling with them, but she trusted the Ferret to honour her promise if the clan seized her.

Avere had displayed her skill with her daggers as they'd carefully wound their way through the forest, skulked along trails, and crawled through bush. They'd fought with aggressive hunters twice. Avere's daggers had always struck true, taking out any archers before Renn and Toe crossed swords with those still alive. Killing those they encountered didn't sit well with the two wild folk, but Avere had convinced them that merely knocking the hunters out would be dangerous. The moment they came around, they'd track those who'd bested them.

If they'd only encountered two groups of hunters, Erryn would have questioned why they needed the Snowlake clan's help. But they'd eluded over a dozen, and had avoided tussling with several others because the hunters had fled at the sight of Zayvang, Lerxis, and Sath.

She stopped moving when Toe held up his hand. "This is as far as we go," he whispered. "I'll approach the clan."

"Alone?" Avere said.

"If they don't agree to our proposal, it will give ye a chance to do what ye have to do," Toe said, avoiding Erryn's eyes.

"If that happens, we'll go to Loring," Renn said.

"No." Erryn's tone was firm. "We'll be outnumbered. They'll never stop hunting us. If you see them coming for me, I want you to do what you promised," she said, meeting Avere's eyes. "And then run. Go back to your lives." She turned to Renn. "I mean it. Anything else would be throwing away your life."

Renn shook her head and touched Erryn's arm. "I said I'd help ye get to Loring."

Erryn had the sudden urge to grasp Renn's fingers and squeeze them. She had to get through to her, make her see that she'd already fulfilled an obligation she'd never had. "You've done all you can. I'd release you from any obligation you feel you have to me, but you promised to do this for Toe, right Toe?" She pleaded with her eyes for him to follow her lead.

"Ye're no longer in my debt, Renn," Toe said gruffly. "If the clan won't help us, then we've done all we can."

"You'd better go." Avere glanced around. "There may be scouts. The longer we're here, the more vulnerable we are."

Toe nodded. "Give me the book."

Avere frowned. "What?"

"The book. They'll want to see it."

Avere hesitated, then unhooked the book from her belt and handed it to him. "I want it back. It belonged to a friend."

"Ye'll get it back." Toe tucked the book under his left arm. "I don't know how long I'll be." He grimaced. "When I come back, I won't be alone."

"How will we know if they're coming to help?" Avere asked.

"If they're coming to kill the Fallener, I'll shout, 'The Fallener must die.'"

"What if you're not with them?"

"I'll be with them. They'll want me to lead them to ye." Toe touched Erryn's arm. "I will do everything I can."

Erryn managed a smile. "You have a way with folk. If they'll listen to anyone, it will be you. Now go." A lump formed in her throat when he squeezed her arm. She watched him creep into the bush, then looked around for somewhere to sit.

"Thank you for getting me this far," she said to Renn and Avere. "I'm going to go sit over there, with my back to you. Please leave me be."

Renn swallowed. "Toe's a good talker. He'll convince them."

"I'm sure he will," Erryn said, figuring the odds were about even. She nodded to Avere, then went to a fallen trunk and perched on it. She took off her hat and rested it on her knee. She wouldn't hide who she was, not now, not when she may never stand up again.

"You won't feel a thing," Avere said.

Erryn didn't turn around. *Good-bye to you, too.* She gazed at nothing and thought about Fi, and their antics as children, the castle, the life she'd expected to have, Rodney's kindness, and her surprising friendship with Renn and Toe. And the Fallen. They were never far from her mind. If she could, she'd call them all right now and take comfort from their presence, and their love. If she died today, they would have to wait years before they'd be summoned into the physical plane and experience a precious few moments of freedom. Knowing they'd eventually have a new master, someone else they'd obey and love, brought tears to her eyes and hurt her above all else.

Toe entered the Mothers' hut and waited for one of the three women to acknowledge him. He'd thought his years of dealing with city folk and those who'd left the strongholds would make him feel out of place here, but when he'd walked through the gate, it was as if he'd never left. He was his own man now, but the clan's spiritual leaders intimidated him as much as they had when he was a boy. He tightened his grip on Avere's book. Erryn's life depended on him convincing the Mothers that they shouldn't order the clan's hunters to kill Erryn on sight. Lale, Zheir, and Asha would decide whether Erryn would live or die.

Asha. Something *had* changed. When he'd decided that running contracts would suit him better than tracking the same game as ten of his kin, Asha had been learning how to hunt. The sullen girl he'd known had never spoken of donning a Mother's robe. He'd expected her to join those who were leaving the stronghold and its traditions behind. But she looked at peace sitting cross-legged on the floor, stitching two hides together, the flame of a nearby candle casting a glow on her smooth skin. Zheir and Lale's hands were also busy. Did the Mothers know he was here? He knew better than to clear his throat.

He hadn't run into trouble when he'd approached the stronghold. When scouts had challenged him, his voice had been strong when he'd answered them. "It's Toe, your kinsman, here to commune with the Mothers."

"Toe?" one had shouted back. "I was wondering if ye'd ever come home."

Home. He felt at home in Stronghaven and travelling the trade routes, until he returned here.

"Toetril," Zheir said, her hands still moving. "Ye've returned."

"I have," Toe said.

Asha glanced at him. "Welcome home."

He looked at Lale and wasn't surprised when she remained focused on her sewing. Would she ask, or deny herself?

Zheir put aside her sewing and pushed to her feet. "Ye're always welcome here. Ye're our kin. But we haven't seen ye for some years. Why have ye come?"

Toe's mouth felt dry. He swallowed and shifted his weight. "I need the clan's help."

Zheir's brows rose slightly. "Syl told us she saw you in Stronghaven last year."

Toe remembered. He hadn't recognized her at first when she'd called out his name in a shop. Fortunately Renn hadn't been with him—not that Syl and those who'd journeyed with her would have challenged her. Not in the city, where everyone had to abide by city law. The worst they would have done was ignored her.

Meeting his kinsfolk in the city had saddened him. There was a time when the Snowlake clan would never have sent its people into the city to trade, but game had been plentiful then, and bellies full.

"She said ye were still running contracts," Zheir said.

"I am."

"Then why would ye need the clan's help? Nobody here does city work."

There was no reproach in her tone. Twenty years ago, she wouldn't have looked at him. Toe met her eyes. "I'm travelling with someone, someone who saved my life twice. She's on her way to Loring. I'm escorting her there. But the way is treacherous. Ye must know some kin are hunting kin."

Asha's head jerked up. Zheir's face clouded. "Those who hunt human prey are no longer our kin."

"Even more reason to fear them. We've avoided those we can, but we've had to kill others, to protect ourselves."

Zheir's expression didn't change.

"It's still a ways to Loring. The farther north we go, the less game there is and the more desperate they are. We're only four. We won't make it to Loring unless ye mark us."

"These kin who kill human prey are not honourable. Our mark may not stop them, and won't stop an arrow unleashed from afar."

"It will stop some, and if ye allow a few scouts to travel with us, they could help us stay out of range of any arrows. And the mark will help in Loring."

"This woman . . . is she the shamed?" Lale asked. Her hands were still.

"No, but the shamed is one of the three with me."

Lale's head dipped. The needle in her hand rose and fell again.

Asha shifted her position to face him, but didn't stand. "This woman who must go to Loring. Is she shamed from another clan?"

"No."

"Then she must be city folk. Otherwise she would ask for our help herself. She wouldn't send ye."

Toe nodded.

"Why would a city woman want to go to Loring?"

Toe had been sure his own kin wouldn't slay him, but now that it was time to speak of Erryn, doubt knotted his stomach. "I need ye to listen to what I have to say before ye judge me."

"What have ye done, Toetril?" Zheir asked quietly.

"Nothing." He gathered his courage. "The woman I'm travelling with . . . she's a Fallener."

Asha's eyes bulged.

"A Fallener?" Zheir said, her voice shooting up an octave. Lale's attention was still on her sewing, her hands still busy. "Why would ye travel with a Fallener?" Zheir shrieked. "Why would ye lead her to us? Ye would make the Seven's anger burn brighter than it already does. What has she done to ye?"

"Nothing. I told ye, she saved my life twice. She isn't an animal."

"She has done something to ye. She has twisted yer mind."

"No."

"Then why would ye want to help her? Ye should have run yer sword through her the first chance ye had."

"When I met her, I was too busy fighting with slavers who tortured and killed one of our men, burned our wagon, and would have killed me and enslaved the shamed," he said, glancing at Lale, "if she hadn't helped."

"How did she help? Did she call them? The Fallen?"

Toe wanted to answer her, but the words wouldn't come. Zheir interpreted his silence as affirmation. "Ye have brought shame on us! Do ye have any understanding of how sickened the land has become? Why do ye think our kin are so desperate that they abandon their clan and kill anyone who could deny them food?"

"We've asked the Seven why they are displeased, why the withering of the land has grown so much worse over the past few years." Asha's voice was tinged with shock. "We've begged them to tell us. Then we learned that a Fallener walked the land. Every time the Fallen enter our realm, the Seven punish us. How could ye travel with her and bring her here? How could ye turn yer back on the Seven? It's bad enough that ye work and travel with the shamed. We overlook it because we know how sick the land is, and ye were in the city, doing city work. But now ye're travelling with a Fallener?"

"Ye should have killed her," Zheir roared. "Because of ye, we have no hope now."

"We killed the last Fallener. If that earned us any favour with the Seven, it didn't last. The land still sickened," Toe pointed out.

"Falleners are cursed by the Seven. They were pleased

when we offered them the last one. They're allowing the land to wither because we've offended them in some other way." Zheir squared her shoulders. "We must act quickly. We must offer the Fallener to the Seven. Take us to her. Show us that ye respect the Seven, that we shouldn't punish ye for what ye've done."

Toe took a deep breath. "Sacrificing her may not be wise. She can help heal the sickness in the land."

Zheir snorted. "What madness is this? What has she filled yer head with?"

"She wasn't the one who made the claim. The other city woman I travel with believes the Fallener is here to help us," Toe said, stretching the truth. He didn't know what Avere believed, nor was he sure about what he believed when it came to the book he held and a temple in Loring. But he never doubted his eyes and ears. Erryn wasn't a beast. She called the Fallen when she had to defend herself or her friends. She was never the aggressor, and she had a good heart. The stories he'd heard about Falleners were a lie. Could he explain why the teachings that had been passed down from generation to generation vilified Falleners? No. He also couldn't deny what he'd seen with his own eyes. "When I met the Fallener, she told me she had to go to a temple in Loring. Something is there, something that could stop the sickness."

Asha's brow furrowed. "A temple?"

Toe nodded. "The other city woman, she had this book that shows a temple, and the Seven blessing a Fallener."

"Show us this book," Zheir snapped.

Toe handed it to her. Zheir scowled and opened the

book. Her eyes widened. She flipped through the pages. "Where did the city woman get this?" she asked urgently.

"From a friend. Some religious zealot."

Asha stood and peered at the book. Her brows shot up. She exchanged a look with Zheir. Lale didn't move.

"Leave us, Toetril." Zheir's voice sounded strained. "Wait outside."

When he reached the door, Toe glanced over his shoulder. Zheir and Asha were bent over the book. Lale was rising to her feet slower than she used to, and now he could see the gray streaking her hair. The years were racing by and would eventually leave her behind. Stubborn woman.

Outside the hut, Toe rocked on his heels and greeted those who passed him. Shock jolted through him when a child ran by and he didn't recognize her. In his mind, nothing had changed in the stronghold since the last time he'd visited. Returning here had shattered his timeless memory.

He smiled when a childhood friend approached and clasped his shoulder. Their conversation didn't take his mind off the Mothers, whose attitude had changed the moment they'd opened the book. He hadn't been forced to offer them Erryn's life if she couldn't heal the land. Had the Mothers recognized the drawings in the book? If so, then it couldn't be a Fallener in the drawing of the Seven bestowing a blessing. If it were, the clans would respect Falleners, not view them as cursed monstrosities.

They'd made a mistake, coming here. The book wouldn't save Erryn. The Mothers wouldn't believe she could help save the land. He could leave the stronghold and warn her, but he wouldn't. The battle had reached the point where only survival was possible, not victory. He'd already risked much by approaching the Mothers on Erryn's behalf. He'd done all he could. He wished he could do more, but—

Zheir emerged from the hut. Toe swallowed when Asha joined her, and then Lale. Toe's friend nodded to the women and quickly excused himself. Toe turned to the Mothers and tried to appear relaxed, but he could feel the tightness in his jaw. The women's expressions were unreadable. Zheir still had the book and was clutching it to her chest as if afraid of losing it.

"We will help ye," Lale said.

Toe gaped at them.

"If a Fallener is to enter our stronghold, she must do it under our watchful eye. Ye'll return to her now. Zheir and eight hunters will go with ye."

Toe mutely nodded. He was so surprised and relieved, he would have agreed to anything.

Still sitting on the tree trunk with her back to Renn and Avere, Erryn stiffened when she heard them whispering. *Don't think about it. When it happens, it'll be quick. I won't even know.* But her assurances failed to stop her hands from shaking. Her chest felt as if Cheturrak were sitting on it. She couldn't breathe and pulled on her shirt collar. She wished she had a lute to strum, but she hadn't wanted to trouble Toe and Avere with buying one while she'd remained holed up in the rooming house with Renn. They'd had more important supplies to gather.

Suddenly she felt warm, but it wasn't her skin that burned. The warmth was inside her, comforting and soothing. It calmed her fear. Tears stung her eyes. The Fallen. They'd be with her when she took her last breath. They never left her.

"They're coming," Renn hissed.

Erryn closed her eyes.

"Hunters and Zheir." Renn said. "And Toe."

"Who's Zheir?" Avere asked.

"One of the priestesses. To us, they're the Mothers."

"What does it mean that she's with them?"

Silence, then, "They come to talk."

"Are you sure?"

"Toe isn't shouting, and if they were coming to slay us, a Mother wouldn't be with them."

"I'm not turning around until we're sure," Erryn said, her eyes still squeezed shut.

"I agree," Avere said. "Wait until they reach us."

Erryn strained to hear footsteps. Minutes dragged by. Just as she was wondering if Renn and Avere were hallucinating, a voice made her jump.

"Which of ye is the Fallener?" a woman asked.

Erryn opened her eyes, stood, and turned around. Her breath caught in her throat. A group of wild folk stared at her. She could feel their hostility, see it in their hard eyes. They were itching to strike her down. She counted them. Eight hunters and a robed woman who must be the priestess Zheir. Why were they looking at her? The

Fallener could be Avere. Then she remembered that she'd taken off her hat. "I'm the Fallener," she murmured, not wanting to appear afraid.

Zheir studied Erryn's forehead, then turned to Toe. "Ye didn't mention that." She approached Erryn, at first tentatively, then when Erryn didn't move, boldly.

Erryn forced a smile. "I'm not—"

The blow to her head took her words away and made her ears ring. She staggered back a step, then a second blow drove her to her knees. She raised her hands to protect her head.

"What are ye doing?" Toe shouted. "Ye said ye'd help."

Someone grasped Erryn's hands and jerked them down and behind her back. They bound her wrists with a scratchy rope.

"Ye said ye'd help," Toe said again, this time less forcefully. Erryn could hear the bewilderment in his voice. Her heart raced. *Calm yourself.* There was still Avere and her daggers. She'd promised.

"She's a Fallener," Zheir said. "I know ye trust her, but we don't."

"Are you going to kill her?" Avere asked. Erryn tensed, even though she knew Avere wouldn't throw a dagger right now. She'd wait until she could escape from the others.

"We might, but not yet."

Erryn slowly raised her head. Zheir looked down at her with disgust.

"Ye had to ask which one of them is the Fallener," Renn

said with a sneer. "Ye couldn't tell, because she's not what ye thought she'd be."

Zheir ignored her and looked over Erryn's head. "Get her on her feet."

Hands grasped Erryn's arms and hauled her upright. Avere met her eyes and winked.

"I could take yer blades, but I won't," Zheir said to the others. "We haven't come to hurt ye."

"Taking our blades wouldn't do you any good anyway," Avere said cheerfully. "Do you think binding her hands will stop her from calling the Fallen and having them rip every one of you to shreds? You're what, eight and an unarmed woman? If we decide to turn on you, we're three and a Fallener. I saw her," she pointed at Renn, then jutted her chin toward Erryn, "and her pets fight off eight men." She grimaced. "And trust me, you wouldn't have wanted to see the bodies they left behind. She really doesn't need us. The Fallen against you?" She snorted. "How do you think that would turn out? Have you seen Cheturrak?"

Several hunters glanced apprehensively at each other.

"But you see, you don't have to worry, because she only ever calls the Fallen when she's being attacked. I suppose you're very lucky that she showed restraint when you rudely smacked her head," she said to Zheir.

Erryn wanted to snap at Avere to hold her tongue. She wouldn't be able to call the Fallen if she was dead. These hunters didn't need much encouragement to run her through.

"I'm not telling you this to frighten you, but to point

out that if she was the animal you think she is, she would have called the Fallen when you struck her. But she didn't. I'd think about that, if I were you."

Renn nodded. "Ye acted more like an animal."

Zheir's eyes bulged. She gestured to the hunter closest to her. He unsheathed his sword and warily stepped toward Renn. "Renn!" Erryn shouted. Renn reached for her sword.

"Don't!" Toe yelled.

Panic surged through Erryn. She wouldn't allow them to cut Renn down. She cried out to the Fallen, desperately wanting to unleash them, then gritted her teeth. She couldn't . . . release . . . them. She couldn't . . . She slowly exhaled when Renn drew her sword, turned it around, and offered it to the hunter. A second hunter, who'd started to circle behind Renn, took it.

Relief made Erryn's shoulders sag. She would have expected Renn to stand with her clan, even though they'd exiled her. She wanted to tell her how much her support mattered and how much she wanted Renn to live. Renn mustn't die for her. She mustn't.

"I won't fight ye," Renn said through clenched teeth. "Just as she isn't like ye think she is, neither am I. I—" The air went out of her when the hunter in front of her punched her in the gut. Erryn's jaw clenched. *No*, she said to the Fallen, as much as she wanted to call them.

"Do not disrespect the Mothers," the hunter growled.

Renn doubled over and coughed, then straightened and glared at him. He reached for the rope hanging from his belt, but Zheir shook her head and turned to Avere. "Ye gave Toe the book."

"Yes, I did," Avere said.

"We have questions for ye." She shifted her attention to Erryn. "We won't harm ye, and ye won't bring the Fallen into our midst."

Erryn nodded, despite her fear. She could sense the loathing under the forced civility. Avere had better be ready with her daggers.

Zheir looked down at Erryn's hat. "Put that back on her," she murmured. "And remember to keep this to yerselves. We want her alive—for now."

One of the hunters who'd grasped Erryn's arm plunked her hat on her head and pulled it down over her branded forehead. She gave Erryn's back a shove. Erryn stumbled forward. As the group marched to the stronghold, Renn fell back to walk near Erryn, but didn't speak to her.

Fi read the notice nailed to the board in Persh's main square and turned to Dann, who was beside her. Duncan, one of the two Tolin men travelling with them, stood a few feet away, keenly watching those strolling past or stopping to read the news from Darroth. Enkelo and Mason, the second Tolin man, had gone to meet the Ferret contact they'd been given in Moss. Fi had wanted to go with them, but the men had insisted on going alone. "It could be a trap, Your Grace," Enkelo had warned. "You and the duke must not expose yourselves unless it's absolutely necessary."

"I'm not the duke," Dann had mumbled. "My older brother may still live."

Fi's stomach knotted. Jared wasn't on the list of executed traitors she'd just read, but that didn't mean he was free. He could be rotting in the castle's dungeon.

"He's not there," Dann said brightly, but his shoulders were hunched.

She wanted to touch his arm and tell him there was still hope, but how could she give him what she didn't have? She wanted to be kind, not dishonest. She wasn't at court. She would likely never be at court again.

"I feel ashamed," Dann said.

"Why?"

"Because not seeing him there . . . I'm relieved, but also dismayed."

"I know it's difficult, not knowing." They moved away from the board to let others have a closer look. "I feel the same about Erryn. I desperately hope she's alive, then I'm almost certain she's not."

"She was here."

Fi smiled wanly. "Yes." They'd heard about her escape on Quon's back, but that had only deepened Fi's fear that Erryn was dead. Those telling the stories described fire shooting from Quon's nose and fur on the backs of Erryn's hands. Fi suspected they were only tall tales. Bards would exaggerate and embellish here as much as they did in the Royal City. But the gist of the stories were likely true. Run out of town by guards? And all because of the mark on her forehead. Anger surged through Fi. Guilt quickly eclipsed it. *I'm sorry, Father. I know you felt it was the right thing to do.* But it meant Erryn would never be safe unless she learned how to survive in the wild. And then what? Never saw anyone? Lived like an animal? Was she still alive?

"I need to find her because she'll tell me the truth," she said to Dann. "She won't be concerned with what I'll do for her if I take the throne. She can't be. There's little I'll be able to do for her. Which is why this is so selfish, to her, and to you and your men."

"May I tell you the truth?" Dann asked softly.

She swallowed. "Please do."

"She's probably dead."

Fi's eyes welled up, not because of Dann's words, but because she could share her burden with him now. "I know. So you see how selfish I am, forcing you and the others to chase after her. But I have to know, Dann. I need to know."

"It's not selfish. You won't be able to take the throne and rule with it hanging over you." Dann looked back at the notice board. "I understand."

She nodded. "We'll find out what happened to your brother, I promise you. As for the throne . . . I don't know if I have the stomach for it."

"But you'll fight for it. You can't let them get away with it."

"Who? I still have trouble believing the Primacy was behind it." Fi blew out a sigh. "I'll take it back for Father and Mother, and Henrick and Surann. It won't be for me. Perhaps eventually it will be, but right now I can't seem to care and I know I shouldn't feel that way, but—" She drew a shuddering breath. "I shouldn't be telling you this, especially when you have your own worries."

"Of course you should tell me," Dann said gently. "You have to appear strong before everyone else, but not before me. I know that here, inside," he tapped his chest with his fist, "you're always strong."

Her throat tightened. "Thank you," she whispered.

"We'll find out what's happened to Erryn. If she's alive, she'll remind you of why you must reclaim the throne for you."

Fi nodded. If Erryn was still alive. If Erryn wasn't a snarling animal. If Erryn still cared, after Fi had done little to help her. If Erryn was dead . . . Fi would never be able to tell her how sorry she was.

Dann's eyes met hers. "I want to tell you something."

Fi tensed. Her feelings for him were still there, but grief and sorrow prevented them from soaring. It was too soon after the assassinations and Viren dying on the rack. To seize any joy or happiness would feel selfish. Guilt would taint every touch and heartfelt word. Guilt that she'd survived, that she was here, speaking to the man she'd coveted while the man she was betrothed to had died on the rack, protecting her. In her darkest moments, she wondered if the assassinations were her punishment, but that was selfish too, thinking so many good people had died to teach her a lesson.

"Terry, my captain," Dann said, bringing Fi back to their conversation. "He's my half-brother. My father's son."

Fi was surprised, but not because Dann's father had strayed. She wasn't naïve. "Viren never told me."

"They weren't close. Terry's only a year older than I am, so he's always been there for me. I've always known."

"Does your mother know?"

"Yes."

This time Fi wasn't surprised. Had Father ever taken a mistress? She didn't think so, but then, he would never have let her know. She was certain she didn't have any half-brothers or half-sisters she didn't know about. Nobles kept their bastards close, as the Duke of Tolin had, and Father had never remarried after Mother had died. He could have. Early on, everyone had expected him to, but he never had.

"I didn't want to mislead you into thinking that I'm in the same situation as you are with Erryn, that Jared is my only surviving brother."

For a second, her gratitude and love for him banished the darkness. He understood that Erryn was her sister. The lack of a blood connection had never made a difference to Fi. "Promise me something."

Dann's brows drew together. "What?"

"Promise me that no matter what happens, you'll always be honest with me. I mean it. I need someone who'll tell me the truth—in private."

"I'll always tell you the truth, Fil—Calindra, and not because I'll want something from you when you reclaim your rightful place."

"If you wanted something from me, you wouldn't

always tell me the truth." Her desire to take his hand made her clasp her hands together. "I appreciate—"

She stepped away from him when she heard Enkelo's voice. "What news?" she asked him.

"She's headed east," Enkelo said.

"East? I thought the spymaster said she was heading to Stronghaven."

"He said he thought so, but he's sent word that she was spotted in Bexley."

"Then we go to Bexley," Fi declared, eager for them to be on their way. "She's alive!"

"We don't know how old the information is," Enkelo cautioned her. He looked at Dann and grimaced. "I'm afraid there's other news."

Dann's Adam's apple bobbed. "Jared?"

"No, your father. I'm sorry, but I'm afraid he's with the Seven. It was peaceful. He was never arrested."

"Only because they knew he was on his way to the Seven and innocent, though I suppose they still could have interrogated him." Dann's voice cracked. "Perhaps they haven't lost every shred of decency they had."

"I'm sorry," Fi murmured.

"I expected it," Dann said, but his eyes were dull and his voice flat.

Fi wanted to comfort him, to take him into her arms and hold him. But it would feel dishonest. The numbness brought on by her own shock and grief would prevent her from sharing his pain. They were both wounded, both limping through their days. Perhaps one day their love for each other would help them heal. Today, it only hurt.

Erryn's skin crawled as everyone followed Zheir through the stronghold's gate. She was surrounded by hunters and Toe kept shooting her reassuring looks over his shoulder, but the wild folk guarding the gate had stared at her with hostile eyes. Now that they were inside the stronghold's tall walls, more eyes were upon her. If not for her hat, it would be worse. The wild folk watched their kin escort a prisoner, some breaking off a conversation to ogle, or stopping in their tracks to crane their necks. Without the hat, they would see more than a city woman with her hands bound. If one of the hunters next to her suddenly knocked her hat off her head, would Zheir be able to prevent a mob from tearing her limb from limb?

Occupied with her thoughts, she almost bumped into the hunter in front of her when he stopped walking. He stepped to his left. Now she could see three priestesses standing shoulder to shoulder, gazing at her. "Does she speak?" the older one asked.

Someone snorted. Erryn glanced to her right. It hadn't sounded like one of the hunters or Toe, so it must have been Renn or Avere.

"She does," Zheir said.

"The Fallen?" the younger priestess asked, her voice uneven.

"She hasn't summoned them."

The older one's eyes glinted. "Still. She can't walk freely among us."

"She has been marked, on her forehead."

"Ye didn't tell us about this," the older one said to Toe.

She spoke to the hunter nearest to her. "Ye will take the shamed to the pen."

"Is that necessary?" Toe asked. Renn's lips parted, but she didn't speak.

"Ye know it is," the older one said. She looked past Erryn. "Ye, and ye, go with them. If she gives ye any trouble, beat her."

Renn gaped. "Ye cannot mean it."

The older priestess turned her back to Renn. The two others quickly followed suit. Renn stared at them, then shook her head. When one of the hunters who was to escort her grasped her arm, she jerked it away from him. "I won't give ye any trouble," she spat.

Erryn tried to catch Renn's eye when she marched past, but Renn's eyes were downcast and her face crimson. Erryn wished she could tell her that she had nothing to be ashamed of, and that she had two friends who'd always stand by her. As she'd said to Toe some time ago, she could relate to how it felt to be an outcast, despised by your own people.

The priestesses turned and faced her again. "Ye will also go to the pen," the older one said. She shifted her gaze to one of the remaining hunters. "Drop those bags ye're carrying and take her."

"Should we put her into the pen with the shamed?" the younger priestess asked. "If she summons the Fallen, the shamed would be trapped."

"The shamed travels with her, the shamed can die with her," the older priestess said.

"Renn is my friend," Erryn said, compelled to speak up for her. "She has nothing to fear from me."

The older one's eyes flashed. "Take her," she snapped.

"Should I go with them?" another of the hunters said. "If she calls the Fallen—"

The priestess barked a laugh. "Here, in the stronghold? She has shown she still has her wits about her. But Doran, ye go as well."

Unlike Renn, Erryn didn't jerk away when one of her escorts grabbed her arm. As she walked away from the group, she heard Zheir say, "Come with us," presumably to Toe and Avere. What did Avere make of all this? Did she regret coming with them, rather than burying a dagger in Erryn's heart back in Stronghaven?

On the way to the pen, she kept her eyes forward. What she could see reminded her of a village, but with thatched and wooden huts instead of stone buildings, and none had a second or third floor. When a boy and girl ran up to her, their eyes filled with curiosity, the hunter shouted for them to move away. He clapped the girl across the head when she was slow to obey him. Erryn wanted to look behind her to see if the girl was all right, but she was worried about her hat falling off.

Eventually no huts dotted the side of the dirt trail they were walking. It led to what Erryn guessed was a makeshift arena. A roughly circular area of dirt was surrounded by wooden benches, and the end of one bench was splattered with blood. Did they fight each other here?

In the distance, on the other side of the dirt arena, stood a solitary wooden hut. As they approached it, Erryn could see only a single tiny window. One of the hunters drew back the iron bolt that barred those inside the pen from escaping. He swung open the door and pushed her inside. She stumbled and fell to her knees. If her hands hadn't been bound, she would have regained her balance, but instead momentum propelled her forward. She fell flat on her face and grunted, the air knocked out of her. The door slammed shut. Erryn blinked into the dim light.

Unable to push herself away from the ground, she struggled to stand up, but couldn't. She rolled to her side, then back onto her stomach when Renn said, "I'll untie ye." Erryn felt tugging at her wrists, and then they were free. She pushed herself to her knees and looked around. A fire burned in the pit in one corner. Now she could also see several bedrolls. "Is this a prison?" she asked Renn.

"No. Young ones hoping to hunt come here to meditate before their time in the ring, for their initiation, but sometimes it's used to keep someone away from the clan. Not very often, though." Renn looked away from Erryn. "Not many are shamed." She went and sat in front of the fire.

Erryn could tell that Renn wasn't in the mood for conversation. She decided to watch the fire too, but from a distance. She lowered herself onto a bedroll and hugged her legs to her chest. That she was trapped in here wasn't panicking her yet. The fire helped, but what about food? How long did the priestesses intend to keep them here? When would they see the sun again? When they finally came for her, would it be to help her, or to torture and kill her?

* * * * *

Sitting cross-legged on a woven mat, Avere strained to listen to the priestesses, who were huddled together in a corner, whispering. She couldn't pick up anything. Her eyes went to the book in Zheir's hand. She'd better get it back. How had she ended up here, inside the priestesses' hut in a wild folk stronghold? To think she'd muttered to herself about the number of wild folk in Stronghaven. Now she was surrounded by them. The only one nearby who wasn't wild was a Beast Master. Avere's predicament would almost be comical, if she wasn't deep inside wild folk territory.

Why, oh why, had she agreed to meet Malina for supper that day? If not for the old bat planting doubt in her head about the Primacy's teachings and Beast Masters, Avere would have ended Erryn's life the first day she'd seen her in Stronghaven. She'd be back in Darroth by now, and with the throne under contention, would be a very busy woman indeed. Instead she expected to push on to Loring, find out that Erryn couldn't help heal the land, and do what she should have done in Stronghaven.

Still, she couldn't stop herself from hoping their journey to Loring would prove fruitful. If Erryn could really heal the withering of the land—*steady, Avere*. It would be best for her to assume that Loring would be where she'd end Erryn's life, slink away, and return to civilization. She glanced at Toe, who sat a few feet away from her, staring at the priestesses. She hoped to leave Toe and Renn alive, but that might not be possible.

The priestesses parted. The older one, Lale, now held the book. "Ye say ye received this from a cultist."

"Yes, I did," Avere said.

"She told ye the Fallener is blessed by the Seven."

"Yes."

"Did ye believe her?"

Avere considered her answer. She wanted Erryn to reach Loring, not to die here. "I don't know. That's why I agreed to travel with her to Loring. To find out."

"Me, too," Toe said. "She saved my life. I feel I owe it to her."

Good, he was sticking to their story. He and Renn had agreed to travel with Erryn to Loring before Avere had shown up, and not because he believed Erryn could revive the land, but because he felt personally indebted to her. He wasn't lying, and neither was she. Malina had made a good point. Why would the Seven allow Beast Masters to summon their pets, only to curse them for it? There must be a reason, but healing the land probably wasn't it, per se. The Seven were capable of doing that themselves, and the Primacy had never taught that the land and its bounty sickened whenever a Beast Master walked Daros. Given how much the Primacy hated Beast Masters, surely someone would have noticed and written it into the Holy Texts. But perhaps bringing the Fallen into the physical plane affected it in a way that wasn't visible to those who dwelled here. Avere was keeping an open mind.

Lale glanced at Zheir and Asha. "What we are about to tell ye, ye must never tell anyone else. Not the Fallener. Not the shamed. We only tell ye to explain why we're not cutting the Fallener down, and to impress upon ye that if ye see in Loring that she can't heal the land, ye must help her no longer. Ye must give her to us. Ye must promise us that, or we won't help ye."

Avere kept her expression neutral. Stop helping Erryn? Yes. Give her to these people? No. She'd made a promise. She'd see Erryn dead, but not tortured.

"Do ye agree to this?" Lale asked.

Since this was precisely the deal they'd agreed to make before approaching the clan, Avere looked to Toe to answer, but his mouth was set. He considered Erryn a friend. He'd be a fool to try to save her if they found nothing in Loring, but that wouldn't be her problem. She gazed at Lale. "We agree. We only agreed to help her get to Loring because we believe she can help. If she can't, well . . ." Avere shrugged.

"This cultist made an impression on ye," Lale said.

Avere lifted her chin defiantly. "She reminded me that I should think for myself."

"I've always believed what I can see and hear, not what I'm told," Toe said.

If his words angered Lale, she didn't show it. "Then why did ye take in the shamed? Why do ye travel with her?" the priestess asked. "Ye know what she did. Ye were there when she told us."

Toe nodded. "But she never told us why. Don't ye think we should have known why before judging her? Don't ye want to know why? Don't ye ask yerself why?"

Doubt flickered across Lale's face, but then her voice hardened. "We asked her why. She refused to say, and admitted to striking down Ian. We couldn't allow her to stay, Toetril. Ye know that."

"We're not here to discuss the shamed," Zheir said. "We passed judgement, and our judgement stands. Ye didn't agree to our terms regarding the Fallener, Toetril. Do ye agree to give her to us if she can't help the land?"

Toe stared down at his hands. "If she can't heal the land, we'll give her to ye. She'll want to die," he said, surprising Avere. Erryn didn't want to be torn apart limb by limb; of that, Avere was sure.

"Then we'll tell ye why the Fallener is still alive."

Asha stepped forward. "I'll tell it. I was the last one to see." She looked to Lale, then continued when Lale nodded. "Before we can wear the robe, we must spend three days and nights in communion with the Seven. We do this alone, in a cave a weeks' journey away. Not all return. The first test is to reach the cave. The second is to find the sacred chamber it holds. The third is to light the sacred fire. There are other dangers, such as the creatures that live within the cave. But we believe that once the sacred fire is lit, we have the Seven's protection."

Avere nodded politely.

"The cave is sacred because we believe the Seven were there many years ago, before we had letters. They marked its walls, so those of us who came afterward could see, would know they were there. They marked its walls with the drawings in yer book."

"You mean the drawings you see in your sacred cave are the same as the ones in the book?" Avere said slowly.

"Yes. But they did not draw the Fallener receiving their

blessing," Zheir said, taking the book from Lale. She opened it to the first drawing. "And there are no skulls," she murmured.

Avere thought back to her conversations with Malina. "I think the skulls represent Death, and by Death, I don't mean dying. According to my cultist friend, Death is . . . well, I'm not sure. Whatever it is, it acts as a balance, prevents the Seven from becoming complacent. But she said things were out of balance, that Death was taking over. That's why the land is sickened. She believed the Seven sends Beast Masters—Falleners, to help restore balance." She paused for effect. "But we keep killing them."

Lale shook her head. "Why would the Seven need Falleners to heal the land? They can do it themselves."

"But they haven't. Maybe the Elder Gods have rules."

Lale frowned. "Elder Gods?"

"Oh, yes, I forgot to mention them. Apparently the Seven and Death serve the Elder Gods. I suppose you could say there's some type of divine hierarchy, with the Elder Gods at the top and the Seven and Death underneath."

Three incredulous priestesses stared at her. Zheir clucked her tongue. "We are allowing ourselves to be misled. These are not our beliefs. This," she raised the book she held, "is a lie. Someone entered the sacred cave, copied the drawings, and added their own."

"That's not possible, Zheir," Lale said quietly, her eyes now thoughtful. "Only those called by the Seven can find the sacred chamber, light the fire, and survive the cave."

"Is there only one sacred cave?" Avere asked, then wished she hadn't when Lale glared at her.

"There is only one. Those called from all the clans must survive three nights there."

Oh, fiddle. She had too many questions racing through her mind to remain silent. "I can understand Zhikinden drawing the spear and sun, but why would she draw Zayvang? And what do the arrow and rectangle mean?"

"Zayvang may be Fallen, but in the heavens, she is also Zhikinden's loyal pet. The Seven loved the Fallen. That's why they lowered them, rather than exterminating them."

A shiver ran down Avere's spine. Keeping an open mind about Erryn suddenly felt like sticking her tongue out at the Seven. But then, Malina was right. The Seven must allow Erryn to summon the Fallen, but why? Did Beast Masters play a role in maintaining the balance between the Seven and Death, or was it some type of game? She'd asked herself this question many times since meeting Malina and was no closer to an answer. Hence her open mind. Her instincts told her the answer lay in Loring, and her instincts rarely failed her.

"I don't know what the other symbols mean," Lale continued. "I don't claim to know the minds of the Seven."

Well, that was refreshing. The Primates never hesitated to speak for them.

"Could someone called by the Seven have entered our cave and copied the Seven's work?" Asha asked. "Perhaps long ago."

"We didn't have paper long ago," Zheir said. "And those of us called now don't carry paper and ink with us."

"My friend was from Westerfox," Avere said. "She claimed that when the Seven walked the land, they visited Westerfox first. They could have left their mark there, too."

"The Seven came to us first," Lale said. "But they travelled all over. They could have left their mark somewhere else, yes, but why draw the Fallener?" She turned to Zheir. "I know ye have doubts about the book. I do, too. But these doubts also stop me from calling for the Fallener's death. We must help her get to Loring. If the book is a lie, there will be nothing there and we'll sacrifice her."

"I say we sacrifice her now," Zheir said. "We don't know anything about this book, or this woman who spoke of Death and healing the land."

"Ye're right, but we know the land is dying. What will be left for the children? If there's a chance the Fallener can help, we should let her go to Loring. If she can't help, she won't leave there alive. She will not return here, or hurt any of us, and we will have sent her to the Seven."

Zheir drew a deep breath. "All right," she said, but her skepticism weakened her voice.

"Ye will go with them," Lale said to Asha.

Asha's eyes widened. "Me?"

"Ye are the youngest and heartiest. If Loring proves empty, ye will sacrifice the Fallener."

Asha nodded. "I'll honour the Seven."

Lale shifted her attention to Toe. "We'll mark ye, and we'll send hunters and scouts with ye, to protect ye. But not tonight. Tonight ye'll both eat with us, and we'll commune with ye."

"What about the Fallener and the shamed?" Toe asked.

"A night in the pen won't hurt them."

"They'll need to eat. If ye're serious about helping the Fallener to Loring, ye don't want her to start her journey weak."

Lale sighed. "We'll send them food. At dawn, we'll mark ye outside the stronghold. Then ye'll go, and ye will obey Asha."

Toe nodded. Avere didn't. Toe was beholden to these priestesses. Avere would do whatever she liked.

Erryn wiped the sweat from her brow and wondered how long she'd sat watching the fire and Renn's back. Two hours? Three? Her stomach grumbled. She shifted position for the tenth time, so her legs wouldn't cramp. Was this some type of test? Had they locked the Fallener in here to see if anger or panic would push her to call the Fallen and rip the shamed apart? They'd be disappointed.

Nobody understood the Fallen like she did. They were inside her mind, always with her, always aware. As she sat here in this warm hut, afraid the clan wouldn't torture her but instead starve her and Renn to death, let their throats parch and their flesh fall away until they were nothing but bone, the Fallen weren't urging her to summon them. They were soothing her fear. They were keeping her calm. If everyone could know them as she did, they wouldn't fear them. They'd welcome them.

Her eyes slid shut. *We shouldn't have come here,* she said to them. They didn't answer her with words. They couldn't speak, not anymore, not after the Seven had lowered them by transforming them into beasts. But she could feel them, feel their concern and their love. Once, she would have done anything to be rid of them, to be free of her ugly secret and be normal again. Now she couldn't imagine being without them.

She cracked open an eye. Renn hadn't moved. "Aren't you hot?" she asked. Her voice sounded unnaturally loud. "I've stripped down to my shirt and rolled up my sleeves, and I'm still sweating." No response. The woman was a statue. Erryn's concern for her deepened. "How long—"

Someone slid the bolt open. Erryn leaped to her feet, then shielded her eyes when the door opened and light flooded the hut.

"So this is the pen," Avere said. "It feels like a hot bath."

Erryn lowered her hand. She'd never been happier to see Avere. "What's happening? Are they letting us out?"

"No, not yet."

"But—"

Avere raised her hand and lowered her voice. "You'll be out on the morrow, at dawn. That's when they'll mark us."

"You mean they're going to help us?" Erryn whispered.

Avere nodded. "They're sending a priestess with us, and enough wild folk that if we don't find something in Loring, you're a dead woman."

Her words weren't news to Erryn. "You promised."

"Don't worry. I keep my promises." Avere's gaze shifted to Renn. "As talkative as usual, I see." When Renn didn't respond, Avere said, "Even more talkative. At least you'll have a quiet night," she said to Erryn. "Unless she snores."

Toe stepped inside the hut. "I've brought you stew," he said.

Erryn had to restrain herself from grabbing one of the

bowls he held. She stiffened when one of the priestesses entered the pen. The priestess hesitated, then said, "My name is Asha. I'll travel with ye to Loring. I've brought ye water." She held out a bulging water skin.

Erryn took it from her. "Thank you."

Asha inclined her head. "We must go. Rest tonight. We'll come for ye at dawn." She motioned for Toe and Avere to follow her from the hut. Toe went to give Renn her stew, then set it down on the ground next to her when Renn ignored him. He patted her on the shoulder and followed Asha outside. Avere flashed Erryn a smile, then left. The door shut, and the bolt slid back into place. Erryn's eyes had to adjust to the dim light again. She crouched to set the water down, then lowered herself to the ground. A minute later she'd already wolfed down half her stew, but then concern tempered her appetite. Renn hadn't touched her meal. "You should eat," Erryn said.

Renn didn't move. While Erryn had stared at Renn's back and hunched shoulders, she'd wanted to go and comfort her, but she'd suspected that showing her concern would have upset Renn more than helped. Coming back to the clan that had banished her, being lumped in with a Fallener... "Were you hoping time had changed the way they'd treat you?" she asked softly.

When Renn didn't answer, Erryn picked up her spoon, then almost dropped it when Renn said, "I didn't know what to expect."

"But you were hoping," Erryn said, resting her spoon in her bowl again.

The silence stretched out, then Renn shrugged.

"Come away from the fire and eat. You'll need your strength on the morrow. When they come for us, don't let them see you defeated."

Renn whipped around. "I'm not defeated!" she spat.

Good. Erryn had intended to rekindle Renn's spirit. "Then stop moping in front of the fire and eat. Come and have a drink," she added, remembering the water. If she hadn't been so hungry, she would have already gulped some down.

Renn let out an exasperated sigh, then picked up her bowl. She stomped over to Erryn and sat next to her. They ate in silence, their spoons scraping against their bowls. When they were finished, they quenched their thirst, but knew not to empty the water skin. It would be hours before the pen door opened again.

Renn unlaced her leather tunic, removed it, and tossed it away. The shirt she wore underneath was drenched with sweat. Erryn wrinkled her nose. They could both use a wash. "Do you have family here?" she asked. She didn't want to pick at Renn's wound, but she was curious.

Renn nodded. "My mother."

"Do you think she'll want to see you?"

Renn snorted, but she also hugged her legs to her chest so tightly that her knuckles turned white.

Erryn struggled to resist her curiosity. Provoking Renn while locked inside this hut with her wouldn't be prudent. She should bite her tongue. Renn would rebuff her anyway. But the question kept intruding, and her desire to know was strong. "Why did you kill your friend?" she asked, sounding stern because she didn't want to sound tentative. "You lost so much. I didn't really understand how much until we came here. You shouldn't be locked in here with me. You're not a murderer." Renn could be hotheaded, but she wasn't a cold-blooded killer. "He must have done something to you. Did he . . . force himself on you? If he did—"

Renn's jaw tightened. She went back to the fire and sat cross-legged in front of it. Erryn wasn't offended. She'd expected as much and pushed herself to her feet. She'd had enough of sitting. She'd stand until her legs were tired, then claim one of the bedrolls and try to sleep.

"It was for a friend," Renn said. "I did it for a friend."

Erryn gaped, grateful that Renn's back was to her. "You killed for him . . . or her?"

Renn nodded.

Erryn forgot about wanting to stretch her legs. She sat next to Renn and gazed at the fire. "Why?"

Renn didn't answer. Erryn wouldn't push her. She'd already learned more than she'd expected. Maybe Renn would tell her more on their journey to Loring. If she didn't, Erryn's questions would die with her. She picked up a piece of wood from the pile next to the stone pit, added it to the fire, and closed her eyes.

"Ian wasn't forcing himself on me."

Ian . . . he was the friend Renn had killed.

"He was forcing himself on her. My friend."

"So you killed him?"

"Yes."

More questions raced through Erryn's mind. "Why

didn't you tell someone what he was doing? Why didn't she kill him?"

"She's like ye, not a hunter, not a scout, would hurt herself if she swung a sword. She wouldn't have had the stomach for it."

Erryn opened her eyes but didn't look at Renn. "So she asked you to do it?"

"No."

"You took it upon yourself?" When Renn didn't respond, Erryn finally turned to her. "Why didn't you tell someone, like the priestesses?"

"Because she was promised to Jory. She loved him. She probably still does."

Frustration threatened to raise Erryn's voice. She took a deep breath. "Why did that matter? And why didn't Jory kill him, then?"

"She didn't want Jory to know. He might not have wanted her anymore."

"But she was the one being wronged. He wouldn't have been much of a man if he'd rejected her."

Renn shrugged. "That being so, she loved him. She would have been hurt. And the clan would have known what had happened to her. She didn't want that."

"So she went to you, instead of him."

"No. I found out." Renn's voice dropped. "I saw them one day, when I was coming back from hunting. She would leave the stronghold to gather wood and herbs. Sometimes Ian went with her, but I didn't think they were—I ran away. I didn't know she didn't want it. But the more I thought about it, the more I couldn't believe what I'd seen with my own eyes. She loved Jory. She'd always dreamed of pledging to him. Ian . . . it didn't make sense. I told her I'd seen." She drew a shaky breath. "That's when I found out."

But why—was Renn talking about herself? Was this "friend" of hers a way of distancing herself from her own terrible experience? "Couldn't you have told someone privately, so Jory would never find out? The priestesses could have come up with another reason for punishing him."

Renn's eyes bulged. "Punish?" she bellowed. "He should have been banished. No, strung up for everyone to see."

Erryn hesitated, then touched Renn's arm. "So why didn't you tell? Why did you throw everything away by killing him? You were punished more than he was. He lost his life, but you live with the loss every day. You're the scorned one. I know it would have been hard to tell, but—" Who was she to question Renn? Back in Moss, when Kell had kissed her and grabbed her breast, she hadn't shouted at him, spat on him, or told anyone about it since. If she'd been in Renn's shoes, and had Renn's temperament and pride, she might have done exactly what Renn had done. "I'm sorry. I shouldn't second guess what you did. I wasn't there. It wasn't me."

Renn stared at the fire. "I've kept this secret for so long, even now it's difficult for me to open my lips and speak of it. But I'll tell ye the rest. She was with child, and it wasn't Jory's. It was Ian's."

With child? Erryn quickly reconsidered her earlier conclusion. Renn wasn't talking about herself, unless she'd left a child behind. No, Erryn didn't believe that, but now she needed to be sure. "I thought maybe you've been talking about yourself this whole time, that your friend is you. But now I realize that's not true."

Renn's nostrils flared. "I'm not talking about myself. I would never have let Ian do it to me. I would have killed him the first time he tried. And I wasn't promised to Jory. I've never wanted to promise myself to any man. I killed Ian because Anasi was with child and knew it wasn't Jory's, and knew that if he found out, he wouldn't want her. She probably would have been forced to pledge to Ian."

Erryn put her hand on Renn's arm again. "Okay, so it wasn't you. You were protecting a friend's honour. Don't get upset, but wouldn't Jory have assumed the child was his?"

"He would have known it wasn't his. When you're promised, you don't lie together until you pledge. It has always been that way with us. Anasi and Jory honoured that tradition. When I told Anasi what I'd seen, she told me about the babe. Their pledge ceremony was only two weeks away, so she'd hoped to pass the babe off as his."

"The baby would have come a little early."

Renn nodded.

"Then why—"

"Ian wanted her to break her promise to Jory and pledge to him. He said if she didn't, he'd tell Jory that she'd coupled with him because she wanted to. He would have done the same if we'd told anyone. He would have said she wanted to, and everyone would have known the babe was his, not Jory's."

"So you killed him."

"It was the only way."

"And she pledged to Jory?"

Renn nodded. "Toe told me. I was gone by then. There was no doubt about my guilt, so I was judged quickly and banished."

"You confessed so that nobody would ask questions."

"Nobody could know it was for Anasi. Nobody could ever know about the child."

Anger surged through Erryn, directed not at Renn, but at Anasi. She knew it wasn't fair. What had happened to her in the tavern in Moss paled compared to Anasi's horrible experience. She should feel sympathy for her, and she did. But if only Anasi had told someone what Ian was doing. "Couldn't you have told her family?" she asked Renn. "I'm sure they would have kept it quiet. Why did it have to be you? And how could she have stood by while they condemned you? She could have saved you."

"But she would have lost Jory," Renn said quietly.

"But it wasn't up to you to make sure she was happy, especially when it meant being shamed. You gave up your life for hers. Why would you—" A sudden flash of insight answered several questions for Erryn at once. *I've never wanted to promise myself to any man.* Erryn felt the same way. She'd dreaded the king telling her that he'd found a husband for her.

Renn's brow furrowed. She met Erryn's eyes. "Why would I—" Her face flushed. She swallowed and turned away.

She knows. She knows I've realized why. Erryn scrambled

for something to say, anything that would ease Renn's embarrassment, and perhaps shame. "Anasi didn't know how fortunate she was to have you as her protector. Not many would give up everything for someone else, no matter how . . . deeply they care about the person."

Renn didn't look at her. Erryn forced herself to continue. She wasn't as sure about what she was about to say, but if she was right, it needed to be said. "Don't do the same thing for me. Don't throw your life away for me. I'm a Fallener. I was doomed before we met. You mustn't speak up and defend me. You can't save me."

"I've upset you," Renn said, still refusing to look at her.

"No! No, Renn, you haven't upset me. I just don't want to see you hurt, especially for me. If I wasn't a Fallener, well, if I—I wasn't a Fallener, we wouldn't have—have met. I'd still be in Darroth. I—" She was tripping over her words and could tell by Renn's face that Renn didn't believe her. "I'm not upset," she said emphatically. When Zheir and the others had come for her, she'd known not to call the Fallen, but she almost had when she'd thought Renn was in danger. If they'd harmed Renn, she would have unleashed the Fallen, summoned them all, ripped every last hunter apart, and Zheir too. Now she understood why.

She should have seen it sooner, realized how much closer they'd grown since Renn's attitude toward her had changed, and especially since they'd spent days in the rooming house together while Renn's arm was healing, playing cards, eating in comfortable silence, and talking about their pasts—well, her telling Renn about her life in

Darroth. She should have seen it sooner because of how she felt—had felt—about Fi. She still loved Fi. She still longed to see her. But the fantasy she'd dreamed about and written about in her diary, the one in which she and Fi would always be together, was just that: a fantasy. She'd always known, deep inside, that it would never come to pass, and the many months away from Fi had allowed her love for the princess to become the love one felt for a cherished sister and friend. If Erryn somehow survived Loring and still wanted to live, she'd find Fi, not because she was in love with her, but because she loved her dear sister and missed her terribly.

She looked down at her hands and willed herself to go on. "When Zheir and the others came for us, I was calm until one of the hunters threatened you. I almost called the Fallen. I *would* have called them, if you hadn't offered your sword but had fought him instead, or if—" *Say it. Tell her.* "If he'd killed you, I would have summoned them all, even though it would have meant I'd never make it to Loring. So, no, you haven't upset me. Not at all."

She could sense Renn looking at her and forced herself to meet Renn's gaze. She'd never felt so exposed, but she also felt safer than she'd felt in a long time. She searched for something to say, but the reflection of the flickering fire in Renn's eyes mesmerized her. She moistened her lips. "I'm a dead woman. We both know that."

Then Renn leaned in, and their lips touched, and Erryn had never felt so alive.

Leap of Faith

The priestess Lale dragged her finger along Avere's left cheek, marking it with two thick black lines. Everyone going to Loring was kneeling outside the stronghold, including the scouts and hunters who'd protect the Fallener until they reached their destination, and then kill her if the journey was for naught. Asha was the only one still on her feet. Apparently her robe and walking stick would be enough to deter others from attacking her.

Lale stepped back and appraised her handiwork, then stood in front of Erryn and clucked her tongue. "Marking ye won't help ye."

"She'll have her hat on," Toe said. "Seeing the mark on her cheek should be enough for most to leave us alone. If she's not marked, they'll wonder why she was left untouched."

Zheir nodded. "Asha will be with ye, but they may sense the Fallener."

Erryn doubted it.

Scowling, Lale dipped her finger into the ink she'd mixed. Erryn remained still while the priestess marked her cheek. "Thank you," she murmured. Lale's answering nod was so slight that Erryn almost missed it.

The priestess stepped away. "I'm not marking the shamed."

Zheir's brows shot up. "Why not?"

"The shamed isn't one of us."

Erryn wanted to look at Renn, but she kept her eyes forward.

"Ye need to mark her," Toe said. "They won't know she's shamed. If she's not marked, they'll ask questions. Don't make it difficult for us."

"He's right," Zheir said.

Lale's face darkened. "If it were up to me, she wouldn't be going with them. She would be sent back to the city to scrape before city folk. That's where she belongs. She wouldn't be allowed to travel with our kind in our lands."

Erryn's desire to look at Renn grew stronger. She gritted her teeth. She was already having enough trouble not dwelling on the night they'd spent together, one of discovery and ecstasy. She'd woken this morning within the warm cocoon of Renn's arms, and when she'd emerged from the hut, she'd viewed the rising sun with new eyes. How closely would the wild folk watch her? She wanted to hold Renn again before she died.

"Consider her city folk, if ye must," Zheir said. "But ye must mark her. If ye don't, ye'll endanger everyone."

"I'll mark her, then," Lale muttered, "but she is not welcome here." Her gaze shifted away from Zheir. "Did ye hear me? Do not come back here with the others. Do not come back here again. Ye're not welcome. Ye should never have come. Ye are shamed."

"Do ye think I came to see ye?" Renn said. "I came because I made a promise to Toe. I'm only here because we needed yer help."

A loud slap made Erryn twist to Renn before she could stop herself. An angry red welt marred Renn's right cheek. Renn glared at Lale, who glared right back. Erryn forced herself to turn away.

"We need to be on our way," Toe said.

Erryn kept her eyes forward while the priestess marked Renn. Lale strode to Zheir and handed her the ink. She raised her hands. "Ye have the blessing of our clan. All who see the mark will know that yer deaths would offend us, and we would avenge ye." As she lowered her hands, her eyes bored into Erryn. "Ye will help heal the land, or ye will die."

Lale motioned for Zheir to follow her. The two priestesses strode away. Erryn let out her pent breath and pushed herself to her feet. She hoisted her bag onto her back and watched the others pick up their loads. All but Asha. She took the lead, marching at the head of the group with only a walking stick in her hand.

The other wild folk formed a circle around Erryn, Avere, and Renn. Toe walked on the periphery, among the wild folk, but Erryn didn't doubt his friendship for a moment. He was still well-regarded by his clan. Right now, he could best help her by aligning himself with those who were eager to kill her.

She fell into step with Renn. "Are you sorry you didn't see your mother?"

Renn didn't look at her. "I saw my mother."

But Renn had rarely been out of Erryn's sight since they'd arrived at the stronghold. Erryn couldn't resist meeting her eyes. "When?"

Renn's eyes were bleak. "At the same time ye did, Erryn. My mother is the priestess Lale."

The back of Arrick's neck tingled as he listened to the grand primate welcome him to the Primacy's estate. He couldn't help but feel like a moth who'd flown into a web, despite having no reason to suspect he was in danger. They weren't even meeting indoors. If he'd been eager to walk the hallowed halls that more noble feet than his had trod, he'd have been disappointed. The garden behind the grand temple was beautiful, though.

When Otane sat on a marble bench and motioned for Arrick to join him, Arrick complied. He'd keep his eye out for the distinctive mitre of a Westerfox primate, but he didn't expect to see one. Anyone who counted would know the spymaster was on the grounds.

"Have you received any information that would lead us to the Lyos traitor?" Otane asked.

Arrick shook his head. "I have all my people searching for her. Someone must be hiding them."

"Someone who'll rue the day they harboured an enemy of the crown and the Seven." Otane's brow furrowed. "We must find her, Master Inel. While she's still alive, whoever sits on the throne will be vulnerable. Daros will not be at peace."

"It might be best for the Primacy to continue its regency until the girl isn't a threat." Arrick wasn't surprised when Otane nodded. "What about the Beast Master? The Lyos girl has offended the Seven by upsetting their chosen dynasty, but the Beast Master thumbs her nose at them every time she calls the Fallen. Perhaps the assassinations are a sign of their wrath." He didn't believe that was true for a second, but he was curious about how Otane would respond. The Primacy should be more concerned about the Fyler girl and let the nobility deal with the power void the king's assassination had created. A Primacy that wasn't corrupt would do exactly that.

When Otane didn't respond, Arrick said, "All my people are focused on finding the traitor, but before the assassinations, we'd been searching for the heathen. I was led to believe that finding her should be my priority. I was under the impression the Primacy was most interested in ridding Daros of her presence."

"I'm aware that my former colleague came to you with an offer for the heathen. He did so at the request of the High Council."

Arrick already knew that. If Enkelo hadn't told him, Arrick would have guessed. Enkelo wouldn't have dared go against the king's wishes and offer wine from the High Council's cellar if he hadn't had the grand primate's blessing. "The king had wanted her found and brought back for trial."

"He'd wanted her dead, Master Inel. If he'd known the daughter he was trying to appease would betray him, he never would have let the heathen go, and he never would have entertained a trial, even one with a predetermined outcome."

"Perhaps we should honour the king's wish and find the heathen," Arrick suggested, not wanting to jeopardize his rapport with Otane, or raise his suspicions, by insisting that finding the Fyler girl was more important than finding the princess.

Otane turned to him. "Don't think we've forgotten about the Beast Master. Her capture is still of the utmost importance. Our search for the princess won't hinder our search for the heathen. Quite the contrary. One capture will lead to the other. And so we must capture the traitor." His voice hardened. "Push your people harder, Master Inel. Instruct them to take whatever measures they must to loosen tongues. The trio we seek has to be somewhere. As you said, someone must be hiding them. Find out who, and soon."

Otane rose and gestured to the servant standing out of earshot. "Malcolm will see you out. Good day, Master Inel."

Arrick inclined his head. "Good day."

On the way to the gate, he turned the brief conversation with the grand primate over in his mind. Otane hadn't overtly threatened him, but his message was clear. If Arrick didn't produce a lead to the princess soon, or better yet, the princess herself, he could suddenly disappear. A Ferret wouldn't do the dirty work. He wasn't naïve enough to believe that none of his people would be tempted by the promise of enough coin to retire. One or two would find the offer difficult to resist, but they'd know they wouldn't live long enough to enjoy their newfound riches. Their Ferret brothers and sisters would avenge their spymaster's life. If the Primacy decided he needed to go, it would have to hire a mercenary.

But Arrick didn't feel a blade at his throat just yet. He could easily keep the Primacy satisfied for now by creating a lead to the princess, one that would take some time to investigate. Still, he'd have one of his people shadow him, as a precaution. Right now, something else Otane had said was making his wheels turn. The grand primate may have given away more than he'd intended. *One capture will lead to another.*

Arrick had initially thought the Primacy had assassinated the king and prince and framed the princess because it wanted the throne, but that motive had never made sense to him. The Primacy couldn't act as regent forever. He'd also wondered why it was so determined to hold a trial when the princess couldn't possibly be found innocent of the charges against her. Now he had his answer. How long would she have rotted away in the dungeons waiting for her day before the judges? The Primacy would have let her stew a long time, for the same reason it wanted her captured alive. *Bait.* Three assassinations, other lives lost, and the princess framed so the Primacy could get its hands on who it really wanted.

But the princess had escaped. It had all been for nothing, unless they recaptured her alive.

Arrick wiped the sweat from his brow with a clammy hand. Avere was with the heathen. He had to warn her, otherwise she could be caught within the same net and treated as a blasphemer. The notion was so funny he almost laughed. It wasn't that Avere was devout—quite the opposite. She was too indifferent toward the Primacy to stand against it. But something had happened, something that had her shadowing or travelling with the Beast Master, rather than killing her. He believed she must have her reasons, but the Primacy wouldn't see it that way. He couldn't allow her to be painted with the same brush as the heathen.

When he reached the Ferret base, he went straight to his study and ordered Jack to pass along a verbal message to several nearby Ferret contacts, who would then give that message to Ferrets who checked with them daily. And so the chain would continue. The men and women Arrick had summoned would meet with him at the Ferret base. He'd tell them they were now responsible for watching every gate into Darroth, day and night. Under no circumstances were they to allow the Beast Master into the city. They were to kill Fyler on sight. No hesitation. No mercy. He would personally deliver her head to Otane.

With a fur draped over her shoulders, Erryn sat on the bank of the river a minute's walk away from camp and watched the water rush by. The sun had only just risen. She'd gotten into the habit of sitting alone in the dawn light, away from the others. It was the only opportunity she had to be alone, the only opportunity to do this.

Zayvang, come. The air shimmered. Zayvang leaped into existence next to Erryn. *Sit with me.* The saber-tooth cat did as she was told. Erryn poked her arm out from underneath the fur and wrapped it around Zayvang.

She wasn't worried that one of the wild folk would see. The two who were tasked with watching her at this hour had grown used to her wandering away every morning. They probably assumed she was going to relieve herself, and she always did. But then she snatched a few precious minutes with Zayvang, and occasionally, Lerxis and Iss. The others were too risky to call. They'd attract attention. *But not you. You always sit quietly.*

She pressed her cheek against Zayvang's and closed her eyes. How many more times would she sit with Zayvang like this? If they reached Loring and found nothing . . . she wouldn't be the only one who'd die. Zayvang, Sath, Lerxis, Cheturrak, Iss, Quon, and Rachagha would die with her—but only for a time, and only on this plane. She opened her eyes and gazed directly into Zayvang's. *Will you remember me? Will I see you, or will I be somewhere else, because I offend the Seven?*

The cat stared back at her. Erryn was convinced that Zayvang understood every word she said. In the heavenly plane, Zayvang sat at the feet of Zhikinden. Erryn must be a letdown in comparison, yet Zayvang always made her feel loved, and strong. Erryn took a shuddering breath. *I don't want to be parted from you.* She couldn't bear the thought and pushed it from her mind. She'd think about Renn instead, because doing so always brought on a smile.

She'd kept her eyes forward when Asha had announced the Fallener and shamed would share a tent. For once, being outcasts had worked in their favour, though sometimes Erryn wondered if it would have been better for her and Renn to be kept apart from each other. She'd been ready to die, until that night in the pen and all the nights that had followed it. Now she had something— someone—to live for. *No, you don't.* Even if she survived Loring, she and Renn wouldn't last. Renn would continue to run contracts. She wouldn't want to live a life on the run, and Erryn wouldn't want her to. The only reason they'd allowed themselves to give in to their feelings was because they knew nothing would ultimately come of it, or at least that was what Erryn told herself when she thought about dying in Loring. She'd only embraced the part of herself she would have kept hidden forever because she had no future to worry about.

She'd struggled, and failed, to see a good side to being banished from the Royal City and everyone she loved, but now she was grateful she'd never have to take a husband. Before being cast out, she would have done as everyone had expected, but that was no longer true. It wasn't forbidden for a woman or man to sleep with their own kind, but it wasn't spoken about, either, and she couldn't have betrayed a husband in such a way, no matter how miserable she was. She would have tried her hardest to be friends with him, to love him as much as she could, and to push aside any lingering feelings for Fi. But now she knew what she would have sacrificed: passion, and the deep, yearning love she never would have felt for a man.

What would Renn have done if she hadn't killed for her friend and been cast from the clan? Erryn had asked her how her people would view them and what Toe would think if he knew. Renn had said they should keep it to themselves, but hadn't said why, and Erryn hadn't prompted her for an explanation. She didn't want to spoil their . . . dalliance? Relationship? She wasn't sure what to call it. She cared about Renn. She liked being with her. But Loring loomed over her, tempering her feelings. It was unfortunate she'd die so soon after accepting her true self. Would she go to the Seven? How would they see her? What would they do to her?

She leaned into Zayvang and buried her face in the big cat's fur. *Will I see you there? Will you know me? Will my punishment be that they'll never let me near you again?* She'd always wondered about meeting her mother and father in the heavens, but now she worried about never seeing the Fallen again. It was bad enough knowing they'd have new masters here on the physical plane. She'd cringed at the thought of the Seven snuffing her out, but there were worse punishments. *We still have time. We—*

Suddenly Zayvang wasn't there. Erryn fell onto her side, hitting the ground with a thud. A dagger skidded to a stop in the dirt, inches before it would have ended up in the river.

"Oh, so they do pass right through them." Avere's voice was low. "I'd seen them disappear when pierced with a sword, but of course, the sword's owner was hanging on to it. I wondered if a thrown weapon would pass through, or be absorbed. Now I know. It's a good thing I threw it at an angle I knew would miss you." She strode into Erryn's field of vision and went to her dagger. "I used an old one, just in case," she said, picking it up.

Erryn pushed herself away from the ground and leaped to her feet. "What do you think you're doing?" she snapped.

The dagger Avere held disappeared inside the folds of her cloak. She folded her arms. "What do you think *you're* doing, calling the Fallen a stone's throw away from camp? You do understand that every wild man and woman we're travelling with, except two, are looking for any excuse to end your life? You so much as sneeze the wrong way and Asha will be calling down the Seven's wrath on you, delivered by her lackeys, of course."

"They don't follow me in the mornings. They know I'll be back."

"That's a terribly naïve belief, Erryn. Any one of them could decide to come after you, or just happen to stumble upon you when they're taking a piss. Do you want to get to Loring? Are you all right, up here?" Avere tapped her temple.

Erryn's jaw clenched. "Of course I'm all right."

"Are they making you call them?"

"No!"

"So you're just being stupid, then." Avere frowned. "Stop being stupid. I don't know what bond you think you have with them, but remember who they are."

"I know who they are." Erryn drew a deep breath. "And yes, I share a bond with them. They care about me."

Avere stared at her. "Nobody else sees them the way you do," she said, after a long silence. "If you want to get to Loring, you won't call them again unless we run into trouble. Give me your word."

Her chest tightened. "I . . ."

"Your word, Erryn. If you want me to keep my promise, give me your word. I know you won't believe this, but I'm doing this for your own good. I want you to get to Loring. I want you to have a chance, however slim. Don't you want to know if there's a temple and if it holds any answers for you? If the Fallen care about you, wouldn't they want the same?"

She couldn't argue against Avere's logic, but her eyes welled with tears. "I give you my word," she said, only because she had no choice and it would be selfish to throw away the opportunity Renn and Toe—and Avere— had given her. They'd disrupted their lives so she could complete what would likely be a fruitless journey.

"Thank you. I trust you'll keep your word." Avere beckoned to her. "Come on. Let's go back to camp and have something to eat."

Erryn fell into step with her, but her appetite was gone.

Fi's fingernails dug into her palms as she listened to those around her shouting for the effigies of the traitors to be set alight. Half of her wanted to clap her hands over her ears. The other half wanted to plead her case to the mob around her.

When she and the others had arrived in Bexley and discovered a festival was being held in the town square, Enkelo had suggested they go listen to the bards, who might offer them clues to Erryn's whereabouts. "The decorations and food may lift your spirits for a time," he'd said. "We'll blend in with the crowds." And they were doing so. But lift her spirits? Poor Enkelo couldn't have known that burning the treacherous princess and the two traitors who'd helped her escape was the main attraction on the evening program.

Was everyone here sheep who just accepted whatever rumours they heard? Perhaps those who believed her innocent had stayed at home. She quietly snorted. More likely, they'd not been able to resist the food and drink, and were now calling as loudly as everyone else for the effigies to be burned. They'd stuck a pig's head on her effigy. A pig! She should find out the names of the men who were lighting the torches, so when she took the throne, she could have them arrested!

Her burst of anger surprised and bolstered her, but fear quickly doused her inner flame. If those around her knew who she was, they'd put the torch to her and laugh as she burned. She'd only visited Bexley once, when she was a babe. Father and Mother had toured the cities in this area. Had Erryn been with them, or had they left her behind at the castle? One thing was for sure—everyone in Bexley would have been clamouring to catch a glimpse of the princess. The same would be true today, but only because they'd want her blood.

Fortunately she hardly resembled the sketch she'd

spotted hanging on public boards, here and in several villages they'd passed through on the way. Her heart had thumped when she'd seen her, Cedric, and Enkelo's likenesses, but her hair was already longer, she was wearing patched clothes, and she was sure she had bags under her eyes. Enkelo, too, looked older than his years. And everyone would be on the lookout for three travellers, not five. She was safe, hiding in plain sight. Nobody here knew that two of the people they'd burn were standing among them.

The men with the torches approached the effigies and set them alight. Flames shot up into the night sky. The crowd roared. For a moment, Fi was mesmerized. Then she turned to Enkelo. His eyes were on the burning effigies, his mouth pinched. The fall from royal primate to vagabond was almost as steep as that from princess to pauper. "Should we find somewhere to sit?" she shouted.

Enkelo nodded, and so did Dann, who stood at Enkelo's other side. Duncan and Mason pushed a path through the crowd. Cool air washed over Fi when she finally broke free of the mob. It had felt as if the entire town had called for her to burn, but most of the square tables set up in the town square were occupied.

Mason made a beeline for an empty one and beckoned for the others to join him. Fi sat down and looked back at those on the edges of the mob and the flames that would light the sky for a while. "I'm sure the fires are keeping everyone warm," she said, pulling her threadbare cloak tighter around her shoulders.

Beside her, Dann smiled. "That's the spirit."

Enkelo didn't smile. "The bards haven't sung any tales of Erryn."

"One sung of the Beast Master," Fi reminded him.

"Yes, but not about anything she did in Bexley, or nearby."

Fear tightened Fi's throat. "What do you think it means?" she asked, not wanting to give her fear a voice by answering her own question.

Enkelo shrugged. "We know she wasn't captured here. They'd definitely tell that tale."

Fi felt her shoulders relax. She wasn't thinking rationally. Enkelo was right. If Erryn had died here, Bexley's people would be bragging about it. Had she passed through without drawing attention, then? No, that couldn't be true. The spymaster had said she'd been seen here. "Did the message say—" She broke off when a man plunked himself down at their table and raised the mug of ale he held.

"To the Seven, and the bards, and . . . and . . ." His brow furrowed. "Where's your ale? You should have ale."

The man's words were slurred. Fi and the others exchanged warning glances.

"And who are you, young lady?" the man said, his blurry eyes settling on Fi. He patted the empty place next to him on the bench. "Why don't you come over here and sit with me?"

Fi stiffened. She didn't know what to say and looked at Dann, but it was Enkelo who stepped in.

"That's my niece and her young man," Enkelo said gruffly.

Her young man? Fi was certain Enkelo wasn't aware of her feelings for Dann, but her cheeks suddenly felt warm.

The man raised his mug to Fi and Dann. "Well, all the best to you," he bellowed. Then he gulped down some ale and wiped his mouth with his sleeve. "Oh, I remember courting my Darla. I miss her, my Darla. She loves festivals like this. I'll have to tell her all about it when I get home. I miss her." He set his mug on the table and stared down at it. "I miss my Darla."

The poor man looked so miserable that Fi felt sorry for him. "Why isn't she with you?" she couldn't help asking.

"She's at home with our young ones," he said, his eyes still downcast. "I haven't seen her for months."

"Why?"

"I've been on the road, haven't I? Got to make coin somehow. I hawk my wares from Stronghaven to Denkirk. That's where my Darla is. In Denkirk."

"You're a travelling merchant," Enkelo said.

The man nodded and lifted his head. "You're not from here," he said, to nobody in particular. "You know how I can tell? You're not drinking!" He roared with laughter and downed more ale. "Where are you from, then?"

Enkelo hesitated, then said, "Persh."

"Oh, Persh. Are you coming or going?"

"What?"

"Are you coming or going?"

Fi stifled a smile at the confusion on Enkelo's face. "We're going to Ableton," Enkelo said.

"Oh, you're going." The man nodded. "Good thing you're going east and not north. You don't want to be going north. No, no, no. I just came from the north. You don't want to be going up there."

"Why not?" Enkelo asked. "Wild folk?"

The man barked a laugh. "If only that were the concern. No, they don't make trouble with you if you don't make trouble with them." His brows shot up. "Or maybe I should say they don't make trouble with *ye*." He laughed again and slapped the table. Fi didn't understand what was so funny. "No, it's the Beast Master."

"Beast Master?" Fi blurted. "What about the Beast Master?"

The man pointed toward the sky. "She's up there. She's up there."

Fi's heart pounded. Did he mean the heavens? "Up where?" she asked, cursing the tremor in her voice. When he lifted his mug to drink more ale, Fi wanted to strangle him. "Up where?" she asked again, sounding shrill this time.

"Do you mean Stronghaven?" Dann asked calmly.

The man coughed into his ale. "That's what I mean. Stronghaven."

"Did you see her there?"

"I heard what she did. Gave me nightmares. I couldn't get away fast enough. Usually I stay a few weeks, but as soon as I heard, I left. A few extra coins aren't worth never seeing my Darla again. I sometimes walk the laneways. It could have been me. She could have done it to me."

Fi swallowed. "What did she do?"

"Ripped apart thirty men. Slaughtered them. Tore

them apart." He swept out his arms. "Blood everywhere. The poor sods didn't stand a chance."

Fi's stomach roiled. Enkelo turned to the man, his face hard. "Take more care with your words. There's a lady present."

The man frowned. "I didn't mean to frighten you, young lady. And don't you fret, you have nothing to worry about. You're not going that way."

But they had been, until the spymaster had told them to come here. "Are—are you sure it was the Beast Master?" Fi asked him. The man across from her was drunk and could be telling taller tales than the bards.

"We'd heard the Beast Master had passed through Bexley," Enkelo said. "We almost decided to stay home."

"No, no trail of blood and guts here," the man said. He winced when Enkelo glared at him, then raised his mug and pointed at it. "You think this is doing the talking, but it's not. They saw Rachagha. Hunters in Stronghaven. No, she's there. Probably killed more people by now." He wagged his finger. "They need to catch her and string her up. The girl must be mental now, not thinking straight. Maybe she'll keep going north and the wild folk will get her. They'll give her what's coming to her."

Father had likely hoped the same. Was Erryn mad? Was she setting the Fallen on anyone who crossed her path? If they managed to find her, would she recognize them? Would she try to kill them? "I'm tired," she murmured to Dann. And sick at heart.

"We should be going," Dann said.

The man drew back. "What? It's early. Get yourself an ale."

Dann gave a curt shake of his head. "We have an early start on the morrow."

"Do you need anything for your journey? I'll be at my wagon at seven, near the board. I'll give you a discount."

Fi wanted to roll her eyes. The chances that this merchant would be up at seven were about the same as her sitting on the throne on the morrow. "Good night," she said to him, but received no reply. He'd put his head down on the table and would soon be snoring.

"We're going the wrong way," she said, as soon as they were out of the drunk's earshot. "Why would the spymaster send us the wrong way?"

"I doubt he intended to," Enkelo said. "Many rumours must reach his ears. He has to sort through them and decide which are true."

"But you said the contact you spoke to earlier told us to keep going east. Surely the spymaster would have heard that Rachagha was seen near Stronghaven, and about this supposed slaughter. Birds travel faster than merchants."

"Do we believe the story?" Dann glanced back at the table they'd left. "Not the most reliable witness."

Enkelo's eyes were thoughtful. "I think we should go to Stronghaven. That's where she was heading when we left the Royal City, and there hasn't been so much as a whisper that she's come east."

"Back to Persh, then?" Fi said.

"No, we'll get there sooner if we go north from here, and then veer west."

Fi wished she'd paid more attention during her geography lessons, and all her other lessons, too. The monarch should know more about Daros and its people than she did. She'd never expected to rule.

"Do you agree?" Dann asked her.

She appreciated him asking for her opinion. Yes, he believed her to be the queen, but until she took the throne, deferring to her was polite, and nothing more. "Yes, I do. Let's head north. We need to find her." If the man's tale was true . . . Fi couldn't bear to think about it.

Toe ran the whetstone along his sword's edge for the last time, satisfied the blade was sharp. He hadn't bloodied it since leaving the stronghold. The scouts he travelled with were helping them skirt around hunters. When they couldn't avoid an encounter, the Mothers' marks had allowed them to continue on their way without bloodshed. They were only a few days away from Loring now. He should be looking forward to the bulging coin purse he'd receive when he delivered the contracts in his pouch, but he worried about Erryn. When Avere had first made her promise and urged him and Renn to promise the same, Toe had agreed with the hope it wouldn't come to that. But now, when they were so close . . . the blade he'd just sharpened could end Erryn's life. She was his friend. He'd be doing it for her, but it would tear him apart.

He looked up when a shadow fell over him. Renn crouched and lowered her voice. "We need to come up with a plan to help Erryn."

He sighed. "No."

"We have to!"

"We've done all we can. I know she's a friend. I know she's not a threat to anyone. But helping her wouldn't be helping her."

Renn's brow furrowed. "What do ye mean?"

"Ye know what I mean. If we help her get away in Loring, then what? What would be next for her? She wouldn't be able to travel with us."

"She's been travelling with us for a while."

"Only because we promised to help her get to Loring. We've done that. She said herself we're not in her debt."

"We wouldn't be doing it because we're in her debt."

Toe could sense Renn's desperation. Somehow he had to make her see sense. "Erryn wouldn't want us to help her. If there's nothing in Loring, she's ready to die."

Renn's eyes flashed. "Ye're wrong."

"Did ye see how quickly she agreed to this plan? Even if there's something in Loring to tell her why she's the way she is, she knows there will be nothing left for her. Her life would be one of running and hiding. She doesn't want that." He softened his tone. "Ye know she wouldn't survive. If we hadn't travelled with her, she'd already be dead."

When Renn lowered her head, Toe hoped he'd gotten through to her. He understood why she still hoped to save Erryn. She'd become fast friends with her, and Renn didn't make friends. She kept to herself. City folk ignored her, and her own kin had banished her. Toe had been her only friend, until Erryn. He couldn't fault her for not keeping her distance, because he'd grown close to

Erryn too. But he knew when to let go, and Erryn knew the same. She wanted to go to the Seven. Others would say they wouldn't accept her, but he believed in his heart they would. She was a good sort. She hadn't asked to be a Fallener. "We all made a promise to her, and we—"

Renn's head snapped up. "Ye just don't want to help her." She leaped to her feet and whirled away.

Toe grabbed her arm. "Listen to me. I know ye're loyal to those ye care about, but this isn't the time to cross the clan. If there's nothing in Loring, we'll make sure she has an easy death. That's all we can do for her now."

Renn jerked her arm from his grasp and stomped away. Toe stared after her, hoping the stubborn woman wouldn't throw her life away for a lost cause.

Erryn accepted her meat and bread from Avere and walked away from the fire, aware of everyone's eyes upon her. She always took her meals in the tent, with Renn. Not only would Asha and her people not serve her, but when she'd sat down to eat the first time they'd stopped for a meal, the muttering and hard looks had made it clear she wasn't welcome. Nor was Renn—the shamed. So they ate in the tent, which suited them both fine. Except Renn was nowhere to be seen this evening. She wasn't waiting for Avere to serve her. When Erryn had asked Toe if he'd seen her, he'd said she wanted some time alone. Erryn had pressed him, but he'd had no more answers for her.

She ducked into the tent and sat cross-legged on the ground. She'd give Renn a few minutes, but then she'd have to eat; otherwise her supper would be cold. Erryn wasn't worried about her yet, but only because Toe hadn't seemed worried. If Renn hadn't returned by the time the sun went down, she'd—

Renn stepped into the tent and folded her arms. "Do ye want to die?" she snapped.

Erryn put her bowl down and looked at Renn, who was silhouetted in the glow cast by the fire outside. "Do ye want to die?" Renn asked again, standing as still as a statue; her tight muscles must be as hard as stone.

"No."

Renn dropped her arms to her sides and shook her head. "I knew Toe didn't have it right. He said ye want to die."

"I don't *want* to die, but if we get to Loring and I can't help heal the land, and I have no reason to believe I can, there will be no reason for me to live."

Renn's shoulders stiffened again. "No reason," she said, her voice too quiet.

Erryn scrambled to explain herself. "No reason that wouldn't hurt others. People I care about. Like you."

"Toe said ye'd have nothing but running and hiding, but ye wouldn't have to be alone. Ye'd have us."

"No, I wouldn't." Erryn pushed herself to her feet, but remained where she was. "I wouldn't do that to you, or Toe. No matter what happens in Loring, we'll have to part ways. You have to go back to running contracts. There's no other way."

Renn stared at her for a moment, then her mouth twisted. "Ye've given up."

"I haven't given up. I'm being realistic. Do you know

why I've wanted to get to Loring ever since I heard about it?"

"Because of the temple," Renn said grudgingly.

"The temple that might not exist. And if it does, all I'm hoping for is an explanation. A reason why I'm a Fallener. That's all I expect. I'll still be a Fallener. I'll still be cursed. I'll still have this." She pointed at her forehead. "I'll still be hunted. I still won't be able to live a normal life. But maybe I'll know why. But you know what? There probably isn't a temple. If there ever was one, it's probably gone. Loring isn't going to change my life."

"Ye don't know what—"

Erryn vigorously shook her head. "No, Renn. Don't start believing the lie we created. I started this journey because I heard another Fallener was on his way to Loring to visit some temple, but now that's been blown into this huge lie about me being able to heal the land. All because of some religious zealot Avere met and probably doesn't believe. It's a lie we created to get the clan to help us. Don't start believing it. I don't."

"But the book . . . it shows Zhikinden blessing a Fallener."

Erryn wanted to shake her. "It shows Zhikinden blessing someone who's holding a whip. I don't use a whip."

"But Zayvang is sitting before the one holding the whip. And whips and Falleners go together."

"Zhikinden's there. She commands Zayvang. And it's a book that belonged to someone who doesn't follow the Holy Texts."

"Yer Holy Texts aren't my Holy Texts."

"But your people and my people agree on the subject of Falleners."

"But—"

"Renn! I'm a dead woman. We both knew that, right? Do not throw your life away for me. When we get to Loring, whatever happens, you have to let happen, and then go back to Sull with Toe. That's what I want for you."

Renn slowly shook her head.

"I wish we hadn't met," Erryn said.

Renn's face fell. "Now ye're telling the truth. Ye don't care. Ye lie with me and tell me ye care because ye've decided ye're going to die, and so ye're taking whatever ye can take. Ye don't care about me." She looked down at her feet.

For a moment, Erryn considered agreeing with her. Renn would be angry with her and maybe even hate her. That could be the quickest way to get her to see sense, so she wouldn't be noble, and loyal, and sacrifice herself for a cursed woman. But Erryn didn't want to die with Renn believing she'd used her, that their feelings for each other meant nothing. She couldn't hurt Renn like that.

"I care about you," she said. "That's why I'm begging you not to fight, not to interfere, if there's nothing in Loring."

"But ye wish we hadn't met," Renn said, her head still bowed.

"Because you wouldn't have gotten mixed up in this. You'd be running contracts, not here, not caring about me. In every other way, I'm glad we met. It's one of the few positive things that's come out of me being a

Fallener." The other bright spots were her friendship with Toe, Rodney's kindness, and discovering what it was like to live free of the royal family's expectations. "If I wasn't a Fallener, our paths would never have crossed. I'd be in the Royal City and married by now, or at least betrothed to someone I'd never care about in the same way I care about you."

Renn didn't speak or move. Erryn wanted to go to her, but if someone were to enter the tent—she and Renn only touched each other when the only ones awake were the hunters who kept first watch.

She listened to the voices of those gathered around the fire. She couldn't distinguish who was who, since most of the wild folk wouldn't speak to her, but it sounded like most were still eating, and even if that weren't the case, nobody except Avere entered the tent occupied by the Fallener and the shamed. Even Toe didn't venture inside, but only because it was important for him to appear to side with the clan. Erryn wasn't particularly concerned about Avere, given that the woman would likely do what she'd intended to do since she'd approached them in Stronghaven. She cared about Renn a lot more than she cared about Avere, and went to her.

"Renn."

Renn ignored her.

"Please look at me. Please."

A lump rose in her throat when Renn raised her head. Renn's eyes were moist. Erryn's eyes welled up, too. She swallowed and took Renn's face in her hands. Renn was the more muscular one, but they were about the same height. "I'm sorry," Erryn whispered. "I've been selfish. I shouldn't have let this happen, knowing that it couldn't last."

"Ye think ye're the one in charge?" Renn snorted, but she didn't move away. "I do what I want to do."

"That's what I'm afraid of," Erryn said, managing a small smile. "You've done enough for me. You've given me the greatest gift—seeing beyond my forehead. You can't do anything more for me. I don't want you to."

"Ye sound like Toe."

"Listen to Toe. It's not because I wouldn't want to stay with you, and Toe, after Loring, but that I can't. I can't have that on my conscience, and it wouldn't be practical. He knows that, and so do you." She hurried on without giving Renn a chance to reply. "We don't have much time left. I don't want to waste it arguing with you. You've done more than you had to for me, much more. Live a long life, running contracts or whatever else you want to do." She gripped Renn's face tighter, wishing she'd never have to let go. "That's what I want for you."

"Ye don't care about what I want for ye."

"I know, it's not fair. None of this is fair. Why am I a Fallener? Why? That's what I hope to find out in Loring, but that's all I've ever hoped for. Now that we've involved your clan, there's only one fate for me. I don't want you to share that fate. I want to die knowing you'll be all right." Erryn hesitated, then went on. "Dying will be hard enough knowing you'll be okay. I don't want to have to worry about you. I . . ." Her voice choked off.

Renn's eyes widened. "Ye don't want to die. Ye don't want to."

"It's not the dying. Avere will be quick. It's the what comes after. Will I see them?" Erryn's voice quavered. "Or will they throw me away?" Not wanting Renn to see her fear, she pulled her into a hug and remained in her arms long after her supper had grown cold.

Striding along a trail wide enough to accommodate two wagons, Avere gazed into the distance. "Are you sure that's Loring?" she said to Asha. It didn't look very impressive. No walls, and she couldn't see any guards from here. She turned to the priestess trudging next to her. She'd wanted to be at her side as they approached Loring, and would stick to her like glue. Asha was the leader. Asha would decide Erryn's fate. Avere wanted to know which way the wind blew, so she could be ready, if need be.

"What were ye expecting?" Asha said.

Something larger. "A city like Stronghaven, I suppose."

"Stronghaven is one of yer cities. Loring is ours."

"I didn't know you had cities."

"Only a few. Some clans joined together and the cities naturally came to be. But some of yer folk live in them, too. Scholars, mostly. They come to study our ways. I don't know why. Yer king doesn't bother with us, and we don't bother with him. If he tried to collect taxes, we'd give him the head of the tax collector."

Avere raised her brows. "The king's dead. He was assassinated."

Asha shrugged. "When I say king, I mean any king. Whatever soft bottom is on the throne. It makes no difference to us."

"Does the Primacy have a presence in Loring?" Avere asked, thinking of the temple Erryn sought.

"No. We have no use for them."

"But—"

"Ye think ye're the only people with temples? We don't have them, but our people and yer people aren't the only people. Where did ye get the book on yer belt?"

"I told you, a religious zealot gave it to me."

Asha nodded. "Maybe her people have temples."

"Maybe, but they're based in Westerfox."

Asha rolled her eyes.

"But there may be other cults with temples," Avere drawled. "I'm following. I'm not slow." Asha didn't respond, leaving Avere to wonder what the priestess thought about her, not that she cared. "How are we going to find the temple Erryn's looking for?"

"We'll ask."

Avere waited for more, but Asha remained silent.

The trees lining the trail thinned out, and they passed a wooden house. As they continued walking, they passed more houses, the only indication they were entering Loring. No guards challenged them. When they reached a fork in the trail, Asha stopped and whirled. The others gathered around her.

Avere searched for Erryn and saw her standing with her arms crossed, appearing calm, except that her fingernails were digging into her arms. Renn stood behind her and could be a problem; she already appeared ready to pounce. The woman had better stay out of it. Avere didn't want to kill her. Toe looked as if he didn't have a care in the world, but his eyes were wary and his shoulders stiff. The rest of the wild folk were alert and waiting for Asha to speak.

"Shila, ye've been here before. Which way to the Mothers?" Asha said.

Shila pointed to the left. Asha spun around and set off down the left trail. Avere quickly fell into step with her. Usually she could hear the murmur of the others softly speaking, and the occasional laugh, but now that they were here, everyone was silent.

Loring certainly wasn't a bustling town. Everyone who passed them acknowledged Asha and ignored everyone else. "Turn here," Shila barked from behind them.

They did so, and then Asha must have spotted something that meant something to her, because she made a beeline to a hut with furs adorning its outer walls. She whirled again and held up her hand. "I will go in. Wait here." She disappeared inside the hut.

If Asha emerged and said there was no temple anywhere in the town, would her people kill Erryn here, or would they want to make a public display of her slow, torturous death? Avere surveyed her surroundings. This may be a wild folk town, but Avere could see the influence of city folk creeping in. Some structures were made of stone. A sign hanging outside a two-storey building up the street displayed a mug, the familiar symbol for taverns. And the locals' tastes in fashion extended beyond leather tunics.

Loring would have a town square or three, somewhere folk could gather to see the Fallener cut open.

Avere had two choices. She could risk the ire of those with her by standing next to Erryn and planting a dagger in her the moment Asha said the game was up, or she could slip away, throw a dagger, and lose herself in the town. She was good at that—losing herself—but it would be more difficult in Loring, where she stuck out like a sore thumb and had only memorized the few potential escape routes she'd seen since they entered the town. There weren't many, but she'd prefer to kill Erryn from afar. It was unfortunate they'd given Renn back her sword when they'd left the stronghold. She was loyal to Erryn. Misfits always stuck together, and this misfit was handy with a blade and wouldn't hesitate to run it into Avere's belly.

Waiting for a better opportunity wasn't an option. The wild folk wanted Erryn's blood. The moment they knew they'd travelled here for nothing, Erryn would be cut, and pummelled, and humiliated. She'd already be bleeding and bruised by the time they started to remove fingers, and toes, and eyes. If Asha emerged from the hut and announced there was no temple, it would have to be now.

Pretending something about the hut across the road had caught her eye, Avere sauntered away from the others and had a better look at where she could run. When her dagger hit its mark and Erryn crumpled to the ground, Avere would take advantage of the few precious seconds of confusion, but that would be the only head start she'd have. She—

Footsteps, behind her. Soft, but there. She turned around and wasn't surprised to see Renn.

Renn's hard eyes bored into her. "Where are ye going?"

Avere considered lying, but only for a second. The woman wasn't stupid. "I'm preparing to keep my promise. Do stay out of the way. And don't look at me like that. We all promised. She made us promise."

"We shouldn't have promised."

"But we did, because it was the sensible thing to do. If there's no temple and you start swinging your sword, you'll die. I'll run. Toe will do whatever Asha tells him to do, but they might kill him, anyway. And then they'll be free to kill Erryn, slowly, and painfully, and she'll die alone, horribly alone, because you were hot-headed and didn't do what she wanted you to do. So if you care about her at all, if you feel indebted to her in any way, you'll go back over there and stay out of the way. Otherwise you'll be responsible for her being ripped open and taking hours to die, while people spit on her."

Renn didn't move. She didn't blink. For a moment, Avere thought the woman was going to grab her neck and snap it. But then Renn turned on her heel and went back to the others.

Avere slowly exhaled. She'd meant every word she'd said, but her daggers suddenly felt heavy. Was it because of Erryn? Malina? Did she not want her gut to be wrong because she'd always trusted her instincts? Had she talked herself into believing there would be something in Loring to justify her listening to an old bat in Stronghaven and disobeying Arrick for the first time?

She didn't have time to ponder her answers. Asha stepped out of the hut. Avere quickly decided which way she'd run and reached for a dagger. She strained to hear what the priestess would say. Asha appeared calm. "... in Loring," she said. "... see a scholar ..."

The wild folk standing farthest away from Asha and behind Erryn turned around. Avere's fingers left her dagger. She smiled and rejoined the group. "Sorry, I didn't hear that. I was looking at the blanket hanging on the line. The pattern is exquisite."

"We're going to see one of yer people's scholars," Asha said. "The Mother doesn't know of anything in Loring that we consider a sacred place, and there are none of yer temples. When I said the temple could be very old, she said there's a scholar here who might know something about yer people that she doesn't. She told me the way." Asha walked past the others to take the lead.

Avere hurried to join her, glancing at Erryn as she passed her. She looked all right, but it must be difficult, not knowing from one minute to the next whether she was going to live or die. "I'm a bit surprised we're going to see the scholar," she said to Asha when she caught up to her. "Even if there was a temple some time ago, it's not here now."

"It may be something else now. And it may have something on its walls that would mean something to us. We must be sure the Fallener can't heal the land before we kill her."

Avere nodded. The lie they'd told had saved Erryn's life twice now. She doubted it would save Erryn's life a third time, but she was in Loring, a wild folk town, travelling with a priestess, a group of wild folk, and a Beast Master, so what did she know?

As the group approached the two-storey structure that served as a college, Erryn's legs felt heavier with every step. While waiting outside the priestess's hut, her mouth had dried up and dread had sickened her stomach. The twenty-minute walk to the college hadn't helped. She felt as if the Seven were toying with her, deliberately stretching out the journey, so she'd have ample time to imagine her fate. What would be next? Another scholar or hut? If this scholar would be their last stop, would those who were eager to spill her blood mob her immediately? She desperately wanted to look at Renn, reach for her hand and draw courage from her, but she stared at Avere's back instead. Avere was her future; Renn a dream.

Asha stopped and lifted her hand. "I will go in. And ye," she said, turning to Avere. "And the Fallener. The rest of ye wait outside."

Renn stepped forward. "Me and Toe have been travelling with her. We should—"

"Ye wait with the others," Asha said, her tone making it clear that she wouldn't back down. She beckoned to Erryn. "Come."

Erryn tried not to look over her shoulder, but she couldn't resist. She exchanged a glance with Renn and stepped to Asha's side.

"Keep yer hat on," Asha murmured. She swung open the door.

Inside, two men sat at a wooden table. One was reading a book; the other was bent over a parchment. Both raised their heads and peered at the newcomers. The one who'd been studying the parchment raised his brows. "You're marked!" He shot to his feet and rounded the table to examine Avere's cheek. "Do you see this, Antony? She's not a Northerner, but she's marked. So is this one," he said, moving to Erryn.

"We've travelled a ways to see ye," Asha said. "We didn't want to fight with those who hunt human prey."

The scholar swung to Asha and inclined his head. "You honour us with your presence, Mother. My name is Boren, and that's Antony. May I know your name? We are so honoured."

Amusement flickered across Asha's face. "I am Asha, of the Snowlake clan. I am pleased to meet ye."

Boren smiled. Antony nodded and set his book on the table. "I have so many questions," Boren said. "Why are the two with you not Northerners? Why have you come to see us? We're honoured, of course, but I don't believe we've ever had a Mother seek us out." When he looked to Antony for confirmation, the other scholar nodded again. "Are you here seeking food? I'm afraid you'll have come for nothing. If it's pretty rocks you want, we have plenty of those, but they don't fill bellies."

"And yet, you're here," Avere said. "If the situation is so dire, why haven't you returned to wherever you're from?"

"Because this is my home now," Boren said. "When I came to study here, I intended to stay for a year, perhaps two. I'm still here for the most glorious and yet the most common of reasons. I fell in love."

"With a wild woman?"

His face tightened. "We don't call them wild folk. That's a disparaging name given to them, to you," he said, glancing at Asha, "by ignorant people. We call them Northerners, and I'd like to know why someone who thinks they're wild is marked and travelling with a Mother." Boren's face was red, and his breath came in quick gasps.

"I'm sure she didn't mean to offend," Asha said calmly. "We're here because my two companions are seeking a temple and asked our clan to help them travel to Loring."

"A temple?" Boren pursed his lips. "For you?" he said, his attention shifting to Erryn and Avere.

"Yes," Avere said, at the same time Erryn nodded.

"That doesn't explain why a Mother agreed to escort you here, and the ones who must be protecting her." He returned his gaze to Asha, clearly more interested in her than in anything Erryn and Avere would have to say.

Asha took a moment to speak. "We believe the temple may hold a clue as to why the land has sickened."

Boren's eyes widened. "Really? How interesting. I'm afraid you may have come a long way for nothing. I don't know of any temple."

Erryn's breath caught in her throat. She felt as if she'd been punched in the gut. For a second, she considered bursting from the hut and running as fast as her legs would carry her, but only for a second.

"Occasionally a primate comes here hoping to educate

and perhaps sway, but they only ever last five minutes. We haven't had one come through for at least ten years now. Those of us who require the Seven's guidance see the Mothers, who have been kind enough to commune with us."

"It might not be one of those temples," Asha said.

"The temple may be connected to this book." Avere unhooked the zealot's book from her belt and handed it to Boren.

He lifted the cover and leafed through the book's pages. "Fascinating," he murmured. "Some of the symbols are familiar, but others . . ." He glanced at Antony. "Come and look."

Antony pushed back his chair and came over to Boren. He studied the book's pages over Boren's shoulder, his brow furrowed. "That could represent a Beast Master."

"Mmm," Boren said absently. "What do you make of the skulls?"

"I think they're supposed to represent Death," Avere said.

"Death?" Boren raised his head. "What do you mean? Where did you get this?"

"A cultist I ran into in Stronghaven."

"Cultist? From where?"

"Westerfox."

"Lightning bolt and book," Antony said. "Death, and Elder Gods."

Avere's eyes lit up. "Yes!"

"Ah." Antony shook his head. "Many years ago, they

tried to bring others around to their way of thinking, but they were unsuccessful."

"Did they have a temple here?" Avere asked, excitement lifting her voice. "It could be very old, and perhaps serve as something other than a temple now."

Antony's eyes grew distant. "There are mentions of the Elder Gods in several texts the Primacy refused when putting together the canon. But this notion of Death only appears in texts the Death Cult considers sacred. "

"A temple, Antony," Avere prompted. "Did they have a meeting place here?"

"Why would they have a meeting place in the middle of territory that has always been the Northerners' home?" Boren asked. "The Primacy quickly dismissed their beliefs. Do you think the Northerners welcomed them?"

Antony raised his finger.

"The Northerners would have been more suspicious of them." Boren snapped the book shut and handed it back to Avere, then gazed at Asha. "Do you mind if I ask why you think anything associated with this cult would help heal the sickness of the land, as you put it?"

Asha opened her mouth, but then closed it, appearing at a loss.

Erryn hadn't wanted to draw attention to herself by speaking, but she couldn't stand by and make Asha lie for her. "You said one of the drawings in the book could—" Her voice was as thin as a thread. She cleared her throat. "One of the drawings could represent a Beast Master. There's a Beast Master walking Daros now. The cultist who gave us the book said the Beast Master could help if she went to a temple in Loring."

Boren's eyes bulged. "The Beast Master could help." His tone conveyed his skepticism.

Antony waved his finger. "Boren—"

"There are two problems with that theory. First, the rumour of a Beast Master has reached our ears, but is it true? And if it is, how would you get her here? She'd likely kill you the moment you approached her."

"Boren," Antony said, more forcefully.

"Second, there is absolutely nothing in any texts accepted by the Primacy, or the teachings of the Mothers, that suggests Beast Masters serve the Seven. If anything, they serve the Fallen. I would expect anyone who could influence the land in any way to serve the Seven." He rolled his eyes. "I don't know why the Death Cult survives."

"She didn't call her people the Death Cult," Avere said.

"Well, she wouldn't, would she?"

Antony shook Boren's arm. "Boren, I may have remembered something."

Irritation flashed across Boren's face. "What?"

"The rubble. To the north."

"We don't know what it was, and they don't want rubble. How would rubble help them?"

"What rubble?" Avere said.

Boren waved his hand dismissively. "Oh, there are ruins of something about half a day's travel from here, but if that's what you're looking for, there's nothing left. Just a few columns that have tumbled over."

"Also what used to be a stone floor, or maybe a roof,"

Antony said. "The land has claimed most of it. Some areas look like an overgrown path. You'll see a stone slab here and there, still poking through the growth. It's not a path, though. At one time, the odd slabs we can still see belonged to a floor, or ceiling, or roof."

"But there's nothing else there. No cultists. No primates. Nobody," Boren said. "I'm sorry, but you've come all this way for nothing."

Erryn consciously controlled her breathing and caught Avere's eye, hoping for a sign that Avere would do what she'd promised, like nod or give her a knowing smile, but Avere turned to Asha and said, "When we leave, I'd like the three of us to speak away from the others before you tell them what was said here."

"All right," Asha said, her face unreadable. "I thank ye," she said to Boren and Antony.

"The honour was ours," Boren said.

Asha tilted her head toward the door and left the building, with Erryn and Avere at her heels. Those waiting outside looked at the priestess, curiosity in all their eyes, bloodlust in some. "The three of us must speak alone for a moment," Asha said to them.

As Erryn followed her a short distance away from the others, she began to suspect what Avere would say. Asha whirled to face them. "Ye want us to go to the ruin because ye're thinking the rectangles in the drawings could be stone slabs," she stated.

Avere raised her brows in surprise. "Yes, that's exactly what I was going to suggest. It's probably nothing, but since we've come all this way . . ."

"We should see it through, but I expect we'll find nothing there. He said half a day's travel." Asha looked up at the sky. "If we eat and then leave, we should arrive before dark. I'll tell the others." She looked at Erryn. "I'm sorry," she murmured, then walked away.

"She'll still rip you to pieces, though," Avere said, when Asha was out of earshot.

Erryn nodded. "I hope this ruin decides my fate one way or the other. Thinking that's it, then getting a reprieve, then thinking that's it again . . . I don't know how much more I can take."

"It will be the end, Erryn. It's a ruin. If there was a sign there pointing us to another place, I'm sure Boren or Antony would have mentioned it. But we have to go and look, to be sure."

"So you'll be sure when you kill me."

"Yes," Avere said unapologetically. "I'll have to run, afterwards. I'm not only worried about Asha's people, but about Renn. She wants to save you."

"I know." Erryn searched for Renn. Her heart swelled. She wanted more time with her, but if she could somehow force her to stay in Loring, she would. "I've told her not to throw her life away."

Avere snorted.

"Try not to kill her," Erryn said, doing her best not to sound as if she were pleading. "I'd like her to live."

"I'll try, but she might take any choice away from me."

But at least Avere would try. Erryn wouldn't ask or expect her to sacrifice her own life for Renn's, but knowing Avere wouldn't kill Renn for nothing offered some comfort.

"Let's go join the others and get this over with," Avere said.

Erryn nodded. As Asha had a minute ago, she looked up at the sky, the same sky that had been here yesterday, and would be here on the morrow. She wouldn't be here to see it.

Carrying a torch to illuminate the way ahead, Fi carefully wound her way through the trees, looking for a good spot to pee. She looked over her shoulder to make sure she could still see the campfire burning. That was the rule: she could go far enough away to have some privacy, but not so far that she couldn't see the fire. Even so, she knew one of the men would be peering in her direction, ready to run to her if he spotted any threats. When they'd first fled the Royal City, Enkelo had wanted to accompany her on these calls of nature and turn his back, a thought that both angered and embarrassed her, even now. He'd only wanted to protect her, but a lady needed her privacy. It wouldn't do for the fugitive royal primate to hear the queen without a crown watering the forest floor.

Here would do; there was enough room for her to crouch. She'd become adept at pulling down her undergarment with her right hand while holding the torch in her left. While she relieved herself, she kept her eyes on the campfire in the distance, the occasional hoot of an owl intruding on the otherwise quiet night and her thoughts. They still had a ways to go to reach

Stronghaven. Would they find Erryn there? Fi couldn't forget what the merchant in Bexley had told them, about Erryn commanding the Fallen to rip apart so many men. He must have exaggerated, but by how much?

A minute later, she started back toward the campfire. A shout suddenly shattered the silence, and then another one. Fi's heart hammered in her chest. She ran—strong arms grabbed her from behind, lifting her off her feet. She screamed—a hand clamped over her mouth. She dropped the torch. Flames sprang up around it. A shadowy figure darted in front of her and stamped out the small fire. He motioned for whoever held Fi to go.

Fi dug in her heels and tried to elbow her captor, but he hung on. Her screams couldn't escape her throat. The shouting from the campfire and the sound of steel crossing steel grew more distant. Fi kicked her legs and strained against the arms that held her, but it was no use.

The man who'd put out the fire had left the torch behind. She could barely see him, but could hear him breathing. The darkness closed in on her. She saw shadowy figures everywhere. Her throat felt so tight, swallowing was difficult. Her captors must be familiar with this forest, or they could see a beacon that she couldn't. It would be too far away for Dann, Enkelo, and the others to see it. They wouldn't know in which direction these men had taken her, and that was if they didn't perish in the fighting.

Fear raged at the thought. She struggled to break free again, lunging forward with all her strength, but the arms holding her refused to give. She focused her remaining energy on not panicking, on not giving her captors the satisfaction, but that was all she could do. Her captors had triumphed. She was at their mercy.

She figured that ten to fifteen minutes had passed by the time they stopped moving. She could make out a covered wagon in the gloom. A horse nickered. The man who'd trailed behind her the whole way drew a strip of cloth from his pocket. "I'm going to gag you," he growled. "Don't scream. Don't say a word, or I'll smash your face in."

Fi blinked at him. The hand on her mouth lifted, but the cloth quickly replaced it, cutting against the corners of her mouth. The one behind her had to move slightly to allow the other man to tie the gag. The pressure on her chest eased. Perhaps she could break free, but there would be nowhere to run. Resigned to her fate, she didn't struggle when her hands were roughly pulled behind her back and bound.

The man who'd gagged her swam back into view and studied her. The captor who'd dragged her here joined him. Shock widened Fi's eyes. A woman! With arms the size of tree trunks and muscular legs to match, and with much paler skin than the man. Fear tightened Fi's throat again. Not just any woman. A wild woman.

"What do you think, Jeena?" the man said.

"She'll clean up well." Jeena leaned toward Fi. "We'll get a fat coin purse for ye. Ye'll be the prize in some lord's house."

The prize in some lord's house? Weren't they going to hand her over to the guard?

"We need one more for the auction," the man said.

Auction? Fi's stomach dropped. They were going to sell

her! They hadn't captured her for the bounty on her head. They didn't know who she was. Anger almost overpowered Fi's fear. She'd heard whispers that an underground slave trade existed in Daros, but the prospect had been too horrible for her to accept and believe.

Jeena grabbed her arm and pulled her toward the wagon. Fi went meekly, knowing she was defeated for now. What had happened to Dann and the others? If they were all dead—no, they must have survived, but they'd have a difficult time finding her.

She didn't resist when Jeena leaped into the wagon and pulled her inside, while the other captor pushed her from behind. He waited for Jeena to light a lamp within the safety of the wagon, then climbed in after them and pulled the door shut.

"Sit," Jeena barked, and helped Fi along by pushing her down. Her captors sat opposite her, their stern faces more frightening in the glow of the lamp. Hard eyes stared at Fi. She flinched when the man reached for her face.

Jeena slapped his hand away. "Keep yer hands off the merchandise," she snapped. "Ye've caused enough trouble already."

He shot her an irritated look. "They should be back by now. There were only four of them."

"I bet they're picking over the belongings." Jeena's mouth pressed into a thin line. "I told them not to do that. It's not worth the trouble. We have what's valuable."

The man leered at Fi. Sweat trickled down her cheek, and her arms and shoulders ached, but her mind was causing her the most distress. The slaver had said there were *only* four, so the others, Fi's precious men, must have been outnumbered. How many slavers had taken them by surprise? How long had the slavers watched them sitting around the fire, sharing a quiet supper?

Jeena shifted impatiently. "I don't like this. We're sitting ducks. If they're not back in five minutes, we'll go back to camp. They can make their own way there."

The man nodded. Jeena appeared to be in charge. A wild woman. Fi had thought they lived in the forests and killed those who weren't wild, but this one was a slaver. Even though the wild folk were citizens of Daros, Father and his predecessors had never bothered with them. "Let them live wild. As long as they don't break our laws, trespass, and steal from us, let them be savages," he'd said. "We have enough animals to tame without taming them." Well, if, by the grace of the Seven, she somehow ended up on the throne, she'd bother with them. Slaving? She'd tame every last one of them.

A knock at the wagon door made her heart race. The man swung it open. Outside stood another man, his breath coming in quick gasps. "They were . . . well trained." He took a moment to gulp down air. "We killed one and . . . almost took another one down, but they slew three. I could see how it was going to end, so I ran."

Killed one. Almost took one down. Fi's eyes welled, and her shoulders sagged with guilt. She couldn't help but think of Dann over the others.

"Did they see where ye ran?" Jeena asked.

The man shook his head.

"Get up front, then. We need to be on our way."

He took one final deep breath and trudged out of view. The man with Jeena swung the door shut again. Fi almost fell over when the wagon lurched forward. Jeena squinted at her. "Something's nagging at me about ye," she said. "I've seen yer face before."

Fi wanted to snort. She highly doubted it.

Jeena suddenly grabbed Fi's cloak and pulled her forward.

"What are you doing?" the man said.

"I want to look at her hands." The wild woman lifted the lamp, crouched next to Fi, and tugged on her hands. Fi desperately wanted to pull them away, but remained still. Jeena grunted and returned to her place next to the other slaver.

"What?" he asked.

"I'll know for sure when we get to camp."

He shrugged.

The wagon jumped when it rode over a bump, almost tipping Fi onto her side again. She wanted to scream, to cry, to smack the smug looks off the slavers' faces. Dann. Enkelo. Duncan and Mason. Who'd lived? Who'd died? If they'd killed their attackers, there wouldn't be anyone to question. If they hadn't . . . Fi wanted to curl up into a ball and howl. Dann could be dead, and if anyone had survived, they'd never find her. She could be anywhere in Daros. There would be no coup. She would not sit on the throne. The Lyos dynasty had come to an end. She was alone. Alone.

Erryn didn't turn to look when someone's fingers brushed

against hers. She could sense Renn and feel her tension. As they'd drawn closer to the ruin site, the group had fallen silent. When they reached the site, the civil masks of those who'd tolerated her would quickly fall away. Eyes would grow feral. Teeth would bare. Erryn wanted to grab Renn's hand and hang on to it, but she'd have to be satisfied with knowing Renn was there and would mourn for her, and would hopefully listen to Toe and quietly return to Sull. If Avere kept her promise, there would be an intact body to bury, rather than pieces, but Erryn didn't want Renn and Toe to worry about her empty shell. She didn't know where she'd be, but she wouldn't be anywhere here, on the physical plane.

The Fallen scratched at her mind, interrupting her thoughts. This wasn't the first time they'd caught her attention since the visit with the scholars. They were growing more agitated. Did they understand what was about to happen? Did they want to be free one last time? Every fibre of Erryn's being wanted to call them, to be with them, but she didn't want to die before reaching the ruin. She wanted to see this through, to know. And when she knew, she *would* call them, but not to kill anyone. She wouldn't care that the wild folk would keep sending them back to the heavenly plane. She'd call them again, and again, until Avere's dagger hit her mark and Erryn fell, her eyes on Zayvang, or Lerxis, or Sath, or Quon, or Cheturrak, or Rachagha, or Iss. She would meet Renn's eyes one last time before she called them. She'd smile, and will Renn to live.

One of the wild folk scouting ahead—Yanik, Erryn

thought—was running up the narrow trail they were walking. "The ruin is just around the bend," he said, not sounding out of breath. His eyes flicked to Erryn, then back to Asha. "Nobody's there. Maybe there was a temple once, but the land has swallowed most of the floor. The columns are broken. There are chunks of stone—"

A great roar ripped through Erryn's mind, drowning out the scout's words. Her head felt as if it would explode. Her surroundings faded away. Zayvang . . . She lifted her hands and stared at them, expecting to see fur and sharp claws. The sensation quickly died, but then she felt as if Zayvang were about to burst from within her into the physical plane, so great was Zayvang's desire to be free. Erryn patted her chest with her hands, half-expecting to feel a gaping hole.

Then, just as suddenly, she felt perfectly normal and blinked at those standing around her. Confused, she looked down at herself and saw her cloak, and felt the bag strapped to her back and the hat on her head. What had just happened? She checked her hands again, confirmed that her skin lacked fur.

". . . go see for ourselves," Asha was saying. "We've come this far."

Dissension rumbled through those gathered.

Asha banged her walking stick on the ground and raised her hand. The murmurs stopped. "Ye will listen to me, or ye will explain yerselves back home," she said quietly.

The wild folk Erryn could see inclined their heads. Yanik sprinted down the trail and disappeared around a bend. Everyone trudged after him. The Fallen were scratching again. Struggling to put one foot in front of the other, Erryn glued her eyes to Asha's back and willed herself to keep up with her. They rounded the bend. Another roar pierced Erryn's mind. She stumbled. Someone caught her arm. Renn. It had to be Renn.

She plodded along, hardly noticing when the trail widened. Asha stopped and turned. Her mouth was moving. Beyond her, Erryn could see a column with a chipped stone sitting atop it. Her vision clouded. Zayvang was begging. *Begging.* The others were scratching, clawing, screeching . . . Erryn's teeth rattled. Her body shook. Then music . . . sweet, soothing music, calling to her. She took a step, then another one, then broke into a run and raced toward the music, feeling freer than she ever had before.

"Erryn!"

No, she had to keep running, had to reach the music and let it envelop her in its embrace.

"Erryn!"

Her vision cleared. Renn was staring at her, grasping her shoulders. "What's wrong with ye?" she asked, her forehead creased with concern. The others were gathered behind Renn, whispering and exchanging glances. They were still on the trail, on the same spot where Erryn's vision had clouded. But she'd raced toward the music. She could still hear it . . . calling to her.

"There's something there." Erryn whirled and hurried up the trail, her legs no longer feeling like lead. She burst into the clearing the ruin had preserved and fell to her knees. "I . . . there's something here. I sense it. They sense it."

"They?" someone barked.

Forcing herself to concentrate, to cut through the music and the Fallen's clamouring, she lifted her face toward the sky. Faces swam into view.

One of the wild folk sneered. "Ye would say anything to save yer worthless life. It's time, Mother. It's time."

"There's something here!" Erryn shouted. In her peripheral vision, she caught Avere moving away from the others. *No, Avere. Don't. Not yet.* She clutched her head. Scratching, and the music . . . were they scratching to the music? Was she going mad?

"There used to be a temple here, but there isn't anymore," she heard Asha say, sounding far away. "All that's here is broken stone, and the land has reclaimed much of it."

The Fallen screeched. "We haven't looked around," Erryn said. "We should look around. If there's nothing, do whatever you will with me, but we have to look."

"She's been lying to us since she came," Yanik said. "Don't listen to her, Mother. She's lying to us. She doesn't know how to tell the truth."

"He's right," another said. Raised voices agreed with him.

"No, there's something here." Erryn started to rise. Her knees hit the ground with a thud when someone pushed her back down. She searched for Renn, then saw Renn's moist eyes and wished she hadn't.

"We should do what she asks, check every stone," Renn said.

"Ye're not one of us," Yanik growled. "Ye're shamed, and ye travelled with a Fallener. We should gut ye."

No. No, no, no, no. Scratching. Screeching. Hands balled into fists.

"I travelled with the Fallener, too." Toe. "Do ye want to gut me?"

"Maybe we should." Yanik lunged and shoved Toe, who stumbled backward and then reached for his sword.

"Stop!" Asha barked, her voice not so quiet. "Ye will listen to me. What I say will be done."

The two men glared at each other, but turned to face Asha.

Erryn squinted up at her. Asha met her eyes. "There's nothing here for ye. We have done all that we can, more than others would have done. We—"

"Before you tear her limb from limb, you might want to come have a look at this." Avere.

Asha looked in the direction of Avere's voice. Erryn did too, half-seeing, half-listening to the music that still filled her mind. "Watch her," Asha said.

"No." Erryn grabbed Asha's robe. Someone kicked her hand away. Pain lanced through her wrist. She gritted her teeth. "I have a right to see. I have the right." Asha had turned to look at her. "Please," Erryn said. "I have the right to see it before you kill me."

The priestess studied her for a moment. "All right," she finally said. "Ye two come as well," she added, looking past Erryn. "But not ye," she said firmly to someone else— Renn, Erryn guessed. Part of her was relieved. Seeing Renn upset made it harder. She pushed to her feet and followed Asha over to Avere, aware of the two wild folk walking right behind her.

Avere was hunched over a square stone sitting atop a broken column. "Look at this," she murmured. "Do you think that could have been a skull?" She moved out of the way to let Asha see.

A block protruded from the stone, with something that had eroded away over time carved into its side. Asha leaned in. "I suppose it could have been, but even if it was, the purpose it served has passed. Ye said the Fallener might be able to heal the sickness in the land, that—"

The music flared. The Fallen's screeching ripped through her mind. Erryn placed her hand against the column, to steady herself. She squeezed her eyes shut and tried to listen.

". . . thinking about what was in the book," Avere was saying. Pages flipping, then, "Remember the arrow pointing at the rectangle? Do you see how it looks like we should be able to push the block? Look here." Silence, then Asha grunted. "I've tried pushing it, but it won't budge," Avere continued.

"Perhaps ye're wrong, or perhaps at one time we could have pushed it, but not now."

"It could be stuck. Let's have one of the men try."

"Ye try it," Asha said, impatience hardening her voice.

Erryn opened her eyes when she sensed one of the wild folk behind her moving. He pushed the block with one hand, then two, then turned and hurled his side against it. Nothing happened.

"Ye're wrong," Asha said.

"But why have this block protrude, and there's room for the block to move," Avere said, sticking her fingers in the gap between the block and the stone from which it protruded. "The book—"

The music swelled. The Fallen were scratching, begging, pleading. She was the Beast Master, the Fallener, the one cursed by the Seven, the one with the bestial soul; this fallen temple was calling to *her*. "Let me try," she said. Asha and Avere gazed at her. "If this temple was here for Falleners, then I should be the one to try."

The wild man who'd tried shook his head but motioned for Erryn to go ahead. Asha nodded. Avere stepped away. Erryn knew that if she pushed the block and nothing happened, Avere would strike. It would have to be now. She stepped to the block and made sure her back was to Avere. She didn't want to see it coming and looked to where Renn was standing, and saw Toe standing next to her, and smiled.

She lifted her hand. *Remember me. Remember that I loved you,* she said to the Fallen. She pressed the block.

Fi's legs were sore by the time the wagon rumbled to a halt. Jeena swung the door open and leaped out, then grabbed Fi's arm and yanked it. "Out," she snapped. Fi almost tumbled to the ground. Voices and laughter reached her ears. Several tents were pitched near a roaring fire that lit the night sky, and an iron cage sat next to another wagon. A sick feeling formed in the pit of her stomach. Women in chains were slumped inside the cage. They didn't lift their heads to peer at the new arrival. Fi wished they would. They weren't dead, but . . .

"Ungag her, Quinn," Jeena said.

The man who'd ridden in the wagon with Fi sneered at her. "One sound, one word, one scream, and I'll give you bruises where nobody can see them. Understand?"

Fi quickly nodded. Quinn removed her gag. Swallowing didn't help Fi's dry throat. She wanted to cough. Her eyes watered.

Quinn jerked his chin toward the cage. "Let's put her with the others."

"Not yet." Jeena let go of Fi's arm. "Watch her for a minute." She strode away.

Quinn's eyes raked Fi from head to toe. He leered at her. She wished Jeena would come back.

"You're a pretty little thing, aren't you?" Quinn murmured. She stiffened when he touched her hair, then ran his fingers through it, making her wince as he forced his way through the tangles. "If you give me a smile, maybe I'll let you stay in my tent."

Fi swallowed and avoided his eyes. He cupped her chin. "Don't be like—"

"What are ye doing, Quinn?" Jeena barked. "Hands off!"

He frowned and spun around. "What, we're not allowed to have any fun with this one?"

She ignored him. A bald man joined them and held a torch so close to Fi that she was worried her hair would catch fire. Jeena held up a paper. "What do ye think?"

Their eyes searched her face. "I think we've just . . ." His voice shot up. ". . . struck it rich!" He shoved the torch at Quinn and grabbed Jeena. They whooped and hollered and danced in each other's arms.

The paper Jeena had held fluttered to the ground. Quinn crouched to look at it. "What's going on?"

The bald man let go of Jeena and slapped Quinn's back. "We just captured the Lyos traitor."

Fi's chest tightened.

Jeena picked up the Wanted poster and thrust it at Fi. "Ye don't look much like a princess now, do ye, but the resemblance is there, and I can tell by yer hands that ye haven't done a scrap of work in yer life."

"She's just sat there stuffing her face and bathing in wine all her life." The bald man turned to Jeena. "She'll stay in your tent. Nobody touches her, all right." He gave Quinn a pointed look. "I'm guessing the Primacy will pay more if we deliver her unblemished."

"If we're smart, we won't give her to the Primacy," Jeena said.

"What do you mean?" the bald man asked.

"We'll take her to Lord Millwood. He wants the throne. Delivering the princess to the Primacy will guarantee he gets it. He'll pay handsomely for that."

The bald man nodded. "This little pig is going to make us very rich. To Millwood, then." He slapped Jeena's bottom and swaggered away.

"Bring me shackles," Jeena said to Quinn. Irritation flashed across his face, but he marched away, the torch bobbing along with his steps.

Jeena smiled at Fi. She looked feral. Savage. *Wild.*

"Look at ye, all high and mighty. A princess, and now, a queen?" Jeena snorted. "A queen of the dirt, maybe."

Fi kept her face blank. She'd learned long ago how to mask how she felt. Who would have thought her skill at court would serve her here, among savages and slavers?

Quinn returned with the shackles. Jeena untied Fi's hands. "I'll be nice to ye," she said. "I'll chain yer hands in front of ye. Ye can thank me." When Fi didn't speak, Jeena slapped her head, making her ears ring. "I said, ye can thank me."

"Thank you," Fi said through clenched teeth.

Jeena laughed and gestured to Quinn. "Did ye hear that? She just thanked me."

Sudden loud cheering from the direction of the fire made Fi jump. She could see those around the flames jumping up and down. No doubt they'd just been told they had the Lyos traitor in custody and were already planning what to do with their bags of coin. Fi held her head up, not wanting Jeena to see her defeated, but Jeena's eyes brightened.

"Ye're nothing now. Ye're ours to sell, and we'll be there when they cut ye up and hang ye." She clamped the shackles around Fi's wrists and locked them, then crouched to shackle her ankles. "Come."

Fi hobbled a couple of steps, then stumbled. Jeena gripped her arm and dragged her along. One of the women in the cage lifted her head, the whites of her eyes visible in the dim light. Who would suffer the worst fate? The traitor, or the slave?

Cat calls and whistles pierced the air as Jeena pulled

her past the fire. "Nobody touches her," Jeena shouted. "Anyone who comes into my tent will have his balls cut off."

"Does that include me?" someone yelled. "You've always liked my balls."

Raucous laughter assaulted Fi's ears. She glanced at Jeena. A grin was frozen on the wild woman's face. She dragged Fi between two tents and entered the tent behind those. Jeena shoved Fi away from her. Fi managed to keep her footing and watched the wild woman light a lamp and open a cheap bottle of wine.

Jeena poured some wine into a goblet, took a swig, and gazed at Fi. "If ye know what's good for ye, ye won't try to run away. Even if ye didn't fall flat on yer face, ye wouldn't make it far, and I won't be able to protect ye if the guards catch ye when I'm not there."

Protect her? Fi wanted to roll her eyes.

"I bet ye're thirsty." Jeena didn't wait for a response. She gulped down more wine, then threw the rest into Fi's face. Fi coughed and wiped away the liquid as best she could.

Jeena's face split into a grin, a real one this time. "Don't look at me like that. I'm taking care of ye. I'm making sure nobody lays a hand on ye. Someone pretty and delicate like ye . . . they'd be lined up for ye. Ye wouldn't get a wink of sleep. Ye'd be on yer back, day and night."

Fi lowered her head, so Jeena wouldn't see her fear and revulsion, then steeled herself and held her head high. The wild woman set the goblet on top of a chest and plunked a bucket next to Fi. "That's for ye. Ye can piss and

shit in there. I'm sure ye piss and shit like the rest of us."
She walked in a circle on her tippy-toes, with one hand on
her wiggling hip and the other waving around. "Ye're no
lady. Underneath the fancy clothes and the jewels and the
stylish hair, ye're just like the rest of us."

Jeena looked ridiculous, more like a drunk whore than
a lady. Anywhere else, Fi would have giggled. But not here,
chained like a dog in a slaver's tent, any hope of taking
the throne gone—not that there had been much hope to
begin with. Fi had told Dann she didn't care about the
throne, and she certainly couldn't muster any interest
now, not when she didn't know what had happened to
him, or Enkelo and the others. *"Killed one. Almost took one
down."* Who? Who had sacrificed his life for her? What
about Cedric? Was he still alive and gathering allies for
a queen who would never sit on the throne? She should
never have gone along with any of it. Good men were
dying for her. Good men. And she was here, chained like
a dog, cheap wine mixing with the dirt on her face.

The moment Erryn touched the block, it slid forward.
She felt it leave her hand, then Renn yelped. Erryn's jaw
dropped. The ground had swallowed Renn and Toe right
before her eyes. "Renn!" She pushed past Asha and raced
to where Renn and Toe had stood, ignoring the shouts
behind her.

Yanik and some of the others had also raced over and
were looking down. Two hunters moved out of the way
to let Erryn pass, confusion in their eyes. Erryn peered
into the hole that was too square to be natural. Someone

groaned. Two dark shadows moved in the gloom. "Renn? Toe?" she yelled.

Avere and Asha caught up to her. Avere crouched. "Someone light a torch," she ordered.

"What happened?" Asha asked.

"I didn't see," Yanik said.

"The stone they were on moved," another said. "They were there, and then they were gone."

"It seems you opened the door to the temple, and only you could do it," Avere said. "Malina, you old bat, you. You were right," she added under her breath.

"This doesn't mean she can help the land," Yanik muttered.

Avere's eyes widened. "It certainly means you're not chopping her up. Not yet."

"Renn!" Erryn yelled again. Then she waved her hand and hissed, "Quiet," when she heard a voice.

"Toe hurt his ankle," Renn shouted. "I'm okay."

Erryn's shoulders slumped with relief.

"How far down is it?" Asha asked, at the same time someone handed Avere a lit torch. She held it close to the hole. Two pale faces peered up at everyone from below. "A bit of a drop," Avere murmured. "What's down there?" she shouted.

"A passage," Toe said. "We can't see very far down it."

Erryn's concern for Renn and Toe had cut through the Fallen's clamouring and the music that still called for her. Now that she knew they were safe, her mind was in turmoil again, making her grit her teeth. "I have to go down there," she said.

Avere nodded. "I'll go with you, and you should come, too," she said to Asha. "I can get down there myself, but we'll need rope for the rest of you, and—"

"Mother, ye shouldn't go down," Yanik said. "We don't know what's—"

"Of course she should go," Avere said. "This is what we came all this way for."

"She's right, Yanik. I need to see." Asha surveyed those with her. "But ye come too. All of ye. Ye should all see."

"We'll need a few to hold the rope and keep a lookout while we're down there," Avere pointed out.

Two of the wild folk quickly volunteered to stay behind, and a third grudgingly agreed when Asha asked them to remain.

Avere patted the bag on her back. "I have everything we need in here, but toss a few torches down for good measure." She waited until a hunter had done so, then handed the lit torch to Asha and leaned over the hole. "Move out of the way. I'm coming down." She lay on her stomach and inched backward into the hole until she was hanging inside it, clinging to its edge. "If you want to do it this way, don't forget to bend your knees when you hit the bottom," she said, then let go.

Erryn watched her land on her feet with a thud. Avere looked up and waved. A torch burst to life. "There's a skull here," she shouted. "On the ground. Well, not the ground, exactly. I'm standing on a stone slab. This skull hasn't been exposed to the elements for years. It must look exactly as it did when it was carved."

"Is this a temple for this Death ye spoke of?" Asha said.

"It could be. We'll move into the passageway so the rest of you can come down."

"Ye shouldn't be alone with the Fallener and her friends." Yanik shot Erryn a hostile look. "She could kill ye. Ye go, then I'll go, then she'll go."

"All right," Asha said. Erryn couldn't tell whether Asha believed Yanik's warning or was appeasing him. One of the wild folk dropped a rope into the hole. When three were holding the end of the rope, Asha shouted a warning down the hole and dropped her walking stick into it. Then she grabbed the rope and climbed down. Yanik followed her, then it was Erryn's turn. She'd never had to climb down a hole or cliff using a rope before, so her progress was slow and she almost fell once.

Her feet eventually touched the stone. The moment they did, Erryn heard rumbling up above, and the dim shaft of light coming from the sun winked out. She looked up, then raised her hands to protect her head when something struck her cheek. "Watch out!" she shouted, her voice ringing through the utter silence. No wind, no birds singing . . . the only sounds were her own breathing and the music soaring through her mind.

She lowered her hands and looked up again. "The stone . . ."

Avere stepped to her side and lifted the torch she held. "What happened?"

"I don't know. When I reached the bottom, the stone . . . it slid closed. Something hit me."

Avere lowered the torch. Erryn searched near her feet. She picked up the rope the closing stone had cut and held it up. Avere took the rope from her and studied its clean-cut end.

"The stone under yer feet must have recognized ye, just as the one outside did," Asha said.

Erryn could see her just inside the passageway she now noticed. "But how? How could a temple built who knows how long ago know who I am?"

"I don't know, but if ye step off the stone and then step on it again, perhaps the stone above will open."

Avere went back into the passageway to give Erryn room. She stepped off the stone and then back onto it. Nothing happened.

"We're trapped down here!" Yanik said, panic sharpening his voice.

Another torch flared to life. Renn hovered behind Yanik, the shadows cast from her torch dancing on the passageway walls. Erryn couldn't see Toe.

"The ones above know we're here," Asha said calmly.

"That won't do us much good." Avere jutted her chin toward Erryn. "The only one who can get the stone open is right here. They can try to break through it, but it looked rather thick to me, and they'll have to return to Loring, to find men and proper tools. It could take them days, weeks."

"Then we see where this takes us," Asha said, glancing over her shoulder.

Avere nodded. "We have to find another way out, or we've come all this way to find our tomb."

Erryn moved to enter the passageway, but Avere grabbed her arm. "We don't know what's waiting for us, and I'm assuming you're the only one who'll be able to open any doors we find. I'll lead the way. And you." She pointed at Yanik. "The rest of you, stay behind us." She snaked her way through the others. Yanik looked at Asha, then brushed past her when she nodded.

Now Erryn could see Toe sitting with his back against the passageway wall, his right leg outstretched. "How bad is it?" she asked.

He grimaced. "Don't worry about me. I can walk."

Renn went to take his arm and help him up, but Asha waved her away. "I'll help him. Ye keep yer sword at the ready." Toe slowly got to his feet, using the wall and Asha's arm for support. Asha handed him her walking stick. "Use this." He took it from her and murmured his thanks.

Renn moved aside to let Asha and Toe pass her, then gave Erryn's fingers a quick squeeze.

"Are you all right?" Erryn murmured. Renn nodded.

"Let's go," Avere said.

Erryn peered into the blackness waiting to greet them. The light from the torches only revealed what lay a few paces away. Avere set a slow pace, pausing with every step to examine where her foot would land next. The Fallen had calmed down. Erryn wasn't sure whether their silence should offer her hope, or if they were quiet because they knew all was lost.

"Look here," Avere said, making Erryn jump. She'd turned toward the left wall and held the torch closer to it. "It's a skull, next to a spear."

Asha leaned in to have a look. Her brow furrowed. "Zhikinden and Death. Like yer book."

"Is this a temple for Zhikinden, or Death?" Avere mused. "If it's a temple at all. Maybe it's something else." She turned and took another step.

"I don't understand why, if they are in opposition to each other, someone carved their symbols together," Asha said.

"I don't understand any of it," Avere said. "I'm glad we have no choice but to move forward."

"Erryn, do ye understand?" Asha asked.

Erryn was surprised, but only for a moment. She'd proven something by opening a door to this temple, but what? "I don't. All I know is that another Fallener was looking for a temple. You know as much as me, now."

"I think we're descending," Avere said.

Yanik and Renn murmured their agreement. Erryn hadn't noticed, but she was focused on listening for the Fallen. The music . . . it was growing louder, but she wouldn't tell the others unless she had to. They'd think her mad.

They trudged along the passageway, leaving the darkness they briefly banished behind them. Avere kept pointing out the skulls and spears that adorned the passageway walls. Erryn wondered if she was doing it to keep her panic at bay. They must have walked for at least fifteen minutes when the passageway abruptly ended and they faced a wall of stone. Nobody said a word, but frightened faces were all Erryn saw in the glow of the torches.

"There must be something that opens a way through," Avere said, the only one who didn't look cornered. She held her torch close to the ground, then shook her head. "Nothing. Maybe it's on the walls." She handed her torch to Yanik and ran her hands along the stone wall blocking their way, then turned to her right and felt the wall there. Erryn pressed her palms against the left wall's smooth stone and slowly dragged her hands along it, the flicker of the torch Renn held casting shadows on her fingers. The spear carved into one of the stones caught her eye. Erryn's heart thumped. The spear was elevated. She pressed her palm against it. The stone wall barring their way rumbled open.

Erryn stepped toward the revealed passageway, but Avere grabbed her arm. "No. Remember what happened last time you passed through a doorway you'd opened? The stone overhead closed. You go through last."

"The stone could close behind us," Yanik said.

"And if it does, she'll be able to open it again. But if she goes through and it closes, we could be trapped. There might not be a way to open it from the other side." Avere stepped across the threshold and motioned for the others to follow her. Yanik hesitated, then stepped through the doorway the stone had hidden. She took the torch from him. Asha and Toe went next. Erryn gave them a small smile. Toe managed one in return, though his face was tight as he limped forward, clutching Asha's arm for support.

Renn patted Erryn's arm and followed the others. Erryn wished she could hug her, feel the safety of her arms, and draw strength from the encouraging words Renn would whisper into her ear. Would they make it out alive, or share this tomb?

When she was sure that everyone was on the other side of the stone that had rolled away, she stepped through the revealed doorway. The stone rumbled closed behind her. Though they'd half expected it, nobody spoke for a few seconds, perhaps grateful to still be with the only one who could open doors in this place, or pondering what would have happened had Erryn passed over the threshold before them.

"There are more symbols here," Avere said, breaking the silence. "Zayvang, and you."

Everyone knew who she meant. "How can it be me?" Erryn asked, stepping to Avere's side and peering at the symbols etched into the stone.

"Not you, exactly, but what you are. This is Zayvang." Avere pointed at a sharp tooth. "This is you." A whip. "Here's a sun and a spear. There were only spears up until now. And there are no skulls."

"What do you think it means?"

"Perhaps we're getting closer to wherever this leads," Asha said.

"And no skulls might mean we won't die down here," Avere added. "That's how I'm interpreting it. Let's find out if I'm right." She led the group again, her every step measured.

They were still descending. As they progressed deeper underground, Erryn found it increasingly difficult to block out the ever-present music. And the

Fallen . . . no, Zayvang. The cat was alert, but not because she felt threatened. *What is it?* Erryn asked, wishing Zayvang could answer. Whatever this place was, it was connected to her master—one of the Seven.

Asha called for a rest and helped Toe sit on the passageway floor. Avere had water in her bag and passed it around. Nobody needed reminding that they hadn't brought food, and nobody felt compelled to point it out to the others. "I wonder how far underground we are," Avere said, sounding as if they were all out for an afternoon walk, not traipsing through a passageway that might never end, at least not in time for them. She leaped to her feet and slung her bag onto her back. "Shall we carry on?"

"Let me help him," Renn said, when Asha offered Toe her support again.

Asha waved her away. "I'll do it."

Renn's mouth tightened, but she nodded. They walked silently along the passage, though Erryn's mind was anything but silent. The music was growing louder, but it soothed, rather than irritated. Still, she worried that she'd soon be deafened to anything the others might say. They'd have to shout, or gesture, and wonder if she was losing her mind.

"Another dead end," Avere suddenly said, jarring Erryn from her thoughts. It didn't take them long this time to find the tooth that was the key. Erryn pressed it; the stone slid away.

Avere passed over the threshold first. "Something's changed," she quickly said. "I think it's a room."

Erryn sensed the others' excitement as they walked

past her. When she could see them all beyond the doorway she'd revealed, she stepped into—

Torches burst into flame, revealing a circular chamber with a smooth stone floor. Erryn had to crane her neck to see the ceiling. The stone door rumbled shut behind her, as the previous ones had done. "My torch just went out, but I don't feel a breeze," Avere said. She dropped it.

"So did mine," Renn said, quickly dropping hers too, as if it would bite her.

Everyone gazed around in wonder, except Avere, who was walking the perimeter, her brow furrowed. "The switch to open the door must have somehow lit the torches, but after so many years . . ." She shifted her attention to the centre of the chamber. "Zhikinden," she said, pointing.

Erryn looked in that direction. The music only she could hear was making it difficult to focus, and Zayvang was now agitating . . . begging again. She wanted to come into this plane. Erryn could feel the cat's desperation.

A rectangular stone altar stood in the centre of the room, with the same painting on the two sides Erryn could see. She studied the familiar image of Zhikinden with her long, flowing black hair and pale skin, drawing back her spear as if to throw it at the sun. But there was one major difference between this depiction of Zhikinden and the ones Erryn had seen in the castle, inside temples, and carved into stone. In this one, Zayvang was with her.

"The Fallen," Asha murmured.

"How intriguing." Avere walked to the altar and crouched to have a closer look. "I've never seen any of the

Fallen depicted inside a temple before, and the ones I've seen outside a temple . . ."

She didn't have to say the Fallen were always depicted as grotesque, predatory, evil. This painting of Zayvang was accurate and respectful. Zhikinden's free hand was resting on Zayvang's head. "Whose temple is this?" Erryn said to nobody in particular. "Is it meant to honour Zhikinden? Zayvang? Death?"

"There aren't any skulls in here," Avere said. "I haven't seen any skulls for a while."

"Then it must be Zhikinden's," Asha said, her voice hushed.

"Or Zayvang's." Avere smiled. "I'd be accused of heresy anywhere else, but we're all friends here."

Erryn turned to look for Renn. She was preoccupied with helping Toe sit down. Asha's walking stick leaned against the wall near him.

"We're trapped," Yanik said, his voice shrill again.

"There's no obvious way out, but I'm sure we'll find one. It might be on the altar. Perhaps you should check," Avere said to Asha. Then she went to the wall encircling the chamber and ran her palms along the stone.

Asha knelt next to the altar. Everyone else but Toe helped Avere check the wall, which was smoother than the ones in the passage. Erryn should easily detect any jutting stone, but the music and the Fallen—Zayvang, in particular—were drowning out what her fingers were telling her. She didn't feel as she had on the trail, when she'd expected her fingers to be clawed, but since entering this chamber, she'd had to scream to hear herself think.

"We're trapped," Yanik repeated, after everyone had searched and found nothing. He turned to where Erryn stood. "Ye brought us here. Ye trapped us here." He suddenly lunged—Renn barrelled into him. He stumbled but regained his balance.

"Stop!" Asha shouted. "Ye almost touched the altar!"

Yanik whirled and leaped away from it.

"You do understand that if there is a way out, she's the only one who'll be able to open it," Avere drawled, shaking her head. "Only a fool would destroy the key while he's still locked inside the room." She muttered something else under her breath, too low for Erryn to hear. "Let's think. So far, there's always been a switch of some kind—"

Erryn straightened and walked closer to where Renn stood, wanting to be near her. As she approached the centre of the chamber, her vision swam and her heart pounded. Zayvang roared again, pleaded, begged . . . "It's the altar," Erryn said, suddenly understanding. "I have to stand on the altar."

Asha's eyes widened. "Ye can't. Ye would disrespect Zhikinden."

"No, she's right." Avere pulled Malina's book from her belt and opened it. "Remember the rectangle and the arrow. It could be about the switches she's been pressing, but the arrow is pointing down to the rectangle." She gazed at the altar. "The altar is rectangular."

"When she came down the hole and her feet touched the stone, the doorway to this temple closed. That could be what it means," Asha said.

"Perhaps, but it could also be telling us how to get out of

here. We've checked the walls and the altar for switches. We can't reach the ceiling," Avere said, looking up at the high ceiling, far out of anyone's reach. "The altar is the only remarkable thing in this chamber."

"I don't know," Asha said. "To step on the altar for one of the Seven . . ."

"If you're worrying about angering them, we're in a chamber with no door. We can sit here and slowly die, or she can step on the altar. If nothing happens and Zhikinden does get angry, maybe she'll give us a quick death. I'd prefer that to doing nothing and watching my flesh waste away."

Asha appeared unconvinced.

"It's the only way, Mother," Yanik said, spreading his hands in a pleading gesture. "Would the Seven wish that we lie down and quietly die? They would want us to try."

"All right, "Asha said, "but we should stand apart from each other, in case the floor opens up somewhere."

"Stay near the wall, Toe," Renn said.

Erryn waited while the others moved away from each other. Renn, Avere, Asha, and Yanik stood different distances away from the altar. Erryn took a deep breath. *I'm sorry*, she said, wondering if the Seven could hear her. Then she strode to the altar and climbed on top of it. She almost stumbled and fell off when the altar dropped a couple of inches. Her mind still noisy, she glanced around, to see if a door had rumbled open anywhere. The others were doing the same, but no door appeared in the circular wall, and nobody dropped through the floor.

"Nothing happened." Yanik's eyes were growing wilder.

Avere threw him a disdainful look. "Something happened, but not what we were expecting. The altar moved." She stared at it with thoughtful eyes. "It responded to you."

"Maybe it would have responded to anyone," Erryn said, her disappointment and sense of failure making her sound surly.

"Move out of the way," Avere snapped. She waited for Erryn to step aside, then leaped onto the altar. Nothing happened. "No, it's you. It responds to you. But then why didn't anything else happen?"

Erryn opened her mouth to say she didn't know, but another roar from Zayvang stopped her. She would have clapped her hands over her ears, if doing so would have helped and not made her appear as if she were losing her mind. She gazed at the altar and—Zayvang! "Zayvang has to step on it. That's why she's in the painting on the altar," she said, excitedly jabbing her finger at it. "She's what's different about it. It's telling us that Zayvang has to stand on the altar."

Avere's excitement matched her own. "Yes, she's here, on the page." She tapped the page she'd turned to in the book again. "Call her. Tell her to stand on the altar."

Erryn nodded, eager to bring Zayvang into the physical plane. It was what Zayvang wanted. She'd wanted it from the moment they'd approached the ruin. "Stand away," she said.

"No," Yanik shouted. "Ye can't bring the Fallen into a sacred place. Tell her, Mother. Don't let her. Zayvang will kill ye, because ye serve the Seven."

"So does Zayvang," Avere snapped. Erryn sensed Renn moving to her side.

"Not because she wants to." Yanik's lip curled. "Only because she has to, because the Seven made her into an animal."

Avere rolled her eyes. "Fine. We'll all sit here and die, then. In the end, Asha will die anyway. And so will you, and me, and all of us. If Zayvang does rip us all apart, it will be a merciful death."

"She won't hurt anyone," Erryn said, bristling. "She obeys me while she's in the physical plane."

Yanik shook his head. "Ye could command her to kill everyone."

"No, Yanik," Asha said. "If she wanted to kill us, she would have done so by now. She could have called the Fallen when we were in the passage." She turned to Erryn. "Call Zayvang. But promise ye'll send her back quickly."

"I will. After she's stood on the altar, I'll send her back, I promise you."

Asha inclined her head. "Then we'll go back to where we were standing."

Erryn waited until everyone had moved away from the altar. *Zayvang, come.* The air shimmered. Zayvang leaped into the physical plane, landing next to Erryn. "I need you to do something for me," Erryn said, for the benefit of everyone else, especially Yanik, whose fear was plain on his face. She didn't have to speak to communicate with Zayvang. They were connected. Bonded. She ruffled the saber-tooth cat's fur. If the others weren't watching her, she would have hugged Zayvang and buried her face in her fur; her desire to do so was strong. She gazed into Zayvang's eyes and marvelled at the intelligence and warmth that burned in them. Zayvang would see love in Erryn's.

Wishing she could stretch out her time with Zayvang, Erryn reluctantly straightened and faced the altar. Her mind was suddenly quiet. It was as if Daros and the heavens were holding their breath. She pointed to the altar. *Stand on the altar, Zayvang.* "Go stand on the altar."

Zayvang bounded toward it. Just before she leaped into the air, she turned back and looked over her shoulder. Shock jolted through Erryn. She could swear Zayvang had nodded to her, but—

Zayvang landed on the altar. A great flash of light forced Erryn's eyes to close. Blood pounded in her ears, and it suddenly felt as if a huge weight were pressing down on her chest. She fell to her knees. Her shoulders hunched, she covered her ears, struggled for breath, gritted her teeth. For a moment, she felt as if she were being ripped apart.

The pressure on her chest eased. Her head stopped pounding. She cracked open an eye and realized she'd turned away from the altar. She could see Renn on her knees, her head bowed. Beyond her, Avere was lying face down, her hands stretched toward the centre of the chamber. Erryn couldn't tell if Avere was breathing, but panic suddenly gripped her because she couldn't sense Zayvang.

She whirled back to the altar. Time stopped. Zayvang wasn't there. In her place, a tall woman was down on one knee, her arm resting on her knee and her head bowed. Black hair flowed to her waist, her biceps strained at her tunic's sleeves, and a golden spear was strapped to her back.

Erryn struggled to accept what she was seeing. It couldn't be, but it was.

Zhikinden.

Author's Note

Thanks for reading *Pawns and Puzzles*. For information about *Fate or Folly*, the second volume in the Daros Chronicles, visit:

sarahettritch.com/the-daros-chronicles-epic-fantasy

While you're there, sign up for my email list, and I'll notify you when I release a new book. I won't share your email address with anyone, and you can unsubscribe at any time.

Thanks for reading!

Other Titles by Sarah Ettritch

The Salbine Sisters

The Missing Comatose Woman

The Rymellan Series

Threaded Through Time

The Deiform Fellowship Series

The Voice in My Head

The Perfect Christmas Gift